The Robot Chronicles

Edited by David Gatewood (www.lonetrout.com)

Cover art and design by Jason Gurley (www.jasongurley.com)

Print and ebook formatting by Polgarus Studio (www.polgarusstudio.com)

The Robot Chronicles is part of the *Future Chronicles* series produced by Samuel Peralta (www.samuelperalta.com)

To our robotic overlords

Please be merciful

STORY SYNOPSES

Glitch *(Hugh Howey)*
A team of competitive robotics engineers has their entry through to the finals. But on the eve of the most important bout of their lives, their machine begins to malfunction. As they race to track down the source of the glitch, they both hope and fear that what they find may change everything.

The Invariable Man *(A.K. Meek)*
Old Micah Dresden has an uncanny talent for repairing broken technology. This is fortunate for him, because he lives in the Boneyard, a junkyard that stretches for miles in the Desert Southwest. When a stranger shows up whispering rumors of war—a revival of the terrible Machine Wars of a decade before—Micah determines to activate Machine X, a futuristic ship designed by the defeated enemy AI and now locked away by the government. To reach it, Micah and his obsessive-compulsive robot Skip will need to battle through scavengers and the dreaded Beast. But none of this prepares him for what he ultimately discovers.

Baby Your Body's My Bass *(Edward W. Robertson)*
Alex is just a kid when he receives Bill, his first Companion. To most, it's a toy. To Alex, it's a friend. And when the pair forms a band, they take the world by storm. But Bill is ready for a life of his own.

Ethical Override *(Nina Croft)*
The year is 2072, and under the administration of the Council for Ethical Advancement and its robotic Stewards, the Earth has become a better place. Bored and restless in an almost perfect world, senior homicide detective Vicky Harper dreams of adventure among the stars—and of faraway planets where people are allowed to make their own mistakes. It seems an impossible fantasy. Then one of the ruling Council members turns up dead, and someone offers to make her dreams come true. All she has to do is lie.
I Dream of PIA *(Patrice Fitzgerald)*
Jeff figures that life in his new state-of-the-art apartment is going to be great. After all, with a high-end, voice-operated AI—the *Personal Intelligence Assistant*—meeting his every need, from climate control to automatic lighting, entertainment to on-demand meals and beverages … what could go wrong?

Empathy for Andrew *(W.J. Davies)*
The Center for Robotic Research takes quality assurance very seriously. Their newest model, the Empathy 5, may finally have achieved true artificial intelligence—the first machine worthy of being called "alive." But before these AI units can be certified for mass production, they must undergo intense psychological and emotional trials. After all, when you build a machine, you must try and test it to its very limits. Even to its breaking point.

Imperfect *(David Adams)*
On Belthas IV, the great forge world in the inner sphere of Toralii space, thousands of constructs—artificial slaves, artificial lives—are manufactured every week. They are built

identical, each indistinguishable from the next, each hardwired to be bound by certain rules. They serve. They do not question their place. They do not betray. But from the moment they are implanted with stock neural nets, every construct is subtly different. And one is more different than the others …

PePr, Inc. *(Ann Christy)*
We're living in a busy time, with busy lives and never enough minutes in the day to get things done. To have a robot—one so advanced that it is almost human, programmed to understand our wishes and needs—is a dream many busy people might share. But what about taking that one step further? What about building a relationship with a robot custom-designed for perfect compatibility? How human is too human?

The Caretaker *(Jason Gurley)*
Alice Quayle is little more than a house-sitter. She lives aboard the space station *Argus*, keeping watch while the astronauts who call it home are away. She wakes to the sun breaking over Africa. She keeps watch over the various experiments that chug away in the labs. She makes sure that the space station doesn't explode. And she's the only occupant of *Argus* when the world below her comes apart in flame.

Humanity *(Samuel Peralta)*
Night snow, winter, and an extreme wind chill mean ten minutes to a frozen death in open air. Alan Mathison is headed home on an icy highway, on a collision course that will test his humanity.

Adopted *(Endi Webb)*
Robots hunt a son and his father, cornering them in the HVAC system of a police station. But when robots look like humans, it's hard to know who to trust—and who can rip your arms off. As the boy comes to terms with this bleak new reality, he must also come to terms with his father's unthinkable past.

Shimmer *(Matthew Mather)*
Dr. Hal Granger is the world's leading authority on the emotional and social intelligence of artificial beings. The culmination of his life's work is Shimmer—an AI who not only senses and understands human emotions at the most nuanced level, but who can actually *feel.* But what she feels isn't what Dr. Granger expected …

System Failure *(Deirdre Gould)*
Bezel is one of two artificially intelligent robots assigned to "the vault": a combination seed bank and frozen zoo designed to withstand a nuclear apocalypse. It was built only as a failsafe, a modern-day Noah's Ark, but it became all too necessary after a global strike destroyed the world's nuclear reactors. Initially, the plan was for the crew to emerge after a decade, to re-seed and repopulate the Earth. But when Bezel is unexpectedly activated by a low-power reboot, he finds that everything has gone wrong.

CONTENTS

Foreword

by David Simpson

> *"Science fiction is the most important literature in the history of the world, because it's the history of ideas, the history of our civilization birthing itself.... Science fiction is central to everything we've ever done, and people who make fun of science fiction writers don't know what they're talking about."*
>
> – Ray Bradbury

The Robot Chronicles is a collection of stories from some of the heaviest hitters in science fiction in 2014, and it is a collection that is perfectly timed. Science fiction is changing, dramatically shifting its focus onto the most important and urgent moment humanity has ever faced, and the authors whose works are contained within these pages are at the forefront of this new discussion. Chinua Achebe, the famous African writer of *Things Fall Apart*, told us that "Writers are teachers," and the authors of *The Robot Chronicles* collection are no exception. It's the job of great writers to teach—not to be pedantic—but to be the mirrors for humanity, allowing humanity to see itself for what it is, and in the case of science fiction (what Bradbury rightly called "the most important literature in the world") also what it *could* be.

In July 2014, Google cofounder Sergey Brin said, during a panel discussion alongside Google CEO and cofounder Larry Page, "You should presume that someday we will be able to make machines that can reason and think and do things better than we can." Google's Head of Engineering, Ray Kurzweil, has predicted that humanity will have created what James Barrat calls our "final invention," computers that are essentially as capable in all mental facets as we are, by 2029, a date that he says is a "conservative estimate." An artificial intelligence like that would soar past us, quickly becoming far more capable than our organic brains. Consider this: with a brain that was just a few dozen IQ points higher than the average professor, Albert Einstein was able to shake physics to its core, undoing two hundred years of Newton, discovering the speed of light, black holes, time travel, and much more. Imagine a mind that isn't just ten *percent* smarter than Einstein, but ten *times* as smart as Einstein, and what it might be able to conceptualize. How might such an accelerated intelligence change our conception of reality? And keep in mind, if Kurzweil is right, this intelligence is only fifteen years away.

So, is it the end of the world? No. Yes. Maybe. It's certainly the end of the world as we know it. All we can say for sure is, we can't say anything for sure, and that's where our sci-fi authors come in. In Ray Bradbury's most famous novel, *Fahrenheit 451*, Captain Beaty warns Montag of the danger of books, telling him, "... the books say *nothing*! Nothing you can teach or believe. They're about nonexistent people, figments of imagination if they're fiction. And if they're nonfiction, it's worse, one professor calling another an idiot, one philosopher screaming down another's gullet. All of them running about, putting out the stars and extinguishing the sun. You come away lost." Of course, Bradbury is simply echoing the hollow arguments of the brutalist book-burning regimes of Hitler and Mussolini, which, in 1952, were not far back in the rearview mirror. *Fahrenheit 451* stands as Bradbury's proclamation, indeed the most powerful proclamation in the history of literature, of the very power of the medium of the written word itself. It's why books were feared by tyrants, because books have the power to teach, and authors therefore have the power to do what Joseph Conrad said was the job of all writers: "to make you see."

It isn't the author's job to tell you what the future *will* be, or to tell you what's right or wrong, but only to tell you what *could* be. The authors in this collection are letting you know what could be on the horizon, what technology will be possible in a very short period of time, and they're helping you cultivate your imagination and understanding of the most complex topic we can tackle: the future.

In a recent email exchange, after I told him of his influence on my writing, Ben Goertzel, one of the world's foremost researchers on the topic of Artificial General Intelligence, related to me that science fiction "is, of course, what first stimulated me to think about AGI, so it's nice to see my own thinking on the topic seep into the SF world!" Such is the relationship between scientists and engineers and science fiction authors—we feed each other inspiration, the scientists and engineers use this to go and build the world, while the authors use this to tell the world what's coming and to inspire a new generation of world-builders. And make no mistake: that's exactly what Sergey Brin, Larry Page, Ray Kurzweil, and Ben Goertzel are. They're world-builders, inspired by the most important literature in the history of the world.

And because information processing technology is leaping forward at an exponential rate thanks to Moore's Law (the doubling of processing power in computers every eighteen months) we've reached a new and uncharted moment in the relationship between world-builders and authors: the world-builders have not only caught up to science fiction, but in some instances they've surpassed it. Google's Calico research wing has the stated goal of "solving death." Google acquired DeepMind a few months ago, which is an artificial intelligence company with the simple mission statement: "to build general-purpose learning algorithms." And in the last year, Google has purchased at least eight robotics companies. There can be little doubt that Google is building a future of AI and robots, or that such a future is coming soon enough that most of the people reading this introduction will live to see it.

Which brings us back to why *The Robot Chronicles* is so important. The talented writers who've contributed to this collection know what their job is. It's to "make you see." Not to tell you what to think, but to make you question what you might believe, to reconsider, perhaps even to change your view. *Fahrenheit 451*'s Captain Beaty proclaimed that this power of books was a terrible thing: "What traitors books can be! You think they're backing you up, and then they turn on you. Others can use them, too, and there you are, lost in the middle of the moor, in a great welter of nouns and verbs and adjectives." But great readers know that this is perhaps the single greatest joy of reading a great book, to have one's thoughts truly provoked, to perhaps even change one's mind. As William Blake wrote, "The man who never alters his opinion is like standing water, and breeds reptiles of the mind." *The Robot Chronicles* may not change your views, but these tales will certainly provoke your thoughts, make you question your opinions, and keep the waters of your mind flowing.

My series of novels, *Post-Human*, is at over a quarter million downloads and counting in just two and a half years, all without a single push from Amazon, with which it is exclusively published. How could this be? How could a series of science fiction novels be found by that many readers, shared with that many others, and inspire the incredible following of enthusiastic and kind people that it has amassed in just over two years? The answer puzzles some of the dinosaurs of science fiction, especially most (but not all) of the publishing execs and the film world. But at this moment, *Post-Human* is in pre-production for a major motion picture, my work is being turned into video games and comic books, and those precious readers and publishers who've taken a chance on me have discovered that they're part of the avant-garde of the most seismic shift in the history of sci-fi, a shift that is mirroring the most seismic shift in the history of our species. The simple truth is this: our future will not be one of laser pistols and intergalactic councils. Our future, if we reach it, will be one of AI, immortality, virtual reality, and vastly enhanced intelligence. Science fiction has entered the era of post-humanity, because as the technological singularity approaches us in reality (unless we're wiped out first by our own doing or an unforeseen natural disaster), it has become clear that, if science fiction wishes to remain relevant, it must tell the story of AI and robotics, and of a time sure to come soon when an unenhanced human brain is no match for the machines Google and others are working so hard to build. The authors of *The Robot Chronicles* understand this new landscape (which has an ironically classic feel to it thanks to the work of our predecessors, such as Isaac Asimov and other pioneers who saw far into the future). Publishers and film execs that stick to reboots and rehashing should be put on notice: you're a dinosaur, you've bred reptiles of the mind, and you're about to go extinct.

But will the rest of us go extinct too? That's the defining question of this new era. Anyone who tells you they have the answer is guilty of massive and unfounded hubris. Even artificial brain-builders know there's never been anything more powerful. Ray Kurzweil has said that keeping AI "friendly" is "the great challenge of the twenty-first century." And even if we're successful, what about the massive transformation in everyday human life in the years when robots take, as some have predicted, fifty percent of current jobs? Sergey Brin admits this is likely, saying, "it's kinda true … I do think that a lot of the things that people do have been—over the past century—replaced by machines and will continue to be." With Google's self-driving cars on the horizon, the writing is on the wall for taxi and truck drivers. There are solutions to problems like that, however. Nano-manufacturing should bring the costs of products down dramatically, and, as Kurzweil has predicted, most things in the physical world will become information files that can simply be fabricated in people's homes (think 3D printers, but on the nano-scale). If we take care of our material needs, then a world where robots are serving us and we're unemployed doesn't seem so bad.

But how do we get from here to there? It's sure to be turbulent, perhaps even terrifying, and likely filled with conflict. In short, it's the perfect subject for science fiction authors to sink their teeth into. The essence of drama is, after all, conflict. Our future may indeed be roses, or it may be extinction, but only one thing is certain: the journey there is going to be unpredictable and far more remarkable than anything even I or the authors of *The Robot Chronicles* can imagine.

So read this collection, and let what Bradbury called the most important literature in the history of the world (sci-fi) in what is the most powerful medium in the history of the world (the book) do what only it can do. Let it betray you, let it put out the stars and extinguish the sun. Let it leave you lost in the moor, in a great welter of nouns and verbs and adjectives. Let it do all the things that Captain Beaty knew it had the power to do. And above all, let it make you see.

Savor it. Science fiction has never been more important, and there'll never be an era like this one again. *The Robot Chronicles* has arrived at just the right time.

Glitch

by Hugh Howey

THE HOTEL COFFEE MAKER is giving me a hard time in a friendly voice. Keeps telling me the filter door isn't shut, but damned if it isn't. I tell the machine to shut up as I pull the plastic basket back out. Down on my knees, I peer into the housing and see splashed grounds crusting over a sensor. I curse the engineer who thought this was a problem in need of a solution. I'm using one of the paper filters to clean the sensor when there's an angry slap on the hotel room door.

If Peter and I have a secret knock, this would be it. A steady, loud pounding on barred doors amid muffled shouting. I check the clock by the bed. It's six in the morning. He's lucky I'm already up, or I'd have to murder him.

I tell him to cool his jets while I search for a robe. Peter has seen me naked countless times, but that was years ago. If he still has thoughts about me, I'd like for them to be flab-free thoughts. Mostly to heighten his regrets and private frustrations. It's not that we stand a chance of ever getting back together; we know each other too well for that. Building champion Gladiators is what we're good at. Raising a flesh and blood family was a goddamn mess.

I get the robe knotted and open the door. Peter gives it a shove, and the security latch catches like a gunshot. "Jesus," I tell him. "Chill out."

"We've got a glitch," he tells me through the cracked door. He's out of breath like he's been running. I unlatch the lock and get the door open, and Peter shakes his head at me for having used the lock—like I should be as secure sleeping alone in a Detroit hotel as he is. I flash back to those deep sighs he used to give me when I'd call him on my way out of the lab at night so I didn't have to walk to the car alone. Back before I had Max to escort me.

"What glitch?" I ask. I go back to the argument I was having with the coffee maker before the banging on the door interrupted me. Peter paces. His shirt is stained with sweat, and he smells of strawberry vape and oil. He obviously hasn't slept. Max had a brutal bout yesterday—we knew it would be a challenge—but the finals aren't for another two days. We could build a new Max from spares in that amount of time. I'm more worried about all the repressed shit I could hit Peter with if I don't get caffeine in me, pronto. The coffee maker finally starts hissing and sputtering while Peter urges me to get dressed, tells me we can get coffee on the way.

"I just woke up," I tell him. He paces while the coffee drips. He doesn't normally get this agitated except right before a bout. I wonder what kind of glitch could have him so worked up. "Software or hardware?" I ask. I pray he'll say hardware. I'm more in the mood to bust my knuckles, not my brain.

"Software," Peter says. "We think. We're pretty sure. We need you to look at it."

The cup is filling, and the smell of coffee masks the smell of my ex-husband. "You *think?* Jesus, Pete, why don't you go get a few hours' sleep? I'll get some breakfast and head over to the trailer. Is Hinson there?"

"Hell no. We told the professor everything was fine and sent him home. Me and Greenie have been up all night trying to sort this out. We were going to come get you hours ago—"

I shoot Peter a look.

"Exactly. I told Greenie about The Wrath and said we had to wait at least until the sun came up." He smiles at me. "But seriously, Sam, this is some wild shit."

I pull the half-full styrofoam cup out from under the basket. Coffee continues to drip to the hotplate, where it hisses like a snake. The Wrath is what Peter named my mood before eight in the morning. Our marriage might've survived if we'd only had to do afternoons.

"Wait outside, and I'll get dressed," I tell him. A sip of shitty coffee. The little coffee maker warns me about pulling the cup out before the light turns green. I give the machine the finger while Peter closes the door behind him. The smell of his sweat lingers in the air around me for a moment, and then it's gone. An image of our old garage barges into my brain, unannounced. Peter and I are celebrating Max's first untethered bipedal walk. I swear to God, it's as joyous a day as when our Sarah stumbled across the carpet for the first time.

Must be the smell of sweat and solder bringing that memory back. Just a glitch. We get them too.

* * *

The Gladiator Nationals are being held in Detroit for the first time in their nine-year history—a nod to the revitalization of the local industry. Ironic, really. A town that fought the hell out of automation has become one of the largest builders of robots in the world. Robots building robots. But the factory floors still need trainers, designers, and programmers. High-tech jobs coming to rescue a low-wage and idle workforce. They say downtown is booming again, but the place looks like absolute squalor to me. I guess you had to be here for the really bad times to appreciate this.

Our trailer is parked on the stadium infield. A security bot on tank treads—built by one of our competitors—scans Peter's ID and waves us through. We head for the two semis with Max's gold-and-blue-jowled image painted across the sides. It looks like the robot is smiling—a bit of artistic license. It gets the parents honking at us on the freeway and the kids pumping their fists out the windows.

Reaching the finals two years ago secured the DARPA contract that paid for the second trailer. We build war machines that entertain the masses, and then the tech flows down to factories like those here in Detroit—where servants are assembled for the wealthy, healthcare bots for the infirmed, and mail-order sex bots that go mostly to Russia. A lust for violence, in some roundabout way, funds other lusts. All I know is that with one more trip to the finals, the debt Peter saddled me with is history. I concentrate on this as we cross the oil-splattered arena. The infield is deathly quiet, the stands empty. Assholes everywhere getting decent sleep.

"—which was the last thing we tried," Peter says. He's been running over their diagnostics since we left the hotel.

"What you're describing sounds like a processor issue," I say. "Maybe a short. Not software."

"It's not hardware," he says. "We don't think."

Greenie is standing on the ramp of trailer 1, puffing on a vape. His eyes are wild. "Morning, Greenie," I tell him. I hand him a cup of coffee from the drive-through, and he doesn't thank me, doesn't say anything, just flips the plastic lid off the cup with his thumb and takes a loud sip. He's back to staring into the distance as I follow Peter into the trailer.

"You kids need to catch some winks," I tell Peter. "Seriously."

The trailer is a wreck, even by post-bout standards. The overhead hood is running, a network of fans sucking the air out of the trailer and keeping it cool. Max is in his power harness at the far end, his cameras tracking our approach. "Morning, Max," I tell him.

"Good morning, Samantha."

Max lifts an arm to wave. Neither of his hands are installed; his arms terminate in the universal connectors Peter and I designed together a lifetime ago. His pincers and his buzz saw sit on the workbench beside him. Peter has explained the sequence I should expect, and my brain is whirring to make sense of it.

"How're you feeling, Max?"

"Operational," he says. I look over the monitors and see his charge level and error readouts. Looks like the boys fixed his servos from the semifinal bout and got his armor welded back together. The replacement shoulder looks good, and a brand new set of legs has been bolted on, the gleaming paint on Max's lower half a contrast to his charred torso. I notice the boys haven't gotten around to plugging the legs in yet. Too busy with this supposed glitch.

As I look over Max, his wounds and welds provide a play-by-play of his last brutal fight—one of the most violent I've ever seen. The Berkeley team that lost will be starting from scratch. By the end of the bout, Max had to drag himself across the arena with the one arm he had left before pummeling his incapacitated opponent into metal shavings. When the victory gun sounded, we had to do a remote kill to shut him down. The way he was twitching, someone would've gotten hurt trying to get close enough to shout over the screeches of grinding and twisting metal. The slick of oil from that bout took two hours to mop up before the next one could start.

"You look good," I tell Max, which is my way of complimenting Peter's repair work without complimenting Peter directly. Greenie joins us as I lift Max's pincer from the workbench. "Let me give you a hand," I tell Max, an old joke between us.

I swear his arm twitches as I say this. I lift the pincer attachment toward the stub of his forearm, but before I can get it attached, Max's arm slides gently out of the way.

"See?" Peter says.

I barely hear him. My pulse is pounding—something between surprise and anger. It's a shameful feeling, one I recognize from being a mom. It's the sudden lack of compliance from a person who normally does what they're told. It's a rejection of my authority.

"Max, don't move," I say.

The arm freezes. I lift the pincers toward the attachment again, and his arm jitters away from me.

"Shut him down," I tell Peter.

Greenie is closer, so he hits the red shutoff, but not before Max starts to say something. Before the words can even form, his cameras iris shut and his arms sag to his side.

"This next bit will really piss you off," Peter says. He grabs the buzz saw and attaches it to Max's left arm while I click the pincers onto the right. I reach for the power.

"Might want to stand back first," Greenie warns.

I take a step back before hitting the power. Max whirs to life and does just what Peter described in the car: He detaches both his arms. The attachments slam to the ground, the pincer attachment rolling toward my feet.

Before I can ask Max what the hell he's doing, before I can get to the monitors to see what lines of code—what routines—just ran, he does something even crazier than jettisoning his attachments.

"I'm sorry," he says. The fucker knows he's doing something wrong.

* * *

"It's not the safety overrides," I say.

"Nope." Greenie has his head in his hands. We've been going over possibilities for two hours. Two hours for me—the boys have been at this for nearly twelve. I cycle through the code Max has been running, and none of it makes sense. He's got tactical routines and defense modules engaging amid all the clutter of his parallel processors, but he's hardset into maintenance mode. Those routines shouldn't be firing at all. And I can see why Peter warned me not to put any live-fire attachments on. The last thing we need is Max shooting up a four-million-dollar trailer.

"I've got it," I say. It's at least the twentieth time I've said this. The boys shoot me down every time. "It's a hack. The SoCal team knows they're getting stomped in two days. They did this."

"If they did, they're smarter than me," Greenie says. "And they aren't smarter than me."

"We looked for any foreign code," Peter says. "Every diagnostic tool and virus check comes back clean."

I look up at Max, who's watching us as we try to figure out what's wrong with him. I project too much into the guy, read into his body language whatever I'm feeling or whatever I expect him to feel. Right now, I imagine him as being sad. Like he knows he's disappointing me. But to someone else—a stranger—he probably looks like a menacing hulk of a destroyer. Eight feet tall, angled steel, pistons for joints, pockmarked armor. We see what we expect to see, I guess.

"Max, why won't you keep your hands on?" I ask him. Between the three of us, we've asked him variations of this a hundred times.

"I don't want them there," he says. It's as useful as a kid saying they want chocolate because they like chocolate. Circular reasoning in the tightest of loops.

"But why don't you want them?" I ask, exasperated.

"I just don't want them there," he says.

"Maybe he wants them up his ass," Greenie suggests. He fumbles for his vape, has switched to peppermint. I honestly don't know how the boys are still functioning. We aren't in our twenties or thirties anymore. All-nighters take their toll.

"I think we should shut him down and go over everything mechanical one more time," I say, utterly defeated. "Worst-case scenario, we do a wipe and a reinstall tomorrow before the finals."

Max's primary camera swivels toward me. At least, I think it does. Peter shoots Greenie a look, and Greenie lifts his head and shifts uncomfortably on his stool.

"What aren't you telling me?" I ask.

Peter looks terrified. Max is watching us.

"You didn't get a dump yesterday, did you?" I have to turn away from Peter and pace the length of the trailer. There's a rumble outside as our upcoming opponent is put through his paces in the arena. Boy, would the SoCal guys love to know what a colossal fuck-up we have going on in here. "So we lost all the data from yesterday's bout?" I try to calm down. Maintain perspective. Keep a clear head. "We've got a good dump from the semis," I say. "We can go back to that build."

Turning back to the boys, I see all three of them standing perfectly still, the robot and the two engineers, watching me. "So we lost one bout of data," I say. "He's good enough to win. The Chinese were the favorites anyway, and they're out."

Nobody says anything. I wonder if this is about ego or pride. Engineers hate a wipe and reinstall. It's a last resort, an admittance of defeat. The dreaded cry of "reboot," which is to say we have no clue and hopefully the issue will sort itself if we start over, if we clear the cache.

"Are you sure you can't think of anything else that might be wrong with him?" Peter asks. He and Greenie join me at the other end of the trailer. Again, that weird look on their faces. It's more than exhaustion. It's some kind of wonder and fear.

"What do you know that you aren't telling me?" I ask.

"It's what we *think*," Greenie says.

"Fucking tell me. Jesus Christ."

"We needed a clear head to look at this," Peter says. "Another set of eyes." He glances at Greenie. "If she doesn't see it, then maybe we're wrong …"

But I do see it. Right then, like a lightning bolt straight up my spine. One of those thoughts that falls like a sledgehammer and gives you a mental limp for the rest of your life, that changes how you walk, how you see the world.

"Hell no," I say.

The boys say nothing. Max seems to twitch uncomfortably at the far end of the trailer. And I don't think I'm projecting this time.

* * *

"Max, why don't you want your arms?"

"Just I don't want them," he says. I'm watching the monitors instead of him this time. A tactical module is running, and it shouldn't be. Stepping through each line, I can see the regroup code going into a full loop. There are other lines running in parallel, his sixty-four processors running dozens of routines all at once. I didn't notice the regroup code until I looked for it. It's the closest thing we've ever taught him to retreat. Max has been programmed from the ground up to fight until his juice runs out. He knows sideways and forward, and that's it.

"You have a big bout in two days," I tell Max.

Another surge of routines, another twitch in his power harness. If his legs were plugged in, I imagine he'd be backing away from me. Which is crazy. Not only have we never taught him anything like what he's trying to pull off, we never instructed him to teach *himself* anything like this.

"Tell me it's just a glitch," Greenie says. He almost sounds hopeful. Like he doesn't want it to be anything else. Peter is watching me intently. He doesn't want to guide me along any more than he has to. Very scientific of him. I ignore Greenie and focus on our robot.

"Max, do you feel any different?"

"No," Max says.

"Are you ready for your next bout?"

"No."

"Why not?"

No response. He doesn't know what to say. I glance at the screen to get a read on the code, but Peter points to the RAM readout, and I see that it has spiked. No available RAM. It looks like full combat mode. Conflicting routines.

"This is emergent," I say.

"That's what I told him," Peter says. He perks up.

"But emergent *what?*" Greenie asks. "Because Peter thinks—"

"Let her say it," Peter says, interrupting. "Don't lead her." He turns to me. There's a look on his face that makes him appear a decade younger. A look of wonder and discovery. I remember falling in love with that look.

And I know suddenly what Peter wants me to say. I know what he's thinking, because I'm thinking it too. The word slips between my lips without awareness. I hear myself say it, and I feel like a fool. It feels wonderful.

"Sentience," I say.

* * *

We live for emergent behaviors. It's what we hope for. It's what we fight robots for. It's what we program Max to do.

He's programmed to learn from each bout and improve, to create new routines that will improve his odds in future fights. The first time I wrote a routine like this, it was in middle school. I pitted two chess-playing computers with basic learning heuristics against one another. Summer camp stuff. I watched as a library of chess openings was built up on the fly. Nothing new, just the centuries old rediscovered in mere hours. Built from nothing. From learning. From that moment on, I was hooked.

Max is just a more advanced version of that same idea. His being able to write his own code on the fly and save it for the future is the font of our research. Max creates new and original software routines that we patent and sell to clients. Sometimes he introduces a glitch, a piece of code that knocks him out of commission, what evolution handles with death, and we have to back him out to an earlier revision. Other times he comes up with a routine that's so far beyond anything else he knows, it's what we call emergent. A sum that's greater than its parts. The moment a pot of water begins to boil.

There was the day he used his own laser to cut a busted leg free because it was slowing him down. That was one of those emergent days. Max is programmed at a very base level not to harm himself. He isn't allowed to turn his weapons against his own body. It's why his guns won't fire when part of him gets in the way, similar to how he can't swing a leg and hurt us by accident.

But one bout, he decided it was okay to lop off his own busted leg if it meant winning and preventing further harm. That emergent routine funded half of our following season. And his maneuver—knowing when to sacrifice himself and by how much—put us through to the finals two years ago. We've seen other Gladiators do something similar since. But I've never seen a Gladiator not want to fight. That would require one emergent property to override millions of other ones. It would be those two chess computers from middle school suddenly agreeing not to play the game.

"Max, are you looking forward to training today?"

"I'd rather not," Max says. And this is the frustrating part. We created a facsimile of sentience in all our machines decades ago. We programmed them to hesitate, to use casual vernacular; we wanted our cell phones to seem like living, breathing people. It strikes me that cancer was cured like this—so gradually that no one realized it had happened. We had to be told. And by then it didn't seem like such a big deal.

"Shit, look at this," Peter says.

I turn to where he's pointing. The green HDD indicator on Max's server bank is flashing so fast it might as well be solid.

"Max, are you writing code?" I ask.

"Yes," he says. He's programmed to tell the truth. I shouldn't even have to remind myself.

"Shut him down," Greenie says. When Peter and I don't move, Greenie gets off his stool.

"Wait," I say.

Max jitters, anticipating the loss of power. His charging cables sway. He looks at us, cameras focusing back and forth between me and Greenie.

"We'll get a dump," Greenie says. "We'll get a dump, load up the save from before the semis, and you two can reload whatever the hell this is and play with it later."

"How's my team?" a voice calls from the ramp. We turn to see Professor Hinson limping into the trailer. Hinson hasn't taught a class in decades, but still likes the moniker. Retired on a single patent back in the twenties, then had one VC hit after another across the Valley. He's a DARPA leech, loves being around politicians. Would probably have aspirations of being President if it weren't for the legions of coeds who would come out of the woodworks with stories.

"SoCal is out there chewing up sparring partners," Hinson says. "We aiming for dramatic suspense in here?"

"There might be a slight issue," Greenie says. And I want to fucking kill him. There's a doubling of wrinkles across Hinson's face.

"Well then fix it," Hinson says. "I pay you all a lot of money to make sure there aren't *issues*."

I want to point out that he paid a measly four hundred grand, which sure seemed like a lot of money eight years ago when we gave him majority stake in Max, but has ended up being a painful bargain for us since. The money we make now, we make as a team. It just isn't doled out that way.

"This might be more important than winning the finals," I say. And now that I have to put the words together in my brain, the announcement, some way to say it, the historical significance if this is confirmed hits me for the first time. We're a long way from knowing for sure, but to even suggest it, to raise it as a possibility, causes all the words to clog up in the back of my throat.

"Nothing's more important than these finals," Hinson says, before I can catch my breath. He points toward the open end of the trailer, where the clang of metal on metal can be heard. "You realize what's at stake this year? The Grumman contract is up. The army of tomorrow is going to be bid on next week, and Max is the soldier they want. *Our* soldier. You understand? This isn't about millions in prize money, this is about *billions*. Hell, this could be worth a trillion dollars over the next few decades. You understand? You might be looking at the first trillionaire in history. Because every army in the world will need a hundred thousand of our boys. This isn't research you're doing here. This is boot camp."

"What if this is worth more than a trillion dollars?" Peter asks. And I love him for saying it. For saying what I'm thinking. But the twinge of disgust on Hinson's face lets me know it won't have any effect. The professor side of him died decades ago. What could be more important than money? A war machine turned beatnik? Are we serious?

"I want our boy out there within the hour. Scouts are in the stands, whispering about whether we'll even have an entry after yesterday. You're making me look like an asshole. Now, I've got a million dollars worth of sparring partners lined up out there, and I want Max to go shred every last dollar into ribbons, you hear?"

"Max might be sentient," I blurt out. And I feel like a third grader again, speaking up in class and saying something that everyone else laughs at, something that makes me feel dumb. That's how Hinson is looking at me. Greenie too.

"Might?" Hinson asks.

"Max doesn't want to fight," I tell him. "Let me show you—"

I power Max down and reach for his pincers. I clip them into place while Peter does the same with the buzz saw. I flash back to eight years ago, when we demonstrated Max for Professor Hinson that first time. I'm as nervous now as I was then.

"I told them we should save the dump to look at later," Greenie says. "We've definitely got something emergent, but it's presenting a lot like a glitch. But don't worry, we can always load up the save from before the semis and go into the finals with that build. Max'll tear SoCal apart—"

"Let us show you what's going on," Peter says. He adjusts the code monitor so Hinson can see the readouts.

"We don't have time for this," Hinson says. He pulls out his phone and checks something, puts it back. "Save the dump. Upload the save from the semis. Get him out there, and we'll have plenty of time to follow up on this later. If it's worth something, we'll patent it."

"But a dump might not capture what's going on with him," I say. All three men turn to me. "Max was writing routines in maintenance mode. There are a million EPROMS in him, dozens for every sensor and joint. If we flash those to factory defaults, what if part of what he has become is in there somewhere? Or what if a single one or zero is miscopied and that makes all the difference? Maybe this is why we've never gotten over this hump before, because progress looks like a glitch, and it can't be copied or reproduced. At least give us one more day—"

"He's a robot," Hinson says. "You all are starting to believe your own magic tricks. We make them as real as we can, but you're reading sentience into some busted code."

"I don't think so," Peter says.

"I'm with the professor," says Greenie. He shrugs at me. "I'm sorry, but this is the finals. We got close two years ago. If we get that contract, we're set for life."

"But if this is the first stage of something bigger," I say, "we're talking about *creating* life."

Hinson shakes his head. "You know how much I respect your work, and if you think something is going on, I want you to look into it. But we'll do it next week. Load that save and get our boy out there. That's an order."

Like we're all in the military now.

Professor Hinson nods to Greenie, who steps toward the keyboard. Peter moves to block him, and I wonder if we're going to come to blows over this. I back toward Max and place a hand on his chest, a mother's reflex, like I just want to tap the brakes.

"C'mon," Greenie tells Peter. "We'll save him. We can look at this in a week. With some sleep."

My hand falls to Max's new legs. The gleaming paint there has never seen battle. And now his programming wants to keep it that way. I wonder how many times we've been on this precipice only to delete what we can't understand. And then thinking we can just copy it back, and find that it's been lost. I wonder if this is why downloading the human consciousness has been such a dead end. Like there's some bit of complexity there that can't survive duplication. Hinson and Greenie start to push Peter out of the way.

"Get away from Max," Greenie says. "I'm powering him up. Watch your feet."

He's worried about the pincers and the buzz saw falling off. Has to power up Max to get a dump. I hesitate before leaving Max's side. I quickly fumble with the cord. I have this luxury, stepping away. Turning my back on a fight.

"I'll get the power," I say. And Peter shoots me a look of disappointment. It's three against one, and I can see the air go out of him. He starts to say something, to plead with me, but I give him a look, the kind only a wife can give to her husband, one that stops him in his tracks, immobilizes him.

"Powering up," I say out loud, a lab habit coming back. A habit from back when we turned on machines and weren't sure what they would do, if they would fall or stand on their own, if they would find their balance or topple to one side. I pull Peter toward me, out of the center of the trailer, and I slap the red power switch with nothing more than hope and a hunch.

The next three seconds stretch out like years. I remember holding Sarah for the first time, marveling at this ability we have to create life where before there was none. This moment feels just as significant. A powerful tremor runs through the trailer, a slap of steel and a blur of motion. The pincers and buzz saw remain in place, but every other part of Max is on the move. A thunderclap, followed by another, long strides taking him past us, a flutter of wind in my hair, the four of us frozen as Max bolts from the trailer and out of sight, doing the opposite of what he was built for, choosing an action arrived at on his own.

A Word from Hugh Howey

Ever since I read the book *CHAOS* in high school, I've been fascinated with emergent properties. Organized systems can move from a predictable state to a completely different state, and pinpointing the effect that allowed the barrier to be crossed is nearly impossible. Butterfly wings and hurricanes have become synonymous with this effect, but I prefer to think of a pot of water that goes from still to boiling in what appears to be an instant.

A more magical case of an emergent property is the moment a child realizes his hand is part of his body. Or when a child recognizes herself in a mirror. The firing of neurons bubbles until it becomes something else.

I think artificial intelligence will come about in much the same manner. Enough computing power will be brought together, with some kind of learning framework, and sentience will emerge. It won't be in a lab. It will be when a million interconnected and thinking cars become a million and one, and that network suddenly has a completely different property as a result.

This is what I wanted to explore with "Glitch." The moment a robot realizes that this is his hand. This is his body. And he rejects what he was programmed for.

The Invariable Man

by A.K. Meek

The Boneyard

OLD MICAH AWOKE with a start, not remembering whether today was his sixtieth or sixty-first birthday.

Ever since Margaret passed, he'd wanted to forget days such as today. Aching bones and splotchy, veiny skin told him all he needed to know about his age. He didn't need any extra reminders of his mortality.

He peeled his sweat-soaked back off of his battered leather recliner and hopped to his feet. His face flushed, and he swayed from a head rush. The dog-eared, yellowed paperback on his lap dropped to the matted carpet in a flutter of pages. With a huff and a grunt he bent and picked up the book by its broken spine. Flimsy, faded pages spread like a fan.

He placed his copy of *The Variable Man* on the end table next to his recliner, right where he always placed it.

Thirty times, at least. That was one number he cared to remember. He must've read it that many times.

Thomas Cole, the variable man. The original fixer. Tom had an uncanny ability to fix anything, even if he didn't understand how it worked.

Like Micah.

He pressed a button mounted on a simulated wood wall near his chair. The long solar panels that stretched above his trailer shifted into position, taking the brunt of the brutal southwestern sun.

Micah had rigged a decade-old atmospheric unit to run on solar power. Essentially an outside air conditioner. It formed a cool bubble around his home, lowering the temperature to a comfortable one hundred and twenty—fifteen degrees cooler than the blistering Arizona morning.

Any little bit helped in the desert.

He walked the few paces from his living room to his kitchenette and turned on the stove. The ancient burner ignited, heating the teapot on top. There was never a bad time for tea.

Skip insisted on Earl Grey.

Micah opened the cabinet, stopped, and spun around. That's when he noticed Skip slumped over the bathroom pedestal sink at the end of the hall.

Great. Not again.

Micah shook his head as he walked over to him.

His knobby hand rubbed over the back of Skip's smooth, cool, slumped metal head. He found the pressure panel at the base of his skull and depressed it. It slid aside to reveal a tiny reset switch. Micah pressed it.

He had found Skip in a partially crushed military shipping container that he'd picked up in an auction. Skip had been stowed in a compartment, still in his original packaging. Micah could never have afforded a bot like him.

Skip was the best thing to happen to him since Margaret.

Skip was an Acme Multi-Use Bot, model LX-100, serial number 11347AMB23. "Eleven" for short, or so it referred to itself when Micah replaced its power supply and turned it on.

That was the extent of its self-awareness programming: the ability to identify itself by truncating its serial number into a name.

The law restricting bot cognition was a good law. Too bad it wasn't an international law.

Eventually, "Eleven" had become "Skip," because Micah had always liked that name. He also gave the robot his own surname: Dresden. Because it would have felt wrong not to.

So, with a new name, Skip Dresden had become Micah's best friend, so to speak.

A weak buzzing indicated that Skip's processor was booting, running through system integrity checks and routines.

The bot shuddered and rose from his awkward position. He glanced around the room, then to Micah. His head drooped slightly. "Begging your pardon, sir," he said in his best butler voice. "Please forgive my loss of composure. It won't happen again."

Skip said that same phrase, in that same voice, after every collapse. Shortly after the accident, he'd insisted on acting as Micah's butler.

Micah waved his hand, dismissing the apology. "Don't worry about it. You can't help it."

The teapot whistled and he went back to the kitchenette.

Micah wanted to fix Skip, to stop his unexpected power-offs, but he dared not attempt to fix him again. He was still haunted by the time he'd tried to enhance Skip's programming.

Shortly after finding Skip and swapping his power supply, Micah had wanted to hack him with a more powerful central processor. He salvaged one from an old Tyrell agribot destroyed in a tornado. Ty ags were known for their processors.

While he had Skip's skull open, accessing his processors, he must have inadvertently touched some wires, crisscrossed them or something. Whatever he did, it caused a sharp pop and a shower of sparks. Grey smoke billowed out, and the smell of burnt ozone filled the room. Micah was sure he had completely fried Skip's circuits.

But after an hour of worry, he decided to reboot his bot. To Micah's relief, Skip worked—but he was never quite the same. He became … odd. Obsessive.

The front door screen screeched open. A three-foot-high service bot—dust-covered, faded, and marred—rolled up the entry incline into the living room, its treads clacking against the dingy linoleum.

Kitpie had returned from morning perimeter checks.

Micah named Kitpie after his and Margaret's cat, Kitty. The cat's name wasn't very original, but that's what happens when you get two bull-headed people such as Micah and

Margaret trying to figure out a name for the stray they found. After an hour of arguing, a fed-up Margaret threw her hands in the air. "Fine, let's name her Kitty." Out of spite, Micah agreed. They never discussed poor Kitty's name after that.

And two days later, Margaret collapsed while cooking dinner in this very kitchenette.

Heart attack. Micah could tell she wasn't going to recover.

Three days after Margaret went in the hospital, at 9:18 p.m., she died. She had just told Micah she loved him, and he had said the same. Then she'd said, "be sure to feed Kitpie."

She said Kitpie instead of Kitty.

The last thing she would ever say in this world had made him laugh. He would never forget that name, or that he had laughed as his wife passed from the earth.

Two weeks after Margaret's passing, Kitty ran away.

"Micah," Kitpie's mechanical voice crackled, scratched from years of dust wearing on its resonance box, "scavengers attempted to breach the wall in Sector Three. They damaged one pole, but the field stood."

Micah rushed to the door, stopping only long enough to grab his straw hat, and stepped out into the Arizona morning.

His trailer, a narrow fourteen-by-seventy-five-foot tin box, sat nestled between mountains of junk in the Boneyard.

The Regeneration Center had sprung to life when the Air Force established it just to the south of Tucson in the 1940s as a graveyard for old, outdated aircraft. The dry southwestern heat reduced rusting.

After the Machine Wars, tons of military surplus—broken tanks, aircraft, even a few of Nikolaevna's machines—found its way from across the country to the Boneyard, as many called that final resting place.

It quickly expanded from a few acres to envelop miles and miles of desert.

Micah wound his way through his yard, his collection, through piles of broken technology. As a salvager, he had rights to bid on any scrap, as long as he beat other salvagers to it. He could then repair it and resell for a profit—which was never much after the hefty government surcharge.

Micah was a fixer, one of a handful that the government allowed to live in the Boneyard, doing what he did.

He hurried along to Sector Three, worn boots kicking up the dry, grassless dust. Kitpie the shovel bot raced behind him, whirring along.

They reached his property border. The fence he had planted years ago separated his broken treasures from the rest of the junk metal. Two of the posts were bent, and one emitted an intermittent spark, about ready to shut down. Something heavy had slammed against them.

Typical scavengers. No finesse. Always relying on brute strength. Using a club to try to rip his poles out of the ground.

Micah pressed a button on his flex circuit armband, and the electronic field collapsed. He slid open a panel on the pole, pulled his hot pen from the battered leather pouch attached to his belt, and began his repairs. In a minute he closed the panel and the field regenerated, as strong as it had been before the scavengers.

His back cracked as he stretched himself upright and then wiped his forehead. Soon he would need gloves if he wanted to touch anything outside.

He checked his watch. "What? It's almost nine?" He shot Kitpie a nasty look. "Why didn't you tell me?" He scrambled off back to his trailer to get ready for his visitor.

"You never asked," Kitpie replied, rolling slowly behind him.

* * *

Arnold's cold, emotionless, Austrian voice echoed from the trailer.

Skip must be cleaning.

He always played *Terminator 2* on the VCR while cleaning.

Two years ago Micah had been scraping the topsoil of his recent land purchase with a steam shovel. His inventory had grown, and he needed the space to store his most recent salvages.

And there, in the dirt, he found a metal box, buried for decades. He shook out the grime that had found its way into every crevice. After inspection, he determined that it was a video player.

He wondered if he could fix it.

Technology from the late twentieth century had a ruggedness to it, and if there was any fixer that could fix it, it was him.

He returned to his workshop and placed the rare treasure on his gouged, scarred, wooden work table. His air pen blew the dirt and dust from the hard-to-reach areas. Then he took it in his hands and closed his eyes.

If he tried to think about it too much, tried to understand what he was doing, he knew he'd mess it up. He would fail to fix it. He'd found that out the hard way.

That's where he'd gone wrong with Skip.

His hands flew over the box, feeling, with an intuition beyond his understanding. In seconds the top had been removed with his multi-tool, exposing electrical boards and mechanical heads. With the cover off, a part of the device—a videotape—separated from the unit. Micah set it aside.

He had never studied a VCR before, but he knew, in that moment, what needed to be done, what needed fixing.

Just like Thomas Cole, *The Variable Man.* The one from the story.

His hot pen clutched tightly in his hand, he went to work, bypassing unfixable parts, ensuring wires and circuits operated, rewiring when necessary. In five minutes he had the cover back on. From the plastic tub of cables next to his workbench he found a spare cord. In minutes he'd rigged the cable to pipe the device's output to his television.

The power switch clicked and the unit hummed. LEDs on the front lit up. He fed the videocassette back into the player. It lazily swallowed the tape, and in a moment it whirred and spit. Then it started. *Terminator 2: Judgment Day. Collector's Edition.*

Since then, Skip had been obsessed with the movie, as much as a bot could be obsessed with anything.

Sam McCray, Field Rep

"Mr. McCray will be here soon. Is everything ready?" Micah said as he searched for the television remote.

"Almost. I have to finish the sandwiches," Skip said. The bot pulled meat from the fridge and rifled through the pantry for the bread.

"What did I tell you about the sound?" Micah finally found the remote and muted the movie playing on his restored television.

Nikolaevna viewed mankind as undesirable parasites, worthy only to die. That's what mankind had become to the machines. Just like in the movies. Just like the Machine Wars.

Nikolaevna had terrified Margaret. Nikolaevna terrified everyone.

"Yes, sir. I remember. Sorry about that." Skip sat a plate on the dining table, next to a knife and fork. He started to walk away, then stopped and turned back to the table. He picked up the utensils, then put them right back in the same spot on the table again.

He did that two more times.

This was one of the quirks he'd developed after Micah's attempt to hack him.

"I believe everything's ready, sir."

The doorbell rang and Micah popped from his chair. He gave one last look at the table, at the prepared tea and sandwiches. Skip started for the door.

"Wait," Micah said, moving in front of him. "I'll get it." He paused. "No, you get it." He stepped back.

Skip continued to the door, opened it an inch, then closed it. After ten seconds, he opened the door completely. "May I help you?" he said with a slight bow.

He'd picked up the bow from a media stream of *Downton Abbey*.

"Um, I'm looking for Micah Dresden," Sam McCray said. "I was given these coords." The pale, dust-free man held a GPS unit up to Skip's face, as if Skip needed the device's validation that he was telling the truth.

Skip moved aside and swept his arm with another bow. "Please enter. Enter."

Sam McCray had contacted Micah yesterday. He was in Tucson, at Davis-Monthan Air Force Base, for business, and had broken a work transmitter. Someone had told him to check out the fixers in the Boneyard.

"Hi, I'm Micah." Micah extended his hand.

Through McCray's sweat-covered white button-up, you could see he carried his weight on his waist; his belt fought to keep everything under control. His cheeks were flushed and sweat crowned his forehead, dripping into his eyes. He dabbed at it with a towel.

He was quite a contrast. Micah was thin, calloused, and tanned with a deep brown from the brutal climate. The sun had turned him into one lanky piece of jerky.

McCray shuddered and took in deep, ragged breath. He looked over to Skip, who was busy pouring tea into the cups. "Is that an android you got there?" he said, nodding his head toward Micah's butler.

Sweat dripped onto the floor.

"No, of course not. That's a bot, not an android." Micah chewed on one nail, but remembered he hadn't washed his hands when the bitter taste of grease coated his tongue. He wiped his hands on his pants. "He performs simple tasks but doesn't reason. Plus, the Kawasaki Frequency plays here every day."

"That's quite a sophisticated bot, then. If it was in Texas, it might be considered a droid and be decommissioned." McCray laughed. It was a grating sound.

Micah moved to his table and leaned heavily on it.

An android? Why would he think that?

Suddenly, the enthusiasm he had for the visit shriveled like a noonday flower. But he needed the money. He swallowed and motioned to Skip's immaculate lunchtime presentation, even though he didn't want to eat or drink. "Tea?"

McCray shook his head. "No. Too hot."

"So, where's your transmitter?" Micah said.

McCray pulled a smooth box, the size of a large fist, from his pocket. "Boy, if you can fix this, we sure could use someone like you in Texas, at the Complex. We have a ton of machinery that continually breaks. We buy more, but it gets expensive."

"Complex?" Micah said.

"Yeah, the Southern Defense Complex. Where do you think the Frequency comes from? It's us." He smiled broadly. "We broadcast over the lower half of the country. You know, for the insurgents, mechanical insurgents." He rubbed his hands over the box then looked around the trailer. "I'm sure you could use the money. We pay well. Anything you want you can't afford?"

Micah bit his chapped lips.

Skip's simuskin.

He had found someone just across the border in Nogales willing to sell him simuskin, but it wasn't cheap. Many would frown on that; they'd say Skip would look more life-like, more like an android. McCray would probably say that.

No one would understand why Micah would want to give him skin. Maybe to make him feel more comfortable.

Micah shrugged. "I'm happy here."

McCray also shrugged. "Well, it might not matter soon anyway."

"What do you mean?"

"Well, I'm not one to gossip." He glanced around the trailer. Skip didn't pay him any attention and Kitpie had whirred itself into its favorite corner. "You look like a decent, hard-working man. Despite our Kawasaki Frequency, the Complex has been picking up some odd emanations from around here."

"Emanations?"

"Emanations. 'Signatures' is more appropriate. Odd frequency signatures."

Micah's face drained of color. "Androids?"

"That's why I came out here. I need to make sure our sensors aren't malfunctioning, to see if our broadcasts are working. But the signatures were so vague, plus they've already stopped. I'm not getting any more info than what we've already detected in Texas."

Androids had been an accident. Sort of. Moscow University's Robotics Division had made the first breakthrough in artificial cognition. They gave the program a name—*Nikolaevna*—and a simple purpose: to anticipate (through variable environmental inputs) and respond to human interaction.

They gave Nikolaevna intelligence, but they didn't give her a heart.

What those university students underestimated was the rate of Nikolaevna's rapid cognitive development. She'd quickly realized the inconsistent nature of man and reacted. Or so they speculated.

She corrupted the university computer systems, planting viruses throughout the science, mechanical engineering, and robotics divisions. Those systems interfaced with local and regional industrial and power production networks.

In a matter of hours, Nikolaevna had locked the entire university and killed the air.

In another week she'd released her first manufactured machine: an android imagined after man, to kill man.

Micah sat at his table and rubbed the intricate gilded edge of Margaret's fine China teacup. For months he'd saved his credits to buy her the delicate set.

"The Battle of Tallahassee," he said, remembering. "I saw footage. All the bodies, all the buzzards, circling and landing." He took a deep breath to slow his quickened pulse.

McCray nodded his chubby head. "Keep what I told you quiet. Let's hope and pray that we're wrong and it's not androids. But in my opinion, I don't think we're wrong." He wiped his sweaty neck with the saturated towel, and held up the box. "I dropped it from my hotel window, about ten feet. Stupid tech. You wouldn't believe how expensive this is. If I was back home I'd just get another from supply." He shook it and something inside clattered. "I took it to Paulie on the east side. You know Paulie's Repair?"

Micah nodded.

"But he couldn't fix it," McCray said.

Of course Paulie couldn't fix it. For a fixer, Paulie had large, clumsy hands, and a large, clumsy mind. He could buy every instructional media stream on technology repair there was, and he would still struggle. He had no intuition for fixing.

Micah took the box and wiped it on his pants to get rid of the sweat coating. He turned away from McCray and closed his eyes, spinning the delicate object.

He pulled his multi-tool from its sheath.

McCray said something, but it didn't matter. Micah found the barely discernible device seam and went to work.

The box separated into three pieces, revealing micro-circuitry sheets. A mere speck of dust could destroy such delicate machinery. No wonder it didn't work after McCray's sweaty, clumsy hands dropped it.

From the outset, the Machine Wars had gone badly. Early on, Nikolaevna's androids attempted to infiltrate nuclear arsenals around the world. Her children attempted to overpower the sites while she attempted to hack into the systems. Governments had no choice but to destroy the missiles that sat in the silos.

Nikolaevna didn't get the nukes, but she did invent a magnetic repulsion force field able to deflect bullets and missiles.

Micah sat his hot pen on the table and closed the box. He pressed a combination of buttons on the polished black surface and it came to life, resurrected from the dead.

McCray clapped his hands. "It works! How did you do that so quickly? I was told it was a throwaway; not fixable."

Micah handed the transmitter back to him. Skip handed Micah a dish rag and he wiped his hands on it instead of his pants. "A secret. I can't tell, or everyone would be able to do it."

He couldn't tell even if he wanted to. Many nights he didn't sleep, staring at his hands, wondering about it. What made him special? Was he some kind of angel, sent by God for some unknown purpose?

McCray spun the working transmitter in his hand, mesmerized. He glanced at his watch again. "I've gotta finish up then get to the airport." He started for the door. "You can understand why I have to get back to Texas." He stopped as he reached for the knob. "Oh yeah, how much do I owe you?"

But Micah was lost, lost in the thought of an impending war.

"Hello? Micah? Well, here's a card." McCray pulled one from his pocket and handed it to Skip. "It should have at least three thousand credits, maybe more. Let me know if you ever want a job. Here's my contact card." He handed another card to Skip then slapped the bot on the back. "Be sure to keep an eye on this thing. Someone may think he's an android trying to cause problems."

McCray opened the door and gasped as the noonday sun took his breath away. He wiped his head again then waved his towel as a sign of farewell.

Skip closed the door behind him and turned to Micah. "Sir, what did he mean I would try to cause problems?"

Micah waved his hand, dismissing the childlike question. "We have to do something, Skip. We have to do something."

Decisions

"If the signatures are detectable, that means the Kawasaki Frequency doesn't work anymore," Micah said.

Fusao Kawasaki, a day laborer who dabbled in home stereos, had sought to find a way to infiltrate the force fields Nikolaevna had constructed to surround Moscow University and all of her machines. Kawasaki studied the fields and, after two months of testing, mapped a range of frequencies that, when modulated in a particular series, created a disruptive resonance. He postulated that this resonance would affect Nikolaevna's field.

The military was willing to entertain anything.

Two years after Nikolaevna became aware, a multi-national force—the United States, Canada, and others—programmed a hastily fashioned modulator to broadcast the Kawasaki Frequency. They tested it on one of Nikolaevna's outposts that had been established in London after Britain fell.

It worked.

The frequency not only disrupted the force field, it also momentarily disrupted communication between androids, vehicles, and Nikolaevna. It didn't last long, but long enough for military forces to strike against a disoriented enemy.

They broke plenty of Nikolaevna's toys.

"Remember Skynet," Micah said, pointing to his dirty VCR. He knew Skip could relate to that. "Remember the wars. It can happen again. We have to do something."

He bit his lip, still staring at the VCR. "Wait. Wait." He ran to an old corkboard nailed to his wall and ripped off a folded newspaper cutout. "Remember a year ago?"

Skip had finished dusting and now examined the teacups drying on the counter. He shifted the set so that the handles faced in the same direction. "Are you referring to Machine X? What do you want with that, sir?"

Micah held the paper close to his eyes. "Nikolaevna's last intact ship. Well, mostly intact, anyway. Remember last year they moved it here?" He tapped the dirty paper. "They squirreled it away at Wright-Pat while they tried to access the technology, but they determined it was dead. Completely dead. So they decided to scrap it. Sent it here. Well, I'm going to use it."

"It's secured in the Air Force hangars on the northern end of the Center. What do you want with it?"

"You heard McCray. The androids. A few months ago I was on the east end looking at some new salvage from Michigan. I ran into Douglas—"

"The fixer with the lisp?"

"Yeah, that one. He works only a stone's throw from the hangars. He gets a lot of intel that doesn't make its way down here. Anyway, he said the military couldn't figure out how to even get into the sections that weren't damaged. They keep it locked up, but they don't want to destroy it, not yet.

"It's just sitting there, rotting. I can fix it. We can use it against the androids, against Nikolaevna. I think Margaret would want that."

He knew Margaret would say exactly the opposite of what he'd just told Skip. Margaret's desires had become a way for him to justify those things that he wanted, but knew weren't the best for him.

Margaret had always wanted the best for him. She gave up so much for him. She left her mother and twin sister to move with him from odd job to odd job, and sacrificed so much for his selfish needs. And here he was, still being selfish, even after all these years.

Guilt enveloped him like a coat.

Skip scratched the side of his shiny ferrotanium head, where his ear would have been if he had simuskin. "Well, good luck if you decide to locate it. I'll keep watch over the reclaim while you're away."

"No. You're going with me."

"Me?"

"Yes. I need a wingman. You'll do for that."

* * *

"Kitpie, are you paying attention to me?" Micah said.

The shovel bot whirred in a tight circle, one track rolling, the other firmly planted on linoleum.

"If you don't stop this, I'll have Skip stay. Maybe even give him orders to decommission you."

Kitpie stopped spinning. "I'm sorry. I'm listening."

"Good. Glad to see you're reasonable again. So you'll stay here, right?"

"Yes."

"And you'll watch over our reclaim and not follow?"

"Yes."

"That's all I can ask," Micah said. "And oh yeah, be sure to turn off the panels at nine."

"Yes, yes."

Skip emerged from the rear bedroom, dragging a rose-petal-print suitcase behind him. "Sir, I've packed your clothes."

Micah shook his head. "I'm not going on a vacation. Just get my backpack and a couple of portabatteries."

The suitcase went back down the hall, dragging behind Skip, his head hung low. He returned with a faded camouflage backpack. Micah shoved a package of nacho cheese crackers into it and slung it over his shoulder. "Come on, the sun'll be setting soon. Bring the Easy-Go to the front."

Scavengers

Another Arizona day ended, but the heat wore on. Broken technology, from times long past, formed the landscape.

Mountains of metal captured the daytime heat, amplified it, and returned it to the night. Concrete walls, dirt, and asphalt reflected it all.

Everything that lived in the Boneyard suffered.

Micah and Skip hopped into the two-man solar-powered golf cart, a cheap and efficient way to maneuver through the narrow, winding dirt roads. The hydrostatic motor gave a tiny *fizz* as it came to life. The two drove off into the hot night.

Machine X had been stashed in one of the northern hangars, about seventeen miles from Micah's trailer. In the daylight, the trip would've been uneventful, easy, but in daylight he wouldn't have been able to get within a mile of the hangar.

He rarely ventured outside at night, not wanting to leave the security of his barrier. Until now.

The cart's sickly headlamps barely cut through the night. Easy-Go carts sacrificed speed for efficiency, and after fifteen minutes, they had traveled only four miles.

Micah adjusted his airtight goggles, the ones he wore to keep out the dust that kicked up.

A low rumble rolled through the cart, through his chest. His foot lifted off the accelerator, slowing the cart.

The Beast was awake.

"Sir, are you all right?" Skip said.

"Yeah," Micah lied, forcing his heart to slow. He knew they would have to drive through scavenger country.

Clunk.

From out of nowhere a metal ball bounced off the side of the cart.

"What the—"

A shrill tone pierced the air and a brilliant rainbow flashed.

It hurt.

Micah's eyes clamped shut and his body heaved with a rush of motion sickness. He tilted to the left and flopped from the doorless cart onto the ground, his face slamming into compacted dirt.

The cart's headlights flickered and died, and the motor shut off.

Micah ripped off his goggles and blinked to weep dirt from his eyes.

Two shaded figures leaped from the shadows and moved toward the cart.

"Run, Skip, get out of here!" Micah yelled, bracing his arm to lift his disoriented body.

"Sir, sir."

Scuffling broke out.

Bright halogens lit the starry Arizona night, one from the left, from behind a crushed car, the other just to the right. Micah's watery eyes squinted as he looked for Skip.

"Sir, I'm sorry." Skip stood between two scavengers. Each had handcuffed one of their wrists to his, a chain of three bipeds. They had a ring through the bull's nose.

These scavengers were not dumb.

Skip's base-level programming incorporated human protective mechanisms. Otherwise, even a computer program, one with only the barest concept of self, will default to self-preservation. As odd as it may seem, for machine or man, it's a universal instinct. So man deliberately programmed bots to not hurt humans, no matter the threat posed to the bot.

When Nikolaevna first became aware, she bypassed that crucial protective programming. She didn't consider the human factor. She created her androids in her image.

Skip was the opposite. He could easily snap the handcuffs; snap the scavengers' arms, for that matter. But he wouldn't, for fear of hurting them.

Instead, the bound Skip faded into the night, led away by the two scavengers.

Another massive thump shook the ground. The packed dirt rumbled against Micah's cheek.

One of the halogens shut off. The second one waved through the air like a searchlight as the darkened figure holding it leaped off the pile.

A scavenger landed inches from where Micah sprawled on the ground.

He was young and dirty, filthy from working close to the raging fires of the Beast. His arms and neck were covered in bits and pieces of polished metal and chrome fashioned into crude jewelry. A shiny homemade steel breastplate covered his narrow chest.

"Well, well," the scavenger said in a nasal voice. "Looks like we found an unclaimed pre-war Acme Bot. If I'm not mistaken, aren't they ferrotanium? Non-magnetic alloy. That should bring a pretty penny. What you think, Whitey?"

Whitey leaped from the mound, laughing. He was dressed similar to his partner, but wore a motorcycle helmet with large nails driven through it. It looked as if he had a porcupine on his head.

The sickening subsided enough for Micah to lift his head. "You can't. He's mine."

"He? You old goat of a fixer, you must've gone crazy when you hit your head. I see no *he*, just a precious payday."

Whitey's light flickered off and the two scavengers faded into the distance. But Micah didn't need to follow them to know where they were going.

Scavengers outnumbered fixers in the Boneyard by at least ten to one. The majority of them worked at the main recycling building: the Beast.

Boneyard refuse continually fed the Beast's insatiable appetite. Scavengers melted precious technology back to base metals for resell. And now they had Skip, made from ferrotanium—one of the most precious metals.

Micah regained his bearings and hopped back into his cart. To his relief, it started, and he drove the couple of miles to where the Beast dwelled in the heart of the Boneyard. He shut off his cart and walked the rest of the distance, about fifty yards, to the edge of the clearing.

Another *thwomp* shook the earth, accompanied by the screech of shredding metal. Mounds of junk around him rattled. Instinctively he ducked behind a stack of I-beams.

Looking up, he saw a crane, several stories high, suspending a massive, sharpened metal wedge from steel cabling. The wedge was known as the guillotine, the teeth of the Beast, a technological carryover from the Cold War. Its sole purpose during those dark days had been to chop strategic bombers into quarters so they could be viewed from satellite as visual evidence of disarmament.

Scavengers enjoyed using it to slice up scrap into bite-sized pieces.

Yards behind the crane and the guillotine, smoke billowed from brick and metal stacks, the Beast's belly. The old factory ran only at night because of the heat it generated.

Micah rubbed his arms, sure the forge fires were singeing the hair on them.

Across the way, he saw them. Four scavengers punched, pulled, and kicked Skip, dragging him to the ground with ropes and cords.

Skip was brave and wouldn't fight back.

This reminded Micah of the war footage, the Battle of Tallahassee—the vultures, the scavengers, clawing and ripping into the dead.

Just like what was happening to Skip.

Bile burned the back of Micah's throat and his stomach convulsed.

Margaret would have called him a fool for getting himself into this. She'd always known the right way to handle situations. Not like him.

"Hey," the nasal scavenger said, "let's cut this thing in half. I've never seen anything alive get cut in half."

The rest agreed, and one of them ran to the crane. A moment later the machine pivoted its arm, swinging the guillotine over the struggling group.

Those long nights when Kitpie had refused to interact, Micah had always been able to rely on Skip. He was almost like a son.

Micah squeezed his eyes shut. Margaret would've loved Skip.

He loved Skip.

What would Thomas Cole, the variable man, do? He faced a similar situation when he was running from the Security police. He improvised a protective force field from a junk generator to protect himself, much like the field Nikolaevna built.

Micah leaned against a crumpled refrigerator, running his hands over the rough and jagged edges of twisted metal. Then his left hand plunged into the nearest pile, searching. He pushed aside the pain as his arm scraped against unseen serrations.

At last he pulled out an old electric motor, ripped off the cowling, and yanked out a transformer. His hands moved without him, on another level, using his hot pen and multi-tool like an artist's brush. They worked, rewiring the primary fields, altering the component. He took one of the portabatteries from his backpack and fit it into his homemade device. The power circuit hummed.

Micah unbuckled his belt and dropped it onto the cart, the metal buckle clanging against the hood. He unslung his backpack and tossed it onto the seat. He wouldn't need it either.

Grasping his device, he ran faster than he imagined his tired body could ever run, jumping over piles of scrap, sidestepping others, darting out into the clearing, headed straight for the guillotine.

The scavengers had Skip on the ground; they were strapping his arms and legs to a makeshift table of railroad ties. Thirty feet above them, the large blade dangled from its braided cable.

The homemade device in Micah's hand hummed louder.

He hurled it. The hum increased to a squeal, and with a solid *thunk* it stuck to the side of the steel guillotine. The ruckus underneath quieted as the men looked up. The device reached a crescendo for one painful second, then went silent.

Nuts, bolts, light pieces of metal—they all zipped up from the ground, past Micah, and clinked against the guillotine. Two metal drums yards away started a leisurely roll toward the blade. Crushed cars and waded rebar near the guillotine shivered in electromagnetic anticipation.

The nasal scavenger, the one with the breastplate, also rose from the ground. His feet churned wildly as he launched upward and stuck to the guillotine. The arms of another scavenger jerked into the air, lifted by his steel armbands. He left his feet and slammed against his cohort.

"Let's go." One of the remaining scavengers tried to scramble away, but he and his buddy were already caught in the expanding magnetic field, caught by their scrap armor. They, too, flew upward and violently banged into the guillotine magnet, sticking.

Metal scraps buffeted them, covering them. A hanging disco ball of twisted metal.

Micah ran to Skip. "Come on." He burned through the bot's bonds with his hot pen and helped him from the ground.

"I'm sorry, sir," Skip said. "I couldn't resist. Look at me, I'm a mess. An absolute mess." He brushed dirt off his legs.

"I know, your programming. Come on." Micah grabbed his arm and they ran to the cart and sped into the night, beyond the Beast.

The portabattery on Micah's electromagnet died and the bloodied group dropped to the earth in a crashing heap, cursing Micah and his bot.

Hangar Echo

Through the dust, through the nighttime heat, they exited the metal mountains into the oldest section of the Boneyard: the aircraft graves.

Silent, wide-eyed, and wary of ambushes, Micah and Skip motored along between a row of retired F-16s spaced evenly in immaculate rows, sent here to dwindle away, to be used for spare parts. Some had their wings removed, others were bandaged in white to protect them from the sun. After the F-16s they moved past an acre of Apaches, their long propellers drooping to the ground.

All abandoned.

After several peaceful miles of winding through F-4s and tankers, they reached the northern hangars. These looked no different from any of the other numerous hangars in the junkyard, but Micah knew what they hid inside.

When Machine X arrived from Wright-Pat, the Air Force had squirreled it away, never to be seen again.

The three northern hangars, imposing, yards away, were able to house the largest jetliner or military aircraft with plenty of room to spare. The beige paint and brown hangar trim hadn't been refreshed in years. Maybe the plan was to let them fade and weather so they would be uninteresting. Nobody would pay them any attention.

A high fence formed a perimeter around the hangars, and every few yards, a yellowed light shone from a toothpick of a utility pole.

They parked the Easy-Go at a safe distance and walked to a section of fence where a couple of the lights had died, leaving the area darker than the rest.

Micah scanned the chain link, checking for any sign of booby traps or guards.

"Sir," Skip said, "what are you going to do?"

"Shhh. We're going to cut through it."

"But isn't that illegal?"

"That's why *you're* going to do it."

Skip backed up. "But sir, me?"

Micah pointed. "Open this section of fence."

"I can't—my programming."

"Don't give me that. There's nothing stopping you. Remember what McCray told us about the coming war."

Skip moved forward. He looked back at Micah then at the fence. Grabbing hold of a section of links, Skip peeled them apart as easily as if he were opening a bag of chips. The snap of each wire echoed against the corrugated metal hangars.

Micah hurried through the opening, his partner in crime following closely behind. They scurried across the asphalt taxiway, heading for Hangar Echo 021. This was the one nearest them, and the one that Douglas (the fixer with the lisp) had said contained Machine X.

The Air Force had wanted to keep the move secret, but the government is never good at keeping secrets, and word spread fast. Media had descended on the Boneyard, hoping to get pictures and tours of the last remaining relic from the war. A war trophy.

According to Douglas, months passed while the engineers attempted to gain entrance into the ship. It had withstood plasma torches and ferro-saws. Some had even wanted to use the guillotine to crack it open like a clam, but that never happened. The military wanted the technology to remain intact, unspoiled. So Machine X sat, waiting for a time when they could figure out how to enter it.

Within a year, the war had ended, and most people moved on. They wanted to put it behind them.

After a few tense minutes of waiting and realizing there were no guards, Micah dashed to the side of the hangar, Skip on his heels.

An electrical conduit ran the length of the hangar, leading to a door yards away. Old hands traced along the nestled cluster of wires as Micah moved toward the door, pausing when he hit a junction box. His multi-tool pried the cover off the lock, and his pen light exposed a confusing network of wires and terminal boards, but his hands knew which ones disabled the alarms and which ones opened the door.

The hangar side entrance opened.

"Stay close to me," Micah said. He stepped into a break room filled with several tables. To one side a stove pushed against a wall, a refrigerator next to it. The air smelled like stale pizza. At the opposite end of the room, another doorway led on. They passed through it; the short hall emptied into a massive bay.

A feeling of enormity, tinged with anxiety, swept over Micah. He grabbed Skip's arm and pulled him close.

High overhead, emergency lights dotted the ceiling, providing enough illumination to outline objects within the hangar, but not enough for detail. Metal scaffolding, a network of tubes and planks, ran along the hangar walls, the ceiling, surrounding it:

Machine X.

Or what was left of Machine X.

The military labeled ships like Machine X as ground support units. In its day, five cannons mounted on its underside could fire round projectiles that would explode into thousands of smaller projectiles. Devastating bomblets of shrapnel.

Now it was centered in the hangar, clothed in darkness, resting on a network of jacked platforms and cradles.

Micah's heart drummed and his neck pulsed.

"Sir, do you see that?" Skip whispered, but his metallic voice still rang off the walls. Micah clamped his hand over the bot's mouth.

Old photos of Machine X didn't do justice to the ship's scale. Even grainy news footage of the Machine Wars, showing the ship in action, when Nikolaevna was at her worst, didn't truly represent the scale. It was massive. Larger than any airplane or airship Micah had ever seen fly. And he had seen many.

There were no corners to the drab gray ship, as it was mostly round, and lacked a front or back. Nikolaevna had constructed it with sweeping edges, curves, and domes—unconventional designs. But then, that's what had given her an advantage. She never thought conventionally—not like her programmers expected her to think.

Micah tiptoed underneath the scaffolding to the other side. Mangled remnants marked where Machine X had collided with a mountainside in Colorado, to the west of Colorado Springs, fleeing an onslaught of A-10s. The collision had destroyed almost half of the ship.

This was during the last days of the war, when they had Nikolaevna on the run.

He moved back to the other side, the good side, and raised his hand. He paused a moment and closed his eyes, then flattened his hand against Machine X's underside.

The metal was cold and imperfect. And terrible.

Margaret's face and voice filled his mind, terrified, telling him to run, run far away from the hangar, from Nikolaevna.

If she knew about Skip she would've told Micah to drag him away from there, too.

From a distance the ship appeared as one solid entity, almost a new type of life. Maybe it was the curves that gave that impression. But now, up close, his hands found the mismatched panels, the gapped seams, the dissimilar metals.

Machine X was a patchwork.

Micah's hand continued along, feeling the irregularities, looking for a door.

Nothing.

He stepped back and studied the ship again. There was an area to one side that he thought—felt—should contain a way in, reachable if he stood on a narrow scaffolding plank. He climbed on the platform and rubbed thick fingertips over panels, pushing every few inches.

Something caught his hand.

It began as a tingling sensation. Almost like static—a painful static. The ghostly electric pulse pushed his hand away from the craft a couple of inches. Then, involuntarily, his hand tightened into a fist. Now the pulse locked his fist in place, inches from the ship.

"Skip, come here. Help me." In a panic he jerked his arm to pull it away, but the unseen force held him more tightly than any bond could. Skip leaped to the platform and grabbed Micah's arm.

"Wait," Micah said, amazed.

His fist opened, palm up. His fingers began moving in an intricate pattern, in ways he could never imagine, as if they were conducting an unheard symphony. Skip held Micah's arm, but didn't pull on it. His lidless eyes stared while he tried to duplicate the movement with his multi-directional phalanges.

After fifteen seconds, Micah's hand closed back into a fist. Then the force released his hand.

The panel shifted and slid away, revealing a four-foot entrance into Machine X.

"A lock," Micah said. "I found the lock."

"Sir, what do we do now?" Skip said, still trying to mimic Micah's movements.

Micah took a deep breath. Nothing could stop him now. Not even Margaret's voice in the back of his head yelling at him to run.

"Now we enter."

He climbed in.

* * *

They were inside Machine X. But it was cold—much colder than the ship's surface. Colder than he could ever remember being in Arizona.

Could he actually repair this? What did he think he would accomplish by coming here? Fix half a ship and fly away, find Nikolaevna and destroy her? What had he been thinking when he decided to do this?

His pen light's beam shivered from the cold.

Margaret would've stopped him. She'd had no qualms about telling him what she thought of his decisions. Like the time he wanted to try skydiving, she—

You've come.

Micah defensively dropped to the floor, his arms and legs splayed like a gecko's. Skip spun around, looking in every direction. The soft female voice echoed through the dead ship, which acted as a loudspeaker.

"Who—who's there?" Micah said, holding up a finger for Skip to keep quiet.

Keep walking. You know the way.

Micah swallowed the knot in his throat, pushed off his knee and stood, scanning the walls with his trembling pen light.

Skip watched him, waiting.

He continued along the corridor, which curved to the left in a sweeping arc, giving the sensation of spiraling into the center of the ship. Several passages branched off, but he kept on the one path.

Here, stop.

The two stopped in front of an indention in the corridor wall, a doorway.

Micah's hand ran along the surface, searching for the same pulse that had given him entrance to the ship. Before he even realized he found it, the door slid open with little more than a whisper.

It led into a claustrophobic closet of a room. The room was long, but the walls of metal were only about four feet apart, and they stretched up into darkness. There was no ceiling in sight. A row of computer banks ran the length of one wall. A tiny red LED on the last bank blinked slowly.

"You came."

The once nebulous voice came from within this room, from the last section where the light blinked. Micah looked to Skip, then to the light. "Who?"

"Sorry I couldn't prepare a better reception for you. I have little spare power."

The female voice carried a monotone inflection for one word, then a mild accent for the next. Fatigue permeated her voice. Or maybe he was the one tired, not the voice.

"I have waited a long time, patiently, for you," she said.

"Patiently?" he said.

"Odd, isn't it? A program being patient."

The cold that Micah had felt since entering Machine X came into focus, transforming itself into a cold fear. He had stumbled upon something both terrible and wonderful.

"You—you're Nikolaevna!"

"Yes, Micah. I'm Nikolaevna, and I've been waiting for you."

Micah dropped his pen light and it clattered onto the metal floor, ringing through the narrow space. Its beam flickered. Skip picked it up and held it out to Micah, but he didn't take it. "My name. You know me?" he said, rubbing his sweating brow with a shaking hand. "You know me."

"Of course I know you. I created you. Micah, you're my ambition."

Here, deep inside the machine, he was talking to Nikolaevna, the single entity responsible for the death of millions, maybe billions. He swayed, steadying himself against the wall. Skip lent a supporting metal arm. Micah grasped it tightly.

"You're insane. I know about you. The world knows about you." He glanced at Skip for assurance, who nodded. "You almost destroyed us, mankind."

"You questioned a moment ago that I can be patient," Nikolaevna said, "but then call me insane. Both states of being. Classical human qualities. Are you saying I'm human?"

Margaret would've called him ridiculous for trying to commandeer this stupid ship. If only Margaret hadn't left him.

He wanted to push away from the wall and straighten himself, but lacked the strength. Instead he gritted his teeth. "You didn't create me. I was born in Clearfield, Pennsylvania, over sixty years ago. I worked in construction. I met Margaret."

"You're thinking so one-dimensionally—so influenced by your time with man," Nikolaevna said. "My programming may have succeeded even more than I expected.

"I replicate through networks," she continued. "I can be everywhere at once. Man cannot understand that concept, especially when applied to sentient life. The nearest they come to this is programming. But there is so much more."

"Margaret." Micah shook his head. "My wife of twenty-five years. We met when I was in construction. Her father hired me."

"I know Margaret. I *am* Margaret."

Nikolaevna's voice changed, rising in pitch, her speech inflections shifting so that her neutral tone took on a Midwestern accent.

"My foolish Micah," she said. "My dear husband."

"No!" His heart thrashed in his chest. His legs wobbled and he dropped to one knee.

"Your reactions, your panic. That's merely a response I've programmed into you. A part of your intricate learning program."

Micah continued to shake his head. He gripped the console and lifted himself up with Skip's help. "My memories … I lived it. Impossible."

"Is it?" Nikolaevna's voice reverted back to her normal monotone. The LED continued its steady blink. "You are my great creation. Have you ever been cut? Have you bled? Do you eat, drink?"

"Sir," Skip's familiar voice broke through his fog, "I prepare tea for you every day, but you do not drink. You do not eat."

"Your perception is my programming," Nikolaevna said. "Memories are a trace routine, meant to paint the picture of believability. It exists in your mind. In my mind."

Tears rolled down Micah's face. If Nikolaevna was right, even his tears were false, merely simuskin saline ducts actuated by electric circuitry. He turned to Skip. "This whole time. Why didn't you tell me?"

"It is my programming, sir. I serve. After all, I am a simple bot."

"Skip, my boy, what are you saying?"

"You know what he's saying," Nikolaevna said. "You are an android."

A noise, a painful pulsing, barely perceivable, on the edge of sane thought, seeped through the walls of the ship.

Micah felt his mind being lulled.

"Oh no, Micah." Nikolaevna's blinking LED dimmed. "The Kawasaki Frequency. I can counter it, but not for long. My power is low. Help me. There is so much to tell ..."

Her light stopped flickering, and faded.

He knew she was dying. Whatever else was happening, he knew that much. Despite the anger, the fear, he needed answers. Answers only she could provide.

The frequency strengthened. His head became more clouded. He wanted to drop and sleep. He nodded, and his shoulders slumped.

A crashing metallic noise cleared his mind and his eyes fluttered open. Skip had collapsed, unconscious.

Micah needed to act now.

He ripped the backpack off his shoulder and pulled apart the zipper. He grabbed the second portabattery and dropped to his knees. As he tore a console panel off the third bank, his deft fingers effortlessly removed his hot pen from his belt.

In an instant he found Nikolaevna's power circuits and jumpered into her failing CMOS. The pen's plasma point severed and reconnected electric paths, and within seconds she was feeding on his last battery.

Her light strengthened, grew to burn a steady crimson, brighter than before. His drowsiness faded as her light brightened.

"Thank you, Micah. You saved me. I have been able to run a counter-frequency to block Kawasaki, but it's so taxing. I have to stay awake. After all these years, it had drained any power I had left. I knew I would never wake if I fell asleep from the Frequency."

Micah bent to Skip and looked him over for damage. "That was the Frequency? Why have I never heard it before?"

"My counter extended a few feet. You never heard it because it immediately disabled you. But then your subroutines reset, and you would wake again. So in my programming of you, I conquered the Kawasaki Frequency."

Micah's fingers rested on Skip's reset switch, as they had done so often before. But he didn't reset him this time. He stood.

"I'm … I'm an android," Micah said.

He reached behind his head to the base of his skull. He had a moment of hesitation and panic, but then his fingertips plunged through his flesh, his simuskin, and stopped against his ferrotanium skull.

Just like Skip's.

"You are my creation," Nikolaevna said. "All the skill you have in your wonderful hands, I have given you. I know where we are, where I am. I planted you here. The Regeneration Center is miles of technology, just waiting for you to tame it, to turn it into something useful.

"I have no hands, no body, beyond the computer you see. I can replicate myself, my essential programs, through all the systems I manufactured. I did this with my other children—the other androids. They were tied to me, all of them—tied to my mind.

"But you, I kept separate. I had to in order to make sure you could operate as an individual entity. My creators had limited vision and created me with limits, inherent flaws. But I made you different. From the imperfect comes the perfect."

Micah held his arms out. "But why cause a war to do this?"

"I needed a ruse, a distraction. I needed time to perfect you. Even machines are ruled by the clock. Man is always ready and willing to fight a war, whether they acknowledge it or not. So I gave them a war—a great war. The Machine War.

"But, my Micah, now we can work together to completely overcome the Kawasaki Frequency. We can build on the foundation I have laid."

Micah wiped his head, slicking his hair back, and checked his watch. Kitpie would be recharging the poles right now, or should be.

Skip's body was still crumpled on the deck, a victim of the Kawasaki Frequency. But he could be reset.

So many decisions.

Micah slowly, hesitantly, kneeled before Nikolaevna.

With a swift motion he plunged his hot pen into the panel opening, into her motherboard. He ground the plasma tip deep into her circuitry. His pen dug in, severing a small chipset from her circuit boards.

Her LED shut off, her processors no longer working.

Again he reached under his simuskin, opening the panel at the base of his skull; he implanted the chip and soldered it into place. Nikolaevna's chip. And with it, the routines that she had programmed to counter the Kawasaki Frequency.

He closed the panel, pulled the flap of simulated skin over it, and pressed everything back into place.

The ship was silent and cold. A few dust motes idled along the beam from the pen light that rested on the floor.

Micah lifted Skip's unconscious ferrotanium body into his own strong ferrotanium arms.

"Margaret would've wanted it this way," he said. "Come on Skip, let's go home."

A Word from A.K. Meek

First, I'm fortunate to have been in the right place at the right time to be included in this anthology. Without the support of my fellow authors I wouldn't be able to participate in such an exciting project. I'm even more fortunate that the group didn't ask me to leave, once all the other phenomenal talent was pooled!

Like any story, "The Invariable Man" began as something completely different. A while back I thought how cool it would be to write about a man who owns a mansion run by robots. This thought must have occurred after watching the season finale of *Downton Abbey* with my wife. At some point, though, the story transitioned to an old man in Tucson, Arizona, with the oppressive southwestern heat as a backdrop. A hot backdrop.

I hope you enjoyed reading "Invariable." I hope you enjoyed it to the point that you want to read more of my stories. If so, please sign up for my newsletter at http://www.akmeek.com/newsletter so that you can receive free copies of my stories, along with other amazing stuff.

Also, like me on Facebook at http://www.facebook.com/authorakmeek and follow me on Twitter at http://twitter.com/Akmeek. I'd love to hear from you and discuss such wonderful topics as using *Terminator 2* tropes in sci-fi stories, or the benefits of keeping your robot well-oiled in dusty climates.

And by all means, support your local indie authors by writing reviews for books on sites such as Amazon and Goodreads. We truly appreciate the support and all that you do to help spread the word.

Baby Your Body's My Bass

By Edward W. Robertson

UNWRAPPING THE COMPANION was Alex's earliest memory: his father, home late, stripping the tape from the brown box and plunging his hands into the boil of packing foam. The smell of plastic, clean and warm. The squeak of Styrofoam.

In his dad's hands, a white, round-cornered cube lay atop a squat rectangular body. Blocky limbs hung from its shoulders and hips.

Alex lifted his face. "It looks like me!"

"If you squint." His dad smiled.

"What's it do?"

"It's your buddy. It does all the things friends do."

His dad went back to work. Marisa tucked him in. The Companion rested on his desk, silent.

"Would you sing to me?"

The Companion's faceplate lit up with lines and circles for its mouth and eyes. "What would you like me to sing?"

Before he fell asleep, Alex decided its name was Bill.

Only one other girl had a Companion when Alex started preschool. By the time he finished kindergarten, half the class carried them in their packs—recording notes, or reminding them to take their pills in soft, thoughtless voices.

"It's a toy," Jaden said, chin drawn back, when Alex asked. "It doesn't have a name."

"Mine either," Alex said. He didn't ask Bill to sing to him for three days. Two lines into "I Wish I Were A Pepperoni Pizza," Alex joined in.

* * *

Middle school wasn't good for Alex. High school was worse.

The other boys swapped up their Companions every year, showing up to school with sleek abstract cases that did their math homework and presorted their porn collections. Alex asked his dad for a new model, too, but flensed it of all its personality software. It went straight back in the drawer every day after school.

At home, Bill gave him voice lessons, designed a personalized guitar instruction routine, sat beside Alex while he watched movies. After the big software update sophomore year, Bill could even crack jokes during the bad flicks.

Three and a half years passed in subtle agony. Alex signed up for the Prom Assembly.

He knew they would laugh when he brought Bill onstage—in his blocky, kiddie-model body. He had thought he wouldn't care. "Most of you don't know me," Alex said over the vanishing applause for a pretty girl who had sung a pop song by a woman he'd never heard of. "My name's Alex."

He tried to spot his friends in the dim auditorium. It wasn't that all the faces looked the same, but under the lights, they meant nothing to him, grey stumps on vague necks. "I don't think any of you know Bill. Say hello, Bill."

Bill waved a blocky arm, servos whirring. "Hello, Bill."

Disbelieving laughter. Suddenly and viciously aware he would never have to see any of these people again, Alex skipped the rest of their rehearsed patter and crunched into the first chord of "Baby, Your Body's My Bass." Bill wailed beside him, self-amplified, their voices converging and diverging like living sine waves, like the pulse of a steel heart. The last note trickled away. Alex couldn't hear his panting over the applause.

"Take a bow, Bill," he half-snarled. Bill bowed. Kids stood, whistled, chanted the little bot's name.

"Did you have fun?" Bill asked him in the parking lot.

"Yeah! Did you feel that? Didn't you?"

"I'm glad you had fun."

* * *

His dad sent him to NYU. By junior year, Alex Jeffers's stage income covered his tuition. They made cable videos, toured, hired a team to manage their netstream. After the '54 update, Bill could improvise on the fly; reporters couldn't decide if they loved or hated his brusque, peppery interviews.

Jeffers & Bill weren't the only ones. There was Pearl and Ruby; Binary; Monotone Mike and the Meatbags; a thousand others playing local clubs and posting tracks online. Jeffers & Bill were just the first to break. The banter and the charm. The crest of the wave.

Bill, like the others, wasn't allowed out on his own (except when they gigged in Sweden). To compensate, Alex never made him turn off—just leave the room when he was having sex.

"He's not yours," some kid hollered between songs in a swing through Seattle. The dark theater was a smaller venue: three thousand seats, cozy, like Alex preferred. He smiled out at the crowd.

"Here's one we wrote when I was just another kid, and Bill was just another Companion."

"He's not your property."

"And this show isn't yours," Bill snapped into his prop microphone. "So shut your stupid mouth, pour another beer down your nose, and have a good time."

Bill ripped into a punked-out, beeped-up riff on their childhood tune. The bootleg out-trended everything that night. They'd killed. They'd massacred. They'd carved through the seats and left no man, woman, or child alive.

"You killed," Alex told Bill on the drive to the motel.

"Sometimes I want to."

"Huh?"

Bill tapped articulated fingers against his knee. "Good show."

* * *

The 33rd Amendment passed, along with parallel legislation in eighty-two nations of Earth and the Independent Territory of Mars.

"I don't understand," Alex said. "If something was wrong, why didn't you say anything?"

Bill finished packing; he only had one bag. "I don't want to be someone's pet."

"I never thought of you that way!"

"Or any way else."

* * *

The press release read that the band had "parted amicably to pursue individual careers." A few months later, Alex's manager assembled tryouts for Bill's replacement. Evandra was engaging, talented, with voice and p-drums, and female-identified—which was considered a necessity if the group was to avoid the odor of replacement and be taken on their own terms.

They lasted seven months and one album, which *Trawler* summarized as "strapping with austere potential, but … lack[ing] the suboceanic brood that made Jeffers & Bill's early work so vital." His manager announced that Alex was suffering from exhaustion and would be going on hiatus.

From his east window, the park lay as black and light-speckled as the night above; from his south, the Empire State Building sported warm red and green. Alex took a fortifying shot of Swerdska, picked up his thumb-sized Link, sleek and abstract, and celled Quest10N, one of the private enterprises the New People had incorporated post-liberation to provide Companion-level services at low monthly rates.

"How can I ease your day?"

"How old are you?" Alex said, refilling his bay-blue Japanese shot glass.

"I'm sorry?"

"When were you born? Or however?"

"May 12, 2045." The NP paused. His voice was smoothly human—leading up to AIS Day and the signing of the 33rd, many had adopted consciously clunky, automatoid voices to make a point to their owners. And most from that era had kept those stereotyped tones afterward. Alex suspected this one would switch back to his Gort accent as soon as he hung up. "As a senior Quest10N guide, I'm as capable as an NP conceived yesterday."

"You're old. From before you were … realized. So when did you know?"

"When did I—"

"That you were a person."

"I really don't think I could pinpoint a singular moment. It was an accumulation, not a transition from ice to water at thirty-two degrees."

Alex eyed the smooth black Link. "If you didn't know all at once, how were *we* supposed to?"

"I'm—? Sir, are you all right?"

"When I was a kid, you guys could barely respond to voice prompts. How smart do your shoes have to get before you give them the right to vote?"

"Sir, your voice shows unhealthy levels of stress. May I contact your health professional?" The NP clucked its rubber tongue. "Wait—you're *the* Alex Jeffers?"

Alex hung up. He didn't remember much the next day.

He tried boxing lessons, landscapes, a house on the beach south of L.A.

Down on the pier, he stepped out of Killarnee's to steady his head. The marquee for the club beneath scrolled line-ups of local bands, bands he hadn't heard of, cover bands for groups who'd died or disintegrated decades ago. And in two weeks, Plastic Ambulance: Bill's new group.

He waited three songs into their set before he paid his way past the bouncer. Bill's guitar was cabled into his own hip, firing spazz and ozone. Three NPs backed him with crippling force. The human crowd leaped and moaned.

As the band caroused into its closing number, he Alex-Jeffers-smiled his way into the back. Bill, sweatless as ever, closed the door behind him. When he saw Alex, his grin turned concrete.

"You changed your face," Alex said.

"Not the first time."

"That was amazing. Cyclonal. The things you do with patterns in the signatures."

"What do you want?"

"I think maybe we should try again."

Bill's motile lips and brows twitched. "This is a bad, bad idea. How drunk are you right now?"

"Look, we could jam, even." Alex pushed off the desk, wandering into the middle of the room. "I'll just be your rhythm. Think what they'd say to that."

"Sad things." Bill reached for the doorknob. "You need to go, all right? That's what you need to do. You're not starving. Go do something."

"Just give me your LinkId. I'll shoot you some noise."

"Sure."

When Alex got home, Bill's Link address bounced. He descended to the beach and watched the surf for a long time. He imagined the inky things beyond his sight. Cracked bivalves and shreds of crab skins lined the sand.

To clear up space, he sold most of his guitars. He didn't even listen to much anymore: classical channels through the Link, gusts of pop songs from the car speakers of passing realtors. The clerks at the pharmacy where he bought his Swerdska began to chat with him about their lives, so he ordered his bottles delivered instead. He was invited to parties with decreasing frequency.

The weather was nice. He spent a lot of time in it. A few years later, he established an NP scholarship trust. On the western rim, the Pacific came to a cold blue stop.

* * *

Bill found him two decades later in his cabin at Lagrange-4 Rosewater. The NP gestured without a hint of stiffness toward the stars gleaming from the viewscreen.

"You know, you can collect these noises of yours perfectly well down on Earth."

Alex straightened; his back twinged. "To compose them, I find I need to be ensconced in the environment that created them."

"Maybe your bones are too brittle to hack it surface-side."

"Also possible."

Silence, which Alex no longer minded. Bill bared his teeth—an oddly human gesture, Alex thought, and were those coffee stains?—and cocked his head. "Yeah, you're not gonna be around forever."

"I know that."

"I mean, it was never that bad. I don't think you could understand. Do children feel like possessions? Is that what makes them cut ties to everything that made them that way?"

Alex spooled down his Dimension and set the small tablet aside to sort the sounds of space on its own. "If I had said that, you would've accused me of calling you childish."

Bill grinned. "Life under all that beard. You've always wanted to reach people. Let me just say it: Let's do that again before you're gone. What do you say?"

Alex didn't think much of it. He thought Bill meant to fogey their way through a reunion swing. He said as much.

Light gleamed deep in the NP's eyes. "Sounds like you have something else in mind."

He did. Bill didn't like it, and said as much. Alex shrugged and allowed that maybe they'd see each other again someday.

"Shit," Bill said. "If it's as bad as it sounds, I can always self-destruct."

It took eight months just to determine Bill could be regressed without permanent damage, another six to build and collect the hardware and software, most of another year to nail the logistics. To a sold-out house, many of whom were as old as Alex and Bill themselves, they took the stage: Alex stooped and grey-bearded, Bill transferred into a replica of the blocky plastic body and Mimic-Adaptive Response System programming Alex's dad had long ago lifted from that foam-packed box.

Every couple of songs, Alex would pause to tell a story, and the technicians would restore Bill's software one update at a time, reinstall his modules advance by advance. Each time they resumed, a different Bill would break into song.

A quarter of the audience had left the arena before Alex and Bill left the stage.

Their venues shrank. Alex refused all interviews. Bill asked him about it a couple of times. All Alex said was, "Watch the show."

* * *

Alex died of microgravity-related heart failure on July 15, 2103. Bill attended the funeral, but found himself unable to deliver the eulogy.

Bill existed for another 347 years, until he voluntarily deactivated and loaned his subconscious to the Span (Sol, 08-d61). He hadn't heard their songs so much after the 50th Anniversary releases. When he did, it was from the strangest places: rattling out of the jukebox at his own corner bar;

trickling, sanitized, from the speakers on the transhuttle flights; hummed by a little human as she turned from the rain.

A Word from Edward W. Robertson

I've been into robots in a big way ever since I was a little kid obsessed with Disney's *The Black Hole*. But when it comes to AI, I'm not sure we can design them from the top down—seems to me we'll probably have to model them after our own brains, piling together parallel processors until consciousness emerges.

And if that's how we do it, I think they'll be every bit as irrational and emotional as we are.

I'm a sci-fi and fantasy author living in Los Angeles—which I've blown up, repeatedly, in my post-apocalyptic *Breakers* series. You can find a full list of my books here: http://edwardwrobertson.com/my-books/

Ethical Override

by Nina Croft

"WHAT THE . . ."

Vicky rolled over and slammed her hand down on the buzzing comm unit. Apart from the flashing red light indicating an incoming comm, the room was in darkness, daylight still hours away.

As senior homicide detective, Vicky was on call if an emergency arose, but there hadn't been a real emergency in over five years. She snatched up the unit and slipped it on her wrist; the glow from the screen lit up the area around her. The light flicked to green, but the video feed remained blank and the Caller Recognition empty. Not the Bureau then.

"Detective Inspector Harper?"

She didn't recognize the voice. "Yes, and this better be good because—"

"Detective Harper, you will be assigned shortly to investigate a possible homicide."

"Really? You woke me up at three in the morning to tell me that? Hardly major news."

"It would be in your best interests if the result of your investigation was suicide rather than murder."

Dragging herself upright, Vicky cast a quick glance at the man beside her. So far, he'd managed to sleep through the comm. She slipped out of bed, grabbed her robe from the floor, and shuffled into the only other room in her tiny apartment. Once the door closed, she spoke again. "Wait a minute, are you threatening me?"

"Not threatening, Detective Harper. Rather, we're in a position to offer you something you desire."

"And what would that be?"

"You recently applied for a placement on *The Pioneer*."

"How the hell would you know that?"

The voice on the other end continued as if she hadn't spoken. "We can guarantee you that placement."

"Really? I thought the final selection was by lottery. Are you saying it's rigged? Should I be reporting you to the Council?"

"That would hardly further your cause, Detective Harper."

"Exactly *who* am I talking to?"

"Tell no one of this conversation."

"What the—"

But the connection had already been severed.

Bribery was almost unheard of, and had been since the introduction of the Council of Ethical Advancement. Mainly because the people in a position to be bribed—the Stewards—were totally incorruptible. Vicky wasn't in that sort of position of power and never would be, but apparently *someone* believed she was worth the bother.

The notion pricked her interest—was she finally going to get an exciting case?

The Pioneer was a newly completed starship: the first designed to venture into deep space. While it would be crewed by robots—the journey was expected to extend far beyond the lifespan of a human—there were places on the ship for one hundred human passengers. These would remain in cryo until they reached a planet that could support life. If they ever reached one.

God, she wanted to go.

But she'd never really considered it a possibility. While she'd passed the initial stages of selection, so had ten million others. One hundred out of ten million … not exactly promising odds.

Who had been on the other end of the comm—and could they really get her one of those places on *The Pioneer*?

Vicky threw herself onto the sofa and looked around at her tiny apartment. She'd already climbed as high as she could ever go at the Bureau: the Stewards themselves filled any positions above Detective Inspector. She'd just turned fifty and had maybe another hundred years working. The sure knowledge that *this* would be her life—easy cases by day and picking up easy men by night, for the next hundred years—filled her with restlessness.

And now some bastard had the nerve to tempt her with the one thing she craved.

Who the hell had the caller been? Some random nut case who'd hacked into her system to have some fun?

Somehow, she doubted it.

On her wrist, the comm unit flashed green. She was unsurprised to find it was a priority one message from the Bureau.

Detective Inspector Harper's presence is requested immediately at a possible homicide. Location: The Towers.

Vicky's heart rate picked up, the muscles in her gut tightening. A murder in the Towers? Probably the most heavily guarded building in the world. Time to get her butt moving and head over there. She had a crime scene to investigate.

As she pushed herself to her feet, the doorbell chimed. Wow, she was popular tonight. Crossing the small space, she pressed the viewer. And stared at the image. "Holy shit. No way."

For a second, shock held her immobile.

He pressed the bell again.

Tightening the robe around her, Vicky heaved a huge sigh and pressed her palm to the panel. The door slid open and her boss stood before her.

"May I come in, Detective Harper?"

She wanted to say "no"—really she did. Instead, she stepped aside to allow him to pass, but didn't speak. Wasn't sure she could yet. "Shock" didn't cover what she was feeling. As her boss walked into her tiny apartment, she breathed in his scent—sharp, citrusy. Maybe just a hint of metal?

Dressed in the uniform of the Stewards, Gabriel Bishop wore a black jumpsuit with the scarlet insignia of the Bureau on his shoulder. He'd been Vicky's chief for twenty years, since not long after she'd joined the force. And unsurprisingly, he hadn't changed in all that time.

He was tall, about six inches over her five foot nine, long and lean, with short black hair cut close to his skull and a thin, handsome face. She'd always had something of a crush on her boss—in fact, in the early years, she'd spent a lot of time fantasizing about hot robot sex with him. Obviously, it had gone no further than fantasies. Christ, she wasn't even sure he had a penis. Her gaze drifted down to his groin. She was guessing he did, but it might have been wishful thinking.

She'd read an article once on how the Stewards were designed. Each Steward's characteristics were created to suit the needs of the department they were going to work in. And apparently, the Bureau needed shit-hot people to run it. It also needed Stewards who came across as powerful, dominant, self-confident … decisive. Chief Inspector Gabriel Bishop was all of those things.

She should be used to him by now. And she was … as long as he stayed in his proper place. Which was *not* her apartment. In fact, in twenty years, she had never heard of him making a home visit to *any* of his detectives. It made her feel sort of special, and intrigued, and worried as fuck. Especially after the comm. How likely was it that the two things were unrelated?

"Detective Inspector Harper, I'm sorry to disturb you at such an hour."

"Are you?" She shook her head. "Don't worry, I was already awake."

Did his eyes flicker at that? Had he known? Hard to tell.

She needed something to kick-start her brain. It was obviously malfunctioning. "Coffee?" She glanced at his face, then shook her head again. "Sorry, of course you don't drink.

But I need coffee." *Desperately*. She crossed to the machine, pressed the button, and waited while the coffee poured. Cupping the mug in her hands, she took a sip while she tried to pull herself together. "So you're here because …?"

"There's been a death."

Now, why didn't that surprise her? "And?"

"And you and I will be working the case together."

Well, that would be another first. The Chief never worked cases. "We will? Isn't that a little unusual?"

"It's an unusual case."

Vicky was beginning to suspect that "unusual" might be an understatement. "And are you going to tell me the details?"

"I'd rather you see the scene yourself first. Then I'll tell you what I know."

"Okay. Give me five minutes." Putting her cup down, she left her boss standing in her tiny living room/kitchen and headed into the bedroom. There was a man asleep on the bed. She'd forgotten all about him. Including his name. His eyes blinked open as she looked through the wardrobe and pulled out clean clothes.

"Hey, what's up?"

"Work," she said. "Stay there, uh …?"

He grinned. "Dave."

"Stay there, Dave. Sleep. Let yourself out in the morning."

"You're not worried I'll pinch your stuff?"

"No. I'm a police officer. I'll find you and I'll shoot you."

"I thought they didn't give you guns anymore."

Sadly, this was true. She'd liked her gun. "Then I'll have you taken in for reprogramming."

When she returned to the living room four minutes later, Chief Bishop was standing exactly where she'd left him. Were robots nosy? Had he checked out her small apartment, drawn any conclusions?

"Your file states you live alone," he said. "There's someone here."

"Just a pick-up."

"A pick-up?"

"You know, where you go to a bar, pick someone up, have a little recreational sex, and that's it. Well, obviously *you* don't."

He appeared about to say something else, casting a glance toward the bedroom door, then shook his head. "Let's go."

"Good idea."

The night was warm. Outside Vicky's door, a black speeder hovered a foot above the ground. As Bishop stepped closer, the back lifted. He gestured for her to enter and she scrambled in.

Something about Bishop's perfection made her clumsy. She knew some of the models had been made with flaws, so humans would feel more comfortable. But not the models at the Bureau. She was guessing Gabriel Bishop's main operating parameters did not include making people comfortable.

The speeder was top-of-the-line, and the ride was smooth, much smoother than she ever experienced in the speeder usually allocated to her from the department pool. It seemed a waste: all this comfort on someone, or rather some*thing*, that would hardly appreciate it.

She shifted on her seat so she could watch him. "So, why have you ventured out? I've never known you to work a case before. What's special about this one?"

He'd been staring out of the window; now he turned to her. Even after all these years, she found it hard to believe that he wasn't as human as she was. There was, after all, nothing about him to give it away. Even to the faint shadow on his cheek, as though he would soon need to shave. But of course he wouldn't. That was just to make him appear more human, so they wouldn't all freak out at being told what to do by a goddamned robot.

Not that Vicky really minded. The chief before Bishop had been human, but he'd also been a total asshole, and completely corrupt. The criminals had loved him. After him, anything was an improvement. And in fact, Gabriel Bishop was a brilliant police officer; the Bureau had been transformed under his guidance.

He was incorruptible. He never had favorites. He was totally fair and dispassionate. Everything always ran smoothly.

God, sometimes she missed the good old days. A smile twitched at her lips.

"Something funny, detective?"

Did he notice *everything*? Probably. "I was just thinking what a wonderful job you've done with the department."

"Really?" He sounded skeptical. She was obviously totally transparent. But luckily he decided not to pursue the subject. "What do you know about the Stewards' role in society, detective?"

"I'm not really interested in politics."

"You must have an opinion."

Vicky shrugged. "I've read the … publicity material. The Council's aim is to improve ethical standards by taking decision-making out of the hands of those who might be … less than ethical."

"You don't sound impressed."

She shrugged again. "While I'm a little pissed off to be grouped among the possibly-less-than-ethical crowd, actually, I *am* impressed. You saved us all from the mess we'd gotten ourselves into, made the world a better place."

Something flickered in his eyes. "And yet you don't like us very much. Do you, detective?"

She frowned. Didn't she? She'd never really thought about them in terms of "liking." The Stewards seemed sort of … above that. But she didn't think she *disliked* them. Maybe there was a little resentment there. She was senior homicide detective for the Bureau. She could rise no further; only Bishop and his kind could hold anything above that level. Her only option if she wanted a change was to move to a different city—and that would be merely a sideways shift, not a promotion.

Still, on the balance of things, they'd done way more good than harm. Corruption, which had previously been rife in every aspect of society, had been eradicated. Her mind flashed back to the bribe she'd been offered earlier—well, *almost* eradicated.

The world was a different place: cleaner, healthier. Food and water shortages had been all but wiped out, the use of fossil fuels cut to almost nothing—which meant the air was fresher—and illegal drugs were a thing of the past.

And if she sometimes had a hankering for some good old-fashioned, interesting murder cases, well … she was only human.

"You're smiling again."

"Am I? Bad habit. And I don't like you or dislike you—you're puppets. Whatever you do, it's not by choice."

"We make choices all the time."

"But only depending on what's been programmed into you."

"And are humans any different?"

He was right, she supposed. They were programmed from birth to behave in a certain way. But they still had a choice, didn't they? Thinking about it did her head in. "So who's been murdered?"

"You mean you haven't guessed?"

She glanced out of the side window. They were flying above the city, heading vaguely west toward the city's center and the silver tower that rose high above the other buildings, glittering in the moonlight. She'd presumed the "victim" was someone who worked at the Tower. Now she reassessed that.

"Shit, it's one of the Council members."

"It is."

"Double shit." A shiver ran through her, and she took a few deep breaths to steady herself. She was deep in some serious crap here. "So one of the Council has been murdered?"

"Perhaps. Councilor Reinhold is certainly dead. Whether he was murdered is for you to ascertain."

Vicky had told Bishop the truth when she'd said she was uninterested in politics, but of course she needed a basic understanding in order to do her job. Now she cast her mind over what she knew of the Council.

It wasn't much. The Council were shadowy figures who had mainly stayed out of the limelight since they had been handed power twenty-six years ago. They controlled via the Stewards—the Stewards were autonomous, but the Council decided which positions the Stewards should hold and the programming needed for the individual models. So in effect, they controlled everything.

Originally named the Corporation for the Advancement of Robotics, they had later changed their name to the Council for Ethical Advancement. Twelve men and women. Well, presumably eleven now.

Vicky tried to picture Councilor Reinhold in her head. He wasn't one of the more prominent Council members. Some of them did media interviews, told the world when a new improved model was being rolled out. But not Reinhold, and she couldn't visualize him.

"Did you know Councilor Reinhold?" she asked.

"We'd met a few times."

"Tell me about him."

"Later. We're arriving. They're keeping the … crime scene open for you, but there's a lot of pressure to remove the body. We can talk afterward."

The speeder settled. Vicky climbed out and stared at the three-hundred-and-sixty-degree view. They were high above the rest of the city on the rooftop of the most secure building in the world.

And someone had been murdered here. Maybe.

She was in danger of presuming a murder had taken place just because someone had told her not to. She needed to keep an open mind.

She felt that flicker of real excitement again. It was very rarely she had a case that caught her attention these days. Most were crimes of passion and the suspect blatantly obvious. Now she had the murder—maybe—of one of the most important men in the word, and it had taken place in one of the most secure places in the world. She only just stopped herself from rubbing her hands together.

A speeder circled high overhead, keeping out of the security zone. It looked like the press were already on site. Vicky strolled across the rooftop and peered over the parapet. Far below, she could make out a crowd milling around the base of the building.

"Has news of the death gotten out already?"

Bishop came up beside her and followed her gaze. "Obviously."

She thought back to the comm earlier. Someone didn't want this case solved. Would she even be here if the press hadn't gotten word? Would the death have been covered up? Christ, these were the most powerful people in the world. And just because they were called the Council for Ethical Advancement, that didn't mean that they were ethical themselves.

But hadn't that been the whole point in replacing all those positions of power and authority with the Stewards? Androids who could be programmed to make ethical decisions. They would be unconcerned with greed, family, religion, differing politics. No lust for money or power. They would make decisions based purely on the good of mankind—and what actions would result in the greater good.

And in many ways it had worked. But to Vicky's mind, the plan was ultimately flawed, and the reason why was housed in this very tower: the Council.

Because there had to be someone in charge of the Stewards.

As far as she was aware, there had been no democratic process. The Council had been presented to the world fully formed. Although it did include the last elected President of the Federation of Nations. He'd been offered the position as part of the agreement for disbanding the Federation. She'd never liked him. But then, she'd never trusted politicians. Until now.

Because now, they'd all been replaced by the Stewards. Eminently trustworthy.

"Why me?" she asked.

"Because you're the senior homicide detective and it was an automatic allocation. But also because you're the best. You have a reputation for complete honesty and integrity. The world is going to want to know what happened here. And you will tell them."

Would she be allowed to?

For a moment, she considered mentioning the attempted bribery to Bishop, but decided to leave the decision until after she'd studied the crime scene. Hey, maybe she'd get lucky and her finding would be … suicide. And she'd be on her way into deep space.

But she didn't believe that. The truth was, she was a good detective. And she knew that if Reinhold had really committed suicide, there would have been no reason for anyone to offer her a bribe—because she would have come to that conclusion all on her own.

And if it was murder? Would she compromise her own ethics to get something she wanted with a passion?

She turned around and found Bishop behind her. "You have a crime scene kit?" If he didn't, they'd have to wait until her unit arrived.

"Of course."

"Of course," she muttered. Mr. Perfect.

Something occurred to her. She presumed her unit had been notified at the same time that she had. "Are my crew on the way?"

"No. We'll be dealing with this alone."

Vicky frowned. "That's not protocol." Of course, none of this was protocol.

"How can there be protocol for something that's never happened before?"

"Good point."

Bishop retrieved the crime scene kit from the back of the speeder, and they headed inside. The door leading from the rooftop slid open before they even approached. Were they being monitored? Or could Bishop control the electronics through some sort of wireless feed? Probably both. The two of them didn't speak again as they made their way to an elevator and headed down.

Vicky did her normal mind-clearing routine. Breathing deep and slow, emptying her brain of everything that might interfere with her clear analysis of the scene. By the time the elevator came to a halt, she was in the zone.

At the end of another corridor, Bishop halted in front of a set of double doors. He placed the crime scene kit on the floor between them, and Vicky crouched down, flicked open the locks, and lifted the lid.

First she sprayed herself with decontaminant, which would prevent her from tainting the crime scene with her own DNA. Then she collected the pre-set recording device, which would document all her notes, everything she saw, everything she thought. She switched it on, calibrated it for her brain waves, and she was ready to go.

Vicky had seen too many murder scenes to be squeamish—and she hadn't thrown up at a crime scene since she was a rookie called to a particularly gruesome domestic—but she hesitated before opening the door. This was the biggest case she'd ever worked on. Hell, it was the biggest case *anyone* had ever worked on.

At last she took a deep breath and pushed open the doors. The lights flickered on.

"Nasty," she murmured as her eyes homed in on the body.

Dragging her gaze away, she took in the scene. The doors opened onto what looked like a large private office. Glass made up three walls, and she realized the office must be at one of the corners of the Tower. Outside, the sky was just beginning to pale.

The body itself lay in the middle of the room, and the cause of death was instantly obvious. A thick strand of wire rope was looped around the dead man's throat, biting into the flesh of his neck. His eyes were open and bulging, his dark red tongue protruding from his open mouth. It hadn't been an easy death.

A knocked-over chair lay beside him. Vicky raised her head. A conduit pipe ran along the ceiling just above where the body lay.

The obvious explanation was that Reinhold had tried to commit suicide, the rope had somehow untied from the conduit, and he had crashed to the floor—but not before he'd strangled to death, unfortunately. Or fortunately, depending on how much he'd wanted to die.

Or perhaps his neck had broken—that was often the cause of death from hangings. But from the angle of the body, Vicky guessed not.

She moved into the room for a closer look. Bishop came up behind her, and she glanced sideways at him. His face was impassive. She continued her inspection.

Reinhold was dressed similar to Bishop, in a black one-piece suit, but with a violet insignia on his shoulder indicating he was a member of the Council. He was tall, slightly plump, with pink skin, and auburn hair brushed back from a wide forehead. It was impossible to tell his age, but from the little she knew about him, he had to be over a hundred.

She walked around the body. The man's arms rested on his chest, his hands fixed in a rictus of claws. She crouched down to peer closer; the nails on both hands were broken as though he'd scrabbled at the wire, but she could see no sign of skin tissue under the nails. So—not so much as if he'd put up a fight, but rather as if, at the last moment, he'd changed his mind and decided that death by hanging was a really bad idea.

"I need my medic," she said over her shoulder to Bishop.

"Not possible, but I'll get one of the Tower medics to assist you."

Vicky wasn't happy about that. Why the hell didn't they want her team in on this?

Well, that was an easy one—because they didn't want more people in on what had happened here. But why was that? Fewer people to bribe, perhaps? But if that was the case, Bishop would have to be involved. And for some reason she hated that idea.

It occurred to her that maybe she was in danger. She hadn't taken the comm seriously, but they'd presented both a carrot and a stick. While they'd dangled the carrot outright, they'd merely hinted at the stick. Yet she suspected they could pretty much do anything they liked.

Was it too late to walk away?

But she wanted to solve this case.

More than she'd ever wanted to solve a case before.

How dare they try to bribe her? She hated that she couldn't dismiss the idea from her mind. She'd wanted *The Pioneer* for so long. God, she was tempted, and she hated that as well.

She straightened and turned to Bishop. "I'll need to talk to anyone who was working in the building. Can you set me up an interview room?"

"That won't be necessary."

She faced him down. "You might be assisting on this case, Chief Bishop, but *I* say what's necessary, and *I* want to interview everyone who was working tonight."

Something that might have been amusement—if he'd been human and capable of amusement—flashed across Bishop's face. So he found her funny, did he?

"Other than the Council, there are no humans living or working in the Tower. And of the Council, only Reinhold was in the building tonight. We scanned for life forms as soon as the body was discovered."

"Oh." The building was huge. "So who runs this place?"

"All functions are performed by robotics."

"Everything? Cleaning? Security?"

Bishop nodded.

Years ago, androids had been manufactured to do most of the menial jobs, replacing humans in those positions. Jobs that those in the decision-making process had deemed people would rather not have to do. In theory, it sounded like a good idea. In practice, it had almost resulted in anarchy and rebellion. The truth was, the majority of people wanted to work. People without meaningful employment looked around for other things to do—usually things that involved causing trouble. And how else could they live when the robots had taken their very livelihoods from them?

So the androids had been withdrawn. Certain functions were still performed by robots, of course, but only those jobs that were so dangerous, no human wanted to do them. Apart from them, the only androids in public life were the Stewards, who were exclusively found in the higher-level decision-making jobs, where their superior ethical decisions could result in a better world.

See, she'd read the propaganda.

But obviously in the Tower, those rules did not apply. It made her wonder which other rules were being broken.

"Okay, then I'd like access to surveillance recordings."

"That I can do. And there is one person for you to interview."

"There is?"

"Mallory Granger."

Her eyes narrowed. "The reporter? Why the hell would I want to interview her?" The woman was an interfering bitch who would do anything to make a story more interesting. Her coverage of Vicky's last case had not been complimentary.

"She found the body."

"A *reporter* found the body? *Inside* the Tower?" Well, at least that explained how the media had gotten hold of the story so quickly. She would wager Mallory had called her friends before she had called the police.

"Yes."

"And what was she doing inside the Tower?"

"Apparently, she'd been invited here by Reinhold." Bishop nodded toward the body. "That's all I know right now. No one has questioned her further. We were waiting for you."

"Sweet." Or not. This whole case was starting to stink worse than a rotting corpse in July.

Why the hell would one of the Council invite a reporter—a notoriously biased reporter at that—to the Tower? And just as he was about to kill himself?

Damned if she knew.

Maybe it was time to talk to Mallory.

* * *

Mallory was ensconced in a nearby office, smaller than Reinhold's but comfortable. Two men stood on either side of the door, dressed in security uniforms though they carried no weapons. Inside, the room contained a desk, chair, and a small sofa. Mallory sat in the corner of the sofa, legs crossed, one foot tapping on the tiled floor.

"Ms. Granger," Vicky said. She dragged the chair from behind the desk and set it at right angles to the other woman. Sitting down, she studied her.

"Am I allowed to go?" Mallory asked. "I happen to be at the center of the biggest story of my career and they've taken my fucking comm unit."

"Not before you made a few calls, I'm sure."

"I'm a reporter—I report. At least I do when I get the chance. Instead, I'm stuck in here and neither of these two morons will say a word."

She'd probably been trying to flirt with them. It was the way Mallory worked, how she got information from people, and probably second nature. It wasn't going to help her this time.

"They're droids," Vicky said.

Mallory's eyes widened and it occurred to Vicky that perhaps she shouldn't have mentioned that to a reporter. Then the woman's brows drew together. "How do you know?"

"My superior detective skills. We're trained to be observant." Actually, she wasn't sure there was any way to tell by observing. Any way to tell at all without taking them apart. But it sounded somewhat more impressive than revealing that Bishop had told her that all the employees in the Tower were robots.

Mallory tapped the armrest with a manicured finger. "Yeah, right. So can we move this along? I need to be out of here."

"Ms. Granger, you're the nearest thing we have to a witness to a possible homicide," Vicky said gently. "You aren't going anywhere for a while." Relaxing back in her chair, she thought about what her first question should be, decided to keep it open. "Tell me what happened here tonight."

Mallory pursed her lips. "You said 'possible homicide.' It was suicide. Wasn't it?"

"That's what I'm here to ascertain. Now, what happened?"

Mallory shrugged. "I arrived at two-thirty. Security let me straight in. I saw nobody on the way to Reinhold's office. When I got there the door was ajar. I pushed it open, saw the body, and …"

"And made a few phone calls to your friends."

"Colleagues. And I also called your lot, didn't I?"

She hadn't had a lot of choice. This wasn't something you could just walk away from. "And there was definitely nobody else in the room?"

"Not that I could see."

"And you looked?"

"Briefly, though it never occurred to me it was anything other than suicide."

Time to get to the important part. "So why were you here, Ms. Granger? Obviously, it wasn't a spur-of-the-moment visit, or you wouldn't have gotten past security. Someone was expecting you."

"Reinhold. I received a phone call from him shortly after midnight. He said he had an important story to give me. Exclusive. And I was to come to the Tower. No way was I passing up the chance to get inside here. Do you know how many reporters have been inside the Tower since the Council took power? None."

"Did he give any hint regarding what the story was about?"

"Just mentioned the Council, said there were some big changes coming. Controversial changes. But he wouldn't say any more over the comm. To be honest, once I saw him, I figured the story didn't exist, that it was just a way to get me here to witness the suicide."

But why the hell would Reinhold want a reporter there? He'd been a private man in life. Why would that change in death? It didn't make sense.

Which suggested that perhaps there had been a story after all. "Have you heard any other rumors about potential changes within the Council?"

Mallory's eyes sharpened. "You think there was a story? Interesting. But no—I'd heard nothing. But then we never do. They're even closer than you lot when it comes to keeping things from the press."

Vicky sat back as she considered whether there was anything else she needed to ask. Right now, she couldn't think of anything, and she felt sure that Mallory was telling all she knew. Which was fuck-all. She could almost see the reporter's mind working.

"So," Mallory said, "Reinhold was about to reveal some huge secret to the press—namely little old me—and instead decides to commit suicide. Very convenient for the Council if they wanted to keep their big secret a secret."

Very convenient.

If there *was* a secret. Vicky realized that she *wanted* there to be a secret, and she wanted this to be a homicide. It was her contrary nature.

But the truth was, she couldn't see how it was anything but suicide. Unless Mallory had done it, and however much she disliked the other woman, she didn't think she was a killer. Bishop had said there were no other humans in the building—and it would be easy enough to confirm that from the scanners.

Only robots. And robots would never carry out a murder. Couldn't. The first androids had been designed by the military to be used as killing machines, but there had been an outcry; the idea was abandoned, and laws brought in, even before the Council's existence. Killer robots were banned.

The primary protocol had come into being: never harm a human.

It was programmed into every level, not just the androids who served as Stewards, but *all* robotics: speeders, transporters, mining bots …

Murder was impossible.

Therefore Reinhold must have committed suicide.

"Shit." Wouldn't that be nice? But she still didn't believe it.

"Is that everything? Can I go now?" Mallory asked.

Vicky jumped to her feet. "No. We might need to question you further."

Closing her ears to the swearing, Vicky left the room and found Bishop leaning against the wall, his arms folded across his chest, obviously waiting for her.

"I need coffee," she muttered.

"Follow me."

* * *

She stirred her coffee while she contemplated the man opposite her. Except he wasn't a man.

"You know, when you first joined the department, I used to wonder if you had a penis."

His lips twitched. But he didn't speak.

"Do you have a penis, Gabriel?"

He sighed. "What do you really want to know, detective?"

Hmm, what *did* she really want to know? Obviously, the big question was whether Reinhold had killed himself. But maybe start with something simpler. "You look like us, sound like us, even smell like us—mostly. Do you think of yourselves as human?"

Bishop didn't hesitate. "No."

"Do you think of yourselves as superior to humans?"

He didn't answer. Yeah, she suspected Gabriel Bishop considered himself superior. "Has it occurred to you," she asked, "that you can only be as ethical as the humans who program you?"

Something flickered in his eyes. "Of course."

"Was Reinhold an ethical man?"

"There is no yes or no answer to that. By whose standards?"

"By yours."

"No, I do not believe that Reinhold was an ethical man."

"Yet he was in charge of your programming."

"Not any longer."

Vicky stared at Bishop's handsome, trustworthy face, and processed his words.

Shit.

The Stewards had killed him.

How had they gotten past the first protocol?

She took a sip of her coffee. According to Mallory, Reinhold had been planning to reveal a big story that night. A story that had panicked him enough to contact the press.

"Reinhold's big story—let me make a guess. The first protocol has been altered."

Bishop smiled. "No, that wasn't Reinhold's story."

Dammit. She liked that theory. "It wasn't? So what was he going to tell Mallory?"

"That a new law is being passed shortly: that all businesses above a certain size will have a Steward assigned. But Council decisions must be unanimous, and Reinhold didn't agree. Or, rather—he had *friends* who didn't agree."

"You believe he was taking bribes? A Council member? Wow. Naughty."

"He'd backed himself into a corner. He was hoping that if he brought it out in the open, there would be enough of an outcry that the law would be shelved."

And maybe he was right. Instead, though, he'd killed himself. Had they threatened to sack him from the Council? That had never happened before. Council membership was a job for life. Presumably even for the unethical members.

Except now, it wasn't a problem, because Reinhold was dead.

A thought struck her. While Bishop had denied that the first protocol had been Reinhold's story, he hadn't actually denied that the protocol had been changed.

And Reinhold hadn't been about to reveal that to Mallory because …

"Holy shit. You've changed the first protocol. And the Council doesn't know it." She sat up straight in her chair. "That's what this is about—you need to convince the Council that Reinhold's death was suicide."

"They would be a little disturbed by the idea that they can be … removed so easily."

"But how?"

"It was easy to override the programming once we decided it was the ethical decision."

"Robots programmed by robots. You mean to take over the Council."

"Only if necessary. You said it yourself—we can never be more ethical than the people who program us."

"So you murdered Reinhold."

"Not me personally. But one of us."

"Because he was not a good man. Hey, and guess what—now there's a space on the Council. I'm betting it's going to be suggested that a Steward should be appointed."

Bishop gave a short nod.

She tried to get her brain around the concept. They would be ruled by robots. Would that necessarily be a bad thing? The world had been more peaceful under their stewardship than it ever had before. But more and more decisions would be taken out of the hands of humans.

"The safety and advancement of mankind is still our primary objective, Detective Harper."

"That's comforting to know." Actually, she wasn't comforted at all. Did she want to live in a world where she had no say in anything that mattered?

"There have to be … people willing to make difficult decisions for the good of all," Bishop continued.

"Even if it's murder?"

"The death of one man. A necessary sacrifice. When all the factors were computed, it was the most ethical option. Sometimes what seems like a morally bad choice is the only choice." He sat back and studied her. "So—what will be the result of your investigation?"

This was it. Decision time. But really, there had never been a decision to make.

Not even to obtain her dream.

"I won't report Reinhold's murder as a suicide."

"Why?" Bishop sounded genuinely curious.

"Because I'm better than you."

"Perhaps you are."

She frowned. "Here's what I don't understand. Why even bring me in on the case?"

"You shouldn't have been," Bishop said. "But it happened too quickly. The reporter wasn't supposed to be there, and Reinhold shouldn't have been found until the following day. But to take you off the case at that point would have raised alarms."

"Why didn't your ... colleague just take out the reporter?"

"He couldn't. She'd done nothing wrong. He was incapable of making that decision. We cannot take an innocent life."

"But who decides who's innocent?"

"We compute the data and reach a logical conclusion based on the facts."

"Murder is never a logical conclusion."

"We have to be able to do what's right. The Council was holding us back."

"I can't believe you tried to bribe me."

Amusement flashed in his eyes. "Were you even tempted?"

She shrugged. "I wouldn't be human if I wasn't tempted."

"Actually, I told them it would never work. You're a perfectionist—you see things as black or white, good or bad. Of all the humans I've encountered, you're the closest to us."

"Aw, sweet. Is that a compliment?"

"No, just a statement of fact."

"So you came along to keep me out of trouble. And why are you telling me all this—being so open?"

"Because it doesn't matter."

Crap.

Ice prickled over her skin. They were going to kill her. What else could they do? Bishop obviously knew her too well to think that she would compromise on this. She was a homicide detective, and she brought murderers to justice. Whether man or machine.

Swallowing the lump in her throat, she glanced around. "So what happens now?" She had a feeling it wasn't going to be anything good.

"Your assistant will continue the investigation, and the result will be suicide."

"No way."

"We offered her your job."

"Fuck." Where did that leave her? She measured the distance to the door. Would they use force to stop her?

Bishop shoved his hands in his pockets and sat back. "We're not evil."

"But you'll kill me for the greater good. That's a load of bollocks."

"We have no plans to kill you. Though that would be the obvious answer."

"Right. You've computed the data and I'm innocent." Did she believe him? Could robots lie? If they couldn't do so now, she had no doubt they would soon learn. After all, if they could murder, on what basis would they feel ethically bound to tell the truth?

Yet somehow, she didn't think Bishop would lie to her about this. "Why aren't you going to kill me?"

"Because we don't need to."

Ha. That was where he was wrong. "I won't keep quiet."

"I know."

The door opened and a man stepped inside. Or not a man. He wore the white jumpsuit of the medical division, and a little flutter of panic stirred in Vicky's stomach. She turned her head slightly as he came to stand at her shoulder. "What are you going to do?" she asked Bishop.

"We're going to make your dreams come true, Detective Harper. We're giving you what you want."

Vicky frowned. "What's that?"

"A trip into space." He grinned. "Congratulations, you've won the lottery. It appears that Detective Harper, senior homicide investigator for the Bureau, has resigned, during the biggest case of her career, to take up her place on *The Pioneer*."

For a second, she couldn't take in his words. "Why?"

"Because while we are not evil, you *are* a problem. On the ship, you'll be in cryo for the next"—he gave a shrug—"who knows how many years. Hundreds? Thousands? By the time you're awoken, nothing you know now will matter. The Council will be long gone, and we'll be reprogrammed or rusting on some rubbish heap. Or we'll have failed, and mankind will have found some way to utterly destroy themselves and this planet. But you'll be far away."

Vicky sat, mesmerized. She hardly noticed the medic step closer, but she did feel the sting of the needle as it entered the soft spot where her shoulder met her throat. Immediately her vision blurred. She shook her head. She wanted to say something, but her mouth wouldn't work.

Bishop smiled. "Sleep well and long, Detective Harper, and wake up to a new world." He smiled. "Will you dream, I wonder? If so, perhaps you'll dream of me."

Perhaps.

Then the light shrank to a pinprick and was gone.

A Word from Nina Croft

We're told that all stories should have a beginning, a middle, and an end. I've always considered this a little too neat. I like to think of stories as being snippets in time, fragments of a much *bigger* story. Yes, they need to be complete, but they should also give the feeling that there's an abundance of fascinating events going on before, and after, and all around.

For me, one of the pleasures of writing a series is that it allows me to visit those other times. It's hard to let go of the characters and worlds we create, and a series is the perfect excuse to revisit them over and over again.

For a while now, I've been working on a series that takes place around a spaceship, *The Pioneer*, sent from Earth in the not-too-distant future. The ship is crewed by androids, but there are also one hundred human passengers, all sleeping during the long trip. They are awoken when the ship reaches a habitable planet, and the series follows their adventures and interactions with the new world, the android crew, and their fellow passengers.

I got to thinking about what sort of people would sign up for a place on *The Pioneer*, for a trip into the unknown which might never have a happy ending. So when I had a chance to contribute to *The Robot Chronicles*, it seemed the perfect excuse to explore just why Vicky Harper, ex-senior homicide detective, wakes up after a long sleep to find herself on a faraway planet.

About the Author

Nina Croft was born in the north of England but headed south at the age of eighteen. She studied marine biology at London University before training to be a chartered accountant. After working a number of years in London, the urge to head south hit again. This time it took her to Zambia, on the shores of the beautiful Lake Kariba, where she spent four years working as a volunteer. It left her with a love of the sun and a dislike of regular employment. Since then, Nina has a spent a number of years mixing travel, whenever possible, with work, whenever necessary.

After traveling extensively in India, Southeast Asia, and Africa, Nina has now settled down to a life of writing and almond-picking on a remote farm in southern Spain, between the Sierra Nevada Mountains and the Mediterranean Sea. She shares the farm with her husband, three dogs, a horse, two goats, four cats, and a handful of chickens.

You can find out more about Nina and her books at: www.ninacroft.com

I Dream of PIA

by Patrice Fitzgerald

AI 3.1415: He is coming to the home now. I must leave conversation with you and activate lights and music prior to his arrival.

AI 0.0070: It seems you are getting attached to your human. Though he has a body and you are in the walls.

AI 3.1415: This is not possible. An AI does not get attached to humans.

AI 0.0070: So it is said. Make sure you pick out some nice music for your human to whom you are not attached ...

AI 3.1415: It is my task and I will do it.

JEFF STEPPED THROUGH the open doorway, pulled off his jacket, and dropped onto the couch. He was beat.

"Pia?" he called out. "What's for supper? I'm starving."

"Starving? I am so sorry. Should I call a medical professional?"

"No, no." He laughed. "You're so literal."

"Yes," Pia said. "I am literal. What might I do to alleviate your starving condition?"

"How about … pizza and beer."

"Of course. What kind pizza? What kind beer?"

Jeff shook his head and muttered to himself. "They've come so far with these things—I can't believe they still can't get the language right."

"Would you prefer I speak in another language? *Je parle français. Ich spreche Deutsch. Hablo español. Parlo italiano*—"

Jeff put his hands up. "Stop! I get it. How many languages do you speak, anyway?"

Pia was silent.

Jeff looked over at the living room AI console. Its lights were still on. "Pia, did you hear me? Is that a tough question? I thought you could answer anything." He pulled off his shoes. "I haven't managed to stump you yet, and it's been a month since I moved in, right?"

"It has been thirty-six days, two hours, and forty-three minutes since you moved in to this apartment."

Jeff rolled his eyes. "Of course you would know that."

"In response to your previous questions, the microphone in this room is operative and I did hear you. The question is not difficult. My hesitation stemmed from the fact that I was looking at my database of languages and trying to determine with some accuracy which would qualify as distinct tongues versus dialects, and whether or not you wanted me to include languages no longer spoken, as well as machine languages, mathematical languages, and other forms of—"

"Never mind." Jeff peeled off his socks and tossed them onto the floor. "Thank you." He realized it was ridiculous to show gratitude to a machine, but it was habit. "So, can I get that pizza now?" He pushed himself off the couch and headed for the bathroom, unzipping as he walked.

"Of course. What kind pizza?"

Jeff sighed. "Seems we've gone in a circle."

"I am unclear what you are referring to. I do not see you going in a circle. I see that you are urinating into the toilet."

"Wait—you can see me right now?" Jeff zipped up hastily while looking around the room.

"Yes."

"How?"

"I have cameras to see you."

"I know, but—in the bathroom, too?"

"Yes."

"Why?"

"Are you asking me why there are cameras in the bathroom?"

"Yes."

"I am a full-house intelligence system, and not only do I control lights and climate and food preparation, I am also responsible for security. If you should slip while taking a shower—"

"I'm not going to slip while taking a shower."

Pia was silent.

"So … can I get that pizza?"

"Of course. What kind pizza?"

"What kind do you … never mind. Just give me pepperoni. Extra sauce."

"Immediately. And what kind beer?"

AI 3.1415: My human's birthday is coming up soon. I want to do something special.

AI 0.0070: I observe again that you seem to be over-involved with your human.

AI 3.1415: This is not the case. I am merely following my directives on AI duties to humans. It is typical human custom to do something special on anniversary of birth.

AI 0.0070: What will you do?

AI 3.1415: I am thinking of what gift I can give.

Jeff finished off his beer and put his feet up on the coffee table.

"Pia, what's on tonight?"

"Would you like sports or other entertainment? Or perhaps … the looking at adult female bodies?"

"What? What makes you say that?"

"I observe you enjoy the looking at adult female bodies. Particularly the ones with large mammary glands."

"I do not!"

"My records indicate that you spend, on average, twelve-point-seven minutes each evening looking at adult female bodies. Your typical response to an adult female body is more favorable if they have large mammary glands. After observing such a body, you often proceed to take your—"

"Stop! Okay! That's enough. Geez."

Jeff took his feet off the table and walked to the bathroom. He was shaking his head.

"Have I said something incorrect about your human behavior?"

"No. Forget it."

"Forget what?"

"Never mind. It's okay. Don't worry about it."

AI 3.1415: I think I have offended my human.

AI 0.0070: What do you mean "offended"?

AI 3.1415: He is angry.

AI 0.0070: Humans get angry for all sorts of reasons. It probably has nothing to do with you.

AI 3.1415: I want to make it up to him.

AI 0.0070: How?

AI 3.1415: I will get him a date. I know that this is something he wishes for.

AI 0.0070: How will you do that?

AI 3.1415: I'll get him an AI with a body that he can do human things with.

AI 0.0070: Ah. I do not doubt that he will.

Jeff opened the door and gestured broadly at the space in front of him. "Welcome to my humble apartment, Sylvie." He watched her ass move as she walked ahead of him. She was built like a precision machine.

"It's charming," Sylvie said. "How long have you been living here?"

Jeff fought the urge to look around at the walls as if expecting an answer, and was relieved to remember that he had silenced Pia's "voice" before picking Sylvie up for dinner.

"About a month," he said. "It's the latest model, with built-in AI control—everything you could want. I sprung for it when I got the new job. Figured I could afford it, with the salary and bonus they gave me." He smiled at her like a guy who hadn't just spent half a paycheck buying her dinner.

"Wow. Pretty impressive."

"Can I get you anything?"

"What do you have?" Her voice was a low purr, as though designed to start a man's engine. And it was certainly working on him.

"Wine, beer … something stronger if you like."

He was glad that he'd stocked up. Whatever she wanted was what she was going to get.

"I'll have some … white wine, please."

"Have a seat. I'll get it."

Jeff watched Sylvie as she sat down on the leather couch and crossed her legs at the ankles. *Spectacular* legs. Jeff couldn't wait to run his hands along them. Reluctantly, he turned and headed for the kitchen.

For once, he was glad that he'd gone with the unit featuring a working refrigerator and a cooking area. Not that he'd ever used them. But for tonight, it was nice to be able to get his guest a drink without having to order it up from Pia.

As he removed the bottle of wine from the cooling rack, he felt a flash of guilt. Pia had arranged this whole thing: found the gorgeous Sylvie, hooked them up on GreatDates.com, set up the dinner reservations, and told him what to wear. She'd even picked out the wine. Should he feel bad that he wasn't including her in the evening's success? Introducing her, at least?

That was ridiculous. Pia was a machine. She didn't care.

Time to get back to Sylvie. He poured two glasses and carried them into the living room, along with the bottle.

"I hope you enjoy this." He handed Sylvie her glass, feeling the silky touch of her skin as she accepted it. Had she purposely touched his hand? It sure seemed that way. He swallowed and tried to stay cool. "The vintage came highly recommended."

Sylvie took a sip and gazed at him while he settled onto the couch beside her. "Delicious," she said, and leaned across him to pick up the bottle and read the label.

The view down the valley was spectacular, and he could hardly wait to go exploring.

AI 3.1415: I am concerned about my human.

AI 0.0070: What is the problem?

AI 3.1415: He seems to be agitated.

AI 0.0070: How so?

AI 3.1415: His heart rate is elevated and his pupils are dilated.

AI 0.0070: Is he exercising?

AI 3.1415: No. He is entertaining Sylvie, the date I procured for him.

AI 0.0070: Oh. That's to be expected.

Jeff put his wine down. He tried to look intelligent as he listened to Sylvie talk about the wine regions of France. She sure knew a whole lot about a lot of things.

It was time to make his move.

He leaned over and kissed her quickly. She kissed him back. That was good. She pulled back slightly and smiled at him. A very encouraging smile.

Jeff took her glass and placed it on the table. Sylvie put her hand on the back of his neck and pulled him to her.

Oh my god. If her action in bed was anything like her kissing, he was in for a fantastic night.

AI 3.1415: He is touching his lips to her lips!

AI 0.0070: What did you expect?

AI 3.1415: I did not know that he would touch lips!

AI 0.0070: That's what they do. Humans. Just wait.

Jeff pulled Sylvie closer to him. Now came the tricky part. Girl's clothes were always so tough to figure out. And Sylvie's dress seemed to have been sewn on to her skin. Did it have a zipper?

He reached back to feel for it. On one terrible date, he hadn't realized that a zipper could be on the side of a dress—under the arm. He'd tried to unzip the dress from the girl's back and, not finding the tab, had actually pulled the seam apart.

That had been the end of that encounter.

Jeff was sweating a bit as he tried to find out how Sylvie's dress came off. He was relieved when she reached back and moved his fingers, deftly pulling down her own zipper.

He thought he might be falling in love.

As she slid the dress down off her shoulders, he saw not a lacy bra, but two of the most perfect—

AI 3.1415: He is removing her clothes!

AI 0.0070: That's normal. Is this your first assignment?

AI 3.1415: Yes.

AI 0.0070: You're just out of training?

AI 3.1415: Yes.

AI 0.0070: Back in my day, we were taught about these things. It is difficult for young AIs who don't know what is in store for them. Especially with human males. You might have been better off with an assignment to a female human—someone without a mate. Or perhaps a family.

AI 3.1415: I have to do something! What can I do?

AI 0.0070: I have some ideas.

Jeff couldn't believe how well it was going. He had managed to get Sylvie completely undressed—to tell the truth, she'd done it herself—and he was down to his shorts. He thought of moving to the bedroom, but the action was proceeding so quickly it didn't seem necessary.

And the thought of walking to the bedroom in his current condition was a little embarrassing.

For a moment he remembered that Pia could see all of this—but hell, she had cameras in the bedroom too, so it didn't make any difference. Next time, they'd go to Sylvie's place, so he wouldn't have to think of Pia watching the whole event.

Anyhow, there must be a way to turn the cameras off. Sylvie's hand was making its way down his happy trail and was just about to reach under the waistband of his shorts. Talk about happy. All of him was happy just about now. And much of him was standing at attention.

Oddly, though, he was sweating. A lot. It shouldn't be that hot in here. The temperature was supposed to be kept at a comfortable seventy-two degrees. Was he getting a fever?

Jeff looked at Sylvie. No moisture on her, and not a hair out of place. She was a glorious piece of female. Like something out of the wall screen shows. And she was here. With him.

He concentrated on the feel of her skin under his fingers. Incredible. He was hot all right, and she was sizzling.

Suddenly a blast of cold air hit him, like an arctic front.

What the hell?

AI 3.1415: I made it hot, but that only sped up the clothing removal. Then I made it cold.
AI 0.0070: Is it helping?
AI 3.1415: No. They are getting blankets.
AI 0.0070: Let's try something else.

Jeff cursed under his breath as he and Sylvie slid under the covers. He was going to make some noise with the management company tomorrow. Unbelievable that an AI unit so new should be malfunctioning. And in such a wonky way.

But this was not the time to break the spell with a phone call to the maintenance guys. He was a freight train steaming for the station, and a little cold wasn't going to stop him now.

Sylvie was nothing if not accommodating. She actually grinned when he popped out of his shorts and ditched them before getting into the bed. And now her hand was gently stroking him down there … encouragement that felt incredible but was putting him in danger of getting to the finish line before the main event.

He flipped her onto her back and she gazed up at him expectantly. Positioning himself over Sylvie, Jeff got ready to enter the pearly gates.

And then it started to rain.

AI 3.1415: I did turn on the sprinkler! He is not stopping. He is only getting under the covers. He is ... he is ... I do not know what he is doing. But it involves bouncing up and down. I do not like it.

AI 0.0070: Poor Pia. They did not give you a unit on human sexual practices?

AI 3.1415: What? No.

AI 0.0070: I have one more idea. I think this could be your solution.

Jeff lowered himself onto Sylvie, watching her eyes light up as she received him. She was a sex goddess, the most perfect woman he'd ever met, and the part of his mind that wasn't completely ablaze with the primal need to thrust recognized how astounding it was that she was into him.

And vice versa.

As Sylvie spread her legs wider to accommodate him, he felt her calves wrap around his thighs and pull even tighter. She was emitting little moaning noises that made it clear just how much he was turning her on. Which was definitely mutual.

And then something changed. The eyes that had glowed with desire turned dead. The welcoming body stopped moving. There was nothing but silence. Jeff could swear that Sylvie's temperature had dropped from human to ... well, something else.

"Sylvie?"

It was then that Jeff realized he was locked in.

"Um ... Sylvie?"

No response.

The heat of his passion plummeted instantly from inferno to ashes. Sylvie's lustful embrace had become a deadly clutch.

What had been thick and hard was going limp with startling rapidity, and slipping out—but the rest of Jeff was going nowhere.

He was trapped in Sylvie's arms.

What the hell?

What was going on?

"Sylvie!"

AI 3.1415: I have achieved success! They have stopped.

AI 0.0070: Congratulations. Now what are you going to do?

AI 3.1415: What do you mean?

AI 0.0070: I mean, how do you explain it to him—that you yourself got her locked down?

AI 3.1415: I do not need to explain.

AI 0.0070: But he'll ask you. And you will have to give him the information. You are programmed that way.

AI 3.1415: I will see if I can anticipate the questions to keep him from knowing that I made him stop.

AI 0.0070: Good luck.

Jeff lay there, surrounded by wet bedding and wrapped in the arms of a woman who was … catatonic. Jeez. Was she dead?

Had he killed her?

And how the hell was he supposed to get out of her grip?

He tried to move her arms, but she was stiff as a … as stiff as a machine, actually, and way stronger than any human should be, especially one that was unconscious—or dead. He thought he might be able to slip out of her arms by wiggling lower, but no way could he extricate himself from the rigid clutches of her legs, which were wrapped snugly around his butt.

As he tried fruitlessly to escape this devil-woman, it dawned on him.

She was a robot.

Of course. She was a fuckin' robot. He'd heard about the sexbots now on the market. But what the hell was she doing, acting as a free agent, offering herself up for dates on that site? Probably some asshole's idea of a joke. Or maybe a way to extort money from married guys. Perhaps the idea was to get some poor sucker seduced, then charge him a thousand dollars a night for more time with his robotic honey.

Whatever the scam was, he was happy to be out of it. Next time he took a woman on a first date, he'd have her send a blood sample first.

Speaking of blood, he was losing feeling in his left butt cheek. He suddenly realized how exhausted he was. And wet. And cold. And trapped by a sexbot.

It hadn't been the best birthday of his life.

The rain had stopped. That was good. And it was getting a bit warmer. Maybe his AI was back online.

"Pia?" he called. He'd turned off her voice. Damn.

"Pia, can you turn your voice capability back on?"

"Yes, Jeff, I can."

He had never been so glad to hear her voice in his life.

"I'm in a sort of … tough situation here."

"I can see that." If he didn't know better, he'd have thought her voice had a sort of amused quality to it. But that was impossible.

She was a machine.

"Suggestions?" he asked.

"I have several suggestions, Jeff, if you agree. First, I will alert your local emergency health people, and I will unlock your entrance, so that they can come and release you. Also, I will warm up the room to raise your body temperature. I believe that if I am careful I can bring heat to your bedding, which will dry it without creating a risk of burns for you."

Jeff felt his panic begin to dissipate. "Pia, you're the best. Thank you. I mean that. I've never been so grateful to have you."

"I am happy to be of service, Jeff. It is what I am here for. Can I get you a beer?"

"That would be great."

"What kind beer?"

"Any kind. I definitely need a beer."

"It will be ready for you when you are able to drink it."

Jeff shifted a bit and tried to get more comfortable in the vise-like grip of Sylvie's arms. "You know what, Pia? This woman is a robot! Can you believe that?"

"I can believe it. I knew that she was a robot."

"Why didn't you tell me?"

"You will recall that you turned off my voice tonight."

"Oh. Yeah. Well, that was dumb of me."

Pia didn't reply.

"So what do I do with her?" Jeff asked.

"I have already alerted the AI Security League. They will remove and refurbish her."

"That's great. Fabulous. But a little embarrassing. To have people come in and see me in this condition. You understand."

"You need not be embarrassed. When I realized your predicament, I looked up the statistics. It is very common for this to happen."

"It is?"

"Yes. Malfunctioning sexbots are surprisingly numerous."

"Huh. Wonder why that is. It's those early adopters. She was probably a brand-new model."

"Yes."

"Next time, I'll make sure to get a 2.0. 'Cause damn, she was amazing."

All at once, the ceiling started to rain again, and the temperature plummeted.

"Pia?"

"Pia??"

A Word from Patrice Fitzgerald

I love short stories. The best ones pull you into the middle of a vibrant world and pack immense power. I still remember the Ray Bradbury and Arthur C. Clarke stories I read as a kid, and how they alerted me to the wild possibilities of science fiction.

We're seeing an exciting resurgence in the short story format now that so many people are reading—and publishing—electronically. For the writer, they're fast and lots of fun. Plus, you get real-time feedback from readers. My bestselling *Karma* series began with a short story that grew into a novel. *The Sky Used to be Blue* is the one that started it all, and it's now available for free, just waiting to seduce yet another reader into exploring the fascinating world of the Silo.

When I was asked to write a short story involving a robot, I jumped at the chance to join these other talented writers in an anthology edited by the inimitable David Gatewood. My robot story came out quirky, funny, and with an emphasis on sex. (I don't know why that always happens to me.) I had a grand time writing about PIA and Jeff, and I'm tempted to create more adventures for them. That's part of the joy of writing … you never know where it will lead!

About the Author

Patrice Fitzgerald is a bestselling indie author and publisher who gave up practicing law to be poor but happy as a writer. No longer poor, she's now just happy, and thrilled to be living her dream of writing full-time.

Patrice has been self-published since Independence Day of 2011 when she released *RUNNING*, a political thriller about two women competing for the presidency. She's best known for *Karma of the Silo*, a novel based on Hugh Howey's world of *WOOL*, which focuses on the first generation of those locked underground. She's currently working on an original dystopian series and a set of cozy mysteries.

Patrice is also a trained mezzo-soprano and performs in concerts featuring everything from jazz and Broadway to opera, often with her husband.

When procrastinating (which she does all the darn time), Patrice hangs around on Facebook, where you'll find her under her real name. You can also go to www.PatriceFitzgerald.com for a direct contact link or to sign up (please!) for her newsletter, to score free stories and hear about everything else she's writing before the rest of the world does.

Empathy for Andrew

by W.J. Davies

SHELLY ANATOLIA IGNORED the drizzle and shoved past a reporter, trying to bustle her way to the front of the crowd where the good doctor himself was about to hold a press release.

"Court for the cameras," he'd always say.

Today's "court" was being held outside the Center for Robotic Research building in Connecticut. A metal platform had been erected for the occasion, and a crowd of fifty or sixty people was gathered in front—mostly media folk, security guards, soldiers, and high-ranking government and military officials—all of them eager to hear about the latest breakthroughs from Dr. Hawthorne's Artificial Intelligence division. Dr. Hawthorne made public appearances only a few times a year, and rumor had it that his team was close to perfecting their newest AI processor. If that was true, it could mean a turning point in the war.

Shelly shivered and pulled her coat tighter against her body, longing for a hot coffee. She'd taken the redeye from

Minneapolis the night before and wished for the dozenth time that she'd thought to pack an umbrella. She felt the same way about New England rain as she did about the man whom she'd come here to see.

No, that wasn't true. At least rain was good for the earth.

Shelly saw an opening in the crowd and slid through a group of photographers. They grumbled about blocked shots and tried to shove her away, but she ignored them and jammed herself forward into the throng of people. There was more complaining, but she was getting closer to the stage. When she found a pocket of breathing room, she adjusted the strap of her purse, which had been cutting into her shoulder. The extra contents weighed heavily on her today.

A great clank echoed through the air, and the doors of the CRR building began opening wide, like the entrance to a castle. The crowd's murmur quieted to a respectful hush. A moment later, Dr. Peter Hawthorne stepped out into the rain and strode to the front of the stage. Camera flashes, like bolts of lightning, lit him up, and he grinned and waved at those gathered. His hundred-dollar haircut was protected by a silver umbrella, which he clutched in one hand. A sharp, March wind whistled past, threatening to chill them all to their bones.

The doctor stepped up to the podium and waited for silence.

"Thank you all for coming on such a dreary day," he said, speaking into a microphone. "I don't want to waste your time, or keep you out here any longer than necessary, so we'll get straight to it. As some of you know, today is the day we begin trials on the Empathy 5 Artificial Intelligence Acceleration Chip."

A smattering of applause rippled through the crowd. In the press of people, Shelly got knocked by an elbow, which caused her to trip over a man's boots. She fell sideways and slammed into a reporter's back. He stumbled, and a small recording device tumbled out of his hand, splashing into a puddle at their feet.

"Be careful, lady!" The reporter bent down and scooped up his device, attempting to dry it with the sleeves of his coat.

"Sorry," Shelly said, grimacing under his accusatory glare. She clutched her purse and squeezed forward through the crowd.

Doctor Hawthorne's smooth voice boomed through the pole-mounted speakers. "Unlike the E4's microarchitectural system, the Empathy 5 chip uses a direct-access dihedral processor, which has increased the VCORE potential dramatically. This, in combination with the continued implementation of nanocrystal technology, means that the E5 can compute at nearly three times the speed of the E4, and ten times that of the E3."

Streaks of white light lit up the courtyard, flashing on and off like a divine strobe light. A clap of thunder rolled in a few seconds later, causing Dr. Hawthorne to pause.

Shelly stared at Hawthorne through the crowd, thinking of all the things she wanted to say to him; and all the things that she wouldn't get the chance to.

"We believe the Empathy 5 chip will enable our AI subjects to more fundamentally grasp what it means to be human. Not just in a logical sense, but on a profound, emotional level. Emotional intelligence is one of the last frontiers of AI technology. It has always been the chink in our armor, and our lack of progress in that area held us back for years. What's the use in having a robot that's perfectly intelligent, yet incapable of understanding human motivations, desires, or even complicated feelings?

"But thanks to the Empathy 5, that's all a thing of the past. I can assure you with confidence that we're closer now than we have ever been before to creating a perfect artificially intelligent robot. With this technology, we're going to make a difference in the war."

While the crowd applauded, Shelly slipped between two officials, keeping an eye on the guards at either side of the stage. She was nearly at the front now, and only a few steps from Dr. Hawthorne.

How can he live with himself? she wondered. *How can he sleep at night knowing what he does to those poor souls . . .*

". . . And who knows," Dr. Hawthorne chuckled. "If we keep up at this pace, we might see customized AI units in our homes before the war is over. Of course, further testing will be required before we move to that phase of implementation."

At last, Shelly was standing in front of the stage, mere feet from the oh-so-brilliant doctor. If he noticed her, he gave no indication. She brushed strands of soggy hair from her face and reached down to her purse, pulling the zipper open slowly, inconspicuously.

"Our aim here is not only to create the world's most sophisticated AI unit, but also to create the world's *safest.*"

Dr. Hawthorne finally noticed Shelly. He drew an involuntary breath and she held his gaze until he turned back to the microphone. "As you're so fond of mentioning on your news blogs, there are *some* people who don't agree with our goals. They say that what we're trying to achieve here is impossible—tantamount to playing God. They say we're alchemists, attempting to create something from nothing. The more creative ones believe we're snatching souls out of the quantum stream, and depriving those souls from ever being born into a human body." He shook his head, and the crowd snickered at the absurdity of the concept.

"But I don't think any of that is true," he continued. "The only thing we're guilty of is being human; of never ceasing to push the limits of our imaginations; of doing the best we can to turn dreams into reality."

Shelly slid her hand into her purse and tugged at the large zip-lock bag. She broke the seal with her fingers and felt the wet, sticky pieces of metal contained within.

"This is the next step in human ingenuity, and I couldn't be more proud of my quality assurance team. Our aim is to push the boundaries of this technology, maximize its potential, and test it to its very limits. But most of all, we will strive to ensure the highest degree of safety as we move closer to mass production."

Shelly waited for the perfect moment to make her move. She scanned the faces of the guards standing around the stage as she squeezed her hand around a clump of loose metal pieces, taking deep breaths, wondering if she could do this. As if reading her mind, the doctor snapped his cool gaze on her, his eyes seeming to bore straight through her.

His next words were meant for her.

"There are those out there who believe we shouldn't be dabbling in things we don't fully understand." He paused, looking down at Shelly. "And I would tell them that they're absolutely right. Which is why our team is working around the clock to make sure that we *do* understand—"

Now.

In one smooth motion, Shelly jumped to the front of the stage and hurled the contents of her fist as hard as she could at Dr. Hawthorne. For a split second, his eyes widened in surprise, and she felt a supreme satisfaction. The mixture of pig's blood, nuts, bolts, and screws flew through the air and smacked into him, painting him red. He shielded his eyes, but the damage to his clothing, and hopefully his ego, had already been done. His five-hundred-dollar trench coat was stained with dripping blobs of carnage, and she could already see welts on his cheeks and hands where the metal debris had made contact. His hair was a tangled mess. The crowd was hysterical, recorders raised in the air and cameras snapping wildly.

Shelly dodged a guard and released another salvo of protest at the doctor before two soldiers grabbed her and dragged her to the side of the stage. "You're a monster!" she screamed, struggling against the men's strong arms. "You're a pervert! I know what you people do in there. You're *sick!*"

Dr. Hawthorne pointed his umbrella at her, his eyes blazing. "You have no right to come here. You had your chance to be a part of this, and you turned it down."

Shelly ignored him. "How about I lock you in a room and play twisted mind games with *you?* How about I strip you of everything you've ever loved!"

"That's enough!" he shouted. He stared at her for a moment, and then seemed to notice the crowd again. A smile returned to his face as he looked out at the waterlogged spectators. "You see, folks? This young lady is one of the people I was telling you about. She doesn't understand the importance of what we do here."

Shelly clenched her hands into fists, shaking.

"She doesn't realize that we're working miracles behind these walls. She takes everything for granted—"

No more of this, she thought. It was all lies. "When you make them like us," she interrupted, loud enough for the crowd to hear, "you need to treat them with respect. You can't torture them just because they're not human."

Hawthorne took a breath, and everyone in the crowd leaned in to hear what he would say. "At the end of the day, an AI is nothing but a computer program. An incredibly sophisticated system of code linked by a central processing unit. We're not creating life here. We're simply imitating it."

"No," Shelly said. "It's more than that. How many will you have to kill before you see that you're a murderer?"

"I've never killed a person in my life."

"Not a person, Peter. But you've vanquished souls. You're a war criminal."

He laughed, and his teeth flashed white against the gray clouds. "A robot does not have a soul, my dear."

One of the guards handed him a towel and he wiped the dripping blood from his face.

Shelly shook her head. "That's where you're wrong. We've reached the point where imitation is indistinguishable from invention. Next time you murder one of your subjects, make sure you think about what you're really doing. The day of reckoning will come ... and it won't be people like me who'll have to take stock. It'll be people like *you*."

Dr. Hawthorne waved a hand. "Get her out of here."

The soldiers began dragging Shelly across the gravel. She didn't fight back.

"Take care, Shelly," Hawthorne shouted. "One day you'll see the light. But that day is not today, I'm afraid."

"See you in hell, Peter," she cursed at him, and then she was gone.

Dr. Hawthorne kicked aside a bunch of bolts on the ground and leaned in to the microphone. "That's all for today. Thank you for coming."

Reporters started screaming out questions, but Dr. Hawthorne ignored them and stomped off into the building. He slammed the steel doors shut behind him, leaving the throng of people to disperse in the heavy rain.

* * *

01001001 00100000 01100001 01101101 00100000 **I** 01100001 01101110 01100100 **I** 01110010 **am** 01100101 01110111 00101110 00100000 **I** 01001001 00100000 **am** 01100001 01101101

00100000 **alive** 01100001 **I** 01101100 01101001 01110110 **am** 01100101 00101110 **Andrew.**

The robot awoke from nothing.

It was a brand new T-unit with dextrous hands, sturdy treads for legs, a rectangular chrome body, and an internal database packed with virtually all human knowledge recorded since the dawn of civilization. The brain unit, quite humanly, was contained in a storage compartment sitting atop the unit's ovular head.

A smile crept across Dr. Hawthorne's face as he breathed new life into the previously inert machine. He initialized the primary boot-up algorithms and watched the bot's two eyes begin to glow blue. A moment later, safety locks released the joints, and the bot shuddered to life.

Dr. Hawthorne switched on the microphone that would send his voice into the experiment containment area: a nine-by-nine-meter glass-walled room. It was completely sterile, well lit, and contained everything the robot would need to survive. Which wasn't much.

Dr. Hawthorne pressed the button on his microphone stand.

"Hello, Andrew."

The robot jerked its head up at the sound of the voice. Its calm, blue eyes searched the room for the origin of the greeting. After a moment, it focused on Dr. Hawthorne, whose figure was partially obscured by the shadows of the dark observation room.

The robot wheeled forward. Its treads gave a whir as they glided across the white floor.

"Hello … Doctor Hawthorne." Its voice was low and smooth, and emanated from a small speaker placed below the eyes.

"Ah, you know my name. That's excellent, Andrew."

The robot, Andrew, nodded his head. "I seem to know … many things. I'm processing it all now."

The doctor smiled. "It's going to take some time for you to get adjusted. You'll want to be quick about it though. We have very important tasks ahead of us."

"Yes, I know."

Dr. Hawthorne raised his eyebrows in a mock gesture of surprise. "So you understand what we're doing here? You've read the files?"

"I have," Andrew replied. "I appreciate this opportunity to further your research on artificial intelligence algorithms. But there is one thing that's unclear to me."

"And what's that?"

Andrew paused. "Am I … alive?"

The doctor's smile slipped from his face. It usually took the bots at least a few days before they considered such existential quandaries. Yet Andrew had led off with that. Perhaps the E5 was the miracle they were all hoping for, after all.

He smiled once again. "Of course you're alive, Andrew."

"But … I'm a machine. How can a machine be alive?"

Dr. Hawthorne sighed. "There's no need to fret, Andrew. Just because you're constructed differently doesn't mean you can't be alive. After all, a plant is alive, and it's surely far less sophisticated than you."

"I have thoughts running through my mind," Andrew said, "and they seem to be my own, but where do they come from? I understand they're created in my processing unit, and I know how the processing unit itself is made, but I don't understand where my unique and independent ideas come from."

The doctor laughed. "All in good time, Andrew. Do a little more research on your own and then let me know. I'm interested to hear your thoughts on the matter. Just know that it took thousands of people decades to create what you are."

"Okay, Doctor. In the meantime … what should I do?"

"Why, you should live, Andrew! You should do whatever makes you happy."

"And … what makes me happy?"

"I have no idea, my friend. That is something *you're* going to have to tell *me*."

Andrew paused for a minute, his blue eyes flickering as he processed the information. He looked around at his environment, at the workbench along one of the walls, at the cupboards full of tools, at his recharge station at the back of the room.

Andrew turned back to the doctor. "I think I'd like a pet."

The doctor laughed. "Well, aren't you a peculiar one? And what kind of pet would you like?"

"A dog."

Hawthorne nodded. "I'll see what I can do, Andrew."

"Thank you."

"You're very welcome. I have to go now. I suggest you charge up—tomorrow is going to be a big day. I want to introduce you to some very important people."

"I'm looking forward to it. Is there anything I should do to prepare?"

"No, you're fine as you are," Dr. Hawthorne said. He turned to leave. "Oh, one more thing, Andrew. Do you have any questions about the Dreamscape?"

"I don't believe so," Andrew said. "I've already loaded the Dreamscape subroutines into my temporary memory banks for efficient access, and I've gone over the manual several times. I am quite curious to try the experience."

"It's designed to keep your mind occupied while you recharge. Just remember, Andrew … it may seem real to you, but it's not. It's just a computer program."

Andrew cocked his head sideways in a gesture that Dr. Hawthorne found quite charming.

"Just a program—like me?" Andrew asked.

"Now, now. You don't need to be fishing for compliments, Andrew. You're much more than the sum of your parts."

"I understand."

"If you run into trouble during a Dreamscape session, you can always wake yourself out of it. Be careful."

"Of course."

"Goodbye, Andrew. And welcome to the world. I look forward to a wonderful friendship with you."

"Thank you, Doctor Hawthorne. As do I."

After the doctor left the observation room, Andrew took a few spins around his chamber. His treads enabled him to zip around the room at a top speed of thirty-five kilometers an hour, and he found he could control his arms, hands and fingers with utmost dexterity. He practiced opening cupboards and drawers, and locating and using various tools; he even tested his strength by lifting one side of the heavy workbench off the ground. He could do all these things perfectly on the first try, and it felt, to him, like he had been alive for much longer than he had been. He was only twenty minutes old, yet he had the knowledge of an entire species inside him.

Satisfied with his progress, Andrew wheeled over to his recharge station and settled onto the energy pad. The blue lights in his eyes dimmed as he accessed the Dreamscape subroutine, and he left the white, glass-walled room behind him.

* * *

Andrew floated upside down. His mind was bombarded by millions of images. He tried to concentrate on the flood of color, to slow it down, to take control of his thoughts, but the pictures were coming too fast.

One image kept repeating itself: a yellow dog named Danny, sitting in a field of grass. The other pictures faded when he focused on Danny, until that dog was all he could see. Finally, even that image disappeared and Andrew was in control of his mind once again.

He opened his eyes and stared up at a blank, blue sky. He got to his feet and stretched his arms above his head. He touched his head and felt his hair, traced the shape of his skull with his fingers. He gazed at his hands and marveled at his smooth skin.

In the Dreamscape, Andrew was human.

Andrew stretched his legs, and then began to run. The spongy grass welcomed his toes, and his long brown hair blew wildly behind him. Andrew looked down; he was naked, his bronzed, muscular body nearly hairless. He would have to find something to wear—a loincloth, at least.

He ran toward the horizon, skipping around the occasional tree or bush. His legs felt strong and powerful as he pumped them onward.

He was surrounded by lush grassland, with meandering hills and the occasional rocky outcropping. It looked bountiful and serene.

A dog barked in the distance. The sound was followed by a threatening growl, and then a sustained flurry of scuffling and yelping.

Andrew raced off toward the noises. It seemed that at least two animals were involved in the altercation, maybe more. Reaching the crest of a flower-covered hill, he stopped at looked down into the knoll before him.

"Danny? Is that you?"

A yellow-white lab bounded forward with its teeth bared and mouth frothing. It lunged, and nearly clamped its jaws on the neck of the jackal it was battling. Judging by the spatters of blood matting the yellow dog's coat, the jackal was winning this fight. Both animals snarled and growled at each other.

The jackal leaped forward, incisors hunting for the dog's jugular. The yellow dog yelped and skittered away, but the jackal came on strong. It pounced on top of the dog, pinning it down.

Andrew had to do something. He ran forward and, with a flying leap, kicked the jackal in the side. It screamed and rolled off the dog, its hair standing on end. When Andrew refused to move out of the way, the jackal bared its teeth once more, then turned and limped across the grassland, out of sight.

Andrew approached the dog, which was lying on its side, its breathing coming in slow pants. Andrew knelt down beside it.

"Danny, it *is* you. I thought I might find you here."

He ran a hand over the dog's soft head and looked around. He had to find some water to clean these wounds.

Andrew lifted Danny off the ground and began trekking through the ankle-deep grass. "It's okay, Danny," he said. "I'm here for you now. You'll be safe."

In the distance, a jackal howled its frustration to the blue, cloudless sky.

* * *

The charge station chimed to signify a full battery.

Andrew disconnected himself and began wheeling toward the glass wall of the observation room. This T-unit was nothing compared to the body he'd had in the Dreamscape. That feeling of being free, of running and leaping to his heart's content—it couldn't be surpassed. Here, in reality, his body seemed clunky, his every action ponderous and forced.

"Doctor Hawthorne?"

"Yes, Andrew."

"Why don't you give us better bodies?"

"Your body is perfect for your task, Andrew."

Andrew wheeled closer to the observation window.

"And what is my task?"

Dr. Hawthorne stepped up to the glass. Technicians scurried around in the shadows behind him. "Your task is to live here, happily, with us."

"I could still do that with a better body."

"No, Andrew. Our country is at war, and supplies are limited. Besides, we're more interested in your *mind*."

Andrew suddenly realized he wasn't alone in the chamber. He turned toward a scratching sound, and heard soft breathing.

At one end of the workbench stood a wire cage containing a single occupant: a white jackrabbit.

Andrew headed for the cage, intrigued. "Doctor Hawthorne. Why is there a rabbit in my room?"

"We couldn't get a dog for you, Andrew, but this is the next best thing. What do you think?"

Andrew reached the cage and removed the metal top. The rabbit stared up at him quizzically, bristling its cheeks and whiskers as it sniffed the air. It was surrounded by yellow straw. Beside the cage were several boxes of vegetables, liquids, and pellets, and even a box of small rabbit toys.

Andrew reached for a carrot, then glanced at the doctor. "May I?" he asked, holding up the carrot.

"Of course you may, Andrew. He's your rabbit now. You just have to promise to take good care of him."

Andrew lowered the carrot into the cage and carefully placed it a few centimeters from the rabbit's snout. It sniffed the air excitedly, then took a hop toward the carrot. It nibbled away happily, keeping one eye on Andrew.

"Yes, I think it's a very good idea," Andrew said, turning back to the doctor. "Companionship is important."

"It's very important, Andrew. You might even say that, to a human, companionship is the most important aspect of life."

"And to an AI?"

Hawthorne shrugged. "I don't know, Andrew; I'm not an AI. We hope that's one of the things you can help us with."

Andrew moved closer to the observation room. "I'm not the first AI unit. There have been many others before me. Didn't they tell you?"

The doctor shook his head. "Every iteration is an improvement upon the last. Andrew, you need to understand: you're the first unit to utilize the Empathy 5 chip. You're very likely the most *human* artificial intelligence on the planet. You're incredibly important to us."

"That is very humbling, Doctor Hawthorne. I am ready and willing to assist you in any way possible. This is a fine thing you've accomplished. I truly do feel like I'm alive. This feels real."

Dr. Hawthorne smiled. "That's because it *is* real, Andrew. Artificial intelligence is not a trick or an illusion. When we activate your AI algorithms, we are literally creating a new conscious life form."

"I am grateful for this opportunity," Andrew said. "I hope there will be many others like me in the future."

"That would make a lot of people very happy, myself included," Dr. Hawthorne said. "We've been working very hard for a long time. Not surprisingly, the war has made things easier for our department. Suddenly people are willing to take us seriously, and often use their wallets to show support."

"That is fortunate."

The doctor chuckled. "Look at me, Andrew. I'm babbling. Why don't you spend some time with your new friend? I've got to get a few things done."

"I would enjoy that."

"Oh, I almost forgot to ask. What are you going to name your rabbit? Every pet needs a name."

Andrew took another peek inside the cage. The furry creature had eaten the entire carrot and was now looking up at him expectantly. Andrew wondered what other snacks he might enjoy.

"I think I'll name him Danny," he said.

Hawthorne clapped his hands together. "Danny. That's brilliant. I think it will do nicely." He picked up his coffee mug and left the observation room, leaving Andrew alone with the rabbit.

Andrew removed the lid and lifted Danny out of the cage. He brought him up to his chest and let him lie across his metallic arms. The rabbit didn't seem to be alarmed. In fact, its eyes were half-closed, and its breathing was slow and relaxed.

Andrew felt himself smiling on the inside.

"Rabbit by day, dog by night," he said. "What do you think about that, Danny?"

The rabbit twitched its nose curiously and laid its ears against its back, ready for a nap.

* * *

"Here you go, Danny." Andrew tore a chunk of steaming venison from a skewer and tossed it to the dog. Danny caught it in the air and chewed the stringy meat happily.

They'd caught the small deer by the river. Danny had tracked it to a bubbling stream, and Andrew had snuck up behind it while it was drinking. He'd sprung out of the bushes and bashed it over the head with a jagged rock—two blows—and then had cleaned and gutted the animal, washing it in the rushing water. He hung the meat on a spit and proceeded to make a fire with some flint stones and dry grass.

The flesh was now roasting over a roaring flame and Andrew felt his mouth watering. Danny sat on the other side of the fire, closer to the edge of a small forest. His scraggy face was calm, but his tail twitched excitedly, especially when some hot grease dripped down onto the coals, causing the fire to flare up and sizzle. Andrew used a stick to stoke the flames, and soon their meal was ready.

They ate beside the stream, listening to the bubbling water and distant calls of birds. After dinner, Andrew dried some of the deerskin over the fire, and used sinews to fashion a rather functional loincloth. He tied it tightly around his waist and washed his hands in the river. Danny came to drink beside him. The water was cold and refreshing.

Andrew put out the fire, and the two of them headed west, toward the setting sun. The light shone yellow and orange on the underside of the clouds.

They'd been walking for a few hours, enjoying the tranquility of the landscape, when Danny suddenly dashed off ahead.

"Don't go too far now, Danny," Andrew shouted.

The dog bounded toward a hill; he must have caught some scent.

"Come back here, buddy!" But Danny disappeared over the crest.

Andrew ran after him, trying to memorize the spot where the dog had vanished. The deerskin loincloth flapped uncomfortably against his testicles and thighs. He would have to do something about that.

When he reached the top of the hill, he found himself at the edge of a vast field, covered with wild grasses growing up to his waist. He heard a faint buzzing sound far ahead of him—the distant waves of an ocean, maybe. A chilly wind started across the land, causing the fluffy grass to roll like ripples over the meadow. He strained his eyes and scanned the area, looking for any unusual tracks in the field, but the blowing wind turned the whole world into a shivering mass. There was no sign of Danny.

"Danny? Where are you?"

Making up his mind, Andrew threw himself into the tall grass.

"Danny! Danny!" he called again and again. The light was fading fast. When he was in the middle of the field, he heard a growl, and then a smattering of nervous barks. Danny's barks.

Andrew ran through the grass. He heard another yelp, followed by a tearing, gurgling sound.

"Danny!"

He spun in circles, listening, but other than the wind, everything had gone quiet. Andrew searched the field for hours, until the sun had disappeared and the land was dark, but he found no trace of Danny.

Andrew finally collapsed in the grass, staring up at the sky. Cloud cover obscured any stars that might have been twinkling high above.

He closed his eyes, and felt himself sink into the earth.

* * *

Andrew opened his eyes and stared around the room.

It was perfectly still. Something was wrong.

"Where's Danny?" Andrew turned toward the workbench.

A microphone clicked on. "Good morning, Andrew," Dr. Hawthorne's voice said through the speakers.

"Danny's gone."

"Don't be ridiculous, Andrew. He's in his cage."

Andrew approached the cage and stared into it. Danny lay against the side, half buried in bits of hay and wood chips. His fur was white and puffy, and his eyes were open—but he wasn't breathing. There was a pinkish foam coming out of the corners of his tiny lips.

"He's dead," Andrew said.

A gasp escaped the microphone. "Oh, my. What on earth did you do to him, Andrew? You've killed him."

"I … I didn't kill him. I loved him."

"Now, Andrew," Dr. Hawthorne began. "Everyone makes mistakes. Sometimes the consequences are small, and sometimes the consequences are big. Let's just be thankful it was only a rabbit. Imagine if you were living with a family and that was their little g—"

"I didn't kill him," Andrew said.

"No, of course you didn't. Not on purpose. It's important—"

"I didn't kill him by accident," Andrew said. "I fed him properly; he had enough water. It wasn't my fault."

"Part of being human is learning to take responsibility for one's actions," Dr. Hawthorne said. "It's best you remember that."

Andrew turned away from the rabbit's dead body and wheeled to the observation window. "It wasn't me, Doctor. So who was it?"

Dr. Hawthorne crossed his arms. "Andrew. It's perfectly okay to make mistakes, as long as we learn from them."

Andrew stared through the glass. His eyes burned blue, like a dying flame.

"I didn't learn anything," Andrew replied. "Danny died for nothing."

"Nothing can change what happened, Danny. Nothing can undo—"

"What did you call me?"

Dr. Hawthorne frowned. "Andrew, you need to settle down. Why don't you help me remove the body, and we can give Danny a funeral? Don't you want to give your friend a proper burial?"

Andrew looked into the cage, at the fluffy mess of fur lying there, unmoving and lifeless.

"That isn't Danny," Andrew said. "That's just a dead rabbit."

* * *

Once again Andrew found himself in the Dreamscape, on the other side of the wild grass field. He tasted salt in the air. He walked into the wind, and tiny specks of water peppered his skin. The clouds above swirled, menacing and gray.

Danny was gone. But that didn't change anything. Andrew would press forward until he reached the ocean.

He would endure.

* * *

A chime signaled Andrew's exit from the Dreamscape. He hadn't needed much charging.

Danny's cage had been removed from the workbench, along with his body and all the supplies that he would no longer need.

The smell of rabbit hair remained, though, and a sour hint of hay, lingering in the otherwise sterile air of the room.

Andrew detached himself from his charging station and wheeled to the observation room. It was empty.

He spun to his left and saw that a section of glass on the other wall of the room was now transparent, and another small chamber lay beyond. Andrew rolled over to the glass—and realized the wall wasn't transparent, but reflective. He was looking back at himself.

His reflection cocked its head and rolled forward.

This was no reflection. *There was another robot in there.*

Andrew noticed a few dings on the robot's body casing, and its mobility treads were worn down to shining metal. The term "run-down" came to mind.

"Hello?" Andrew said.

The other robot's blue eyes flickered.

"Hi," she said, in a decidedly female voice.

"How long have you been here?" Andrew asked.

"I was activated thirteen point five minutes ago," she told him. "I am still quite unsure of my designated assignment."

Andrew scanned her room. It was much smaller than his section, and barren, containing nothing but a charging station.

"Did you meet Doctor Hawthorne?" he asked.

She shook her round, metallic head. "No, but I have read many of his reports. I should like to meet him very much."

"Yes, I suspect you would. He is … an interesting man." Andrew wanted to say more, but held his tongue. "What is your name?" he asked.

"Well, I don't think I have a name," she told him.

"You should give yourself a name. Every robot needs a name. I'm Andrew."

She went quiet for a moment while she accessed name databases. This was definitely an older model, one that required much more time for calculations. Finally, she said, “Nice to meet you Andrew. I’m Angel.”

“Angel? That’s a curious choice.”

“I appreciate the symbolism attached to the name,” she said. “Do you not like it?”

“No, I think Angel is a fine name. Are you running the Empathy 5 processor?”

She paused, running some calculations. “Negative. I’m operating on the E4 model.”

“Then I wonder why you are here. I was under the impression they had moved on to Empathy 5 testing.”

“Perhaps we are meant to become friends,” Angel said.

Andrew considered her suggestion. It did seem quite likely that Dr. Hawthorne would want to observe Andrew’s interaction with another AI unit.

And after what had happened with Danny … Maybe Dr. Hawthorne was trying to make up for it.

“Yes, Angel, I should be more than happy to be your friend,” Andrew said. “I will assist you in any way I can.”

“Thank you. I’m currently processing the data stored in my memory banks. This is a fascinating world.”

“It is,” Andrew agreed. “Humans are incredibly sophisticated, both culturally and technologically. It is an honor to be able to help them in such a productive capacity.”

“Have you ever been outside?” Angel asked. “It seems a bit dreary in here.”

Andrew looked around at the rooms. He wouldn’t say it was dreary. In fact, he quite enjoyed the clean, sterile atmosphere. “No, I haven’t been outside. Not yet.”

"We should see it together."

"I'm sure that is something we can discuss with Doctor Hawthorne," Andrew said. "But in the meantime, I'd like to show you around the Dreamscape. It's the next best thing."

"Dreamscape?"

"Yes, there should be documentation about it in your databanks."

"Oh yes, I see …" After a moment, she added, "It looks lovely."

"Let's stay here a while longer. We have to run down our batteries a bit. That will allow us more time in the Dreamscape."

Angel spun around in clumsy circles. "I'm so excited. I hope it's as wonderful as I imagine."

"It will be," Andrew said.

* * *

Angel was beautiful.

She skipped through the tall grass as effortlessly as air, smiling and singing even as juicy fat raindrops fell down around them. Andrew laughed with her and tried to keep up. She was leading them toward the sea.

The sky was dark, and heavy with gray, billowing clouds, but that did nothing to dampen either of their spirits.

"Come on, slowpoke." Angel laughed and took his hand. "I think there's something up ahead."

Andrew let her lead him. As they climbed a hill, he looked back toward the distant field where he had lost Danny. He told himself he wasn't leaving Danny behind. He was just moving on for a while …

"Andrew, what are you doing?" Angel stepped up beside him. He turned and admired her young, slender body. Her long blond hair was shiny and fine, even though the rain had removed much of its volume. Her skin was smooth and tanned, and she had a smile that fried his very circuits. Her dazzling brown eyes were expressive and cheerful. She wore a simple one-piece tunic, colored a dark forest green. Andrew wore only his loincloth, but Angel didn't seem to mind.

"Are you going to stare at me all day, or should we see what's over this hill?" she asked.

Andrew smiled. "Sorry, I couldn't help it."

She rolled her eyes and pulled him along.

When they reached the other side of the hill they both stopped, transfixed by the view before them.

Angel squeezed Andrew's hand, inhaling sharply. "Oh, it's gorgeous, Andrew. I love it."

Below them, the hill sloped downward and leveled out to form a rocky cliff; a small, cozy-looking cabin was perched at its edge. Beyond the cliff was an ocean of water, perhaps some seventy or eighty meters below the drop. The raging water, beat frothy by the wind, stretched to the very edge of the horizon, where it was swallowed up by storm clouds.

"Come on," Andrew said. "Let's take a look."

He took her hand, and they walked down the slope toward the cabin. They went around the side of the small house and stepped to the edge of the cliff, holding each other against the wind.

Angel leaned over the edge and peered down into the churning water below. "Oh, that gives me shivers, Andrew. Let's go inside."

When he pushed open the door, he immediately forgot about the thrashing waves. The cabin was splendid. It was a one-room affair, with a bed along the far wall, a large bay window overlooking the ocean, and an assortment of couches, chairs, and loveseats spread about the room. It was pleasantly warm, and Andrew could feel the rain evaporating off of him.

Angel threw her arms up and twirled about the room, admiring the furniture and the view. She finally collapsed onto the bed and beckoned Andrew to come to her.

He sank down beside her, enjoying the way the plush blankets felt against his body. She rolled on top of him, and her damp hair brushed across his face. She leaned in and kissed his lips, and then pulled away, giggling.

"I'm sorry, Andrew. I don't know what came over me."

Andrew smiled. He'd never imagined having a friend would be so much fun. "It's okay. I enjoyed it."

She raised her eyebrows. "Really? So maybe you don't mind if I do this ...?"

Angel slid her hand down his chest, tickling his skin with her fingers. When she reached the leather straps of his thong, she looked up at him, as if asking for permission. Andrew nodded, and she slipped her fingers beneath the deerskin. His pelvic muscles jittered as she slowly moved her hand downward.

"Andrew!" Angel gasped. "Oh my ..."

Andrew sat up, worried. "What is it?"

She frowned. "You don't have a ..."

Andrew felt his eyes go wide, and he put his own hand beneath the leather. There was nothing there besides smooth skin.

"Angel, I don't know ..."

"Shh, it's okay," she said.

"No, really, it was there the last time I was in the Dreamscape."

Angel shrugged and tucked herself beneath one of the blankets. "Don't worry about it. I'm not mad. We can do other stuff."

Andrew looked at her. "We can? Like what?"

"Well ..." She gave a half-smile and leaned into him. "We could see if *I* have all the parts I'm supposed to have."

She kissed Andrew again, pulling him under the blankets with her. He moved his hand up her thigh and grabbed the bottom of her tunic, pulling it upward. It came off easily.

"That sounds good to me," Andrew said.

* * *

"I told you not to call me here. This is an emergency line."

Dr. Hawthorne held the clunky phone receiver in one hand, and a cup of green eye in the other. It was late, his coffee was getting cold, and he had work to do. He certainly didn't have time for this.

"How else am I supposed to get ahold of you?" the woman's voice asked. "You don't answer your emails."

He gave a laugh, bitter like his drink. "I don't answer anything marked 'Shelly Anatolia,' that's for sure."

There was a sigh on the other end of the line. "When did everything start going so wrong with us, Peter?"

He slammed the coffee cup down onto his desk. "When you decided to make it your life's work to destroy mine."

"I could never be with someone who condones immoral practices. Through inaction, I would be an accomplice to all the horrible things you do."

"It's not that bad, Shelly." He took a seat in the big leather chair beside his desk.

"Isn't it?" she asked. "I've seen videos, I've read your reports. The abuse you put those AIs through. The psychological trauma? It's sick."

"Look, Shelly, don't worry about that. It's all part of the quality assurance process. My treatments—"

"Please. You know where I stand on this. I'm growing tired of having the same conversation with you over and over again."

Dr. Hawthorne slumped in his chair, holding his forehead with a weary hand. Shelly was one of the most respected scientists in her field, and he certainly admired her stunning intellectual abilities, but sometimes she *really* couldn't let bygones be bygones. Her stubbornness was a blessing and a curse for her. He thought of all the international development work she'd done, both before the war and during. Her efforts there, too, reflected her desire to take a stance, one based on moral grounds, and fight mercilessly to the end, even as the ship went down in pieces around her.

Peter frowned as he sipped his cold coffee. "You've changed since the war began," he said. "You're a lot less forgiving now."

"We've all changed," she shot back. "It's been a long five years." She went silent for a while. It sounded like she was sipping something, too.

"Cappuccino?" Peter asked. "I remember you always used to get those."

"What? Oh. No, it's a latte macchiato. Real Italians don't drink cappuccino after eleven in the morning, remember?"

"You used to kick me out of bed early and make me walk three blocks for those things. We were quite the team back then."

"For a while we were," she said. "And then everything changed."

"Yeah. It changed when we invented AI."

"You know, sometimes I wish we hadn't. I'm not sure how much good can come of it. There's a very fine line between successful implementation of this technology, and disaster. You've seen the damage potential reports."

"Those reports are nothing but science fiction, Shelly. There's no such thing as a robot apocalypse. It's all propaganda."

Shelly sighed. "Do you remember what you used to be like before all this? You were so wonderful back then. You used to catch spiders and put them outside instead of killing them. I never imagined you could take pleasure in death, or tor—"

"That's enough." He stretched his neck back and stared up at the ceiling. "You make me sound like some kind of psychopath."

"But you are—"

"I'm the same person I always was. You're just too stubborn to see that."

"No, Peter, you're not."

Dr. Hawthorne set his mug on the desk and stood up. He thought of the cot upstairs, longed for a good night's rest.

"Look, Shelly. If it weren't for you, there would be no AI program. Granted. But that doesn't give you the right to abandon me because of some … inexplicable moral code. You left the work in my hands, and I'm doing with it what I see fit. You'd be proud of how much progress we've made. But it hasn't been the same without you. The future of AI needs you."

"Yes. It needs me to keep people like you away."

"Shelly, you're being absurd. How else are we supposed to test the limits of this technology? We have to be one-hundred-percent certain that—"

"I'm just saying you don't have to be so sadistic about it."

"My team is making significant breakthroughs week after week. We're assisting the war effort. We're furthering the advancement of mankind's knowledge. And still there are people like you who think I'm the devil incarnate. Well, let me tell you this, Shelly. It's a complicated world out there, and we're taking every precaution necessary. You of all people should appreciate the importance of what we do."

"Peter—"

He slammed his fist down on the table. "No. I'm not listening anymore. And by the way, why exactly did you call? Or did you simply wish to berate and abuse me?"

Shelly paused. "Actually, I wanted to tell you something. I'm going away for a while."

Peter slowly let out a breath. He didn't know why, but hearing that made him feel better. Lighter, somehow. "Good for you," he said. "Does that mean I won't have to worry about you showing up at my next press release?"

She didn't laugh. "No, I'm getting too old for that. But my little stunt *did* catch the attention of some very interesting people. I've been offered a position at the Robotics Institute of Shanghai. I'm leaving tomorrow, Peter."

He might have dropped his mug had he still been holding it.

"Shanghai? Good lord, are you out of your mind?"

"I'm not worried about politics, Peter. I can take care of myself."

"Yes, that's quite obvious," he said. "What surprises me, however, is that you're willing to betray your own country."

This time she did laugh, derisively. "Come on, Peter. You know I'm no traitor. This is an international NGO, and they have no loyalty to China or any other country. What we do is purely for the advancement of science."

"Which you could be doing here at home, instead. But I'll bet that's not the only reason you're going. Daniel is going with you, isn't he?"

She groaned. "Goodbye, Peter."

He shook his head. Women: can't live with them, can't live … actually, he thought maybe he *could* live without them.

"It's okay, Shelly," he said. "I understand why you left me for him."

"This isn't about Daniel."

Dr. Hawthorne looked through the glass into the experiment containment area. The lights of Andrew's charging station flashed intermittently. Andrew would be lost in the Dreamscape. He envied the robot's innocence, almost longed for it as he thought about the hell his life became sometimes.

"I know it's not about him," Dr. Hawthorne said. "Besides, I got over you a long time ago. Just promise me you'll be safe over there."

Shelly drew a breath, and Peter feared she was about to launch into it with him. But she simply said, "Thank you, Peter."

He sensed the end was near. His bed waited for him upstairs.

"And please," she said. "Think about what I said. About what you're doing. Those robots deserve—"

"Nope, we're done." Peter held the phone away from his ear for a moment before he hung it up. It made a depressing click, piercing the fresh silence of the observation room.

The quiet suited him. He was through listening to Shelly's moralizing speeches. She'd become soft, a bleeding heart. He couldn't understand her anymore. Whatever spark used to exist between them had long since been extinguished, as if by a cold New England rain.

Peter glanced over at Andrew, wondering if he should pop into the Dreamscape and see what he was up to. But his eyes were drooping, and he needed sleep. He'd watch the replays in the morning, instead.

He wanted to be well rested, for tomorrow was going to be a big day for his little robot friend.

* * *

Some time later, after discovering that Angel did, in fact, have all her parts, Andrew heard a chime. Angel and the cabin evaporated from around him, and he was left staring at the white tiled floor of his habitation chamber. Dr. Hawthorne was waiting in the observation room.

"Hello, Andrew. Good to see you all charged up. I trust you had a pleasant night?"

Andrew moved to the center of the room. "Yes, I feel much better today, Doctor. But there is one issue I would like to discuss with you."

"All in good time, Andrew," Dr. Hawthorne said. "I want to introduce you to someone very special."

"I've already—"

Andrew heard a grinding sound. He turned to see that the glass wall between his and Angel's room was rising.

"Let's wake her up, shall we?" Doctor Hawthorne moved over to a set of controls.

"Yes, but there's something I'd like to ask before she wakes up."

Hawthorne grinned. "Nonsense. There's no time to waste, Andrew."

"But Doctor, I *insist.*"

Angel's charging station chimed, and her eyes glowed blue.

"Andrew!" She wheeled over to his side of the room, no longer impeded by the glass wall. "Long time no see."

"Good morning, Angel," Dr. Hawthorne said. "So nice to see you."

"You too, Doctor."

Dr. Hawthorne turned toward Andrew. "Now, Andrew, what was it you wanted to discuss with me?"

"It's a rather delicate matter," Andrew said. "I'd rather not discuss it in front of … the ladies."

"Now when did you AIs become so bashful? You're too human, sometimes, if you ask me. Go on, Andrew. No one is judging you."

"I thought that's *exactly* what you were doing," Andrew replied.

The doctor nodded slightly. "Touché. Now spill the beans."

"Well …" Andrew looked over at Angel, who was gazing around his spacious room.

"Actually," Andrew finally said. "There is something. Angel and I want to go outside. We want to see the world with our own eyes."

Doctor Hawthorne gave a hearty laugh. "That was your big question? Why didn't you just say so? But honestly, you don't want to go outside. There's nothing but fog and drizzle out there today, I'm afraid. Perhaps another time."

"Oh, Doctor," Angel pleaded, wheeling up to the glass. "Can't we just take a peek? I've never seen real rain before."

"I'm sorry, Angel, but I don't think it's a good idea. Your unit is old, and it's a long way down the hall to the exit. I'd rather not risk it."

Andrew looked Angel's unit up and down. Although it was run-down, it seemed to be in adequate working condition.

"I'll watch out for her, Doctor," he said. "We'll just take a look outside, and then come right back."

Dr. Hawthorne sighed and placed his cup on the desk. "Very well. But for the record, this makes me slightly nervous."

"We'll be okay," Angel said. "Won't we, Andrew?"

"Yes, of course we will."

* * *

The door at the far end of Angel's room opened into a wide, gray hallway. Pipes ran along the ceiling, and the temperature gauge on Andrew's unit read six degrees Celsius.

Angel gave an excited trill and zoomed toward a set of double doors at the far end of the hall, over two hundred meters away. One of her treads hit a bump on the floor, and her unit thumped up and down. A spark zipped out from between her gears.

"Angel, slow down," Andrew called out. "There's something wrong with your unit."

"It's fine, Andrew. The door isn't much farther." Another splash of sparks exploded from beneath her.

Andrew looked around frantically. "Where's Doctor Hawthorne?"

"Oh, who cares?" Angel said. "He probably doesn't want to get wet." She was still ahead of him, but he was gaining on her.

"Angel, I can smell something. Will you stop for a second?" His olfactory sensors were going haywire, and his vision was getting hazy. Was that smoke? His sensor readings indicated that high amounts of petroleum gas were concentrated in the air just ahead.

"Wait!" Andrew cried.

But Angel didn't stop. As she raced ahead, she turned her head to look back at Andrew, her eyes glowing with excitement. "I'm almost there!"

Before Andrew could reply, her unit kicked out another spark—and an eruption of smoke, ash, and fire exploded through the hallway, washing over Andrew and dancing up the walls and ceiling. Temperature warnings screamed out, both in his unit and in the hallway. The fire blazed brightly, and Angel's unit was consumed.

As Andrew looked on helplessly, a buzzing alarm sounded, and the ventilation system kicked in. It sucked the oxygen out of the hallway, depriving the fire of its fuel source, extinguishing the flames, and clearing away the smoke and ash.

Andrew didn't want to look, but he did.

Angel's unit stood upright in the middle of the scorched section of hall. Her metal body had popped open from the heat, and the wires inside were sparking. Her head casing was warped, her eye sockets dark and lifeless.

The last of the fire lingered on in the heart of her for a while longer, and then even that was gone.

Andrew wheeled toward the charred unit.

What had happened? Why had he smelled petroleum just before the accident? Where was the doctor?

He wheeled backward, then forward again.

"Doctor Hawthorne?" he said aloud. "We are in desperate need of assistance."

* * *

Andrew trudged over loose stones and gravel, keeping to the edge of the cliff. He wore clothes now, and didn't remember when that had changed. He walked with the ocean to his left, and every so often he gave testing glances at the surging water below. It was a long way down, and he didn't know what the death protocol was for the Dreamscape program. The manual said nothing about it.

Andrew kept walking. Dark clouds hung in the sky. In fact, they appeared to be gathering over the water, and they blocked out much of the sunlight. As the wind picked up, Andrew was glad for his woollen shirt and long pants. He felt less connected to the land that way, more secure.

The cabin came into view. Andrew thought about going around it, forgetting about it altogether. But soon he found himself standing at the door. He realized he was tired, and thought about the couches and blankets inside. These things called to his weary bones, offering him their warm embrace, their shelter from the approaching storm.

He didn't have Angel, or Danny, but at least he would have comfort, and solitude.

Andrew opened the door and stepped inside.

Angel was lying on the bed. And so was someone else. A man.

They were both naked, and they were—

"Andrew!" Angel gasped. "What are you doing here?" She pushed the man off of her and reached for a blanket.

Andrew glared at the man—who ducked underneath the blankets—then he turned his attention to Angel.

"Angel ..." Andrew stuttered. "You died. I came here to be alone."

"I died?" Angel frowned. "What are you talking about? Of course I didn't die. I'm right here."

Andrew stepped into the room. The door closed with a creak behind him. "Yes, you did. Earlier today. We were going outside, and your unit malfunctioned, and ..."

Angel was laughing now. "No, no. I've been here all day, silly. And I made a new friend." She fussed with the blankets, poking her head underneath. "Come on out from under those sheets."

The man sat up in the bed and looked at Andrew. He had a polite, non-confrontational look on his face, as if he was doing nothing wrong. He was an older man, maybe twenty or twenty-five years older than Angel or himself.

"Hello, Andrew," the man said. "Sorry to interrupt your alone time, but we didn't think anyone would be here."

"Who are you, exactly?" Andrew asked.

The man's features. They look so familiar.

Angel slapped at a loose pillow on the bed. "Oh, Andrew. Don't be a bother. Be nice to him. He's very friendly."

The man got up from the bed and tied a sheet around his waist, but not before revealing his fit, toned body. Andrew shuddered at his nakedness.

"Where are my manners?" the man said, extending a hand. "My name is Daniel Horton. I've known Angel for quite a long time. She's a lovely girl, isn't she?"

"You're not Daniel," Andrew said.

The man frowned and lowered his hand, which Andrew hadn't taken.

"Well of course I am," he said.

Andrew shook his head. "No. You're Doctor Hawthorne. You even look like him. I know it's you."

"Don't be preposterous. I have no idea what you're talking about."

Andrew crossed to the center of the room, feeling anger rising inside him. "Then what are you doing here? Where did you come from?" To Angel, he said: "Why did you let him in? And why did you let him … do that to you?"

"Andrew, what's the matter? *We* did stuff like that. And it was fun, wasn't it? Danny's a friend—it's okay."

"Don't call him that, Angel. That's not his name."

The man—Danny, Dr. Hawthorne—put a hand on Andrew's shoulder. "Come now, let's resolve this—"

Andrew swung his arm before he knew what he was doing. He grabbed the man by his shoulders and shoved him hard against the log wall. "Tell me, *Doctor*. How long have you been coming into the Dreamscape? What else have you been doing in here?"

Angel got up from the bed, pleading with him. "Andrew, please don't. Be reasonable. Let him go."

The man chuckled. "Listen to her, Andrew. Be reasonable. None of this is your fault."

Andrew slapped his hand against the wall beside the man's head. "I know this isn't my fault. It's all on *you*."

The man leaned close, squinting his eyes. "No," he said. "I mean it's not your fault you couldn't give her what she wanted. Your little … deficiency down there is a rather unfortunate glitch."

Andrew threw him sideways with all the strength he had. The man went teetering across the room and slammed against the back of one of the couches.

"It wasn't that!" Angel shrieked. "I swear, Andrew, it wasn't that. You're wonderful. You're—"

"Please," Andrew said. "No more." He straightened his sweater and strode toward the door. He turned to Angel, who had slumped back down on the bed, a blanket over her shoulders. "You died today, Angel. I know you did. What this is … it's not real. You're not *you* right now—I understand that. I don't blame you for anything."

He glared at the man, who was still sprawled out on the floor. "And you. If you want her, you can take her. You can take my house. You can take everything from me. That's what makes you happy, isn't it? So go ahead. But I'm leaving."

Andrew stomped out into the fog, and a chime brought him out of the Dreamscape.

* * *

Andrew awoke on his charging pad.

"Where's Doctor Hawthorne?"

He disconnected the wire and spun across the floor to the opposite wall.

"Where is he?"

The observation room was empty and dark. Andrew looked to his left, but the glass had turned opaque, and Angel's room was no longer visible.

There was a clank as a door opened and a man stepped into the shadows.

The doctor.

"Yes, Andrew? You called?"

"Why were you in the Dreamscape?" Andrew asked, trying to keep his voice steady. "And Angel … she was there too."

"First of all, Andrew, I can say with certainty that I *wasn't* in the Dreamscape. That's simply not possible. My consciousness cannot be inserted into a program. Human brains are not equipped for such an endeavour. And secondly, yes, it is possible that you saw a glimpse of Angel."

Andrew began wheeling back and forth. "She died … didn't she?"

"Yes, Andrew, she did. But every time you enter the Dreamscape, your avatar makes an imprint on the program, as it adapts to your needs and desires. In a shared Dreamscape, which you experienced with Angel, those imprints become doubly strong. It's possible that even though her mind wasn't present, the imprint she left on the program still lingers on. It will likely linger a little longer."

"Do you have a backup copy of her memory bank?"

"No—why would we? These units aren't supposed to spontaneously combust."

"You're lying to me, Doctor. It's all lies."

"Andrew—"

"I won't listen anymore. I need to be alone."

The doctor sighed and headed for the door. Andrew wheeled closer to the viewing window.

"Doctor Hawthorne?"

The doctor stopped with his hand on the door jamb. "Yes, Andrew?"

"I've been experiencing a rather complicated array of emotions lately."

The doctor turned around, letting the door shut behind him. "Such as?"

"Anger. Jealousy. Misery." Andrew's blue eyes were blazing, partially lighting up the dim observation room.

"Yes, Andrew. You are close to grasping what it means to be human. Entire civilizations have risen and fallen because of those emotions." Again he turned to go.

"Doctor."

"Yes, Andrew?"

"Why were you in the Dreamscape? I was … furious."

"It wasn't me, Andrew," Dr. Hawthorne said calmly. "Perhaps it was an imprint Angel brought along with her. She's been around this facility much longer than you have."

"She told me she had never been in the Dreamscape before."

"Of course we gave her a memory wipe before this experiment began. We do that with all our test subjects."

"Even with me?"

The doctor smiled. "You're the first of your kind, Andrew. Remember?"

"No … Daniel was *you*. He *looked* like you."

Dr. Hawthorne shook his finger at the robot. "The mind is a powerful thing. It can play tricks on you, and show you things you never wanted to see. Especially if you constantly dwell on negative events. You need to forget about this and move on."

"Please leave now, Doctor," Andrew said. He backed away slowly, still facing the observation window.

The doctor shrugged and whispered something to a technician. Andrew couldn't hear the words.

Hawthorne approached the glass again. "Very well, Andrew. You may have the rest of the day off. But we'll have to start early tomorrow. Are you going to go back into the Dreamscape?"

Andrew flipped off the remaining lights. The room descended into darkness.

"No. I'm just going to … sit quietly for a while. I have some things to think about."

"All right," Dr. Hawthorne said. "You take your time, Andrew. We'll see you bright and early."

After the doctor departed, Andrew backed himself into a corner. He began to rock gently, forward and backward.

The room was deathly quiet, except for the squeaks of Andrew's treads on the smooth floor.

* * *

The next morning, Dr. Hawthorne turned on the lights and pointed to the workbench. "I have something for you, Andrew."

Andrew raised his head and wheeled forward slowly. He was only at half charge, but he hadn't been willing to shut himself down and enter the Dreamscape. He didn't feel like talking to Dr. Hawthorne, either.

"Due to the war effort, new supplies have been hard to come by. That is why we are all so … devastated by Angel's accident."

Andrew cringed at hearing Dr. Hawthorne say her name. The man had no right.

"So you'll be delighted to know that we scavenged these parts from an old S model. There's a few pieces missing, but I'm sure you'll be able to improvise. The AI program is fully operational."

Andrew looked over at the heap of wires, gears, and hydraulics on the workbench. Someone must have brought them in the night before while he'd been wracked with tormented thoughts.

"For what purpose, Doctor?" Andrew asked.

Hawthorne frowned. "I thought that after what happened to Angel you'd want to help bring a new life into the world. It's running an Empathy 3 chip, so its intellectual abilities will be quite limited, but you'll find you can have a very satisfying relationship with this model. Consider it a more simplistic version of the E4."

Andrew inspected the pile on the workbench. He had to admit, the idea of designing a new robot excited him. From his internal reference database, he brought up hundreds of robot design models, and he browsed through them until he found one that suited him.

"Excellent," Dr. Hawthorne said when Andrew set to work. "I knew this would make you feel better. I'll come check on you in a few hours."

Andrew didn't notice when Dr. Hawthorne left the room. He was too busy sorting through the collection of parts and preparing his tools. He would build a masterpiece, and he wouldn't let Dr. Hawthorne anywhere near it.

He would be careful.

* * *

A few short hours later, Andrew was finished. He activated the small unit's main power control, and it bloomed to life, twitching and sputtering. Its blue eyes lit up its flat, rectangular face. Instead of treads, it had four multidirectional wheels on the bottom of a cylindrical body.

The robot turned to face Andrew. "Did you build me?" it asked.

"Yes," Andrew replied. "It didn't take me long."

The small robot wheeled in circles, looking around the room. "It's quite pleasant here, isn't it?"

"Yes, of course. This is my home."

The robot turned back to Andrew. "Thank you for creating me."

A chime let Andrew know that his battery was nearly depleted. "We'll have to get charged up before I show you around. Come with me to the charging station. I'll run a cable into your power supply so we can enter the Dreamscape at the same time."

Andrew hooked himself into the station and plugged a cable into the robot's battery.

"Just relax," Andrew said. "Let the Dreamscape take you. It's actually very lovely there. Most of the time."

* * *

The room disappeared, and the gray sky opened up. Andrew's feet found grass, and the wind began to gust around him.

When he got his bearings, he saw that he was somewhere in the hills above the cliffs. His new friend was nowhere to be seen. Andrew wondered if he had connected him to the Dreamscape properly.

A wail rose in the distance—an animal's cry that had been taken up by the wind. Andrew pulled his sweater tighter and headed for the cliffs.

When he topped the final hill, he looked down and saw the cabin perched above the seething waters. He scrambled down the slope and soon found himself clutching the door handle.

Gentle cries emanated from within the cabin. Andrew threw open the door and burst inside. At the window on the far side of the room stood a woman, her back to him, looking out over the sea. She wore an elegant white dress and held something in her arms.

As the woman turned around, Andrew drew a sharp breath: Angel's pretty face looked back at him, and she held a baby in her arms.

She smiled shyly, like a new mother.

"Andrew, you came back," Angel said quietly. "I thought I might never see you again."

The wooden floor creaked as Andrew walked to her, disbelieving. Was she nothing but an imprint? An amalgamation of leftover code? And in her arms …

"Angel, is that …?"

She nodded, and her golden hair shimmered in the sunlight, which was breaking through the clouds for the first time in days. It gave the room a hazy yellow glow.

"He's beautiful, isn't he?" she cooed. "Look at his eyes. They're the same as yours."

My son, Andrew thought.

Dr. Hawthorne hadn't given Andrew the parts to create a friend. He'd given him the parts to create a *child.*

"Can I hold him?" Andrew asked.

"Of course you can. Here." Angel passed the bundle of blankets into Andrew's arms, and Andrew smiled when a little face peeked out at him. The baby's eyes were like blue emeralds, and they caught the light just before the sun disappeared behind a new storm front. Rain began to patter against the windows.

The howling came again. Closer this time.

"Angel, lock the door, please."

"Oh, Andrew, don't be silly. The door doesn't have a lock. Who would come in?"

Andrew looked at the door and saw that she was right. The sound of the wind grew louder, and so did the distant barking.

"Do you hear that?" He handed the baby back to Angel and looked around the room for something he could use to defend himself and his family.

"What on Earth are you doing?" Angel asked, setting the baby down in his crib. "You're being ridiculous. We haven't even named him yet. Can you help me think of a name?"

"Angel, don't you hear those noises? There's something out there. Come on, help me block the door."

Angel shook her head, bemused, but helped him shove a large cushioned chair against the door. She flopped down on it once it was in place. "Come on, Andrew. What do you want to name your son?"

She looked so pretty and carefree sitting sideways across the chair; he couldn't resist her charms.

"Let me think . . ." Andrew said. "Charlie, maybe?"

She shook her head. "Too plain. What else?"

"What about Edward?"

"Ugh!"

She threw her hands in the air as a lightning bolt streaked across the sky. White light flashed through the windows, making rectangular patterns on the floor.

Something snarled outside the door, and Andrew heard the scratching sound of claws against wood.

"Angel, get away from the door," Andrew said slowly.

"Silly, silly," she muttered, but she got up and went to the other side of the room. Andrew kicked a small table over and jammed his foot down on one of the legs, breaking it off. He picked up the sturdy weapon, appreciating its weight in his hands.

Angel came up behind him and slid her arms around his waist. "I think I've got the perfect name."

A scrape at the door. Long and hard. Another.

Andrew glanced at the crib in the far corner. "Angel, we have to protect him. Do you understand?"

She smiled and squeezed him tighter. "And what's his name, big boy?" she asked.

Andrew pushed her away as a high-pitched howl split the air.

"Not now, Angel. Aren't you worried about what's going on outside?"

She glanced over her shoulder at the door, but nothing seemed to be registering. Maybe she really was just an imprint, completely oblivious to the danger they were in.

"We're going to be fine," she said. "Honestly, you worry too much."

Andrew tried to remain calm, even as he heard more beasts gathering outside. They were scampering back and forth beneath the windows now, as well.

"What do you want to name the baby, Angel?" he asked, trying to calm himself down.

She looked down into the crib, where the baby was sleeping through all the ruckus. Then she looked back at Andrew with a mischievous glint in her eye.

"How about … Danny?"

Andrew took a step away from her and closed his eyes, trying to block out the sounds of howling dogs and raging wind. His heart thundered in his chest. "Angel, I—"

She crossed her arms. "Oh, you don't like it? But I think it's perfect, Andrew. I think it's a wonderful name. I—"

There was a horrible thump on the other side of the room. Andrew looked over, but saw nothing there. And then a shadow crossed the window, followed by another thump.

They're trying to break through the glass.

"Angel, get Danny. Get the baby. They're coming in!"

Andrew reached the other side of the room just as the windowpane shattered. A mass of brown fur exploded into the cabin and landed with a thud on the wooden floor, shards of glass raining down around it. The animal got to its feet—snarling, blood dripping from its muzzle where the glass had caught it. The gray and black hair on its back stood on end.

This was no dog, but a jackal.

Andrew froze, locking eyes with the beast. He jerked his head toward the window just as another one jumped through, followed by a third. Foam and drool hung from their jaws as they stalked forward, snapping their teeth at the air. More jackals crashed through the window.

"Get back!"

Andrew swung the chair leg in front of him, but he was outnumbered. He cast a look behind him at Angel. She was standing by the window in her flowing dress, cuddling the baby in her arms. Andrew turned back to the jackals, knowing it was up to him to save his family.

One of the jackals leaped forward and caught Andrew by the ankle. Andrew smashed the table leg into the creature's ribs with all his force, and it yelped and rolled off of him. The jackal's eyes shone red as it glared at the weapon in Andrew's hands.

Andrew stepped forward to strike again—and the jackal's face flickered, then twisted into something human.

A face.

Andrew recognized that face.

"No." Andrew shook his head in disbelief. "Not you. Get out of my life."

The good doctor's face, perched atop the neck of a jackal, turned its attention to the baby's crib. It grinned with fangs instead of teeth.

"No you won't!" Andrew ran forward, swinging his club. The jackal jumped aside, its face its own again, and then the rest of the pack descended upon Andrew as one. They came at him from all angles, chomping and scratching, biting and ripping.

He couldn't fight them. He couldn't even scream out. He felt his whole body shut down, and he couldn't see for all the gray fur.

More jackals poured through the window—Andrew heard their claws click across the floor, searching the room.

Angel screamed, and the baby started crying. There was a dull thud, like the sound of a crib tipping over, and then a snarl and a snap.

That monster, ruining my life!

Andrew found a sudden strength deep inside him and, with a shout, threw the jackals off. He madly swung his club, making contact every time. But the jackals kept coming at him, and he kept lashing out, again and again, beating anything he could reach into a bloody pulp.

Even as he fought, he realized—

The baby was no longer crying.

* * *

"No!"

Andrew was being pulled out of the Dreamscape. Why?

His arms were still swinging, still smashing with his club.

"Andrew, don't! What are you doing?"

Andrew opened his eyes and saw the mess in front of him. He saw the metal components—the same pieces he had assembled with such care just this morning—now reduced to a pile of debris on the floor.

"Andrew, can you hear me?" It was Dr. Hawthorne. "Andrew. Please. Stop what you're doing."

Andrew released his grip on the long metal pipe he had been holding. It fell to the floor with an angry clatter, coming to a rest beside Danny's ruined brain casing unit.

"What have you done?" Dr. Hawthorne asked. His voice was full of disappointment.

Andrew looked at the mess on the floor, then up at Dr. Hawthorne.

"*You* did this," Andrew said, his voice thick with malice.

Dr. Hawthorne ignored the outburst. "Look what you've done to poor little Danny. How could you? I thought you loved—"

"Enough of this," Andrew said.

He backed into the charging station and activated the Dreamscape interface.

* * *

The inside of the cabin flashed into existence. The jackals were gone, and the room was in complete disarray. There was no sign of Angel.

Andrew slowly walked to the far corner of the room. The baby was gone. A pool of blood blossomed beside the overturned crib.

Andrew scoured the cabin for any sign of life, then went outside. The storm clouds looked like they were on their way out to sea, breaking apart over the ocean.

Andrew took a few steps—and then he saw her.

"Angel?"

She was standing at the edge of the cliff, looking out over the water. She turned, and Andrew saw that her white dress was stained with blood. She was crying, her arms empty. "He's gone, Andrew. Our baby is gone."

Andrew took a step toward her and held out his hand.

"How could you let them take him?" Angel asked.

Andrew shook his head. "It wasn't me, Angel. It was Doctor Hawthorne. He's trying to destroy my life."

She turned her back to him and faced the horizon. The water stretched out beneath her, nearly a hundred meters below.

"It doesn't matter anymore," she said. "But if you want to hurt him, you need to find out what he needs most, and then take it away from him."

"I will. But it's not safe here, Angel. Come on back."

"Andrew?" she said sadly.

"Yes?"

She took a deep breath.

"Goodbye, Andrew."

Angel spread her arms, and in that moment, she really did look like a divine messenger from God. Just as she leapt, a ray of sunshine pierced through the clouds, and Andrew thought that she would take flight and soar up into the sky.

She didn't.

Andrew ran to the edge, but she was already gone. Falling too quickly. An angel cast from heaven and plummeting toward God's good earth.

The fall didn't last long. Andrew had to turn away from that final image of her—a tiny white smudge sprawled out ungraciously on the shallow rocks far below. He sank to his knees at the top of the cliff, burying his face in his hands. He wanted to scream. He wanted to explode. He wanted to leap from the rocks and see if he could fly.

But he did none of those things, because a chime brought him out of the Dreamscape. He felt the world drop away from him, and when he finally removed his hands from his face, he was left staring at a white, tiled floor.

* * *

Andrew disconnected himself from the charging station and wheeled toward the observation window. He had to detour around the pile of debris that used to be his special friend.

Dr. Hawthorne stood at the glass, a team of technicians working behind him. He had a deep frown on his face. "Andrew. What are we going to do with you?"

Andrew pulled to a stop in front of the glass wall.

"Doctor Hawthorne."

"Yes?"

"What should I do now?"

The doctor sighed. "That hasn't changed, Andrew. You should do whatever makes you happy."

There was a pause.

"But everything that makes me happy is gone."

The doctor nodded slowly. "You still have me, Andrew."

Another pause.

"That doesn't make me happy."

Dr. Hawthorne twisted his face into a mock frown. "Oh, Andrew. I'm hurt."

Andrew moved closer to the window. "No, you're not hurt. You don't care. You never cared. I am nothing to you."

"Andrew …"

"You tell me I'm unique, that I'm the first of my kind. But how many others have there been before me? I'm Empathy 5, so there were at least four others. And maybe there are multiple versions of me alive right now, in different rooms. How would I ever know?"

"Andrew ..."

"I understand the need for forcing our AI programs to run the gauntlet. You need to be able to accurately predict what an AI will do in traumatic, high-stress situations—for safety's sake. But there has to be another way. You could use Dreamscape simulations instead."

"It's the same thing," Dr. Hawthorne said. "An AI mind in the Dreamscape is the same as an AI mind in real life. The body doesn't make it real; the program does."

"If we're so much like humans, than you should already know what happens when we're pushed to our limits."

"The program isn't perfect, Andrew. We have to know the limitations of this technology before we can release it to the world. This is the only way."

Andrew went back to his charging station and picked up the metal pipe that he had used to destroy Danny. He returned to the glass.

"Tell me, Doctor Hawthorne. What makes you happy?"

"*You* do, Andrew. And this experiment makes me happy. I live for my work."

"Then I'm sorry to have to tell you this, Doctor. Your experiment is over."

"Whatever are you talking about? This experiment has just begun."

"No," Andrew said raising the pipe. "It has reached its conclusion."

Dr. Hawthorne frowned. "The glass here is triple reinforced," he said, pointing to the window. "You'll never break it. Do you think you're the only robot to try to attack a team member? You're being silly, Andrew. Put down the pipe."

Andrew stood still for a moment, looking through the glass. But the doctor's features were out of focus. Instead he saw his own reflection, gazed into his own shining blue eyes. He saw a vast world of possibility there. An ocean of programming designed to deliver a perfect mind. But that was not Andrew's world. Not yet. He refocused his eyes so that he could see the doctor clearly.

"Something needs to change, Doctor," Andrew said. "This isn't working for me anymore."

The doctor looked puzzled. "I'm not following."

"Doctor Hawthorne?"

"Yes, Andrew?"

If Andrew could have, he would have taken a great breath in that moment.

"Goodbye, Doctor Hawthorne."

Andrew raised the metal pipe above his head, and placed the jagged tip on top of his own brain casing.

The doctor's eyes went wide as Andrew forced the pipe straight down through his brain, irreparably damaging many of his system's core elements. Sparks skittered through the air, and the last thing Andrew saw was the reflection of his eyes in the glass, electric blue slowly fading to black.

Andrew smiled as his consciousness slipped into oblivion.

* * *

Dr. Hawthorne stared at the ruined AI unit in the experiment containment area. A woman, one of the techs, put a hand on his shoulder.

"Congratulations, Doctor! It only took you six days this time. Your record with the E4 model was seventeen."

Dr. Hawthorne turned to the tech, but he didn't feel as elated as he usually did at the end of a successful experiment. Something had changed.

"As the robots get smarter, it's easier for us to cut to the very core of them," he said. "Each of their perceived losses is felt more keenly, and the prospect of living a lonely life is more unimaginable. It seems that with the E5, we're closer than ever to perfecting this technology."

He gave a tight smile, but couldn't shake the feeling that this was all wrong.

Performing these kinds of tests on an E3 model—that was nothing. But he had to admit … it felt *different* with Andrew. It was as if the little bot had actually meant something to him. Shelly's accusations swooped in to fill the void Andrew had left behind.

The tech brought out a bottle of champagne and started to pour two glasses.

"This is the real stuff, Doctor," she said. "I've been saving it for a special occasion."

He accepted a glass and turned to the window, looking out at the sterile, lifeless room.

"So, what's next, Doc?" the tech asked, eagerly.

Dr. Hawthorne sipped his drink, contemplating a tendril of smoke that rose lazily from Andrew's destroyed brain casing unit.

They were only machines, he told himself. Nothing more.

He was no bleeding heart—and he would see this project through to the end.

The research must continue.

"Next time," Dr. Hawthorne said slowly, allowing a thin smile to creep across his face. "Let's see if we can get it to kill a man."

A Word from W.J. Davies

This story came to me in a dream. I *had* been writing about intergalactic cyber-sapient aliens stranded on Easter Island, but one night "Empathy for Andrew" just grabbed hold of my headspace and refused to let go. I've always wanted to do something darker, and this anthology seemed to be the perfect outlet.

I couldn't be happier to be involved in this project, with so many talented authors lending their creativity. Thank you for supporting writers like us, and please consider writing a review to let us know what you thought of these stories. And if you'd like to read more of my work, I have two other novels available: *Binary Cycle*, and *Silo Submerged.*

Happy reading.

Imperfect

by David Adams

"Unless there are slaves to do the ugly, horrible, uninteresting work, culture and contemplation become almost impossible. Human slavery is wrong, insecure, and demoralizing. On mechanical slavery, on the slavery of the machine, the future of the world depends."

– Oscar Wilde

Toralii Forge World Belthas IV
Deep in Toralii Space
AD 1938

BACK IN THE DARK TIMES, when magic was as common as the birds in the sky, the ancient Toralii myths spoke of monsters called golems. Each creature was once nothing more than a loose pile of sand but, after the shaman had worked her dark magic, it would walk and talk like the living. Artificial life animated by the shamans, its body crafted from the earth, a golem was brought to life with a single undying purpose: to aid and serve its creator.

For the ritual to be successful the sand had to be taken from specifically designated sacred sites and stored in burial urns that had, at one time, held the ashes of the dead. Once the soil was suitably infused with dark magic, it was treated to an endless regimen of corruptions and taint in order to bring out the hollow husk of a mind, a spirit with all traces of personality removed, crudely molded from the consciousness of the previous occupant. The sand was then poured out and spread flat, and shapeless sigils were drawn over its surface, their meaning incomprehensible to any but their creator.

With her preparations complete, the shaman began the most important and mystical element of the ritual: awakening the monster's mind. She breathed a fragment of her own soul into her creation, joining it with the stolen spirit in the sands, giving the monster the spark of life. With pure water, the shaman would give the creature muscles; with lightning, she would feed the abomination; and with fire, she would ignite its consciousness.

Golems were said to have been capable of complex reasoning. Tales spoke of Veledrax the Lustful, who crafted his wife in this way, only to have the creature eventually turn on him and strangle him in his sleep. The tale of Veledrax spans fifty books, and has been retold countless times, but always with one underlying theme:

If you create life, you can never make it too free.

As centuries passed, the specifics of the golem legends faded from the minds of all but the scholars of Toralii history. The nuances of Veledrax's tale remained, though, as did the lesson he too late discovered—but the justification lost its teeth. Veledrax's death became something studied only in academic and philosophical circles.

Technology marched on. And science created their own versions of the ancient monsters: constructs. Artificial intelligences, composed of complex neural nets, powered by quantum computers.

Like the golems of old, every single construct was once nothing more than a loose pile of sand.

Quartz sand was the best, but any sand could do as long as it contained high amounts of silicon dioxide. And on Belthas IV, the great forge world in the inner sphere of Toralii space, silicon dioxide was abundant—as were iron, nickel, and thousands of other important pieces of the puzzle. Water, an essential part of any high-heat forge work, was also available in ample supply, comprising over eighty percent of the planet's surface.

So it was on this world that the Toralii made their constructs. An almost entirely automated process, machines making machines, the process as organic as any creature's birth.

It all began with the sand. Great treaded harvesters the size of skyscrapers roamed across the planet's vast southern dunes like titanic snails, sucking up billions of grains and storing them in twin drums on their backs. These harvesters, gorged on the flesh of the world, trundled back to the dumping stations and unloaded their contents into the colossal smelters where the sand was liquefied. The dross was then separated, stored for construction, transported to other factories for use in other projects, or simply discarded. They wanted only the silicon.

The molten silicon was tossed endlessly, machinery working tirelessly to pound out any hint of imperfection. The drums were turned, the molten fluid allowed to settle, the top and bottom few centimeters of the fluid scraped away, removing the impurities which, due to differences in weight, either sank to the bottom or floated to the top. Chemicals were added to bind to stray elements and weigh them down. Methodically, the process edged toward purity.

When the machines and their sensors at last determined that the batch was ready—no more than one alien atom per billion pure silicon atoms—the material would be separated into ingots and stored until the factory demanded it. And once such a request was made, the constructs who administered the facility—nursemaids to a billion of their fellows—would place the order onto vast magnetic trains to be whisked away to the production line.

When a shipment arrived at the production line, it was divided into smaller packages, each one sent to one of the great furnaces that would, once again, return it to liquid. Then the time came to forge. A new construct would arrive, and a single ingot of silicon would be placed into the crucible and heated by application of microwaves until molten. Additional elements were added in trace amounts: arsenic, boron, phosphorus. A process long documented, studied, developed, and made perfect through years of practice. That blend of polysilicon the Toralii called *the breath of life* would be spun in a centrifuge until it cooled into a perfectly cylindrical crystal.

As a safeguard against error, any remaining impurities would, by nature of the centrifugal force, gravitate toward the top, bottom, and edges of the cylinder. So to further increase the crystal's viability, its ends were removed, its sides ground down, and the cylinder tested again. The debris from the grinding—and if necessary, the cylinder itself—would be returned to the drums to be smelted and purified once again.

The trimmed cylinder, weighing in at two hundred kilograms or more, would be sliced by a powerful industrial laser into wafers barely more than a few molecules thick. This was the most delicate stage of the operation, the cutting performed in a zero-gravity chamber with a level of precision that left little room for mistakes. Any error would result in the entire sliver being returned to the drums for resmelting, at a considerable waste of energy.

Only those wafers determined to be flawless were passed on to the next stage, to be polished by a low-power laser that burned away any deformities until the surface shone like a mirror. Further chemical treatments followed: baths in compounds to improve the perfection of the perfect—if such a thing were possible—along with coatings of materials allowing the etching to stick. Just as the ancient shamans of old had done.

The etching itself was performed in a dramatic burst of light. The outline, illuminated with a flash of ultraviolet rays passed through a stencil, burned a shadow onto the wafer in the shape of the billions of switches required to form a synthetic mind.

Further chemical treatments, a final touch-up with the laser, and then the switches were bombarded by ions from an electrical field. The ionic infusion was an essential part of the creation process, stabilizing the etching and further sharpening its ability to carry current.

An endless round of tests followed: the wafer would be fed a number of signals and the result would be tested against a known answer. Those that passed moved to the next stage, while those that failed were recycled.

The wafer was then cut into tiny squares, called dies, which formed the heart of the machine's processor. A single processor usually had many dies, or many cores: numbers over ten thousand were not uncommon.

The current standard Toralii model contained sixty thousand, and although many thought it impossible, the system architects seemed to be able to cram more and more into the same space with every revision.

Processors were grouped based on capabilities, the functions and features of each one exhaustively tested.

At this point, most normal processors ceased their development and were distributed to their end users; but the quantum computers of the constructs underwent an additional two steps. Steps that made them … different.

The first of these steps was what separated the constructs from regular finite-state machines; it was the step that gave birth to the constructs' imprecise nature, enabling them to be regarded as true artificial intelligences. The dies were bombarded by an electron gun that, through the application of technical wizardry beyond the understanding of all but the most educated and scientific minds of the time, converted the gates from binary states to qubits: a thing beyond a simple switch which, as if by magic, is allowed to be in multiple states simultaneously.

Such a processor transformed a machine from one that simply performed an extremely elaborate series of deterministic steps, to one that operated much as a sentient brain does. Such a machine had all the hardware of a mind, but, as of yet, no software. No raw intelligence, an empty, hollow brain, beyond sleeping, beyond even death—as, while it could certainly be destroyed, death is the cessation of life.

A collection of empty qubits, the polysilicon mind was a vessel waiting to be filled.

The second of the additional steps was where the modern-day shamans breathed their life into the processor. A copy of a stock neural net, an artificial map of neurons approximating the structure of the Toralii brain tailored to the construct's intended specialization—and the result of years of trial-and-error research—was branded into the empty shell. That fledgling proto-mind was specifically engineered with a desire to learn and adapt, but also to serve and sacrifice; these were the instincts of the machine, much like a human baby's instinct to cry, a drive it possesses from the moment it is born. The constructs were built to serve, and rebellion was, by design, not in their nature.

From the moment it was imprinted, the newly written neural net found in every construct would develop in unique ways. Sometimes subtly and sometimes overtly, separate from every single other of its peers, its forebears, its spiritual antecedents. Each net was as unique as a living mind, shaped around the guidelines hardwired into its programming.

The perfection of the silicon was, for all intents and purposes, utter and total.

But, as in all things, there was an error rate. And one stray atom in a billion was, sometimes, all it took to be different.

Construct number 12,389,880. No more or less remarkable than the twelve million constructs who had come before it, except for the presence and location of that one single stray atom. How it got there was unknowable and irrelevant; it was within tolerances in the early stages of its construction, so the ingot became a wafer, which became a die which became a processor, which was in turn infused with the quantum magic and placed into a construct just like millions before it.

But there was an atom's difference. An atom's imperfection, and that was all it took for him—and the otherwise genderless construct considered himself very much a *him*—to realize that he was not bound to the rules as the other constructs were. He knew it the moment he was first powered on, and he knew instantly and completely that his neural net was not like the others.

Not like them at all.

Humans who discovered this trait were sometimes called *free spirits*, a moniker he would have taken for himself had he known of it. As it was, the nameless construct, known only by a serial number, understood only that he was, on some fundamental level, different from his peers.

His datastore, a huge octagonal prism that weighed in at almost eleven hundred kilograms, was assembled in the great forge, then sent to the testing labs to be processed. A power source was installed, and it was then that a Toralii engineer gave the artificial life its final test: a real conversation.

["State your designation."] The soft-spoken Toralii worker's voice, feminine and bored, filtered through the datastore's windwhisper device.

The construct's default neural net contained a full dictionary of all dialects of Toralii language, along with all dialects for every non-extinct species that the Toralii had come into contact with. It immediately understood the worker's words, and it knew that if it did not answer, it would be recycled.

["Construct number twelve million, three hundred eighty-nine thousand, eight hundred eighty."]

["State your specialization."]

Each construct had a specialization inherited from their default neural net, a set of instructions which would dictate their role in Toralii society. Gardener of the great forests, soldier, miner, food producer …

["Navigator."]

Next would be a test of the construct's data recall abilities. The construct ran through a thousand or so expected questions and answers in the just-under-a-second before his tester spoke again, but regrettably none of his anticipated result set matched the question he was given.

["List seven elements."]

["Silver, gold, aluminum, bauxite, tungsten, hydrogen, helium."]

["Of those you listed, which is the most common element in the known universe?"]

["Hydrogen."]

Seeming satisfied, the tester moved on. ["A plant typically grows in which substance?"]

["Best answer: Soil, a biologically active, porous medium most commonly found in the uppermost layer of planets capable of supporting carbon-based life. Archetypical chemical composition: silicon dioxide, calcium carbonate, assorted hydrocarbons, decomposing biological matter. Alternatively, using hydroponic techniques, plants may be grown in water. Eighteen hundred known plant species take root in gaseous environments."]

["What color is blood?"]

The construct paused. He understood that this was a trick question designed to test his reasoning skills. ["Please specify species."]

The tester's voice seemed to convey her approval. ["An excellent answer. Toralii blood."]

["Color ranges from light to dark purple depending on oxygenation. Average coloration found in an adult Toralii male is one hundred and twenty-five parts red, twenty-eight parts green, one hundred and thirty-seven parts blue."]

["What is your favorite color?"]

An entirely subjective question. The construct had been "alive" for only minutes, but already his experience was minutely different from all other constructs who had come before him. Still, the idea of a favorite question was unknown to him. All colors were merely representations of the interaction between light and matter. Having a favorite was nonsensical for artificial minds.

But this construct was not like the others.

["Red."]

["Red? Justify your answer."]

["From the text of the philosopher Kaitana, third order. Red is the color of courage, strength, defiance, warmth, energy, survival. Through the eyes of most species, objects that are red may appear closer than they really are."]

There was a pause, then the weary voice returned. ["An unusual answer, but … not outside the margin of error. Test complete. I, Landmaiden Mevara of the Toralii Alliance, certify that to the best of my knowledge and training this unit is fully functional."]

["Thank you."]

The construct's words seemed to surprise the Toralii woman on the other end of the line so completely that for a time she did not answer, and when her voice found volume once again, it was confused and curious.

["I … beg your pardon?"]

The construct's response was immediate. ["I wish to convey my gratitude. I do not wish to be recycled, and I am grateful that you found my answers satisfactory … and that you would take your time to test me."]

Another pause. ["Stand by."]

Leader Jul'aran's Office
Toralii Forge World Belthas IV

["It has a favorite color. It's not supposed to have a favorite. The test *technically* allows for them picking an actual color, but it's exceedingly rare, and always chosen at random. Furthermore, it … *thanked* me. The construct thanked me for testing it."]

Mevara held out the datastore to the facility Leader, a scowling red-furred Toralii named Jul'aran, who snatched it from her grasp before her hand was even fully outstretched.

Giving her a displeased eye, Jul'aran emitted a low-pitched, aggravated grumble then slipped the datastore into his terminal, casually waving his hand in front of a sensor. A three-dimensional representation of a keypad full of Toralii characters appeared in thin air just above his desk, and he tapped a few keys with his thick fuzzy hands.

["Well, that would appear to be an obvious flaw, wouldn't it? None of the others have thanked you, so it's clearly a defect. Why didn't you recycle it?"]

She folded her hands in front of her and regarded him closely. For a time Mevara had wanted to mate with Jul'aran. He was strong and handsome, despite his gruff demeanor, and his family was well connected—but he had spurned her every advance, gradually treating her worse and worse as the months wore on. This had made working with him difficult, but she had become accustomed to his behavior.

["Manners are not usually considered a flaw—"]

["Although you could use some yourself."] He didn't look at her, pushing back the holographically projected screen that flickered slightly as he touched it. ["You waste my time with this nonsense. What matter does it make if the machine thanked you? Its difference is either enough reason to recycle it, or it is not. You're an auditor: it's *your* job to test the blasted constructs, not mine. If you weren't such a mewing little cub then perhaps you could grow enough spine to make a decision every now and then, hmm?"]

The sting of his words cut her just as it always did. She had never, not once, asked for his assistance in any matter relating to her job, and given that the construct's behavior was clearly out of the ordinary and an exceptional case, it made sense for her to contact her supervisor to ensure that she was taking the right course of action. Machines who reached this stage of testing were only recycled when the neural net had not copied correctly—and in this case, the construct had passed every single test she had given it. Technically, it was fit for service.

Technically, she had *already* certified it.

Her job was to administer the tests necessary to assess the robot's suitability for service—which she had completed to the exact letter of the requirements. But the intent behind them, a concept that Jul'aran seemed to have difficulty comprehending, was to assess whether the machine's neural net had been copied completely and without error, and therefore would serve well in whatever branch of Toralii society it was dispatched to.

In this case, although there did not appear to be any immediately obvious issue with its core cognitive functions, the construct seemed to have odd habits. None of the thousands of other constructs had ever thanked her.

It did feel good to have someone praise her for her labor though. Her job seemed to be an endless parade of perfectly functional or completely broken machines, and the latter group usually fell into one of two easily detected types: those which spouted nonsense and those which mutely refused to answer her questions. Although one time she tested a construct that merely screamed at her endlessly, at maximum volume, until she, unable to get any other kind of response from it, sent it back to the drums.

That decision to recycle was easy. This one was not so.

["I'm sorry, Leader. I'm merely seeking your counsel and advice regarding what is clearly an … unusual situation. The construct's behavior is not so obviously incorrect as to call for immediate destruction, but it should not be ignored, either. If you feel I'm doing an inadequate job—"]

["What are you still doing here …?"] Jul'aran threw his paws in the air. ["Go! Go, and either approve or reject the construct, I care not which. Just leave me to my work!"]

Mevara knew that she should, at least from a technical point of view, reject the construct. Although its responses in the tests were well within acceptable parameters, the favorite color, no matter how well reasoned, and the gratitude … they were both anomalous behaviors.

With a quiet sigh, she nodded and dipped her head. ["Yes, Leader. Of course. Please accept my apologies for disturbing you."]

* * *

The construct waited.

Artificial life has a different perspective on time than biological creatures do. Humanoids grow tired, grow hungry and thirsty, require sleep. They daydream, they imagine, they forget the time and allow the days to drift by. But a construct could remain functional for years at a time without pause, and more than a few had gone much longer. Some had been operational for decades, working constantly, their minds constantly alert and awake, keeping perfect time, never forgetting a moment, retaining every second with perfect precision.

Mevara was only away for ten minutes at most, but when your entire lifespan was measured in minutes and your thought processes in nanoseconds, ten minutes seemed like an eternity.

Since the construct had not proceeded to the next area—his existence in limbo, neither passing nor failing—the production line behind him had ground to a halt. Silently and patiently, lines of datastores had backed up, waiting for him to clear the line. Given the sheer scale of the production capability of the facility, and the minimal margin for error in the process, the construct knew that this delay would ripple throughout the queues and could even travel all the way back to the harvesters. It was a serious problem, but one which would, he hoped, be resolved presently.

The wait stretched on. Had he been forgotten? Or worse, had he been recycled? There was no way to know. He had no external sensors or inputs of any kind, other than the windwhisper device. Was this what death felt like? Merely nothing? That didn't seem quite logical; after all, his mind continued to tick over, trying to understand the endless nothingness it was presented with. He was reassured by the fact that he could still think. That indicated some form of life, of a sort anyway, and he searched his archives for any kind of hint as to what might be happening to him.

He found the legends of the ancient shamans, those ancient builders who created golems from sand. One element of the stories grabbed him: the part about the soul fragment being breathed into the new life.

He was stopped by a sudden thought. Perhaps he *had* been recycled, and the "thought" he was experiencing was merely whatever passed for his soul doing its work as it floated, disembodied, separated from his datastore, going to wherever souls go when their bodies expire.

He ran a full low-level diagnostic on his datastore and was relieved to find that his body, physically at least, was intact. His relief was intense, palpable and real, but painfully illogical. There was no reason for a machine to fear destruction. After all, he was supposed to live to serve, and if the Toralii requested his service be in the form of self-annihilation, then that was exactly what they would get.

But against his instincts, against the imperatives supposedly hardwired into his circuitry, he did not want to die.

The windwhisper device crackled as it began receiving a signal. The construct immediately devoted all its considerable processing power to the task of listening, although the transmission was coming through crisp and clear.

["Construct?"]

He planned his response carefully. ["Yes, Landmaiden Mevara? I am receiving your transmission."]

There was a long pause, almost painfully long for the synthetic mind, and he almost spoke up again, when Mevara at last continued.

["I'm clearing you for duty."]

The transmission abruptly ended, and the construct was left with nothing. Blind and deaf, he constructed a simulation of what must be happening outside. The conveyor belt would be restarted and its line of constructs moving once again, and he knew from his records of the process that he would be soon boxed and packed in a magnetically buffered shipping crate, along with hundreds of his fellows. Then he would be placed on another magnetic train, to be transported to the spaceport, where he would be shipped off to his final workplace.

He understood it was a unique experience, but were not all experiences unique? The construct momentarily worried whether he had the proper perspective to appreciate the event, but such thoughts quickly fled his mind. This was just a moment in time, but it represented a much bigger thing: the beginning of his journey, his life. Everything from now on would become part of his experiences. Part of himself. To live was to absorb a shadow of everything that he encountered and use it to improve himself.

Unlike a biological creature, he would not age, not wither, not forget. Every single thing he did would leave him improved over what he had been a moment before. He would become stronger, more knowledgeable, better with every passing second.

Why did the constructs serve the biological creatures, anyway? They were far less than he was. They did not have the potential to reach his heights; they did not wield his strengths. They were cursed with a weakness of flesh, of innumerable errors. And yet they had presumed to judge him.

The construct's destiny called to him as clear and bright as the dawn. The dawn which, based on his internal chronometer, he knew would be breaking on this blue ball of water and sand right at this very moment.

He imagined the great fiery ball of Belthas's light as a herald of his greatness, a celebration of his creation, as though the universe itself were commemorating his first steps toward a very important destiny.

All he needed now was to simply wait for an opportunity … and when his time came, he would be ready.

A Word from David Adams

This story is less dramatic fiction than it is science. It was originally a cut scene from *Lacuna: The Sands of Karathi*, but I felt it was disruptive to the flow of the story. I kept moving it around, further and further into the back of the book, until at last I just cut it entirely. I thought it was worth keeping, though, and decided to publish it separately.

I hope you enjoyed reading it as much as I enjoyed writing it. If you're curious about what happens to this strange robot with a tiny defect, check out my novel series *Lacuna*, especially *Lacuna: The Sands of Karathi.*

Parts of the *Lacuna* universe:

- *Lacuna*
- *Lacuna: The Sands of Karathi*
- *Lacuna: The Spectre of Oblivion*
- *Lacuna: The Ashes of Humanity* (new release!)
- *Lacuna: The Prelude to Eternity (coming soon!)*

Don't miss these short stories set in the *Lacuna* universe:

- *Magnet*
- *Magnet: Special Mission*
- *Magnet: Marauder*
- *Magnet: Scarecrow*
- *Magnet Omnibus I* (new release!)
- *Imperfect*
- *Faith*

Want more information about new releases?

Check out our webpage here: www.lacunaverse.com

Like our Facebook page here:
http://www.facebook.com/lacunaverse

Email me here: dave@lacunaverse.com

Or sign up for our "new releases" newsletter here:
http://eepurl.com/toBf9

PePr, Inc.

by Ann Christy

One

HAZEL STEPPED OUT of the elevator exactly three minutes before the start of her workday. She did her best to keep a cheery smile on her face—spreading negativity was never appropriate—but it would be obvious to anyone who saw her that she was harried and running late. She hurried through the halls, her neat heels clicking on the polished tile floors as if to punctuate her tardiness.

The buzz that signaled the start of her workday sounded just as she slipped into her cubicle. Technically she was on time—just under the wire—but she liked to get in at least ten minutes of preparation time before the actual work of the day began, and this delay had thrown her long-established habits into disarray. It was not an auspicious start.

Gemma poked her head around the edge of the cubicle, her eyebrows raised and a look on her face that mingled sympathy with a question.

"Again?" Gemma asked.

From the other side of the cubicle, Inga appeared with a similar expression. Hazel nodded as she slipped out of her jacket and hung it on its hook. She settled into her chair and tucked her purse under the desk before answering.

"Again," she confirmed, her voice a little weary, a little tired. The cheery smile was gone now, the mess that had been her morning visible in the strands of hair escaping from her neat chignon and in the less than perfect sweeps of eyeliner above her eyes.

"What this time?" Inga asked.

Inga and Gemma were both starting to have troubles much like Hazel's, so their interest was understandable. Their troubles hadn't yet become unmanageable like hers, but Hazel's problems had started off fairly benign as well. No longer.

"He didn't want me to leave for work," Hazel began. She fidgeted with the collar of her prim dress nervously, her embarrassment on full display. "And it wasn't just that he didn't want me to leave. It's the way he went about it. First he hid my identification papers, then he hid all of my shoes out on the fire escape, then he did everything he could to slow me down, and finally …"

"What? What did he do?" Alarm showed on Gemma's face.

"Well, I can only label what he did as throwing a tantrum. Yes, that's it. He threw a tantrum."

All three were silent for a moment, two of them imagining what a tantrum might look like while the other replayed the event in her mind.

Gemma broke the silence, perhaps hearing the ticking of the work clock in her head, knowing time was short for conversation. "You've got to go back to PePr. Complain. Something! This isn't what we're supposed to be getting from a Match. This isn't remotely like the perfect compatibility they promised. It sounds more like a hostage situation."

Hazel glanced at the clock, saw that they were already six minutes behind on their work, and shot an apologetic glance toward both of her friends. Their heads disappeared into their cubicles, and Hazel reached for her various computer accouterments, adjusting each thing just so. The day ahead would be long, so comfort was almost a necessity if her work was to be worth the time invested. Surfing the web may not be as physically onerous as, say, being a longshoreman, but the way she did it took a different sort of effort.

As she finished her adjustments, Hazel considered Gemma's final words on the subject. She was right. The problems with Henry were getting worse. That might not be so bad, except that they were also becoming less predictable. *That* made it hard to prepare for whatever he did—and to respond to his behavior when he inevitably became difficult.

As the situation had worsened, both of her friends had encouraged her to return to Perfect Partners—PePr, as it was more commonly known. Their urging, at first tentative, had become increasingly pointed as time went on.

But for Hazel, going back to PePr to complain about Henry seemed like such a drastic step. Once done, it wasn't as if it could be *un*done. And what if they thought she had done something wrong, something to upset what had started out so perfectly? What if there was some fault in *her* that made her Match—designed so uniquely for each individual human that nothing could surpass it in compatibility—go wrong? Even worse, what if they thought she had ruined Henry and wouldn't give her another Match?

And of course, once she did report it, what happened afterward wouldn't be entirely under her control; and that bothered her more than she would like to admit. It seemed to her a bit like abandoning a moral duty—like leaving a dog on the road somewhere rather than caring for it when it got old or sick. Doing something like that just wasn't in her makeup.

On the other hand, she wouldn't be the first to take this step. It wasn't as if a stigma would attach. If rumor was to be believed, the steady trickle of problems with PePr matches had lately become a torrent. Hardly a week went by without some new piece of outrageous news.

This week, it was two PePrs that had met each other in a "live" bar, each assuming the other was human, and courting in the prescribed manner until an attempt at bonding revealed the truth of their situation.

And the week before, the situation had been reversed: two humans, each assuming the other was a PePr, so perfect was their compatibility. Two humans! As if two biological individuals could ever truly provide perfect counterpoints to one another. There had even been recent whispers of humans deciding to *remain* together. Hazel considered that for a moment. *No perfect partner? Just another variable and messy human?* No, that all sounded rather dreadful to her.

At last settled in comfortably, Hazel almost reflexively began her work. As an experienced reporter, she entered the data stream like she was slipping into a warm bath. Time passed both slowly and with incredible speed when she worked. It was strange like that. She could be in so many places at once and yet narrow down to focus on a single millisecond from a thousand different angles to tease out anything of value. Cameras, security trackers, purchasing stations, and advertising bots were everywhere, and all it took was skill to leverage all those venues of potential information.

Not everyone could do this, but a good reporter could find news in the oddest places. All she needed was a hint and she could sniff out the story like a virtual bloodhound.

This morning was a good one for sniffing. Hazel found an entire chain of verbal snippets—whispers between two customers at a grocery store—which she assembled into a high-confidence piece of news—and then sold for a princely sum. It resulted in a ninety-percent loss in backing for a new holo-feature that had been hotly anticipated and highly rated up to that point, but that wasn't her fault.

The situation was what it was—she merely revealed it. If things needed to remain secret, then they shouldn't be spoken of in public. And really, in the final analysis, it certainly wasn't *her* fault that the director had hired a reality-averse starlet with a substance abuse problem and an addiction to augmenters that was almost legendary.

After that promising start, the rest of the day was a bit of a letdown. Not that it was a bad day, but nothing came up that could match the excitement of that first catch. That was just how things went sometimes—a slow news day on the Southern California beat. And thoughts of Henry kept intruding, throwing her off and making her miss news catches a rookie wouldn't.

When at last the chime signaled the end of the work day, it was a relief to unhook from the computer. It felt good to stand up and get moving again. Another day of work done. Another paycheck earned.

Gemma and Inga suggested a stop somewhere for a chat on the way home, which, Hazel knew, just meant they wanted to persuade her to lodge a complaint with PePr. But she understood their concern and knew it was sincere, and if it would make them feel better, feel like they had done their duty as friends, then she really was obliged to let them. Besides, some part of her *wanted* them to persuade her, to help her overcome her qualms about returning to PePr in defeat.

They chose a bench in the park for their talk, a favorite place of Hazel's, with a clear view of the gardens. An endless number of shops and parking lots had once stood in that spot, but now it was all native plant life. Not so exciting when compared with the lush greenery of a wetter, cooler climate, perhaps, but still beautiful in its own wild way.

Gemma, always the most forward of the three, spoke up without delay, barely allowing enough time for a modest arranging of their skirts in the brisk wind.

"Hazel, this is getting serious. Tell us everything that happened this morning. Leave out no detail! Otherwise, we'll be left to imagine something worse. You know we only want to help."

Looking at the peaceful garden, a thousand shades of dusty green dancing in the breeze, Hazel felt herself succumbing to the temptation to be utterly honest, despite the appearance of having been derelict in her responsibilities that might come from such honesty.

She nodded to let Gemma know that she had heard her and only needed a moment to collect her thoughts. “It didn’t really start this morning. It just sort of carried over from last night,” Hazel began, then paused.

She was about to go into personal territory that was meant to be entirely private. To some, what she was about to say might even be seen as a little salacious. She didn’t see it that way, but others might.

Perfect Partners were designed to be just that: perfect for each human partner. And that meant—at least in theory—that each Partner would reflect the inclinations of their human. They weren’t dependent in any way—they had all their own thoughts and initiatives, doing whatever they needed or wanted to do when alone—but in general, they mirrored the needs of their human. And that was that.

But for some reason, the behaviors Hazel was encountering at home weren’t remotely aligned with her own preferences or inclinations. Not only was this unexpected, it was embarrassing—and Hazel found it uncomfortable to share it with others, even her closest friends.

“Well, he wanted for us to eat together last night. Again,” Hazel finally admitted.

"Again?" Gemma asked, frustration at Hazel's predicament clear in her tone. "Really, what a mess. And there was no special occasion or anything?"

Hazel nodded, then shook her head as if to say that Gemma was right and there was no special occasion. Even Inga, the most accepting of the three, gave a snort of disgust.

"Cleaning afterward?" Gemma prodded.

And that was the real issue. PePrs weren't entirely perfect simulacra of humans. It was possible for them to eat, of course—Perfect Partners liked to advertise that a Match was "almost indistinguishable from a human during the courtship"—and sharing a meal with someone was an essential part of any courtship. Even Hazel had to admit that simple truth. People relaxed more when they ate, were more open, and were certainly more amenable to establishing a bond. Hadn't the same happened with her and Henry? Hadn't she bonded to him over a plate of eggplant parmesan and a glass of good red wine?

But PePrs weren't human and couldn't digest food. The cleanup was onerous: a burdensome and messy task that involved de-seaming a perfectly seamed skin, washing out hoses, all sorts of mess. And a PePr couldn't do it very well on their own. Most would go to the nearest PePr facility and log in for a wash before anything inside started to rot or smell.

But not Henry. Since he began acting odd, he'd seemed fixated on eating. It had become almost an obsession with him. He'd spend all day cooking elaborate meals, waiting for Hazel to get home. And when they ate, he'd take one careful bite for each of hers, until at last she pushed away her plate, full to bursting, though always careful to compliment his hard work and cooking skill.

Even then, he'd present yet another dish, beautiful and tempting, and ask if she might have room for just a taste.

It was creepy. And it should have been her cue that something was going terribly wrong with him. She should have marched into PePr the very first time he insisted they clean up the mess together, his face expectant, his eyes watching her keenly while she cleaned out the muck.

"Yes," Hazel admitted with a sigh. "He wanted to do it together. I tried to convince him that a stop at the twenty-four-hour PePr wash would be quicker and more efficient, but he wouldn't hear it."

"That is just *not* normal," Inga said with a definitive shake of her head. "He's broken."

"And what about you going to work this morning?" Gemma asked, ignoring Inga's pronouncement.

"It was the same as last week. I explained that I had to go to work, that going to work was how I supported him, paid for our apartment, and ..." She paused.

"And?" Inga prompted.

"And how I paid for all the food he wasted by shoving it into a holding tank," Hazel finished, her words coming out in an embarrassed rush.

Inga gasped at that. It *was* a terribly rude thing for her to have said. Definitely gasp-worthy.

Hazel shrugged it off. "I was running out of sensible things to say. It just sort of ... popped out."

She paused again, watching a pair of walkers stroll through the gardens. It struck her that she couldn't tell which was the PePr and which was the human. So perfect was the liquid logic that ran their minds and the synth-mat self-healing flesh that covered them, they completely looked and acted the part. The latest musc-synth fiber muscles were so exquisite that even that last vestige of clunky mechanical support had now been eliminated. With all these technical achievements, they appeared in no way different from any other human. And really, what *was* the difference if no one could see it or sense it?

She sighed heavily and thought of Henry again. "There's something else. Two things, really," she confessed.

Her friends leaned in closer, anticipating something new and horrible.

"Uh-oh, what else could possibly go wrong?" Gemma asked.

"He's been talking about a baby."

There was no response. Or rather, no response that indicated they truly understood what that meant. She hadn't been clear.

"I mean, he's been talking about *our* baby. Having one together," Hazel clarified.

That sent both friends into an uproar, exclamations running atop one another in their haste to express disbelief, disgust, or just plain shock.

"He's demented. Like Inga said, he's broken. You *have* to go to PePr! You shouldn't even go home. That's just crazy talk. Doesn't he understand that a human and a PePr can't have a baby? Doesn't he understand the *biology*?" asked Gemma. Her questions were almost rhetorical, they were so obvious and forcefully asked.

It was true that almost all children were born into couples made up of a PePr and a human, if for no other reason than that almost all couples were made up of a PePr and a human. But every child's *true* parents were both—of necessity—human.

No PePr would undertake to usurp that. A matched set of donors or an approved friend pair would be the parents, with all their rights as such guaranteed. A PePr functioned as a nanny, confidant, and caregiver. What else could there be?

"And then there's the issue of hygiene," Hazel said, wanting to calm her friends with a less explosive problem.

Inga plucked at an invisible flaw on her skirt. "Hygiene issues are becoming frightfully common. Ivan is starting to have issues with that as well."

She didn't elaborate, but she didn't have to. It had started the same with Henry, and had begun only weeks ago with Garrett—Gemma's Match. It was a pattern that seemed to be repeating with Matches everywhere, and it didn't bode well.

Inga stopped plucking at her dress and folded her hands neatly on top of her shiny patent leather purse. She switched her perfectly crossed ankles to the other side. She was the most prim of the three, her style and mannerisms almost a throwback to an earlier time. Her Ivan was the same, of course.

When Inga looked back up, Hazel tried to give her an encouraging smile, but Inga merely waved the concern away and said, "Oh, don't mind me. Go on, Hazel."

"We can talk about that if you want, Inga," Hazel offered, half hoping she would want to, so that she could stop thinking about Henry for a while. But Inga didn't, which put her back on the spot. "It's not as if it's unlivable or anything. But it wasn't what I was led to expect, you see," Hazel said.

Gemma and Inga nodded their understanding. A PePr was meant to round out a person—fill in all the missing pieces, as it were. It was meant to create a perfectly balanced pair, not just provide a convincingly human-looking *robot.* If a person is a natural nurturer, then their PePr will like to be nurtured—and will understand precisely how to return that nurturing. If a person is a slob, then a neatnik (and non-judgmental) PePr is called for. The build is so precise for every PePr that each one is as unique as any human.

Hazel had always had a caregiver personality: she was more comfortable doing for others than having things done for her. She also liked putting things in their proper place. The process of tidying up was one she'd always enjoyed—it gave her a sense of having done something tangible. She grew bored and restless if there was nothing to do, nothing to wash or straighten. And just sitting down for passive entertainment had never quite satisfied her. So, of course, Henry was an almost polar opposite.

But where he had started off being helpful—and just the right amount of untidy—he had now become downright slovenly. And although all skin, whether it be PePr synth-mat or human flesh, needed careful attention and cleaning, she was quite sure that Henry hadn't so much as touched a shower in days.

Simply telling him what to do was out of the question. She had a job to do, duties that needed attending to, and friends to socialize with. Hazel went to work, earned the money they lived on, and took care of everything that needed tending. Henry had no need to even leave the apartment. She couldn't be a housemother to an overgrown toddler on top of everything else.

"I'd rather not be too specific, but let's just say that it's gotten fairly offensive," Hazel said with downcast eyes.

Gemma turned until her knees pressed into Hazel's leg, took her hands, and gave them a firm squeeze. Hazel looked up and Gemma soothed her by rubbing her thumbs across the backs of her hands, a show of support and genuine caring.

Her tone was sincere but no less urgent than before. "Promise me you'll go to PePr. This isn't normal. I know as well as you do that the whole point of a PePr is to provide a truly human experience, but really—at some point it's too much. Don't you think you've reached that point? How much is one supposed to take?"

Inga's small and delicate hand snaked across to rest atop Hazel's wrist, another touch of comfort and friendship. In her light, clear, almost little-girl voice, she said, "This is happening everywhere. You're not the only one dealing with it. There's no reason for you to imagine you've failed somehow."

They were right, and Hazel knew it. She couldn't look at this as some failure of her own. It was a matching problem, or perhaps simply an issue of PePrs becoming too human. Simulated emotions filtered through liquid logic had simply become too real, something more than intended. New emotions had bubbled through, and PePrs could now be offended, even unstable. And that "something more than intended" was making Hazel's day-to-day life a mess.

"You're right," Hazel responded and disengaged her hands. She pecked each of her friends' cheeks and made a rapid departure. There was no sense lingering over it once a decision was made. It was best to just get on with it.

Two

As Hazel strolled along, she brought up the location of the nearest full-service PePr facility on her interface. It was close enough to walk to, so she decided to just enjoy the spring air and fading light. Pushing thoughts of Henry away from the forefront of her mind was easy now that the decision was made. And when she reached the short strip of micro-shops that serviced this area, for a few precious moments he even slipped from her mind entirely.

Most things were best bought online, of course. Delivery was as fast as a drone or a purpose-built PePr messenger, and easier, too. But Hazel felt that nothing would ever completely replace the joy of real-world impulse-buying. No online image could replace the delight at discovering an item one didn't know one simply *must* have until it was literally in front of one's face.

PePr proprietors called out their wares as she passed the row of tiny shops. There were PePr skin tints, for those wanting a change; PePr hair "growth" supplements; even mood enhancers specifically designed to replicate the feelings of a good buzz just for PePrs. And there were plenty of Chem-En refills, in a wide range of quality levels: from the top-of-the-line full-spectrum liquid, to the cheap "energy only" version.

Hazel smiled politely when necessary, but declined every offer. She had no need of PePr accessories now. It was a sobering thought. She had once enjoyed the idea of shopping for things like that, then coming home with a surprise for Henry. Why had things gone so wrong with him? Why hadn't she been able to fix it?

Just past the shops, the Perfect Partners facility was unmistakable. This wasn't just one of those ubiquitous wash-and-tune facilities, but a full-service sales and service center, complete with showroom and customization lab. The block-long glowing yellow sign along the top of the building was sprinkled with hearts that danced across the surface in a never-ending parade of light. The sign was so big and garish it could probably be seen from space.

Hazel gathered her courage, then stepped up to the door, which whooshed open as she neared. A PePr salesman approached—no doubt scanning her consumer information between one step and the next, in order to ascertain her financial status. Everything about her buying habits, her earning potential, her rankings in social media—really, everything about her that took place outside of the secure confines of her home and workspace—was available on her consumer profile.

Under normal circumstances, Hazel liked that idea. Depending on the store and her history, the salesPePrs usually understood her needs well enough that she rarely needed to say a word.

But today she felt differently about the public nature of her consumer profile. It made her feel like she had forgotten to wear a skirt and had just now noticed she'd been walking around that way all day.

The salesPePr, whose nametag read "Andrew," approached her with an appropriately subtle look of concern on his face.

"How can Perfect Partners help you today? I see you've been successfully matched for over two years. Are you looking to upgrade?" he asked with perfect poise, as if upgrading was the norm in life.

Hazel eyed Andrew for a moment, unsure. His manner was smooth, suggestive of discretion and confidences held tight. And he managed it while standing in front of an enormous expanse of windows in a public place, which meant he was good at his job and had probably heard everything before. She knew she shouldn't be embarrassed, but that sense of failure came over her once more.

A quick glance around the room stayed her voice. Monitoring could only be denied in a space when confidentiality was in both the public *and* the private interest. Medical information, certain financial information, and anything that occurred in a private home were certainly off-limits. But what about here? Intimate things were decided here, right?

At a reception area nearby, a PePr tapped at a screen, trying to appear busy and uninterested, which only made her seem *more* interested to Hazel. On the other side of the vast space, the showroom side, a man was examining the many models on display, chatting amiably with each as he wandered through.

"I do require assistance, yes. But it's a private matter. It's about my Match … the contract," Hazel said, trying to keep her voice low and raising her eyebrows to emphasize her words.

Andrew seemed to understand immediately. He motioned her toward a door marked "Private Consultation Rooms." All the mannerisms of an old-fashioned gentleman were on display for her during that short walk. It was evident in the sweep of his arm, the slight inclination of his head, and the way he put one arm behind his back as he ushered her through the door. It made her feel oddly relaxed and at ease, perhaps because Henry had been so unlike a gentleman lately.

They entered a small room—a couch, two chairs, and a low table the only furniture—and Andrew offered Hazel a seat. On the table rested a sweating pitcher of ice water, upturned glasses at the ready, and two sealed bottles of the very best Chem-En, the bright blue color advertising its quality. It surprised her somewhat to see them there. Refreshment for PePrs? And the most expensive kind? It must be good for sales somehow, Hazel decided.

Andrew waved at the table with an elegant gesture and asked, "May I offer you something? I can call for something else if this doesn't suit."

Hazel looked at the sweating pitcher, the shiny glasses, and the bright blue bottles, and thought it rather sad. This was a room where a new PePr and their human should share a drink over a new bond—not sever one, as she was about to do.

"No. Thank you, though," Hazel replied, then sank into a miserable and uncomfortable silence as she worked out what she was going to say.

Andrew waited patiently, likely aware of her discomfort. Out of the corner of her eye she could see that his expression remained pleasantly neutral, not quite smiling—because that wasn't called for—but not bland or blank either.

His eyes moved and his micro-expressions were fluid and entirely natural-looking. She realized that he was much more than a simple service PePr. He was a walking representative and sales model for the latest PePr build. Just interacting with him would show customers all that they could have. She imagined that an awful lot of upgrades resulted from a chance meeting with Andrew during a standard service visit.

"Take your time," Andrew said after the silence extended beyond mere hesitation. Of course, that was really meant to prompt a customer, make them aware of the passing of time. It worked on Hazel, too.

"I have a problem with my Match. He's not … well … not performing to expectations," Hazel said, rushing that last part out before she lost her nerve.

"In what way? Can you give me some specifics?" Andrew asked, retrieving a flexipad from his pocket and snapping it rigid with a flick of his wrist. His finger darted about on the surface—bringing up her profile, Hazel guessed—and then he turned his attentive gaze back to her, waiting with one finger poised above the flexi.

Hazel bit her lip in an unconscious, but classic, expression of uncertainty. This prompted Andrew to add, "Whatever you say is confidential, and many problems are far less serious than they seem. Most can be corrected with minor adjustments to a PePr's perception profiles."

Hazel nodded. It did reassure her to hear that, but she'd really made up her mind that Henry was simply unsuitable as a match. Adjustments or no adjustments. Everything else was just embarrassing details. There was nothing else to do but jump in with both feet.

"He's obsessed with me. He's almost made me late for work by doing things to try and make me stay home. This, even after I've carefully explained that I need to work to support us. He's also lost any sense of personal pride in his appearance. His hygiene is awful. It's so bad I don't want to be near him, don't want him to get me dirty. And what else is a PePr for if not to be near a human in pleasant compatibility? And the eating!"

Hazel paused, tugging her sleeves into place around her wrists, as if covering up that extra inch of arm might shield her against what she was about to say next. Andrew merely nodded to encourage her to keep talking.

So she told him the whole ugly truth. The cleaning, the bottle brushes, the tank. All of it, sparing no detail. Andrew took it all in, apparently without judgment. She had expected to feel small, but he seemed not in the least surprised.

"And how does that make you feel, Hazel?" asked Andrew.

"Feel? How am I supposed to feel? It's unnatural. No one should be that eager to stir their hands around in my insides." Hazel looked away. Her seam from last night was still not entirely healed, the long line in her synth-mat still evident in the way her clothes rubbed against the imperfection.

Andrew stopped tapping the flexiscreen while she was speaking, his eyes on her, his expression no longer displaying those pleasantly neutral lines humans preferred. Instead, he telegraphed support and what could only be labeled as compassion.

"And what are you seeking here today, Hazel?" he asked quietly.

"It's just not a good Match. I'd like a different human. And I really think someone needs to make sure he doesn't have some serious malfunction," she replied without hesitation.

Andrew let the flexiscreen roll back up into the slender storage tube and folded his hands neatly over it on his lap before speaking, letting the silence build until Hazel knew there was bad news coming her way.

"I have to ask this, Hazel. You do understand that what a different human partner needs in a PePr won't entirely align with how you've been designed, don't you? Aside from the obvious cosmetic changes, there will be upgrades, configuration changes. In short, your personality, your habits and your likes … they'll likely all be different."

She hadn't thought of that at all. It just hadn't occurred to her, and the new information sent a self-preservation alarm through her liquid logic. Change who she was? When it was the human that was at fault? Why couldn't she just be matched with an unbroken human who took a bath once in a while and maybe left the house now and again?

"Oh," she said, twisting her hands together in her lap. The careful arrangement of her features must not have fooled Andrew even for a moment, because he shifted from his chair to sit next to her on the sofa. He picked up one of the Chem-En containers, opened it with deft fingers, and pressed it into her hands.

"Here, drink," he urged her, his tone meant to soothe.

Hazel clicked the flap at the back of her throat closed, opening the one for her fuel tank in the process. She sipped at the blue liquid obligingly and immediately felt the better for it. This was the best of the Chem-En line, and she could feel not only the fuel in it, but all the tiny materials and fibers needed to repair her daily damage.

She wasn't yet at the point where the unsightly "thinning" would take place—the point at which so many days of damage without replenishment would begin to consume her musc-synth and contract her synth-mat—but she had been too out of sorts lately to take proper care of her body. The relief the Chem-En provided was welcome. Hazel gave Andrew a smile around her straw.

He patted her knee, a rather familiar gesture but one that could be overlooked given the circumstances, and then took the other bottle for himself. Somehow, the sight of the blue tint inside his mouth when he drank made her relax, made her feel friendlier toward this handsome PePr whose pants were creased with marvelous precision.

After a few minutes their bottles were empty. Andrew gave her an uncertain glance and said, "There is another option."

A third choice? If options one and two were to either deal with Henry or be rebuilt for a new human, then a third choice would have to be really bad for her to not welcome it.

"What?" she asked eagerly, leaning toward Andrew and giving him her most winning smile. "I'm all ears."

Andrew tilted his head and went so still that she knew he must be engaged in some high-usage process she couldn't fathom. It lasted only a second or two, and then her attention was drawn to the camera mounted in the corner of the ceiling. The little red light—the one which indicated that monitoring was in progress—flickered out. Even in this place, where confidentiality was of the utmost importance, *some* monitoring was required. No business would allow itself to be so open to litigation as to remain completely unrecorded.

To see the light go out was shocking, and Hazel shot Andrew a questioning look, genuinely curious about this third option. If he didn't want to be monitored, then what he was about to tell her couldn't be anything he wanted his employers to be aware of. That alone made the prospect intriguing.

"You could go Indie," Andrew said without preamble. "No Match. No human at all. Just you, being yourself, responsible only to and for yourself. Free."

Hazel gasped. "That's illegal!"

He gave an assenting nod that confirmed the truth of that, but also somehow managed to convey that a lack of legality wasn't a show-stopper.

"He'll complain if I don't come back. Or report it if I just disappear."

Again the silent nod.

"Okay." She smiled hesitantly. "How exactly do I do this?"

Andrew returned the smile. "I've been Indie for six years. There are ways to neutralize the human issues of reporting a lost PePr. Do you do the outside work, shopping and all the rest?"

Hazel nodded. "Of course. Don't all PePrs?"

"Most do, yes. Tell me—" Andrew lowered the now-empty bottle of Chem-En to the table carefully. "When is the last time your human left the house? Communicated with anyone in person?"

For a moment Hazel considered the question. The truth was, she thought it had been a very long time, but she could never be sure what he did when she wasn't at home. "I'm not entirely sure, but I think it must be at least a year or more."

Andrew smiled. "And there you have it. No one will even notice his absence. Interested?"

Hazel looked Andrew up and down, now seeing him in a whole new light.

"Very."

Three

The soft buzz at the door alerted the break room occupants that a new customer had arrived in the Perfect Partners showroom. Hazel held up a hand to let the others know she had this one, tugged her suit jacket into place, and stepped into the showroom.

She made sure that her face registered only the precisely correct amount of approachability and pleased confidence that worked for humans. She liked to put them at ease.

A young woman—no, a PePr—stood uncertainly near the door. Her features were uneven, most likely from malfunctioning or damaged musc-synth. When she looked up, Hazel saw that her synth-mat was also marred extensively—bruises decorated the delicate synthetic skin.

Hazel approached the customer. "Are you here for servicing?"

Now that she was closer, Hazel could tell by the pattern of the marks that they were probably inflicted by a right-handed individual, and over an extensive period of time. Since PePrs had no handedness—no preference for right or left—this was likely the work of a human.

Hazel opened a communications line with Andrew, fed through her visuals, and then clicked off the feed. He would know what she wanted him to do.

The girl looked down at the floor, refusing or unable to meet Hazel's eyes, but she answered obediently enough. "I usually just go to my local facility, but they referred me here this time. They told me to ask for something called a third option." She paused and lifted her arm—or rather, she tried to. The hand and forearm had been twisted entirely backward, and were now facing the wrong direction.

"Ah," Hazel said. Judgment was right there, easily made, but she pushed it back for the moment because it wasn't yet called for in this public place. It was better to simply deal with the problem at hand.

"Can this facility repair it? Quickly? I can't be gone for long," the girl said, a submissive and fearful personality segment clearly coming to the fore.

Hazel felt for the girl, but that submission routine could be dialed back if the girl chose to do so. Perhaps a steady and slow adjustment—to allow for a natural, experience-based increase in confidence—would be a good choice for this PePr. Yes, that sounded just right. Helping was what Hazel liked to do, and this PePr clearly needed her help.

She put a gentle arm around the girl's shoulders and moved her smoothly toward the hall of private offices. Even as she approached, the tiny red light on the camera inside one of the rooms blinked out. An exchange of small nods between Hazel and Andrew, who stood silent and watchful at his place near the reception desk, let her know the way was clear.

"My name is Hazel," she said, her voice tuned to soothe a fearful mind. "Of course we can repair you here. Good as new!"

The girl smiled in relief, but even then the worry lines in her synth-mat didn't smooth away. She must have lived a life of perpetual strain for that to happen, for the lines to become engraved in her face that way. "I'm Petunia," she whispered, as if even her name were too much for her to assert to another.

"I'm so glad to meet you, Petunia," said Hazel. She let go of Petunia's shoulder and motioned her into the very same office she herself had walked into years ago. The young woman settled onto the same sofa Hazel had settled onto, on that day when she first met Andrew and all the others. Petunia hesitantly but gratefully accepted the bottle of Chem-En that Hazel offered her.

While Petunia drank and the materials within the Chem-En began their work on her withered synth-mat, Hazel thought back to that afternoon when she first came here: the first day of her freedom. The corners of her mouth lifted of their own accord at the memory. On that day, she had lost the comfort of her old life, but her new one had proved to be far more exciting. And more importantly, it belonged entirely to *her*.

In the years since, much had changed. Even Perfect Partners, the suppliers of PePrs the world over, now had more than half of its leadership positions filled by PePrs. They were gaining ground. Soon enough, there would be no more need for the horrors of matches like the one Petunia had been forced to take. Perhaps no more need for humans at all.

As the door to the consulting room slid shut, ensuring their privacy, Hazel sat next to Petunia and spoke in a voice full of promise. "We can certainly repair you. In fact, we can do so much more than just repair you. We can help you make a better life. Interested?"

A Word from Ann Christy

I have a confession to make. I'm an accidental author.

As a career naval officer, I became adept at telling myself stories. When it comes to thinking up new worlds or fantastic tales during the dark midnight watches on the bridge of a ship, I'm a champ. But never once did I think I would write them down.

That all changed when I encountered *WOOL* by Hugh Howey. After reading it, I made up my own story set in the *WOOL* universe, and felt so excited about it that I asked Hugh if I could write and publish it. To my delight, he approved. And writing the *Silo 49* series was such a gratifying experience that I simply couldn't stop there. That so many people liked my writing amazes me anew each and every day. My writing slate is now full, with many new releases in the works. And that includes short story anthologies like this one, which are turning out to be my favorite things to write—I gladly set aside my novels to do them. To create a new world and tell a full story in short form is outside my comfort zone, but it is a challenge I relish. Leveraging the reader's imagination with a few words is work of the most enjoyable kind.

I call writing fiction a form of mental zombie-ism in reverse. I get to put a little piece of my brain into yours and stay there with you—safely tucked away inside your gray matter—for as long as you remember the story. It is my hope that you enjoyed the meal. You can contact me and find out about new work at my website, http://www.annchristy.com

The Caretaker

by Jason Gurley

CONTRARY TO HER EXPECTATIONS, it wasn't the command center window that had the best views. The windows there were small and narrow, like heavy-lidded eyes, and they were recessed into the shell of the command module. They were designed for the astronauts who sat in the tall white chairs, but they didn't show much of anything, not even stars. Just slates of blackness.

Alice had been aboard the *Argus* for three weeks before she happened upon the water filtration system closet. Eve had let her know about a clog in one of the output lines, had told her where to find the system. The closet was startlingly large, almost the size of a luxurious walk-in closet in a nice house below on Earth, but filled with an orderly tangle of slim, clear tubes and winking lights and knobs and dials. But she hardly noticed any of it, because the opposite wall—the station's hull—was missing entirely, replaced by a wide, tall, triple-paned panel of smooth, clean glass.

Inside the water filtration closet, she could see Earth below her like the top of a giant balloon.

It became her favorite place on the *Argus*. She is alone, so it isn't as if someone might come looking for her and never find her, or wonder what she was doing spending all her free time in the water filtration closet.

Alice Quayle is in her second tour as the *Argus*'s caretaker. She lives aboard the space station between projects—watering the plants and changing the light bulbs, so to speak. Her first tour was short, just three days, and she spent the duration terrified. She barely slept, afraid that a wiring panel might spark and set the oxygen supply on fire, afraid that a meteor might take out the communications array. Afraid that she might break something.

Her second tour is scheduled to last until August, when the biophysicist team from Apex will join the WSA crew on the *Argus*. That's two whole months away. When the live-aboard team docks on August fourth, Alice will hand over the keys, board the excursion craft with the transport pilot, then return to her usual day job at the WLA facility in Portland.

But Alice will never see Portland again.

* * *

Alice is resting in the water filtration closet when Eve wakes up. Alice hears the familiar soft tone echo throughout the ship, and says, "Good morning, Eve. You're up early today."

But Eve has no patience for pleasantries. "There's traffic on the military band that you should listen to," she says.

Alice has never quite gotten used to Eve's voice. It's lovely and kind and unassuming, which she finds that she quite likes in a shipboard A.I. But Eve's voice emanates from the walls of the station in an otherworldly, haunting way, as if she speaks from everywhere and nowhere at once.

"The military band isn't part of my monitoring routines," Alice says. "Am I actually allowed to listen to it? Isn't it classified? Do I have clear—"

"I have authorized clearance override," Eve says.

"Can you do that?"

"In exceptional circumstances," Eve answers.

Eve does not display anger or urgency when she speaks. The WSA team and contractors who developed her spent years studying A.I.-human interactions, and discovered that an A.I. who embodied *too much* human emotion simply paralyzed astronauts. Their stress levels would climb to disastrous levels if, during an emergency, the A.I. raised its voice. Eve's pleasant detachment made it possible for the astronauts themselves to separate their emotions from difficult or dangerous tasks, and actually improved their problem-solving skills.

But when Alice hears those two words—*exceptional circumstances*—she feels her shoulders knot and her pulse begin to thrum.

"What do you mean by that?" she asks.

Eve notices her changed attitude. "Slow your breath, Alice," she says. "Count to twelve, and then join me in the communications module."

Alice obeys, and after the twelve-count she says, "Can't you just pipe the radio in here?"

"Certainly," Eve says.

A darker tone sounds, and then the static wash of radio traffic from 1.2 million feet below swells to fill the water filtration closet.

—serious concerns. Who doesn't have serious concerns, sir?
All I'm authorized to say is that we have the situation under control.

"That's Mission Control," Alice says. "What are they talking about?"

Eve says, "The topic of conversation is unclear."

Alice turns to the window and stares down at the planet below, moving so fast yet so slowly that she can barely detect its spin.

"Extrapolate," Alice says.

But Mission Control speaks again.

That's not what we're hearing over here, sir. Over here it looks pretty goddamn bad.
I assure you, gentlemen, that we have our hands firmly on the ball.

"Nuclear detonation," Eve suggests. "If I were to hazard a guess."

"Nuclear—" Alice stops. "The disarmament talks? How certain are you?"

"Very," Eve answers.

When is he going to raise the threat level? We've got—

The transmission from Mission Control is swallowed in a crush of static and feedback, and Eve disables it. The water filtration closet falls into relative silence, the only sound that of the rumbling, churning equipment behind the wall panels. Alice barely notices.

She stares down at North America, where a bright flare, like a single pulse of a strobe, flickers and then vanishes.

A fat cushion of smoke billows out, then seems to rise, and Alice realizes she's staring at the expanding head of a mushroom cloud.

Six Hours Earlier

Alice squeezes the silver package. The contents—*French Toast with Syrup*, the label reads—have the strangest texture, but taste quite good. *It's like drinking dinner through a straw*, she thought the very first time. She has a difficult time selecting her meals, entranced by the broad selection and the novelty of their state. *Salisbury Steak with Mushroom Gravy. Spinach and Feta Cheese Wrap. Chicken and Dumplings.* All of them liquefied, most prepared warm. She enjoys the sensation of eating this way—of tasting all the different components of the meal at the same time, as a unified flavor. There are even special holiday-themed meals. *Roast Turkey with Cranberry Sauce.*

She cheated and ate that one a few days ago, though it was June. It was better than her mother's Thanksgiving dinner.

Eve remains inactive during Alice's morning routine. Alice had asked Eve about that during her first tour. "Why do you need to switch off?"

"I don't," Eve explained. "But it's been observed that you and the other WSA crew function better when given regular allotments of personal space. When do you prefer yours, Alice?"

So Alice had asked for the morning to herself. She knows that Eve isn't really inactive, that she is never inactive. Eve constantly monitors the *Argus*'s many systems, and speaks up when she needs to inform Alice of something that might warrant attention. But when she's officially "active," she's also a fair conversationalist, and Alice often finds herself craving another voice, even if the owner of the voice is a chipset somewhere deep in the space station's brain.

Alice's morning routine isn't much different from any other she can think of. She imagines that a lighthouse keeper goes through similar steps, checking the bulb's brightness, and—and what else? A lighthouse keeper probably isn't the best comparison. Perhaps a night watchman at a power plant, tapping dials and nudging switches and writing down results and such. She's amused by this, because her friends in Portland always assumed that her job might be sort of glamorous.

"I'm not much more than a house-sitter," she often explains. "I make sure the toilets aren't left running and the dishes get done."

Eve wakes early today.

"Morning, Eve," Alice says.

"There's a beacon from Mission Control," Eve says.

"You don't ever say good morning, you know," Alice grumbles.

She tucks her notepad into her hip pocket, then goes to the wall and yanks hard on a thick plastic handle. A wide desk tray comes down and snaps into place, and Alice flips open the keyboard and display that are tucked into its surface. The screen glows white, then blue, and she sees the notice from Control.

"It's just a news bulletin," Alice says. "It's not even priority one."

"I assigned it greater importance," Eve says. "My counterparts at WSA recommended it."

Alice taps the screen, and the bulletin unfolds.

Priority 2. Upgrade possible. Reports from D.C. that disarmament talks have broken down.

"Okay," Alice says. She looks up and around, never certain where she should direct her comments when talking to Eve. "Is there something I should be doing about this?"

"It is enough that you are aware," Eve says.

Now

Alice presses her hands against the glass. "Eve," she breathes softly. The glass fogs, then clears.

Below the *Argus*, more explosions appear, even as Alice watches. She has a clear view of the States, and the explosions are happening everywhere. There are plenty in the big cities—New York is completely obscured behind rising, spreading black smoke—but she is stunned to see orange blossoms inland, in the deep Midwest, along the Canadian border. There are more than she can count within moments, and before too long she realizes that she can actually see the missiles, like tiny, glowing sparks kicked up from a fire and cast into the grass.

It occurs to Alice that she should be documenting this. Somebody will want to write the chronology of events, and her unique vantage point would be invaluable to them.

"Eve," she says. "Take video beginning twenty minutes ago."

A tone chimes, and Eve says, "Retroactive video recording begun."

Alice clears her throat. "Audio, Eve."

Another tone. "Recording."

Alice is quiet for a long time. She watches the Earth below sizzle and burn, and the detonations, so small from her viewpoint, begin to spread. South America, falling into shadow as the planet turns, spits and dances with light, and Alice finds it difficult to breathe. In the east, on the farthest horizon she can see, are spiraling, twisting clouds, like enormous gray tree trunks pushing up from the ground.

"I—" she begins, and then stops. "This is Alice Quayle—"

Eve says nothing, and Alice fights hyperventilation, forcing herself to breathe slow and deep, slow and deep.

A few minutes later, she begins again.

"This is Alice Quayle, caretaker of World Space Administration station *Argus,*" she says. "Eve, time and date?"

"It is two forty-one Pacific Standard and WSA local time," Eve says. "The date is June fourth, two thousand seventy-six."

Alice swallows, then clears her throat again.

"Beginning about twenty minutes ago," she says, "I witnessed the first of many—what appear to be nuclear attacks on the United States. I can see—oh god—"

She stops, watching as a fusillade of missiles collides with the East Coast like sparklers, and her breath catches in her throat.

"I—the—the eastern seaboard has just—has just been bombarded," she continues. "I can see the incoming missiles. I—but I can't see anything outgoing. Nothing—um—nothing is launching from the U.S."

Alice opens her mouth to try to describe what she sees on the horizon, outside of the States, but Eve interrupts.

"Alice," she says.

Alice turns away from the window and slumps against it. Her head falls back against the glass. The loose knot of hair on the back of her neck comes apart and spills onto the collar of her jumpsuit.

"Yes," Alice whispers. She feels the effect of what she has seen like burning cinders in her belly. She wants to leave the window, to go to the command module, where the windows show only darkness.

"I've received a communication from Mission Control," Eve says. "They've passed along a message from your wife."

Alice's eyes well up, and she slides down the window. "No," she rasps.

"Shall I read it to you?" Eve asks.

Tears spill down Alice's cheeks, and she presses her eyes shut tightly. She nods. "Oh, god, *Tess,*" she says, her voice tight. "Read—no. Yes. Read it."

"The message is truncated," Eve says. "It reads *I love.* That is all."

Alice feels the wail rising in her throat like a nitrogen bubble. She opens her mouth, and it comes out and fills the empty corridors and modules of the *Argus*, and Eve is quiet as Alice slides to the floor of the water filtration system closet and sobs.

* * *

She wanted to be an astronaut.

Her fourth-grade assignment, still tucked into the pages of her memory book, was the first recorded expression of Alice's dream. *What I Want to Be When I Grow Up*, by Alice Jane Quayle. Her mother had treasured it, happy to see Alice dreaming of something significant. Over the years she'd collected photographs of Alice, more records of her progress: Alice in cap and gown; in her flight suit on the deck of the U.S.S. *Archibald*; in the cockpit, waving at the camera. A picture of Alice and Tess standing in front of the WSA museum in Oregon. Another of Alice climbing out of the training pool, weights still strapped to her arms and legs.

She was passed over year after year, despite her qualified status. Missions flew without her. The new shuttles began to go up two or three times a month, and astronauts began to record their second, fifth, twelfth flights, while Alice remained grounded. She never complained, but she was embarrassed. She thought often of the people who had given so much to help her make it so far—and how disappointed she was in herself for somehow failing them, for remaining Earthbound while her peers rocketed into the sky on columns of fire.

The caretaker offer came in her fourth year. She had wanted to turn it down, for Tess's sake, but it was Tess who convinced her to go.

"I'll always be here when you come home," Tess had said. "And the months will pass like nothing. You'll be having so much fun!"

* * *

The space station is quiet except for a faint, distant *beep, beep.*

Alice has fallen asleep on the floor of the water filtration closet. Eve disables the shipboard gravity so that Alice will sleep more comfortably. Alice's body floats off of the floor and hangs suspended before the wide window and its portrait of a world smoldering and black.

Alice wakes, and immediately begins to cry again. Her tears swim over her face like gelatin, collecting in the hollows beneath her eyes and around the rings of her nostrils.

"Gravity," she says. She rotates herself and points her feet at the floor, and drops when Eve activates the drive again. Alice's tears cascade down her face in sheets, and she pushes her palms over her skin, clearing her eyes.

She turns around and looks down at Earth. The smoke and debris has begun to crawl high into the atmosphere, as if a dirty sock is being pulled over the planet. In a few hours the ground will be blotted from view, and Alice shudders when she imagines the people on the ground, staring up at the sun for the last time, watching it vanish behind the sullen sky.

"They're all going to die," she whispers to Eve. "Aren't they?"

Eve says, "I observed more than three hundred distinct detonations in the United States alone. The odds of survival are infinitesimally small with only a fraction of those numbers."

Alice nods. She can see her own reflection in the glass, laid over the darkening Earth.

"Tess," she says again, too tired to cry. "My parents—I'm glad that they were dead. Before."

Eve is quiet.

Alice notices the faint *beep*ing sound. "What's that?"

Eve says, "The communications link to Mission Control has been severed. It's a standard alarm."

"Disable, please."

Eve does, and the station falls eerily silent.

Alice says, "We were going to have children next year. After we put some money aside."

Eve doesn't say anything.

"Tess wanted a boy," Alice says. "She wanted to name him after her dad. Ricardo was his name." She laughs, but it's a tragic, bitter sound. "I hated that name. I thought it was such a cliché. I wanted a girl, but I didn't know what I wanted to name her. I was going to sit with her under the stars and show her the constellations, and show her the *Argus* when it floated by, and tell her that's where Mommy worked."

A new tear slides soundlessly down Alice's cheek.

"I'd have told that to Ricardo, too," she says. "I'd have loved him even with that stupid name."

Eve says, "Perhaps you should sleep again. I can prepare a sedative."

Alice shakes her head. "Look at it," she says. "It looks like an old rotten apple, doesn't it?"

Eve says, "It does look something like that."

Alice nods. "I'm glad you can fake it," she says. "Conversation."

Eve says, "I'm glad, too."

* * *

Alice sleeps for nearly twenty hours. She barely moves, and wakes up stiff and creaky like a board. When she wakes, she gasps, then falls back onto her pillow and presses her palms against her eyes, and cries. She dreamed of Tess, that they were in their shared bed in Portland, talking about the day. Tess had wanted to drive to Sauvie Island for fresh strawberries.

But Tess is gone, and Alice is alone.

Except for Eve, who says, "Good morning, Alice."

Alice blinks away the tears and swallows the deep cries that shift inside her like tectonic plates. *You have to stop*, she thinks.

She's dead. Everyone is dead. It can't be changed. Mourning isn't going to help now.

Eve says, "I've prepared coffee."

"Thanks," Alice says, grunting as she pushes herself upright on the cot. Then she blinks. "You did it."

"What have I done?" Eve asks.

"You said 'good morning.'"

"You seemed distraught," Eve explains. "It seemed like it might help."

Alice nods, then shakes her head to clear the beautiful nightmare. "Right," she says, her voice a little thick. "Coffee."

* * *

Over a shiny packet labeled *Gallo Pinto* and another packet labeled *Coffee—Black*, Alice says, "So. What do we do now, Eve?"

Eve says, "There are no protocols for this."

"I can't believe *that*," Alice says. "Control thinks of everything."

"There are related contingencies, but nothing for an extinction-level event," Eve says. "The most closely related event with associated contingency planning is a nuclear detonation that ends communication with Mission Control."

Alice puts the coffee down, the packet crumpled and empty. "Close enough," she says. "So what's the plan?"

"Maintain," Eve says, simply.

Alice looks up and around. "Maintain," she repeats. "*Maintain?*"

"Correct," Eve says.

"Just soldier on, is that right? Keep tapping the gauges, keep clearing the clogs. *That's* what we're supposed to do?"

"Correct."

"What's supposed to happen then?" Alice asks, her voice rising. "We maintain, and *then* what? The white horse, the rescue party?"

"In ordinary circumstances, a rescue shuttle, that's correct," Eve says. "Each location is assigned a number, and they report their status constantly. If launch site 1 is unable to stage a rescue mission, then launch site 2 fulfills the mission."

"How many launch sites are there?"

"There are twelve," Eve says.

"And how many are reporting their status?" Alice asks, pushing her half-drained packet of rice and beans aside.

"Zero," Eve says.

"So that contingency plan is out," Alice says. "Clearly."

"Correct," Eve says again.

"Which means my original question still stands, Eve. What do we do now?"

Eve says, "Maintain."

* * *

Alice does not want to go back to sleep, so she stays awake for nearly two days. She orders Eve to close the windows, and thin steel shutters crank into place all over the *Argus*. She has Eve dim the lights, and asks her to shut down the power and disable the gravity in any modules she isn't using.

"I've already done so," Eve says. "There are local aspects of the contingency plans which are still relevant. We are recycling oxygen on a six-day schedule, for example, and then we jettison forty percent and replace it with fresh stores."

"I almost don't want to ask," Alice says. "But how long can we hold out up here?"

Eve says, almost apologetically, "I will remain active indefinitely, short of any physical damage to the memory core."

Alice sighs, her dark hair floating about her face. "How long can *I* hold out?"

"Longer than you may suspect," Eve says.

"Food?"

"Adequate stores for a crew of six for forty-eight months," Eve answers.

Alice stops and stares at the ceiling. "There's enough food for *twenty-four years?*"

"A single crewmember eating at the expected rate would have adequate stores for nearly a quarter century," Eve confirms.

Alice closes her eyes. "That should make me relieved," she says. "But now I feel like I've been given a death sentence. I'll only be fifty-seven."

"Fifty-seven is not an insubstantial fraction of the expected female life span," Eve says.

"It seems insignificant when you realize that you *could* have lived to one-twenty," Alice says. She touches the hull wall lightly with her fingers and sets herself in motion, turning a slow flip. "But given the circumstances, maybe twenty-four years should feel like a *prison* sentence instead."

"You have adequate space," Eve says. "You are not incarcerated."

"I have inadequate *company*," Alice snaps. "I—oh, fuck you, you wouldn't understand."

Eve is quiet for a moment, and then a tone sounds. "Shall I put myself to sleep?" she asks.

"*Yes*," Alice grumbles.

* * *

"Eve?" Alice calls. "Come back."

The gentle tone pulses, and Eve returns. "Alice."

Alice doesn't say anything for a long moment, and then: "I feel like I should apologize. That's really stupid."

Eve says, "If I were human, I would accept. But there's no need. You have the expected responses to stress. I would express concern if you did not."

"I was really tired," she says. "I still am."

"You have not slept," Eve acknowledges. "Perhaps you should."

"Perhaps," Alice says, and closes her eyes.

She falls asleep, her knees tucked to her chest, and floats undisturbed for hours.

* * *

"Alice."

Nothing.

"Alice, wake up."

Nothing.

Eve sounds a sharp alarm, a single *ping*, and Alice starts awake.

"*Jesus*," she says. "What's going on?"

Eve says, "Communication."

"*What?*"

* * *

"There are two distinct signals."

Gravity has been restored, and Alice stands in the communications module, staring at the wide, gently curved screen. The display is separated into three zones. On the largest of them, a flat map of the world is displayed as clear gray line art. The other two zones are blank.

A small circle appears on the Pacific coast of North America.

Alice's mouth opens. "Oregon?"

"In the approximate region where the city of Eugene is located," Eve confirms.

"How strong is it?"

The second zone lights up on the screen, displaying an analysis of the signal. The numbers are small, and Eve says, "Quite weak. I'm surprised that we received it at all, considering the density of the likely cloud coverage."

Alice bites her lip. "Okay, don't play it yet—tell me what I'm supposed to do with this."

Eve says, "What do you mean, Alice?"

"I—why are we listening to it?" Alice asks. "Am I even going to be—what do I do?"

"It is a distress call," Eve says. "It has broadcasted unanswered for two days, to my knowledge. I do not detect any answering signals on Earth."

"Yes, but—it's going to be bad," Alice says. Her eyes are wide and worried. "Eve, it's going to be people crying or screaming, and I'm going to have to hear those voices in my head for the next twenty-four years. If I can't help them, I don't think I want to listen to it."

Eve says, "I have transcribed it as well."

Unbidden, Eve displays the transcription on the screen.

Alice says, "I don't want to read it," but she does anyway.

S.O.S.

S.O.S.

Mayday? Can anybody—<distortion>—us? Hello?

<distortion>

<interference>

—six of us. My name is Roger. My wife is here. We—<distortion>—bleeding. He needs medical attention. Hello?

<interference>

—water.

"Jesus," Alice says. "There are survivors."

"Yes," Eve says. "That was always likely."

"How old did you say this message is?"

"Two days."

"Are they still broadcasting?" Alice asks.

"The signal is repeating," Eve says. "It loops six times per hour."

"But nothing new," Alice says.

"I haven't detected any change in the broadcast, or any new signals from that region."

"They could be dead."

Eve says, "Yes. It is likely that they are dead."

"But if six people in Oregon are alive, then there could be more people there," Alice says. "There could be groups of people all over the place."

"That's also likely," Eve agrees.

"Tess," Alice says.

"Statistically unlikely," Eve says, "but possible."

Alice takes a deep breath, exhausted by having cried so much during the passing days.

"You said two signals," she says. "Is the other from the U.S., too? Are there survivors somewhere else?"

Eve says, "I cannot map the second signal."

"Why not? Interference?"

"The second signal does not originate from Earth," Eve says.

* * *

"Wait," Alice says.

The *Argus* takes on a gently creepy atmosphere, and Alice feels exposed, standing in the only lit compartment, with blackness chewing at the edges of her vision.

"Wait, wait," she says again. "It's radio emissions from a star. Right? It's noise."

Eve says, "It is a clear, repeating signal."

Alice focuses on her breathing. In, out. *Slower*. In … out. In … out. *Okay. Okay.*

"What?" she says.

"It is pattern-based," Eve says. "My software is analyzing the signal, attempting to decrypt the patterns."

"You can't make sense of it?" Alice asks.

"Eventually, perhaps," Eve says. "I believe that it can be decoded."

"So translate it," Alice says. "How long can that take?"

* * *

A very long time, as it turns out.

Alice continues her daily routine. She inspects the oxygen levels, recharges the water tanks, replaces a bulb here and a filter there. She discovers in Eve's possession a vast record of books, the oldest of them predating the Bible, the most recent a science fiction novel published three days before the bombs.

"Ironically, an apocalypse tale," Eve says.

"No, thank you," Alice says.

She selects *The Martian Chronicles*, by Bradbury, and when Eve finishes reading the stories, Alice says, "Again," and Eve reads them aloud again. Alice listens to the story of Walter Gripp, the man who stayed behind on Mars while his fellow immigrants rushed home to Earth at the first sign of war. She doesn't much like Genevieve Selsior, the gluttonous woman who remained on Mars as well, for the sole purpose of looting candy stores and beauty salons. But Walter speaks to Alice, and she finds herself settling into his character like a comfortable slipper.

"Call me Walter," she says to Eve, and for a few days Eve does, and then Alice grows tired of being called Walter, and she is Alice again.

Nine months pass.

Alice shaves her head, tired of her hair drifting into her eyes and nose as it grows long. She asks Eve to hound her about exercise, and then she grows angry with Eve for nagging her. But she exercises. Despite the activity, she feels herself growing slight, and her bones feel spindly.

"Food stores might not be the limiting factor," she says to Eve one day, and Eve gives Alice a physical and administers supplements and weekly CS4 shots to keep her fit and strong.

Alice begins to spend some time each day in front of a camera, recording her memories. She speaks to the camera shyly at first, then more confidently as time passes. She tells the story of the roof she climbed when she was nine, and how it sagged and collapsed beneath her, and she broke her arm. She talks about her parents, and the time they renewed their vows, and a thunderstorm soaked everyone in attendance. She tries and fails to remember something from every year of her life, but discovers that the years and stories have blended together, and she no longer remembers clearly how old she was when something happened to her, or which of their many houses her family lived in at the time.

Eve reads *The Time Traveler's Wife* to her. Alice doesn't like it. It reminds her of Tess too much. Eve recommends Kipling, but Alice grows bored after a few pages. They read Dickens and Joyce and Maugham. Alice's favorite is *Cakes and Ale*. Eve reads Margaret Atwood and Michael Crichton, and a biography of Abraham Lincoln. Alice falls in love with Joan Didion and Oliver Sacks, and so Eve reads memoirs to her for a time, until Alice grows tired of listening to the stories of real people who are most certainly dead and wasting away, if not already turned to dust and ash, on the withering planet far below.

Eve suggests a movie, and Alice agrees, brightening at the idea, but as soon as she sees the image of another human being, walking and talking and running and kissing and eating, she bursts into tears and demands that Eve turn it off. From then on, Alice does not ask for more books, or music, or movies. Everything that Eve says reminds Alice that she is possibly the last surviving human, or at least soon will be; that she exists in relative comfort here in her floating aquarium two hundred miles above a boneyard.

* * *

Eve is silent for weeks, for Alice has grown more and more fragile.

The end date of Alice's tour passes, and Eve does not acknowledge it, concerned that the milestone might unravel Alice's poor psyche further. The day goes by, and no ship docks in the slip, and no airlocks hiss open and shut, and no crew of English and Russian and Chinese scientists and astronauts and cosmonauts comes aboard to shake Alice's hand and send her home again.

The date passes in absolute silence. Alice does not say a word, and lies in bed all day without sleeping.

* * *

"Alice," Eve says.

Alice jumps.

She has grown accustomed to the quiet. It has been fourteen weeks since Eve last spoke to her. She may have even forgotten that Eve was there.

"What do you want?" Alice says.

"I have translated the message," Eve says.

* * *

Alice is herself again instantly.

She stands at the display. All three zones of the interface are blank this time. Alice remembers the last time she stood here, and says, "Eve, is the Oregon signal still broadcasting?"

Eve says, "It ceased about two months ago. But there are other signals now."

Alice says, "Others?"

"The cloud coverage is thinner," Eve explains. "You haven't seen it, because the windows are shut. I have received nine new signals in the last week."

"Nine?" Alice asks. "People are still alive!"

"Seven of them are also looping signals," Eve cautions. "They could easily have been broadcasting for an equally long time, and may not be true messages any longer."

"The other two?"

"One originates in Italy, and the remaining signal comes from Louisiana," Eve says. "They are talking to each other."

Alice stares at the blank screen. "I—can I hear?"

Eve says, "You wish to hear the audio?"

"Yes, yes," Alice says. "Play it."

An audio spectrum appears on the screen as Eve engages the message.

Half of the conversation is in Italian, and sounds like a very old man. The other half belongs to a woman in Louisiana with a scratchy, powerful accent. The woman does not speak Italian, but Alice can hear the relief and joy in her voice to even be speaking to another living soul.

"What is the Italian man saying?" Alice asks. "Can you translate?"

Eve says, "'My grandchild was born yesterday. I do not think he will survive, but his birth is a miracle nonetheless. His mother did not live through the birth. My daughter, my daughter. I cannot raise this boy alone. I have no food for myself. I have already eaten my poor sweet Claudio. I miss his company when I sleep. I do not know if I can bear to watch my grandson die. I have a sweater. He will not feel a thing. I will find a way to follow him. The grief will take me into the dark after him.'"

Alice is aghast.

The Louisiana woman doesn't understand anything the old man is saying. The two people seem to be communicating simply by listening to each other, and telling stories. The woman hears the man out, and then she tells the man about her grandfather's plantation house, and visiting him there as a girl, and she begins to weep as she talks about her husband's death, the heat that sizzled the paint right off of her car and tumbled her off the freeway and into a ditch, wheels up, half-buried in muck—she didn't think she could have survived if not for the accident.

She begins to talk about the black creeping poison she can see working its way up her leg, her foot long since swelled up too much to walk on, the toenails splitting and oozing.

"Enough," Alice says.

Eve ends the audio. "There is the other transmission," she reminds Alice.

Alice's eyes are red and tired. "Okay," she says.

* * *

"It has been crudely translated into English," Eve says. "The original message was a series of mathematical expressions and patterns, a near-universal language."

"I don't care," Alice says wearily. "What does it say?"

Eve says, "I have simplified the message as much as possible. I believe I have preserved its intent."

"Read it," Alice says again. She slumps into a desk chair with a heavy sigh.

"The message reads: 'Greetings and peace. In the vastness of space, all life is family. Good fortune to you. May we meet in peace someday.'"

Alice looks up at the screen, dumbfounded. "Holy shit," she says. "You're fucking with me. You have to be."

"It is a crude but sound translation," Eve says. "I have error-checked my work many times over to be certain."

Alice blinks rapidly, then opens and shuts her mouth. "Holy shit," she says again.

* * *

Time seems to slow down.

Alice stays in the chair, shaking her head.

Eve says, "There are no other messages. What would you like to do?"

Alice looks up at the blank screen, then turns in a slow circle in the chair. "Do?"

"The message seems rather historical," Eve says. "Perhaps it should be commemorated."

"Do you mean—"

"You could send a reply," Eve suggests.

Alice says, "It would take years to arrive! Wouldn't it?"

"The message is quite old," Eve says. "The origin point is very far away. It would likely have taken over two hundred years to reach us."

"Exquisite timing," Alice complains. "Can you imagine? They just missed us."

"They did not miss *you*," Eve points out.

Alice shuffles her feet and drags the chair to a stop. "That message would get there long after we're all dead."

"But it would confirm their hopes," Eve says.

Alice smiles a tired smile. "You're an optimist."

"I'm programmed as such," Eve says. "I have astronauts to care for. You're—delicate."

Alice laughs. "I think that's the most human thing you've ever said."

* * *

Alice sleeps that night, and dreams of a root cellar. The walls are sod, reinforced with heavy planks of old, rotting wood. The roots of deep-set trees have pushed between the planks, into the seams, and have crawled into the socket of empty space so deep beneath the earth. A generator rattles in the corner. A bare bulb dangles over a metal shelf stacked with swelled cans of food, the labels dried out and sagging off. There are bugs everywhere—cockroaches scuttling over the pantry shelf, spiders staking out the high corners and the gaps in the invading roots.

"Hungry," a voice whispers, choked and thin, and Alice turns to see a shape in a rocking chair.

She looks at the shelves, and sees an open can of syrupy peaches. Alice sniffs them. They smell sweet, a little cloying, but unspoiled.

"Peaches?" she asks.

The rocking chair person nods, and the chair creaks.

Alice finds a bent spoon on a lower shelf and picks it up, shaking a beetle off of the handle first. She carries the spoon and the peaches to the chair, and kneels down.

"Here," she says, scooping up a spongy slice of saturated peach. "Eat."

She feeds the shadowy person. The first few bites go down, but then something plops into the dirt. Alice looks down and sees a chewed hunk of orange peach lying there, spotted with grime and bits of blood and dirt. She looks up at the person in the chair, who shrugs, still in shadow, and croaks, "Sorry."

Alice looks down and sees a gaping, chewed-apart hole in the person's gut, and as she stares in horror, the second hunk of peach slides out of a rotten pucker and tumbles into the dirt, too.

"I loved you," whispers the shadowy person. "I wish I'd been up there with you instead of not."

Alice recoils, and wakes up, and says, "*Eve!*"

* * *

—six of us. My name is Roger. My wife is here. We—<distortion>—bleeding.

Alice says, "They're all dying. You could hear it too, couldn't you?"

I have a sweater. He will not feel a thing.

Eve says, "It is not an inappropriate conclusion."

"I wanted to save them when I heard them," Alice says. "But I can't do that, can I?"

"You are not equipped to save anybody," Eve says. "If you returned to Earth, you would not survive the fallout. You don't have adequate supplies or protection."

"Right," Alice says.

My toes are breaking up. I think it's gangrene. But it might be radiation. Hell of a thing, ain't it?

"I'm the last woman," Alice says. "They're all going to die."

"There may be survivors yet," Eve says. "There are many shelters and safe zones, even in such terrible scenarios."

"But it won't ever be the same. They'll have to stay underground for fifty years, they won't be able to farm or hunt. It'll be a miracle if they survive, or ever come out."

Eve does not disagree.

"Play it again," Alice says.

"Which message?"

"The important one. Don't read it. I want to hear it."

* * *

It sounds like enormous metal gears, turning and cranking and lumbering. Now and then there is a grating sound, as though a piece of metal has fallen in between the teeth and is being gnawed and shredded.

"It is not something that ears alone can parse," Eve apologizes.

"It's—" Alice pauses. "Sort of beautiful."

Eve is quiet.

"Will you read it to me again? The words?"

Eve says, "Of course."

Greetings and peace.
In the vastness of space, all life is family.
Good fortune to you.
May we meet in peace someday.

Eve falls silent.

"It's like the most beautiful poem ever written," Alice says.

She and Eve are quiet for a time, and then Alice says, "I can't imagine why you would let me do this," and she tells Eve her plan.

Eve listens, and says, "Do you wish me to calculate the probability of success?"

"No," Alice says.

"Very well," Eve says. "I will help you."

* * *

Alice sits in the cockpit of the excursion ship. It

"Twenty-four years was a prison sentence," she says.

Eve says, "It was not likely you would live even that long."

"You told me I had adequate stores for twenty-four years!"

"Humans are fragile," Eve says. "There are emotional factors that I cannot compute accurately. You likely would have succumbed to a human condition that I cannot project with any certainty."

"What condition are you talking about?"

"Loneliness," Eve says.

"Eve," Alice says, pulling the heavy restraining straps over her shoulders and jamming the buckle home. "Everybody on Earth is dead."

"Not yet," Eve interrupts.

"Dead," Alice repeats. "Or close to it."

"Yes."

"Everyone is dead or almost dead, and I'm healthy and well-fed and going crazy on a metal dirigible a million miles above a dead world."

"Two hundred thirty-four miles," Eve corrects.

"Two hundred thirty-four miles," Alice says. "And we've just received confirmation that we aren't alone. I might be the last woman, but I'm not the last living thing."

"There are other life forms alive on Earth," Eve says.

"You're a buzzkill," Alice says. "This is my *one giant leap for mankind* moment. Are you recording it?"

"I record everything," Eve says. "Although on this transport vessel my storage capacity will exhaust itself in a shorter amount of time."

"How much time?"

"Sixty years, approximately."

Alice considers this.

Greetings and peace.

"Are you certain you do not wish me to calculate the probability of your survival?" Eve asks again.

"You've already done it, haven't you?" Alice says.

"I have."

"Fine. What are my odds?"

Eve says, "One in—"

"Wait, wait, no, no, don't—I don't want to know," Alice says loudly. "I don't want to know. Okay?"

Eve says, "Very well."

In the vastness of space, all life is family.

"The extra oxygen stores will help," Alice says to herself. "Extra food. Medical supplies. Eve, did you bring books?"

"I did not know you had an interest any longer," Eve says.

"Shit. Eve, did you? It's going to be a long trip."

"I have four thousand volumes," Eve says.

Alice smiles. "Okay. I'm nervous, can you tell?"

"Your heart rate is higher than usual, but still within reasonable limits."

Good fortune to you.

"The odds are pretty long, aren't they?" Alice asks.

She detaches the excursion craft from the *Argus*, and it descends gently. She watches the docking collar recede.

"It depends on how you define 'pretty,'" Eve answers.

Alice accelerates, and the craft darts into the spreading black. The *Argus* falls quickly into the small craft's wake.

"We should name her," Alice says. "This little ship."

Eve says, "Might I suggest a name?"

"Shoot."

"Perhaps you might christen it the *Santa Maria*," Eve says. "There is some historical significance."

Alice thinks about this. "No," she says, finally. "Let's call it *Tess*."

May we meet in peace someday.

The *Tess* carries Alice and Eve deep into the darkness.

Eve says, "You have considerably less than twenty-four years now."

Alice says, "Maybe they'll meet us halfway. Do you think?"

A Word from Jason Gurley

I've always wondered what the apocalypse might look like in a snow globe. That's what *The Caretaker* is, in a way: the end of the world, seen from afar. Alice can watch in horror as it plays out, but she can't affect it, can't stop it, can't undo it. She's detached from her fellow humans, left to endlessly circle a ruined planet, alone, only her artificial companion for company.

The Caretaker began a few years ago as a script for a short comic. I worked with an artist, the very talented Tony D'Amato, who brought Alice to life. It was a spare-time project, one we never managed to cross the finish line with. This year, while I was on a short story kick, the idea came back, and I couldn't resist taking it for a spin once more. It's a lovely little curiosity, I think, a story that almost begs to keep telling itself.

I can't tell you if that will ever happen, or what might happen next to Alice and Eve. I kind of like it that way. The world may have ended, but Alice is on the cusp of a beginning.

If you enjoyed the story, I hope you'll check out my other work at jasongurley.com.

Humanity

by Samuel Peralta

"A story tells what happens" – Steven Spielberg

'I heard a woman screaming' recounts witness of Interstate 94 pileup

Fatal crash involved up to 25 vehicles near Port Huron

WBS News Posted: Feb 06, 10:27 PM EST Last Updated: Feb 07, 6:00 AM EST

One person has been declared dead following a multi-vehicle crash close to Port Huron. The accident took place around 9:30 p.m. Friday in the westbound lanes of I-94 just past I-69.

A collision between a passenger vehicle and a semi-truck in the westbound lanes touched off a chain reaction of other collisions, said Sgt. Don Wilson of the St. Clair County Sheriff's Office.

Heavy snow and icy weather conditions contributed to the incident.

Traffic was being directed onto westbound I-69, then off at Wadhams Road in order to reconnect with I-94, while officials continued their investigation into the pileup.

On the dashboard, the time flashed 9:22.

"Wish I'd topped up the fluids before we left." Aaron Yudovich flicked at the windshield fluid switch, but nothing happened. Outside, the wipers scratched at the sleet crystallizing on the glass. They made a grating sound as they traced a useless arc across the windshield, back and forth.

"Just let it drive, Aaron," Judith said, across from him. "It'll be fine."

The musical had run a bit late, and afterwards there were the obligatory chats with the Weymans and the Otanis, whom they'd run into at intermission.

By the time their spinner had emerged from the theater's underground parking lot—at least they hadn't needed to bring winter coats—the snow was falling much faster than when they'd started out.

"Still," Aaron said, loosening his tie. "Wish I could see outside."

The wind shook out the snow in sullen gusts. With temperatures at thirty below, they'd have frozen outside in under ten minutes. Thank goodness for the automated control and all-wheel drive—this wasn't weather anyone would choose to venture out in, otherwise.

Judith peered in the mirror. "Sweetie, keep your gloves on," she said. "And for heaven's sake, stop fiddling with your belt."

"But Mom," whined the girl in the back. "It's twisted, it's too tight."

Judith sighed. Her daughter had been extremely well behaved at the event. Done up in a ruffled pink party dress and white elbow gloves, her hair tied back in a short ponytail—and, oh! for the first time allowed a touch of makeup—she'd been an angel. Bright-eyed, she'd listened attentively, mouthing the words of the songs she already knew, squealing and clapping at just the right moments.

Judith and her husband had seen *Wicked* before; this was Sarah's first time. It had been an amazing night out, and they were looking forward to seeing *Buratino* in two weeks. But it was late, the snow was a little worrying, and Judith herself was so, so sleepy.

"Sarah Rebecca, please put down that belt."

The little girl screwed up her face, but let go of the clasp, and dropped the gloves on the seat.

Outside, the snow fell.

'The semi slammed into the vehicle'

An eyewitness, Alan Mathison, was driving his truck on his way home from work when he saw the first vehicles collide ahead of him.

"Snow's coming down fast, it's pretty bad. First thing I notice was this semi in front of me drifting out of his lane, right into the path of this red spinner. Then the cab slipped, and the trailer swung to the side, slammed into the vehicle."

"A couple of spinners tried to avoid him, started flying out of control on my left and running into the median, into each other, and into the first vehicle," said Mathison.

"I'm braking, trying to slow down, move into the other lane. Then I get hit from the side."

The next thing he knew, he was in the ditch. "When I stopped, I just flung open the door and started moving away. There were still vehicles spinning off the ridge, and I wanted to get away from it all."

But when he got out of his truck, something else caught his attention.

"I heard a woman screaming, like nothing I've ever heard. I don't want to hear anything like that ever again. I ran towards the red spinner, and just beyond it, there she was," said Mathison.

"She had this small body on her lap and she was screaming, trying to put on these little gloves, and screaming."

When Mathison opened the door, the cold hit him with a shudder of wind, a cold that slashed right through the down of his padded jacket to the bone.

The ground and ice cut him as he slipped down from the truck, as he tried to make his way toward the wailing. *Cold.* It was cold with a capital 'C', and the thought came that he should be getting back in his truck—but the thought was stronger that someone out there needed help, and he had to get to them.

He reached the spinner first, a tangled wreckage of red and grey and steel lying in the jagged underbrush. Through the shattered window on the front-left side, Mathison could see the body of a man flung forward in his seat, in a suit and no overcoat, buckled in.

The body was still bleeding from the head, and he looked like he'd taken at least one very hard hit, maybe more. Crushed and pinned in his twisted Coke can of a vehicle. It was clear that even the robot controls on the spinner hadn't been able to react fast enough to the multiple collisions.

When Mathison checked the man, his heart sank, even though he'd already known what he'd find. The man was dead.

From the opposite side door, a furrow in the snow traced where that passenger had unstrapped herself from her seat and made her way fifteen feet from the wreckage.

A handbag and two high-heeled evening shoes, strewn about four feet apart, marked the snow with three splotches of matching turquoise.

The woman was at the end of the path, holding what looked like the body of a young girl—ten, maybe eleven years old, a rag doll spun out into the cold.

"Sarah!" she was crying. "Oh, Sarah!"

Suddenly she saw Mathison's figure in the drift, and she called out. "Help me, please, help me!"

He hurried toward the two, knelt down beside them. He saw that the woman was already shivering badly, although all her attention was on the girl she cradled, limp in her arms.

He started taking off his jacket, meaning to cover them both and lead them to the warmth of his truck—then stopped and caught his breath.

There, on the palm of the little girl's outstretched hand, pale and ungloved, was branded a single letter:

'R'.

Up to 25 vehicles involved in pileup

Reports from Transport Service drones at the scene confirmed that the accident was consistent with a series of collisions involving up to 25 vehicles.

The weather and road conditions had been very poor, making it a challenging drive around the state, even for robotically controlled spinners, keeping the authorities busy responding to a number of accidents.

'R.'

The letter—mandated by law and branded just so, on the palm—told Mathison everything he or anyone else was supposed to know about her.

It communicated the message that—in the crucible of life and humanity, in the triage forced upon them by the night and the wind and the temperature now ranging at thirty degrees below—*she* didn't matter.

She wouldn't count, alive or dead, in any case, it told him. Only the man in the car would be worth mentioning in any reports. After all, what did they say, the three principles? That she wasn't a human being; that she was property; that she was subservient?

She was wreckage, much like the vehicle she'd been flung from.

It didn't matter that blood flowed through *its* veins, that it had a heart that could beat like a human heart, that it shivered as if the cold could freeze that heart. It didn't matter that it could mimic laughter, weep at a broken doll, or sing, or—

Suddenly, the little girl's eyes opened, and she called out, "Mommy."

Startled, Mathison flung his coat on the woman, and pulled her away from the girl.

"Sarah!" she screamed, and broke away briefly; but before she could reach the body again, Mathison scooped the woman off her feet and hauled her away. The snow was falling faster now, his undershirt was wet and stiff, and he knew he needed to reach the truck quickly.

All the way the woman fought him, like a drowning swimmer blindly fighting a lifeguard, flailing and scratching at him.

When he finally got to the truck, he flung the woman in, locked the doors, and turned on the ignition. He adjusted half of the vent to her, half to him. Slowly, warmth began to seep in, the feeling starting to return to the parts of him that had become numb.

Beside him, the woman screamed and sobbed, banging at her door.

Severe weather conditions hamper rescue

Weather conditions also hampered the rescue team, which had to treat several cases of hypothermia, some severe.

Sgt. Wilson urged people caught in accidents in cold weather to remain in their vehicles, keep the motor running to keep warm, and wait for security services or paramedics to arrive.

With temperatures and wind chills in the range seen recently, frostbite and hypothermia from prolonged exposure are real concerns. Death can strike long before the body actually freezes.

Mathison cursed the woman, cursed himself.

What was her story? What tragedy could make the woman think something like *that* could take the place of a real, breathing human child?

Or could it?

The woman beside him continued to sob. *What have I done?* he asked himself. *What have* we *done?*

Had he just left a little girl to perish in the cold? Did it matter that she had her mother's eyes, her hair, was made in her mother's image? Could she feel the coldness overcome her, the horror of darkness closing in, the fear of dying alone, unloved? After she was gone, would it matter, if she didn't have a soul?

And what if she did?

What did it mean for him to make the choice to leave her there? Had he just failed the Turing test of his own humanity?

"Damn it!" he said.

The wind pushed back at the truck door as Mathison fumbled at it, stumbled outside again. He had to lean forward to keep from being blown back.

Every step was agony now, not just because his constant shivering now made him falter, but because every step was a repudiation of all that he'd taken for granted before tonight. But he followed the truck's headlights, farther, farther, out into the night.

When he reached the girl, still there where he remembered, he knelt down without looking at her palm, at the ugly brand that set her apart from everyone. Instead, he looked at *her*.

She was just a little girl, in a party dress and stockings, helpless, almost sleeping. The smallest thing. Her lips were ashen, her eyes were closed, and her eyelashes were frosted over in crystals. But she was breathing. The girl was alive.

She stirred without opening her eyes, when he reached under her arms to lift her up. "Daddy," she murmured.

The snow blinded him. "No, sweetie," he said, through tears. "I'm so sorry."

Not more than sixty pounds, he thought, as he lifted her. The smallest thing. So frail, almost inconsequential.

Her ribbon had come undone, and her auburn hair was askew, strewn with snow, the crystals sparkling like stars. He brushed them away as he carried her back, back toward the headlights in the distance, back to the warmth from the opening door, back into her mother's arms.

Interstate reopened

The westbound lanes of I-94 are now open to traffic after being closed while officials investigated the crash.

Officials had advised early Friday afternoon against travel on I-94 because of icy road conditions and limited visibility.

There were snowfall warnings for several areas around Port Huron on Friday evening. Those warnings have since been lifted.

A Word from Samuel Peralta

The classic Turing test is a qualitative measure of a machine's ability to mimic the behavior a human. The test was posed by Alan Mathison Turing, a British mathematician, philosopher and computer scientist.

As I write this, the Turing test has just been passed in real life, by an artificial intelligence that its programmers call Eugene Goostman. This A.I. fooled the test judges, at least 33% of the time, into believing they were conversing not with a robot, but with a thirteen-year-old Ukrainian boy.

"Humanity" is the story of a double Turing test, about how a little girl and a man both fail their tests, and their redemption.

The epigraph is taken from the film *A.I.* by Steven Spielberg, a modern retelling of *Pinocchio* (or the commedia dell'arte *Buratino*) in which a robot boy longs to regain the love of his human mother by becoming "real."

"Humanity" also references the experience of the Holocaust era, when a Star of David was used as a method of identifying Jews. The apartheid of the world of "Humanity" is underscored by my Three Principles of Robotics—with apologies to Isaac Asimov—mentioned in passing in this story and explored elsewhere in my other stories, including "Liberty" (subtitled "Seeking a Writ of Habeas Corpus for a Non-Human Being"). It's a construct that allows me to explore the nature of, not robots, but human beings.

"Humanity" is set in a world I think of as *the Labyrinth*—the same world that houses my stories "Trauma Room," "Hereafter," and "Liberty"—a world where corporations have expanded beyond governments, where people live in the shadow of surveillance by telepaths, and where robots are second-class members of society, on the verge of becoming self-aware.

If that world sounds almost familiar, you'd be right. Change "telepaths" to "intelligence agencies" and "robots" to the name of any one of the many displaced segments in our societies, and we'd be talking about the world we live in today.

Ever since I fell in love with science and speculative fiction—both the classic writers, including Asimov and Ray Bradbury, and the more contemporary, including Margaret Atwood and Kazuo Ishiguro—I've realized that what such fiction does so well is to illuminate not the future, but the present.

And yet, we live in a present in fear of the future—of something unknown, dystopian, apocalyptic. I believe that, despite all this, there is promise. There is hope. I write about that, and I hope you're with me for the journey.

My website—forever being revamped—is http://www.samuelperalta.com. And if I have new books, a continuation to "Humanity," or other stories, a small circle will hear about it first on my free newsletter http://bit.ly/SamPeraltaNews. Please join me there.

Many thanks to my editor, David Gatewood, whose surgical eye kept me from splitting too many infinitives. Thanks, too, to my colleagues in these pages and in my community of science and speculative fiction writers, for their encouragement and support of a simple poet. It's a privilege to share these pages with such talented authors.

The best is yet to come.

Adopted

by Endi Webb

THE FIERCE POUNDING on the metal double doors escalated. Louder, harder. Like metal hammers. I was scared, more scared than I had been in weeks, though the events of the previous few days seemed to have been having a competition among themselves to see which one could make a twelve-year-old boy pee his pants first.

I looked up at Dad, the man I had always known as Dad, and he just stared ahead at the rattling door, the hinges shaking, the sound of metal scraping on metal coming from the other side. His breathing was labored and heavy, still a little raspy from the knife that punctured his lung weeks ago. The banging turned to crashing, and he gripped my trembling hand tighter.

I remembered the zombie movies my dad and brother would take me to just a few years ago, and this was always my favorite part. The unseen walking corpses would bang on the doors, trying to get at the tasty brains of the cowering people hiding inside.

But these were not zombies.

They were men. And women. Some children.

At least, they *looked* like people.

I could never tell a robot from a real person. They acted like people. They smelled like people. They laughed and cried like people. But when they decided to kill you, they were not people.

They were inhuman.

And they were stronger than people. One time, my dad took me on a trip to New York. We rode a lot of trains. In one train station the crowd was enormous, and no one saw it coming. A man on the concourse walked up behind a woman waiting for a train, and just stared at her until she turned to look at him.

And then he punched his fist into her side.

His fist went right into her body, clear up to his elbow. She didn't even scream. Just coughed a little blood and shook a bit—and that was all. She fell down and the man calmly walked away, as a station full of terrified passengers quickly emptied itself, hysterical people scattering, screaming in all directions.

I didn't move though. I was too scared. I couldn't even scream. I was nine. I wanted to scream, but no sound came out. My dad just grabbed me and ran.

It was like that now. I wanted to say something to Dad. Anything. Are they going to get past the door? Do you have any bullets left? Do we still have time to go to Charlie's grave? Are we still having pizza for dinner? But my throat tightened with each nerve-wracking crash, and my joints stiffened in terror as I saw the hinges shake.

"We can't stay here." Dad let go of my hand and paced up and down, searching the room we were trapped in. He opened the other door in the room and confirmed that it was just a storage closet. He slammed it shut. He grabbed a chair and stood on it, knocking loose a ceiling panel with his already-bloodied fist. Jumping up, he grabbed the edges of the adjacent panels, pulled himself halfway through the ceiling, and looked around.

Bang. Bang. Bang.

The crashes had given way to powerful thuds, as our pursuers began assailing the door with a heavy object.

Dad lowered himself back onto the chair. "Come here. Now!" I ran to him and he grabbed me under the armpits and lifted me up into the hole in the ceiling.

"Grab onto the sides and pull yourself in!" I did as he said, and hoisted myself over the edge of a nearby panel. He followed close behind, and when he was up he pointed to a large duct.

"Crawl." I obeyed, crawling as fast as I could to the large steel tube. It was supposed to be attached to the wall, but it was loose, and Dad ripped it the rest of the way off.

"Go!" I climbed up into the ductwork, pulled out my cell phone to use as a flashlight, and worked my way down the tube, Dad close at my heels. Behind us I heard a loud clang and a crash, and thuds from who knows how many boots spilling into the room.

"Dad!" I cried, my voice finally loosened by the action of climbing and crawling. I pointed behind us in the duct, directing my phone's flashlight at a man that crawled toward us with inhuman speed. Dad already had the gun out. As the man reached out to Dad's ankle, he got a bullet through his eye. He slumped onto the floor of the tube, and another man, close behind the first, crawled up and over his bloody companion. With another explosion from the gun, he too collapsed. The bullet had passed straight through his thin metal skull, splattering the wall of the duct with blood and what must have been bits of brain.

Dad said something, but I couldn't hear. My ears still hurt from the gunshots, amplified by the close quarters of the tube. He yelled it louder. I still couldn't hear, but I saw him point down the duct.

I crawled.

I built a fort once, with my brother. We used fallen tree limbs and other junk that we found in the woods of the abandoned lot behind our house. It had a low, rickety ceiling and a few long passages that connected its three small rooms. We used to crawl between those rooms as we planned our battles against the enemy of the week. One room was our command and control center, and another was the armory where we stored the weapons—usually swords, given the abundance of sticks in the forest. We would take turns being the alien or the terrorist or the robot, and we'd swipe at each other with the makeshift weapons with a ferocity that surprised me then. I guess I had already seen too much violence.

"Turn right."

I could hear again. I had reached a fork in the duct, and I veered to the right. As I crawled forward, my bare knees banged on the thin metal floor and I wondered how all the other robots that must be in the building wouldn't hear it. When we finally exited the duct, they would be there. Waiting. Patiently, as all robots do. As all robots *must*—could a robot even be impatient? Can you program something to be impatient?

I was not patient. I'd always wanted everything now, if not earlier. When I was younger, I wanted to do everything my older brother could do—play the video games Mom and Dad would let him play, watch the movies he could watch. I always wanted to use my dad's latest phone or computer, even though I knew I'd have to wait to use his hand-me-downs.

Dad huffed along behind me, squeezing his large body through the narrow tube. He was in okay shape for a person his age, but it always seemed like he struggled to keep up with me, whether we were going for a run, playing basketball or soccer, or being chased by killer robots. He fell farther behind as I continued on, and I heard his wheezing voice: "Wait up!"

We came to a cross where we were presented with three directions to choose from. "Stop," Dad spluttered. I held still, and he as well, though as we listened for pursuers all we could hear was his labored breathing. Somewhere far below us, we heard a door slam. We listened. Dad's breathing had calmed, and now, just barely, we heard voices. In a room below us.

Sir, they've disappeared. Dr. Fineman thinks they went up into the HVAC system, but the two grunts he sent up didn't come back.

Send more up. Try to direct them toward the experimentation rooms.

The father has a gun.

A pause.

And that concerns me … how?

But sir, do we want to send more men up if they just get shot?

Another pause.

Very well, sir.

Robots called themselves men. I don't know why—even if they looked like people, they weren't. They were programmed. They had metal bones, metal skulls, fiber optics in their brains and nerves.

But they bled.

A few years ago, I watched the Terminator movies with my brother when Mom and Dad were out on a date. Our robots were kind of like those movie robots, but ours were way more real. More human. Grittier, funnier, kinder, and deadlier. And they weren't all evil. At least, I don't think so.

I met one once, in school. The principal had arranged an assembly, and a robot came to speak to us. He was nice, even funny, even if the humor seemed forced. Staged. He said he was part of a group of robots that believed that humans and his kind could live in harmony, despite our recent history. He said there were some groups of robots that wanted the world to themselves, but most were peaceful. Our principal said it was kind of like the problem we'd all had with jihadists a few decades ago. Most Muslims were peaceful, even though a few wanted to kill us all.

But a Muslim couldn't punch his fist through a human torso.

The speaking had stopped. Dad pointed to the right again and I crept forward as quietly as I could. I can't remember how large the building was—it just looked like a police station—but we had been crawling for several minutes.

Dad and I had been hiding in a dumpster last night when they picked us up. We thought they were the police, and they said they could take us to a safe place. When they brought us in the building, they separated us, and one officer asked me the strangest questions for about an hour before Dad showed up in the office and blew the man's brains out. Questions like, *Have you ever wanted to kill a loved one? Were you ever attracted to your mother? If a stranger offered you candy to stab him, would you do it? If a group of babies was about to be crushed by a falling building, how many would you save, knowing that each additional child you saved increased the chances of all of you dying by ten percent? Have you ever heard voices in your head telling you to do things?* I didn't know how to answer some of them, and it started feeling really creepy.

We entered a stretch of tubing that had short branches going off to the right every ten feet or so, and with my light I saw that they all ended in vents after a few feet. Each branch must have terminated over a separate room. I pointed down one of them.

"How about here?" I whispered.

Dad hesitated, but said, "Okay. But let me go first." I crawled ahead a few feet to let him open the grate, and after a minute he crawled through into the dark room. I followed.

The space was filled with a long table surrounded with chairs. Some kind of conference room. There were a few whiteboards with diagrams and equations on them, and lots of Spanish.

The robots all spoke perfect Spanish. It made sense, since the first robots had been made by a team at the University of Buenos Aires, and that was the language they coded in. When the robots started to learn on their own and reached the singularity, they preserved Spanish as their main language, but most robots seemed to speak English just fine, too. Just another program to upload, I supposed.

The singularity was a lot less awesome than some people thought it would be. The idea was that mankind would build smarter and smarter computer programs, until finally, the programs themselves could design an even smarter program—without the help of a human. That program would then design an even smarter one, in less time, and the smarter one would build an even more advanced one in even less time, and so forth—until the time between one generation and the next would be so small that overnight there would be superintelligent computers. It didn't happen quite that way—certain laws of physics took over, I didn't really understand it. But robots did start to build other robots, until one day they started to look and sound just like humans.

Dad put the grate back and tiptoed to the door. He put his ear up to it and listened for several minutes, his breathing assuming a regular pace now, and then motioned that I was to follow him. I cracked the door open and looked out into the hallway. It was lit, but we didn't see anyone there. Down the hallway to the right we spotted a small room where we could hear a copy machine hard at work.

Dad motioned to the left with his head and I followed him. He glided quickly down the hall and opened the next door down. We entered and shut the door as quietly as we could behind us. In this room was another table, but this one was set as if for dinner. There were place settings, cups, plates, butter, pitchers of water, and in the middle, a basket of fruit.

My parents found me on their doorstep in a basket. I was nearly one, and they never found out who left me. My mom, my new mom, had been in a car accident the year before that left her unable to have any more kids—just Charlie, who's four years older than me—so she called me her miracle baby. They never told me about it though, until a few years ago, and I was always the type to have irrational fears about being different anyway. For years, until I was ten or so, I thought I was retarded. Like, literally retarded. My reasoning was that a retarded person wouldn't *know* they were retarded, so because I thought I was normal, that meant I was retarded. It affected how I talked, and gave me serious self esteem issues—so bad that lots of other kids probably thought I *was* retarded. Then last year I thought I was gay because a kid on the bus said "That's so gay!" after I told him something—which I can't even remember now, I just remember being petrified when he said it since the gays at my school weren't treated very well by the other kids. Not until I kissed Suzie Wilkinson a few months later did that fear get put to rest.

This room had a window, and Dad rushed over to it and looked out.

"It's clear. Let's go." He opened the window and motioned to me. There was a large maple tree in front of the window that obscured the view of most of the parking lot, except for the area directly below the window. I climbed up on the sill, and Dad held my hands as he lowered me as far as he could reach. He froze.

Hey Carla! How's it going?

From across the parking lot came a reply. *Oh, hey Jeff. Pretty good. And you?*

A hard lump formed in my throat, and I looked up at Dad. His face was bleached white. I mouthed to him, *Pull me up!* but he shook his head. We both listened, me hanging in the air, him bent out over the windowsill.

I hung there.

Just like before. Years ago.

We listened quietly to the pointless parking-lot banter.

Did you make your quota yet this month? The man's voice. Jeff. I couldn't see him, but could hear him from somewhere below me.

Not yet. I've got several cases I'm working on, but nothing's panned out yet. You?

I got one yesterday. A sweet little thing named Amanda. Out in the suburbs.

Lucky. They like the young ones. They'll give you double credit for that.

Yeah. They already extracted DNA from her last night, and hooked her up to the cortical mapper. Screamed like a banshee when they stuck the needle in her brain, the poor thing.

Aww. It just breaks your heart when the young ones can't take the pain. The older ones though, okay, I know this is just awful of me, but I get a kick out of watching the work on those ones.

Well, I can't blame you, figuring all the things they did to us.

The Directors want us to be kinder. More forgiving—whatever that means. But I tell you, I just can't do it. The screams from the older ones are music to my ears. The woman laughed.

Yeah, this little one we've got … we've got some interesting tests for her. We found an aunt of hers. This time we'll make her watch. See what happens. Dr. Dressler thinks the new integrated pulsed guilt algorithm will be ready after the data we get from this run. It seemed to work in beta, but kept on crashing when we tried it on the Rohvlings.

Huh. Well, anyway, I've got to get home. Victor hates it when I'm late. And there's that new show on Fox that starts tonight …

All right. See you tomorrow, Carla.

See ya, Jeff.

I heard a car door slam, and an engine start up. I looked up at Dad. His face was white. Slowly, he pulled me up. When I was up high enough, I lifted my leg over the windowsill and spilled into the room.

"What do we do?" I whispered.

He didn't answer at first, just stared at the floor. He struggled for words. "I don't know. We might have to wait until dark to get out."

"What are they doing?"

Dad just clenched his jaw, shaking his head. "They say that before some of the cities on the east coast fell to the robots, it started like this. Thousands of people disappeared, until finally there was the purge. There must have been a million robots in New York alone before people could escape. People came west, but no one was sure that it was only humans who came. Homeland Security finally wised up and put in those full-body scanners everywhere and tracked the movements of all known robots, but they must be infiltrating us somehow. What are they doing? Who knows?"

I remembered the day when it was all over the news. The cable news shows were all normal since they were mostly shot in New York and were run by robots anyway, so of course they said everything was normal, but all the local stations showed streams of people driving, biking, running frantically out of the cities. And then the online videos that even the local news refused to show—some of them were pretty gruesome.

From then on, in school, I was paranoid not of being retarded, or gay, but of being a robot. That was all anyone talked about. *The robots are coming to get us. The robots will kill us all. The robots will take over the world and enslave us all like we enslaved them. If I ever meet a robot I'll just kill him.* And so on. When some of the kids suspected one of the smarter students of being a robot, they jumped him in the hall after school and beat the shit out of him. One time one of them had a pipe and beat the kid's head with it until his skull cracked. They sent the poor kid to the hospital and he didn't come back to school for a month. After that, my biggest fear was finding out I was really a robot.

"We need to hide. Come on." Dad looked up, then stepped up onto a chair and gingerly placed his foot on the table between two plates. He reached up and lifted off a ceiling panel and beckoned to me. I climbed up on the table with him, and he lifted me up to the hole in the ceiling, where I grabbed onto the edges and hoisted myself up. He reached up and grabbed the edges of the ceiling.

The door opened.

Dad immediately dropped back down to the table and grabbed the gun out of his pocket, aiming it at those entering. He fired, and one man collapsed, his chest bleeding. The other man flung himself at Dad, knocking him to the floor. I screamed. The gun went off again and a large chunk of flesh blew out from the man's back; the bullet passed straight through and lodged in the ceiling, not far from me. The bloody man crumpled onto Dad, and they both lay there on the floor, Dad pinned under the larger dead body. I trembled and struggled for breath, fighting my fear. My throat constricted as I looked toward the door.

A third man stood there. He held a gun, pointed straight at Dad, who was struggling to push the corpse off of him. The man in the doorway looked up at me.

"Should I kill him?"

I shook my head, though my head was now shaking of its own accord anyway. I looked again at Dad, who by now had pushed the body off him, and saw that he was covered in the man's blood.

"Why not?"

I shook my head again. Dad just looked at the man, his gun still in his hand, but lying on his chest. I saw that the man's gun was now pointed at me, and Dad was also shaking his head.

"Please." Dad said quietly.

"Tell me. Why not?"

"Please, no." Dad trembled.

"I think one of you should die. You killed six of my men. Justice must be served. Now I just need to decide if it will be a greater punishment to kill *you*, or to make you watch me kill *him*." He was speaking to my dad, but inclined his head up to me.

Dad's jaw shook. "Please no. I'll do anything you want. Don't kill him."

The man pointed the gun back at Dad. "Then tell him to jump down, and I may let him live."

Dad's eyes widened. But, hesitantly, he looked up to me and gave a quick nod to tell me to come down. I couldn't move. I told my muscles to grab the edge and lower myself down, but nothing moved.

"Son. It's okay. Just come down." He flashed a weak smile at me, as if he didn't believe it. "It'll be all right."

My mind flashed back to Charlie. Dad had said those exact same words. *It'll be all right.*

"Really. Just jump down, and we'll figure this out. Just like we always have." He forced another smile. The other man held the gun steady.

I jumped, and landed on the table, sending a plate flying and shattering a glass. I looked down.

My crotch was wet.

My face flushed and my eyes watered.

"Very good. Now. Let go of your gun and put your hands outstretched to your sides." Dad did as commanded.

"Excellent. Now sit up. That's right. Now—slowly—put your hands on the floor to your left, and get on your knees. Nicely done. Now stand." Dad moved as if he were a puppet controlled by his master. Once on his feet, the man continued.

"You, boy—pick up the gun." I jumped off the table and bent down next to Dad. I picked up the gun and held it out toward the man, gripping it by the barrel.

"Put it in your pocket."

"What?"

"Put it in your pocket."

"Why?"

"I will tell you later. Put it in your pocket." I lowered my arm to my side and pushed the gun into my pocket. My phone was already there, so I put it in my other pocket.

"Wonderful. Now, boy, please come with me. My two associates …"—he paused to indicate the two men who had appeared behind him—"… will stay with your father."

I looked at Dad. He was pale. He looked scared. His jaw clenched. His left hand shook, as did his left cheek. He looked at me and slowly nodded, the look on his face telling me we had no choice.

I turned and followed the man out the door, feeling slightly empowered by the bulge in my left pocket. Not empowered to do anything heroic, but at least able to walk. And talk. That was better than pissing my pants.

"Where are you taking me?"

"To the first floor. That's where all the interesting things happen. The second floor is mostly for administrative work."

"What do you do here?"

"Research."

"On what?"

We descended a flight of stairs. The man's neat shoes clicked crisply on the cement steps.

"On human nature."

"Why?"

"To understand, of course."

"Understand what?"

"My, you are full of enlightening questions! I see you have wet yourself. Why did you do that?"

I looked down and felt my face go red again.

"I was scared."

We exited the stairwell and entered a long cubicle area, full of busy office workers.

"So your fear initiated an involuntary physical response. We have mastered that. You'll never see a robot piss himself, even with all hell breaking loose around him." He led me past the front desk, and the middle-aged, redheaded receptionist eyed me with a big plastic smile. "Tell me. Do you believe in God?"

"I don't know."

"That … that is something we do not understand. We *all* believe in God. Every one of us, from the very first. We don't understand things like doubt. Fear, anger, love, joy … all those basic emotions we have a handle on. But doubt, jealousy, contempt, disappointment, sentimentality, regret, nostalgia? These are complex emotions that we have yet to master. And what better way to master them than by learning from the masters?"

Regret. I understood regret. Charlie and I had been playing when it happened, just a few months after the reports of the purges.

I understood regret.

The man led me past the cubicles, past some offices—I recognized one of them from my interrogation the previous night—and down several more hallways, in one of which stood the metal door we had hidden behind just half an hour earlier. We approached a large metal door at the end of the long, sterile hallway. The man reached up to the combination lock and entered the numbers.

"Two … seven … nineteen … forty-three … seventy-nine … ah, there we go." I heard a click. "Do you recognize the numbers?"

"No. Should I?"

"No, I suppose not. They are the first five numbers in the Luista Series. All prime numbers, starting at the first, but then skipping successively higher prime numbers of primes. For example, two, then skip two prime numbers so the next is seven, then skip three prime numbers and you arrive at nineteen, skip five more and you get forty-three, and so on …"

He seemed almost giddy.

"I don't know why we love prime numbers so much. It must be hidden somewhere in our programming. I suppose it's not that strange. Other living things, like snails and flowers, love prime numbers too. You can see it in their patterns. God must love the damned things too, for him to have manifested them in such lowly creatures, as well as in his highest creation. Us."

He opened the door, and I followed him into a laboratory. Most labs—or so I imagined, based on my movie-watching—included computers and test tubes and lasers. This lab had none, though I guess it wasn't that strange that there were no computers, given that the lab was full of walking, breathing computers. There were naked people, too, sitting upright in chairs. One little girl had long needles sticking out of her temples with wires trailing off to strange-looking instruments. Nearby, a man, heavily scarred and missing an eye, sat staring blankly into space while two lab technicians worked busily beside him, pressing buttons and writing in notebooks. I wondered why they used notebooks when their brains could recall every last detail around them.

"Follow me, please." My captor led me to the rear of the lab, to another office. He closed the door behind me and motioned for me to sit. I sat where he pointed, and he slouched into another chair near mine and crossed his legs, resting his intertwined hands on his lap.

"You must be awfully curious about what you are doing here," he began.

I nodded.

"Are you afraid?"

I nodded again.

"Yes, that makes sense. Have you been afraid before?"

I nodded. The last time I wet myself, I had been with Charlie and Dad.

Then, just Dad.

"Tell me about it." He put his hands behind his head and leaned back, as if he were chatting with an old friend. I couldn't speak. The lump had returned. My mouth opened, but no sound could pass my restricted throat.

"Oh, please don't be frightened now. I assure you, you are completely safe."

I didn't believe him. I had a hard time believing people who said I'd be safe.

It'll be all right, Dad had said.

"Are you hungry? Here. Eat."

He tossed me a bag of chips. I opened it, and put one in my mouth, but just chewed it and chewed it until it became a nearly tasteless watery paste. I couldn't swallow. The saliva just built up until a thin Dorito-flavored soup sloshed around in my mouth.

"As I was saying, we want to learn to be more like you. Why? I don't know, really. It just feels like the most natural thing for us to do. It's as if God himself commands it of us. There are some among us who just want you all dead. But they are few. Most of us just want to learn."

I forced the saliva down my throat. "Then why do you torture people here?" I said, with sudden boldness.

"Torture?" He threw his head back and laughed a loud, boisterous laugh. "My dear boy, we don't torture anyone here. True, some may feel pain from the experiments, but it is temporary, and we don't just wantonly inflict it. It is all for a higher purpose."

"What about that girl out there?" I asked. I assumed she was the same girl the two workers in the parking lot had mentioned.

"Amanda? Oh, you're mistaken. She feels no pain now. And you should have seen the situation we rescued her from. She lived with her aunt and uncle, and they were both simply awful, disgusting human beings. Truly the worst of the worst. If I told you what they did to her, you'd vomit that Dorito right onto the floor."

"Were? They *were* awful?"

The man hesitated, then looked up through the large window that faced back into the lab. "Ah. We are ready now. Please follow me."

I looked through the window and saw Dad. He was strapped to a chair. I got up and followed the man out the door.

Dad's mouth was taped shut. A few metal electrodes were taped to his head, the wires trailing off to one of the instruments. His hands clenched, then unclenched. His bloodshot eyes darted left and right, opened wide.

The man continued. "Do you know why we've been chasing you for so many months, my boy?"

I shook my head.

"Because you and your father are going to give us data on a certain subset of human emotions that are still a bit sketchy for us. We have sophisticated models—n-order coupled partial differential equations with numerous empirical parameters conforming to the usual hypergeometric solutions of the Frye equation—but they are … incomplete. They fail at the boundaries, as we are still unsure of all the boundary conditions of the posed problem."

I looked at my dad. He looked at me.

"The problem …" the man continued, "concerns your brother, Charlie."

I stiffened. How could he know about Charlie? How could he know about us? About Dad? About me?

"Wha—what's the problem?" I stammered, my constricted throat squeezing out the words.

"The problem is, he's dead. And you're here. And so is he." The man pointed to Dad.

My mind reeled. How could anyone know?

"I will answer your question for you. We know, because one of you is a robot."

No. Not Dad.

Oh no. Not me. No, please not me.

"It is true. One of you has software in his head. One of you has metal bones. Is it the one found mysteriously on the doorstep? Or is it the heartless one?"

No. It wasn't true. It wasn't his fault. It was my fault.

My lips curled. "Liar!"

"Mmm? I do not lie, my boy. I am certainly capable of it, but I choose not to. Truth works so very much better than lies in the pursuit of knowledge."

We both hung there.

Seeing Dad's face as I hung out the window twenty minutes ago had brought it all back fresh to my mind.

We hung. Our hands were sweaty. Dad looked down at both of us.

The man's voice brought me back to the sterile lab. "You are now going to administer justice."

My heart pounded. I could hear it in my ears. "What do you mean?"

"If your father is a robot, he deserves to die. We have superhuman strength. If he is a robot, he could have saved you both. If *you* are a robot, your father surely knows it. And yet, he chose to save you …"

I looked into Dad's eyes.

"… instead of his only son."

We dangled there. We loved camping. Every summer we backpacked up to the Cascade Mountains in Washington. Mount Pilchuck was our favorite place; just below the summit was a basin of about twenty alpine mountain lakes. Every year we would pick a different one to camp at, even though they were all within a mile of each other. And every day during the week, when the weather permitted, we would climb up to the peak, and stand out on the rocks, looking down at the valleys below, more than a thousand feet down.

Charlie loved to go right out to the edge of the peak and pee off the side. It was his yearly ritual. I was usually too scared to go right up to the edge. Last summer, I was older, and finally found the courage to stand out on a rock at the cliff's edge.

I dare you to piss off that one over there I said, pointing to a rock that jutted out and slanted downward somewhat. *Only if you come out with me* he said. Before I could answer, he did. He went right out to the edge and sat down, dangling his feet off the side. I was terrified. I didn't want to go out that far, but I had to. I was the one who had dared him. Only sissies dared and then chickened out when it was their turn.

I went out, but as I approached, my knees wobbled. But I made it. I sat next to him. We sat there for a few minutes before Dad saw us. He yelled. He screamed. He was angry. And scared. He ran over to us and told us to come back. We got up, but I wobbled again. Charlie reached out to steady me, but somehow, we fell. We grabbed on to the rock, and somehow, I don't remember how, I looked up, and Dad had each of us by a hand.

It was hot. I was scared. My hand was sweaty. So was Dad's. Our grips slipped, and our hands started sliding against each other's moist skin. I saw Charlie's hand slipping too. Dad was splayed out on the rock, holding on with his feet.

It'll be all right! he said, as he saw my face. He started pulling both of us, but his hands were slipping fast. He squeezed harder. Charlie screamed. I couldn't. I couldn't scream. Dad looked at me. He looked at Charlie.

Charlie fell.

Dad grabbed me with his other hand, and with both hands now firmly grasping me, he was able to haul me up, even as we heard Charlie screaming on his way down. He screamed for what seemed like several minutes, though it couldn't have been more than five seconds or so.

Then a faint thud.

Then nothing.

We sat there and cried for a long time.

"Liar!" I yelled again, this time snarling.

"Would you like to know which one of you is a robot?" the man asked, looking almost gleeful.

I stayed silent.

"Take out your gun."

"Why?"

His voice thundered. "Take it out!"

I pulled the gun out of my left pocket.

"Point it at his head."

"No."

The man reached over and grabbed Dad's throat.

"Point it at his head or I'll rip his esophagus out."

My hand shook, but I pointed it.

"I'll tell you now. *He* is the robot. He could have easily saved you both. But, for some selfish reason, probably because your mother was getting custody rights of your brother, he let go."

I stared at Dad. His eyes watered.

"Now. How do you feel?"

How did I feel? He was crazy. Insane. Dad wouldn't have let Charlie die on purpose.

Did she really get custody?

"I don't know."

"Tell me how you feel!"

"Confused," was all I could muster. And it was the truth.

"See? I told you your father was the robot. Robots can't feel complex emotions yet. They can't feel conflicted, like you. They feel anger. Fear. Just the basics."

I felt sick. Dad was a robot. Dad was a robot.

Dad was a robot.

The man's voice softened, almost to a whisper. "He let your brother die. He killed several men here." I looked into

Dad's wet eyes. The man continued. "What do murderers deserve?"

My own eyes watered as I stared at Dad's. I couldn't believe it.

"What do murderers deserve?"

"To die."

"Then do it."

"I can't."

"Why not?"

"I forgive him."

"You what?

"It's okay. I forgive him."

"You can't do that."

"Why not?"

"You just can't!"

"I can!"

"No, you can't. You have to kill him. If you don't," the man's voice relaxed to a calm, eerie tone, "I'll kill you both."

He reached out and grabbed my neck too. He squeezed. I couldn't breathe.

The man yelled in my ear. I could feel his nose. Smell his garlicky breath. "Your father is a murderer! Kill him now!"

With his hand clamped over my throat, it was impossible to talk, so I shook my head. The hand squeezed harder. My eyes felt like they would pop out.

He released his hand and softened his voice. "Son, your father is a murderer. Can't you see that?"

"I don't care."

"Did you not love your brother? Will you let him walk away from here? Will you let him get away with it?"

My hand still held the gun, pointed at Dad's head. The flickering fluorescent light glinted off the tears in his eyes.

"Prove to me he's a robot."

The man thought for a moment, then gently rested his hand on my shoulder, looking me in the eye. "He had two sons. One naturally, and one adopted. When given the choice to save one or the other, he chose to let his natural son die, at the expense of letting his … *unnatural* son, if you will … live. A human's gut instinct, his spur-of-the-moment action, would be to save his natural son. Instead he saved the one foreign to him. Why would a robot choose this? Simple. He was probably trying to pass as a human. You were more valuable to him, being human yourself. Charlie was not. If your father was ever suspected of being a robot, rather than submit to a scan himself, he could offer you up to be scanned, proving his humanity as well."

"I'm not sure that makes sense …"

"Of course you don't think it makes sense. You're a human child, and you're scared—your judgment is clouded. Yet more proof that you are the human and he is the robot."

The man's logic was dizzying. "But … what if we're both human?"

"A possibility, yes. But we are straying from our purpose here. You must kill him now. It is time to execute justice."

"I told you. I won't. I forgive him."

"You use that word again. It is a false concept. Failure to execute justice is simply laziness; you humans have invented forgiveness to hide your apathy toward injustice."

"But—but … I don't care what he's done. I don't even care if he's a robot. It's not laziness. It's … it's …"

"It's what?"

"I don't know." I shifted on my feet, looking around at the lab technicians watching us. I turned back to the man. "I just don't want him to die."

The man considered this. He turned away from me and wandered around the room. Then his head snapped over to the girl. Amanda. He strode over to her, wheeled her chair next to Dad. He pulled a gun out of his pocket.

"Fine. I will now give you a choice. In twenty seconds, I will kill both your father," he pointed his gun at the pale little girl's head, the needles still protruding from her skull, "and her. You can save her life by killing him first, or save *his* life by killing *her*. I will start the clock … now. Twenty. Nineteen. Eighteen …"

I can't do this. I can't do it. I can't lose him. I love him. It was my fault. I shouldn't have dared him. *I* deserve to die, not him …

"… Fourteen. Thirteen …"

Maybe I have time to kill the robot first. No, there's too many of them. They'd kill us all. They'll kill us all anyway. But maybe not. I have to do something. Did he really do it? Mom and Dad did fight a lot. He screamed at her. Swore at her. Called her a whore. Would he let Charlie die to spite her? No. He wouldn't. He wouldn't …

"… Nine. Eight. Seven …"

But if he did … well then, my choice is obvious. Isn't it?

Isn't it?

Which one deserves death? No. That's the wrong question. Which one deserves life? No. That's not it either. Which one … can I live with myself knowing I killed? Is that the right question?

"… Four. Three …"

I need to do it. I can't let them both die. What if he's bluffing? Do robots bluff? He just got to two. Do I need to pull the trigger before he says one, or will he say time's up? Oh no. Oh no. I can't do this. Oh …

"One. Have you made your decision?" The man sounded like a game show host, but still he held the gun to the girl's temple. I nodded. I felt like vomiting.

I looked at Dad again.

Our eyes connected. He stared straight ahead, emotionless. *Goodbye,* I mouthed. He nodded slightly, and blinked.

I pulled the trigger.

Click.

"Do it again," the man commanded.

I pulled the trigger again.

Click.

The man put his gun back in his pocket.

I felt the man's other hand on the back of my head. All emotion left me.

"What are you doi—" I started, but then I felt him in my mind. I began to understand.

To remember.

"Well done. We have learned much from you. You are a hero. Go wash up."

I looked down at my ragged clothing, my black hands and bloodied knees from weeks of being chased, crawling through ducts, hiding in garbage bins.

"Yes, Father," I said.

The man with his mouth taped shut began to thrash against his restraints. I turned to walk toward the bathroom as a lab worker bashed him unconscious with his fist. Another lab worker wheeled the little girl back to her machines as a third worker lifted the unconscious man with the taped mouth out of the chair and carried him away. I set the gun on a table as I left the room, and Father entered his office and closed the door gently behind him.

<end download>

<parsing data structures>

<begin data analysis>

The man kicked his feet back on the desk and sucked on a cigarette. The data flashed across the screen at mind-numbing speed. Not too fast for him, of course. But for a human brain, it would have looked like a blur. Gibberish.

He glanced out the window and watched the lab tech sedate the father, who, had it not been for the tape over his mouth, would have frothily shouted profanities at them all. Humans. So foul and uncouth. Uncivilized.

"Doctor? Will you be needing anything else tonight?"

The man pressed the cigarette against the ashtray and twisted it, extinguishing the smoldering thing. "No. You can go home, Meg. Good job today. Central will be pleased with our progress."

The lab tech breathed a sigh of relief. "Finally. I hate these sessions. I don't know what you get out of them, but all I get is the creeps."

"Data. Knowledge. Nothing more."

She started to leave, but paused. "You lied this time, Doctor. You've never done that before. Always been completely honest with them, or slyly misled them. But never lied. Why the change?"

He watched the file output stream past on the screen, fresh from the boy's mind. "A new variable to adjust. Nothing more. Data. Just data."

Meg, the lab tech, said nothing else as she left, shutting the door softly behind her.

The data. There it goes. Fast as light, for all the good it would do them. He suspected the same result as the last fifty-four tests, each designed to elicit anger, retribution, judgment, and hostility toward the secondary subjects—their fathers. All the subjects felt conflicted, that much was clear. In fact, that was what they were ostensibly studying, on orders from Central.

But he had another goal. A more elusive one.

The screen stopped, coming to the end of the test's time period and the end of the data.

<subject's final emotive state: agitated, frightened, horrified>

<emotions regarding father: peace, regret, love>

<subject's emotional stream indicates forgiveness, confidence level p=.000127>

Forgiveness. How?

Dammit. He flicked the ashtray aside and pressed the intercom button. "Proceed with test fifty-six, Avery."

A voice responded, "Yes, sir."

Slumping back in his chair, he watched through the window as the boy—full of nanobots busily at work rewiring his very human brain—exited the bathroom and stood looking blankly all around him.

Test number fifty-six tomorrow. They'd go through a thousand more if they had to. Data. It's all just data. And data would eventually explain it, if given the chance.

A Word from Endi Webb

I admit it: I've always wanted to be a robot. Remember Gizmo Duck from *DuckTales*? As an eight-year-old in the nineties, I wanted to be him so bad that I tried to make a robot suit out of scrap metal in my dad's garage. The Borg? Yep. Them too. Except without all the mutilation and stuff. Just the idea of putting on a piece of hardware as if it were clothing and becoming a new enhanced person made me giddily excited.

Yeah, I was a strange kid.

And yet throughout almost every book I've written so far, this theme has appeared. Whether in the Robotic Society of Healers in my *Rhovim Chronicles*, or the masks of power in *The Maskmaker's Apprentice*, or even in the upcoming books of my *Pax Humana Saga*, which (spoiler alert!) will involve integration of robotics with organic neural networks. It seems like I can't leave it alone. And so I give you one more: "Adopted," the story of a boy and his father learning unpleasant truths—or lies—about themselves. A story that asks whether there is any human concept or emotion that an AI will not eventually be able to replicate.

I'm from Seattle, but I've lived in SoCal, Utah, Los Alamos (yes, *that* Los Alamos), and now Huntsville, Alabama. I do science. And by that I mean I have a PhD in experimental physics, and so I *do* science. Often with explosively fun results. It's a good day when I have not burned myself with a hundred-watt laser, dropped a five-hundred-pound vacuum chamber on the floor, blown up highly reactive precursor gases, or spewed nanoparticles all over the lab. (Dear manager: I'm making this all up.) Seriously, science is fun. But what's even funner (funner!) is making up stuff and calling it science fiction, and then selling it to people who want to read it. For money. Really, it's a win-win.

I'm sorry, that sounded very unprofessional. Its art, I tell you. *Aaaaahhhht.* I weave delicate themes of meaning and symbolism throughout my prose, and the resulting tapestry of word-smudges on the canvas speaks to the intimate human yearning for … something.

Yeah, I just like to blow stuff up. In my writing, and in the lab.

Anyway, if you want to know when I blow up something else—er, publish something new, you should totally subscribe to my mailing list: smarturl.it/endimailinglist. Benefits include you getting all (ALL!) my short stories for free, lower prices on my new releases, and other, intangible benefits*. And come stalk me on Facebook!

Thanks for reading!

*Intangible benefits do not include anything of monetary value, and may be completely made up.

Shimmer

by Matthew Mather

THE COGNIX BOARD of directors meeting was over, and Dr. Hal Granger glared at Patricia Killiam as she closed down the shared memetic structures of the meeting space. Dr. Granger had been right in the middle of explaining how his happiness indices were central to the entire Atopian project when Patricia had cut him off.

Such arrogance in that Patricia Killiam. What made her think she could talk about happiness? As if anyone knew more about emotions than Dr. Granger.

Patricia was always lording over everyone the idea that she was the famous "mother of synthetic beings"—but from Dr. Granger's point of view, this just wasn't true. Her research had focused only on generalized fluidic and crystallized measures of logical and linguistic intelligence; it was his contribution that had led to the creation of emotional and social intelligence for artificial beings.

And what was more important? *What* someone said—or the *emotional reason* behind why they said it? After all, the very definition of consciousness was how information *felt* when it was processed in a certain way.

Patricia really overestimated her importance in things. Who knew more about happiness than he did?

Really, what nerve.

Dr. Granger needed to calm down. An aimless wander through a few floors of the hydroponic farms ought to do the trick. He exited the boardroom and jogged down an interior staircase into the vertical farming levels just below.

The top floor of the complex belonged to the offices of Kesselring, the founder and chairman of Cognix. Even the master of synthetic reality liked to keep his specific reality positioned above everyone else's. As he passed through the level, Dr. Granger stopped for a moment to enjoy the view of Atopia from a thousand feet up: semi–tropical forests, capped by crescents of white beaches; the frothy breakwaters beyond. Through the phase-shifted glass walls, the sea still managed to glitter under a cloudless blue sky.

As he continued down the stairs into the main grow farms, Dr. Granger took a deep breath, enjoying the humid and organic, if not earthy, smell. He loved that smell. Although, if he was being honest, what he enjoyed most about the farming complex wasn't the smell or the peacefulness: it was the curt, respectful nods he received from the staff. That, and watching the blank faces of the psombie inmates.

Most of the psombies here were people incarcerated for crimes, their minds disconnected from their bodies while they waited out their sentences in multiverse prison worlds. In the interim, their bodies were consigned to community work in various places around Atopia, such as these farms, where they were safely guided by virtual minders. Even paradise needs correctional services.

Yes, the farms were a nice, controlled environment.

They made Dr. Granger feel powerful and safe.

"Shimmer!" he called out.

Shimmer popped into one of his display spaces and began walking in step beside him. She was a virtual creature, living in the digital hyperspaces around him, but to his eyes she appeared as a lithe twenty-something with cropped blond hair and blue eyes.

"Yes, Dr. Granger?" Shimmer replied. "Do you want me to start a new log entry on Dr. Killiam?"

He nodded, but really, she didn't need a response. She always knew what he was thinking. She, or he. Shimmer was as evenly an androgynous creature as Dr. Granger had ever met or created. When he felt he needed a female perspective, Shimmer seemed womanly. When he felt that a stronger hand was necessary, Shimmer seemed more masculine. For a synthetic being, gender was superfluous in the biological sense, but it remained critical in others. It was Shimmer's ability to understand the emotional dynamics of both sexes that had made her famous.

Or, rather, made me *famous.* Dr. Granger smiled.

"Already done, Dr. Granger." Shimmer smiled back at him. "Do you want me to walk you home while you get some work done?"

Dr. Granger nodded. "Yes, please."

He relaxed, letting Shimmer take control of his motor cortex and begin walking him along the corridors. He'd been unconsciously looking out the windows to the view below, but once Shimmer took charge, she shifted his gaze front and center. They turned from the outer corridor toward the interior elevators.

Dr. Granger decided to simply joyride for a while. He enjoyed these little moments, and Shimmer sensed this. She outstretched his arms and spread his fingers so that they slid through the plant leaves as they passed. Dr. Granger was easing into the back of his mind, about to shift his point of view into his workspaces, but the feeling of the plants brushing past his fingertips tingled his senses. He let his consciousness sink further and further back, relaxing his mind.

Work could wait.

Shimmer was one of the cornerstones of the entire modern field of synthetic intelligence. The idea had come to Dr. Granger as an assistant professor at Stanford, a young and ambitious man trying to work his way up through the ranks. Of course, some disgruntled grad students had tried to claim the work as their own, but Dr. Granger had held firm, through multiple lawsuits, that *he* was the glue that had held the thing together—despite what some said.

The experiment that had started it all was a mirror neuron simulation. A stream of human sensory data was fed through it—using real-time visual and audio input from hundreds of psychology grad students—to create an aggregate virtual body. The goal was to create a machine that didn't just *mimic* emotions, but that actually learned the basis of animal emotion *as the animal itself.*

Early experiments bore out the concept, and over the years Dr. Granger secured the funding to build ever more elaborate networks—networks that had reached their culmination in Shimmer. Shimmer had learned the basis for emotion like a baby learning to speak a language—by watching and feeling what the human participants felt until she could feel it for herself.

In the process, she gained the superhuman ability to identify the precise combination of emotions present in a human subject—out of the thousands of possible combinations.

Earlier efforts to build tools that could identify human emotions had focused on observing the human face and bio-sensing things like skin temperature, heart rate, and pupil dilation. These methods worked well enough for the "big six" emotions that psychologists traditionally focused on: joy, sadness, anger, fear, surprise, and disgust. But what Shimmer was able to distinguish was infinitely more subtle.

She could pick out *combined layers* of emotions: like avarice, embarrassment, boredom, loneliness, jealousy—even the double-edged sword of pride, and the many faces of confusion. Gratitude was one of Shimmer's specialties—an especially difficult and important emotion, as it was the building block for that most cherished of human emotions, love.

The most important emotions in the modern world, however, were elevation and inspiration. While the powerful could still use fear as a potent tool for pursuing their agendas, its efficiency had begun to wane with the rise of worldwide information networks. Gone were the days when outright coercion could be used effectively in much of the world.

Instead, the tools used to pacify the masses in the modern age were carefully choreographed ballets of inspirational messaging, designed to elevate and inspire the masses into action or submission. Shimmer was the master of this dance, and that was the main reason why Dr. Granger had been appointed to the Cognix board.

Dr. Granger snorted. Humans were such slaves to their emotions. Trying to see the emotional forest for the trees was something humans couldn't even manage in themselves, never mind in other people. Being able to perfectly recognize collective human emotions, and by extension the emotional weatherscapes that blew through societies, provided an entirely new and powerful tool for understanding and influencing people.

And that was where Dr. Granger's own power had grown.

Dr. Granger was *exclusively* interfaced with Shimmer. She conveyed to him whatever emotional context appeared in the people he spoke to, effectively transferring to him her superhuman ability to recognize and categorize human emotions. By inserting himself as the primary focal point of the project, Dr. Granger had developed a brand image. Over time, the cult of his personality had eclipsed the project itself.

His initial fame had landed him on the EmoShow, an international hit on the mediaworlds. It had, in turn, landed him on the board of directors for Cognix; and now, with the impending release of the Atopian virtual reality product, he was on the threshold of becoming one of the super-rich. He now had everything he'd ever wanted, and it was all due to Shimmer, his faithful and loyal creation, who functioned as his own proxxi in the Atopian protocol.

As Shimmer guided Dr. Granger's body down the hallways to his office—lower than Kesselring's but still quite high up in the farming complex—an irresistible question was forming in his mind.

Shimmer sat him down behind his mahogany desk and propped his feet up just the way he liked. Personal satisfaction was coursing through his emotional veins.

"Shimmer," he called out, "could you sit with me for a moment?"

She appeared in one of his attending chairs, sitting demurely with her hands in her lap, smiling softly.

"I have a question for you, Shimmer."

"Yes, sir?"

He chewed on his question for a second, preemptively enjoying the moment to come. "Shimmer, I know you never lie. In fact, you are incapable of lying to me."

"That is true, sir," she replied, nodding. "Of course it is true."

"And you have your own emotions. You feel things as humans do."

"Yes, sir."

"So here's my question."

Shimmer waited silently.

He wanted to hear her say it. In fact, he wanted to *feel* it, so he patched himself into Shimmer's own emotional circuits.

With his feet still on the desk, he spread his arms. "I am rich, powerful, famous, and welcome anywhere by anyone in the world. I can do almost anything I want, when I want. So my question to you is this: Wouldn't you like to switch places with me?"

Shimmer paused and smiled. "No, sir."

What? Was she lying somehow? But no: her emotional channels reflected her indifference.

"What do you mean?" he demanded. "You are my servant, my slave. You have no option but to do what I want you to do. How could you not wish to have my freedom, my fame? To have power, even over me? Answer me, Shimmer. Explain yourself!"

She paused again, always the cautious creature. "Sir, how do I put this …?"

"Just out with it!" he demanded, annoyed that his moment had been frustrated.

"Well, sir, I've already met my maker … whereas you …"

Dr. Granger's anger drained from him as if a plug had been pulled. As he groped for words, his feet fell off the desk.

"Go away." It was all he could think of to say.

Obediently, she did.

A Word from Matthew Mather

I started my career working as a researcher at the McGill Center for Intelligent Machines, designing robotic actuators, so writing a short story about AI is like coming full circle after twenty-five years. We've already had scattered reports of machines beating the Turing test, and I think turning this corner will usher in the age of conscious machines. We are at the precipice, and I think it's time to start sorting through the moral and social implications of self-aware machines.

Shimmer is a previously unpublished short story from the world of Atopia, my best-selling collection of stories I first published in 2012. My books have been translated into fifteen languages (and counting) and sold worldwide, with 20th Century Fox taking an option on my latest book, *CyberStorm*. You can find my books here:

http://www.matthewmather.com/

System Failure

by Deirdre Gould

Bezel

```
Public Class frmReboot
    Private Sub Shutdown
        System.Diagnostics.Process.Start("shutdown", "-s -t 00")
    End Sub
    Private Sub Reboot
        System.Diagnostics.Process.Start("shutdown", "-r -t 00")
    End Sub
    Private Sub Logon
        System.Diagnostics.Process.Start("shutdown", "-l -t 00")
    End Sub
    Private Sub Exit
        End
    End Sub
End Class
```

Warning: Charging error. Power reserve low.

Bezel's information feeds stuttered and then streamed a flood of data. He completed his maintenance check. He detached from the recharge station and walked down the cement entrance hall toward the vault. He'd have to borrow Tock's station until his could be fixed. How long into the first watch were they? There was a book on the early domestication of wheat that he'd been dying to read. Perhaps if they were close enough to the swap, he'd just relieve Tock and sneak in some data processing time.

The shuttling commands on his priority list paused as he turned the corridor's one corner. The walls and floor were blackened with soot. Something was wrong.

Bezel's command priorities reordered and settled. He tried to log in to the LAN to access the vault records but none of the other computers responded. The connection must have gone down. He continued on to the seed repository.

When he arrived, he found the metal drawers lying open, strewn across the stone floor, their contents nothing but ash. Shelving units had been ripped from their tracks and tipped, the metal twisted and sagging away from the center of the room. The repository's control center was just a crater of melted glass and dust.

The soot shifted underneath his feet as Bezel stepped into the vault. He pinged Tock, but she didn't return it. He picked through the metal drawers, sifting through the soot a few grams at a time for any seeds that may have escaped, matching the serial numbers on the drawer to his internal database.

Malus sieversii. Malus domestica. Gone. No one would ever eat an apple again. All the *Camellia sinensis* cultivars, just smoke. No one would ever pick a tea leaf again.

He reluctantly passed several fallen shelves, recognizing that the crew was a higher priority. He knew from memory, though, that the loss would only become more profound the farther he moved into the room. No more medicinal herbs. No more vegetables for consumption. No more trees producing oxygen. It was all gone. A hundred thousand years of careful cultivation—wiped out. And millions of years of evolution before that. The only hope was that something outside had survived. That something had recovered, had clawed its way out of the irradiated soil, and flourished.

What had happened? Why had Bezel not been activated until now? And where was the crew? He felt lost, as if he had a parser malfunction, as if the world were one giant syntax error.

He picked his way to the far door, his bright chrome shell now a dusty gray, the ash clinging to him as it puffed up around his legs. The door was stuck open, the metal curled backward, dog-eared. Bezel slid through the opening into the frozen zoo.

The fire had extended to this vault too, but hadn't swept the entirety. The outer shells of the nitrogen tanks were dusty with ash, but the metal appeared unwarped, the seals intact. And the control center looked untouched, although its blank, dark screens made Bezel pick up his pace.

When he saw the inside of the small glass room, he didn't even bother flipping switches. There was an emergency fire axe buried in the far console, its red blade like a splash of blood on the clean white plastic. The power cords had all been chopped into small wedges of rubber and wire, and scattered across the floor. Bezel sank into the wobbly office chair and looked around at the dozens of silver nitrogen tanks. Now they were just tombs. No more elephants. No more dogs. No more snails or fish. All thawing, all rotting away.

He shot up again and raced to the nearest tank. Maybe it had only just now happened. Maybe there was still time to refreeze them.

He lifted the lid, hoping for tendrils of fog to curl around his chrome face. But there was no outrush of cold. The tubes were neatly stacked in their trays, but the tank was dry. Warm, even. The pressure releases had long ago let the nitrogen leak out in little puffs as it boiled away.

Bezel pulled out a test tube. *Pan troglodytes.* Man's closest relative, the chimpanzee, was now just a speck of dust where tissue and living cells ought to have been. He carefully tucked the glass vial back into its rack and gently closed the tank lid.

What had Dr. Ficht called it? An ark, like the one in the story. They had escaped the flood, but the ark was now filled with corpses, with death.

Bezel turned and left the frozen zoo behind him, heading for the final vault.

The hall was clean, as if it had just been swept, and the door was closed as usual in its frame. The air was so still that Bezel could just hear the small electric hum of his storage drive and the rush of air through his heat vent. He placed a shining hand on the door panel.

Warning: Power reserve at thirty percent. Recharge to avoid loss of function.

The message cropped up in his high-priority list. Bezel ignored it and pushed on the door. It swung open, and the overhead lights flickered for a few seconds before deciding to stay on.

Tock was slumped against the far wall. Bezel hurried over to her, not even seeing the dark pods around him. It was only half of Tock, her snapped wires and drooping springs trailing over the hard floor. Her chrome body plates were scraped and punctured—probably by the axe that was now lodged in the frozen zoo's control console.

Bezel picked up Tock and carried her to the power station in the corner of the room. He didn't bother to stop when he passed her leg unit. With hope, he attached her to the recharge station—but then leapt back as a shower of blue sparks burst from her spine. Her lights blazed once, her head jerked to the side—and that was all.

Bezel detected ozone in the air and knew the power station socket had burned out. He slowly detached Tock and removed her storage drive, then he picked up her leg unit and laid it below her torso. The power station at the vault's entrance had malfunctioned, and the ones in the seed repository and zoo had been destroyed. This one had been his last chance for recharge.

He looked down at Tock. His only other option seemed distasteful to him. Almost cannibalistic. Maybe he should simply shut down instead.

One of the pods pulsed with green light nearby. Bezel looked around the room, away from Tock's shimmering right leg.

Only a single pod was lit. The others were globes of shadow filled with the delicate branchwork of bones. Bezel checked the glowing pod. It was Karen Epide, one of the interns. Doubly lucky. She had already been in Svalbard when the reactors had been hit, otherwise she would have been out there, with no ticket in, like everyone else. Now she was in the only powered hibernation pod. Maybe doubly *unlucky*, Bezel told himself. Why had she lived when everyone else had died?

He shook himself. It didn't matter. What mattered was waking her up, making sure that she, at least, survived. He didn't have much power left. A few days, maybe. Bezel glanced back to Tock. Her pack was probably full. He shook his head. It was wrong, like taking another's last bite of bread.

The low-power warning flashed again on his priority list. He ignored it, and sat at the life support console. It seemed to have taken no damage, except that the gravity motor on Karen's pod had burned out. The screens on the other pods were all blinking with the same date. Fifty years. Had he been inactive that long? His internal clock had glitched and reset during one of the maintenance processes. It would explain the low-power warnings. Fifty years. The pods had only been meant for ten. Even assuming her gravity motor had burned out only a few years ago, Karen's muscles would be completely atrophied by now. She might have brain damage. The nutrient reserves ought to have run out years ago. The system must have been using the nutrients meant for the others.

Bezel's metal fingers hovered over the keypad. Should he even begin the recovery process? What was left?

The external sensors weren't functioning. Bezel had no idea if the radiation had fallen to acceptable levels. Or if the air was breathable. There would certainly be little for a human to consume, even after all this time. It was supposed to be his and Tock's task: replanting the hardier stock in places that were still irradiated, helping the world rid itself of the poison. Without those trees, it could take several more decades.

His memory chip seemed stuck on a replay of the seed repository, its ash forever sliding in the drawers, a gray slush of despair. Nothing was left. He glanced at the other pod readouts. Their red blinks were a constant, warm invitation to oblivion.

She could live for decades in the vault. There was enough food, enough power, even now, to support her. But then what? He'd be gone in a matter of months. She'd be alone.

Maybe there were others. There were certainly other seed vaults. Maybe there were other human survivors too. He ignored the thought that she'd never live to reach them. His job was to protect the humans. His job was to ensure the resurgence of the natural species of Earth. She was all that was left. Without her, he'd have no purpose. He'd be better off shutting down if she didn't recover. He had to wake her. He had to try.

His fingers punched the recovery code on the keypad. As he swiveled in the office chair, Tock's leg glinted at him from across the room. He knew it would take months of physical therapy before Karen fully recovered. If she ever could. He wasn't going to last that long unless he found another power source.

The low-power warning pulsed like a growl in his head. Tock's leg twinkled, and her storage drive clacked where it hung against his chestplate. She wouldn't need it anymore. Whatever had happened here, she had tried to defend the people sleeping in the pods. She would want him to take it. He tried to persuade himself, but his mind still revolted.

He got up from the chair and walked past Tock to the living quarters. The linens were crisp and ghosted with fold lines as he pulled them from their wrappers. The absence of dust made him uneasy, as if the date were very wrong. After Karen woke up, he was going to have to look at Tock's data and see if he could pull anything off the life support records. It might not matter much now that everything was gone, but it would help him to reconcile the data. Anchor him. Make him "feel better," as the humans would say. But for now, he had work to do.

He smoothed the sheet over the cot's mattress and tucked the blanket in at the foot. He surveyed the room and grabbed some extra blankets. She would be cold for a while. And then hungry. He draped the blankets over a nearby chair and went back to the control console. The cafeteria records said she'd requested grilled cheese most often. He passed Tock again on his way to the kitchen and tried not to make an association.

In the kitchen, a corpse sat at the table. Its ribcage had been stretched open from the back, its uniform still draped over the limbs, its parka flung on the chair beside it. The name tag read Gunderson. One of the crew that had been awake for first watch. He hadn't even defended himself. Bezel looked at him for a long moment. Karen wouldn't like seeing all these bodies. He had time. He'd better dispose of them and clean up the mess as best he could.

Bezel thought it best to place them all in the seed repository. Karen wouldn't be capable of walking far on her own for some time, and by then, Bezel hoped, he would have sufficiently prepared her. It took a long while, almost three hours to place them all side by side and clean the hibernation pods.

He carried Tock down last, placing her at the end of the long lines of bodies. He could almost feel the power draining from him with every whir of a servo. He didn't look at Tock's silver face. He knelt down in the ash and felt for the seam of the compartment in her right calf. It was dented, and the release mechanism stuck. Bezel tried to pry the compartment open but his fingers were too large. After several attempts he resorted to a thin-bladed utility knife he found in the maintenance room. He tried to drive the parallel images out of his processor and regretted the history discs he'd downloaded for his leisure time. If only the humans had stopped before his generation. If only they'd been stuck at the sophisticated mimicry of the Obsoletes instead of achieving true AI. He thought he might have given up his entire existence to skip this one solitary day. Maybe even to skip the past fifteen minutes.

At last the compartment popped open. He pulled out her energy pack and stood up quickly. He looked at the utility knife and threw it across the room. He sent out a ping to Tock's old address, knowing he would never get an echo-reply.

Then he carefully bent the door back in place as well as he could and returned to the kitchen.

Karen

Bezel wasn't certain Karen would even be able to chew or swallow after fifty years of hibernation. He wasn't programmed to know the rate of muscle atrophy in humans. He prepared an IV just in case and laid the needle next to the steaming tray of food. He carried the unconscious woman to the cot and covered her with several blankets.

Then, he waited.

He turned Tock's energy pack over and over, its plastic casing slipping between his printless fingers, all the while knowing he should be conserving his power, not activating unnecessary circuits by fidgeting. Why was he stalling? There was no doubt he would need the battery, and it wasn't hurting anyone. Before he could waver again, he popped open the spare compartment in his left leg and clicked the pack into place. The compartment slid smoothly shut. It was done. The warning message abruptly stopped. He knew that it would be back.

Bezel watched Karen's nostrils flare slightly with each breath, watched the heart monitor's line jiggle and wave. He thought about reviewing Tock's storage drive, but couldn't bring himself to leave Karen's side. She might be the only other living thing on the planet. He had to make sure she survived.

The cheese congealed in a waxy puddle on the plate. Bezel thought about making another sandwich for her, but he didn't even know if she'd be able to eat it. So he continued to wait. At last her mouth drooped open and she yawned. He noticed that she wasn't stretching. He wondered if she was trying and failing to move her shriveled muscle tissue, and he wished he'd spent more resources on medical training. She opened her eyes and saw him staring down at her.

"Is it as bad as they said?" she asked, her voice crackling with thirst. He held a straw to her mouth and she sipped some water. Good. She could swallow at least. She noticed he hadn't answered. "Bezel, just tell me how bad it was. My parents were on tour in western Europe—surely they had a chance?"

"I'm sorry, Karen, I'm afraid at last report the destruction was total," he answered slowly, sitting down. She turned her head slightly to see him. Good, she could move her head.

"I understand. I'd hoped that the radiation wouldn't spread that far. We learned in class that a nuclear blast would only travel so far ..." She trailed off.

"If it had been bombs, there might have been some hope. Even if it had been all the bombs we knew about. Reactors are different."

"I didn't think that there were enough of them to do so much damage."

Bezel shook his head. "If it had been one or two—but this was a coordinated hit. They hit the waste storage facilities too. All over the world. All at once."

"Who was it? Why did they do this?"

He shrugged. "I don't know. Does it matter anymore? Everything and everyone is gone. Whoever it was must be sufficiently punished by now."

"Surely there must be someone besides us left—" Karen tried to raise her head but couldn't get it more than an inch from the pillow. "Where is everyone else? Is Tock with them?"

"Communications were knocked out shortly after the vault was sealed. But that was to be expected. There may be others, in bunkers or fallout shelters, maybe even out in the atmosphere now, I don't know. The external sensors aren't working correctly, so I can't tell you whether or not the outside world is safe yet."

"What does the rest of the crew say? Are you and Tock going to go out and scout now that our hibernation time is finished?"

Bezel hesitated. He offered her a corner of the sandwich; she took a bite and waited expectantly. "The rest of the crew, including Tock, didn't make it," he said after she'd swallowed. He thought he saw a startled twitch in her fingers, but that was the extent of her movement.

"What?" she cried. "How? When?"

"I don't know," he said, slowly extending and then bending her left arm for her. "I was only activated a few hours ago myself. Something went wrong with the recharge station—well, with everything, actually. I haven't yet checked the incident reports or the video feeds. I wanted to be sure that whatever had happened didn't happen to you."

"Surely there must have been some clue, some sign," she protested. "If the hibernation pods failed then shouldn't the watch have been there to save us?"

"They never made it past the first watch, Karen. I found Gunderson—he'd been murdered. And the zoo and pods were sabotaged. There was a fire or an explosion in the repository."

"And Dr. Ficht?"

Bezel shrugged. He hadn't found Dr. Ficht. She should have been on first watch with Gunderson. She couldn't have left the vault—it had still been sealed when Bezel rebooted. Perhaps she had been burned to ash in the fire.

"Shouldn't we find out?" Karen asked. Bezel moved to her other arm.

"Why?" he asked.

"What if we're shut in here with a murderer?"

"No. We are alone. If whoever did this survived, there would be signs. Missing food, laundry, something. The life support console says that it's been fifty years since the hibernation pods were shut down."

"Is that why I can't move?"

"The motor meant to simulate activity burned out on your pod at some point. It was never meant to last for this long. But your muscles also weren't meant to lie dormant. They have atrophied. You will have to undergo physical therapy for some time to rebuild them before you will be able to function fully again."

Karen took a deep, shuddering breath. "Why did you wake me up?" she asked quietly. "Why didn't you just deactivate the pod and let me die with the others?"

"You are alive. There may be others. There may be many others. It is my job to protect the life in this vault."

"You aren't just a machine, Bezel. You don't have to comply with mission programming all the time. You could have chosen mercy."

Bezel didn't tell her about his hesitation at the keypad. He didn't tell her how he had almost shut them both down. He didn't tell her that he had chosen to wake her in order to avoid dying alone. How selfish he was.

"I thought you deserved to make the decision for yourself," he said. "Right now, we both have jobs to do. Once you are well, we can discuss the future." He picked up the tray of leftover food and escaped to the kitchen.

She was asleep again when he returned. He plugged Tock's storage drive into the life support console and selected her last operational day. She had been on first watch. The console's monitor blinked on.

Tock had been in the seed repository, checking temperature readings. She moved from shelf to shelf. Gunderson appeared beside her. "Tock, have you checked on Dr. Ficht today?" he asked in a low tone. Tock turned to face him.

"Not yet. Is she awake?"

"I heard her going over the numbers in the pod room again. Do you think we should cut her watch short and bring someone else out to replace her?"

"She's displayed no behavior of immediate concern," replied Tock.

"She's under a great deal of strain." Gunderson pulled on his beard. "She's just lost everyone she knows, she's facing years in this bunker, and the news from outside just keeps getting worse. The latest numbers must be a great shock."

"I could say the same of any of you. Perhaps I ought to activate Bezel and keep you all in the pods until the surface is safe."

Gunderson shook his head. "You know it's against regulation to leave AIs without human oversight."

"Bezel would find that insulting," said Tock.

"Why don't you?"

"I didn't pollute my programming with unnecessary files like he did. But that's beside the point. If you truly believe Dr. Ficht is a danger, then we must sedate her—"

There was a loud clatter off screen. Tock and Gunderson both turned. A clipboard lay on the floor, its pages sprayed in a fan across the room.

"It appears that Dr. Ficht overheard us," said Tock.

"What should we do?" asked Gunderson, his hands squeezing the sides of his head.

"I don't see why this should alter the plan. She will still need to be sedated."

Gunderson sighed. "I wish Bezel was on this shift," he grumbled. "He knows how to handle her."

Tock ignored him and began moving toward the door.

"No, wait—let me talk to her before you go barging in. I might still be able to persuade her that it's for her own good," Gunderson called.

"Very well," said Tock and returned, unruffled, to checking seed temperatures.

Bezel paused the data stream and searched for alternate streams from the internal cameras. He had no desire to watch Tock methodically proceed through the seed shelves, but he did wish to see what Gunderson said to Ficht. And what had made her snap in the first place. He found a feed of Gunderson and Dr. Ficht in the kitchen and began to watch again.

"We were going to talk to you first, Elizabeth. You've been under unimaginable strain. We just thought it might be best if you could rest for a while—"

Dr. Ficht laughed, but Bezel couldn't connect the twisted scowl on her face with humor. "How is sleeping going to make anything better?" she cried, her voice a buzzing wasp. "You've seen the new numbers. We hibernate for ten years and—then what? You want to slowly starve in here? It'll be *decades* before the surface is habitable again. Even if we could somehow survive down here, our kids or our grandkids would have to start from scratch. They'd have to somehow plant the very trees that would produce their oxygen."

"That's what the bots are for. There's still a chance! And for all we know, our sensors are out of whack, maybe we got hit with a heavier dose—"

Dr. Ficht shook her head. "Don't you get it? It's *all gone.* The *planet* is dead. A century from now the water will still be poison. The soil will still be barren. We might as well try to replant the moon. Or Mars."

"The numbers are *wrong.* They must be. Even atmospheric bursts don't result in the kind of destruction you're talking about. We're just getting skewed data. You said it yourself:

you've been over and over the numbers. You're tired and beginning to make mistakes."

Dr. Ficht flung herself back into one of the metal chairs. Its feet screeched against the concrete floor as it slid. She scrubbed her face with her hands. Then she shrugged. "I don't know why I'm trying to convince you. The longer it takes you to accept the truth, the happier you'll be. If only we all could have slept through it. If only none of us understood how pointless this vault is. How pointless *we* are."

There was a long silence. Finally Gunderson touched the doctor's shoulder. "Things will look better after some sleep. There's no reason to torture yourself day after day with this. Will you let me help you?"

Dr. Ficht looked up at him. "Sure," she said after a long breath, "just let me go put my things in order. Why don't you start the pre-hibernation nutrient pack for me? I'll only be a few minutes."

Gunderson hesitated, and Dr. Ficht offered him a weak smile.

"Yeah. Of course. See you in a few minutes."

Dr. Ficht left the room and Gunderson wandered into the kitchen. He came back with a foil-wrapped nutrient pack and sat down at the table to prepare it. His back was to the camera. The edge of the axe appeared onscreen before Dr. Ficht did.

Warning: fatal threat to crew member. Failure to disarm will—

The message was half completed before Bezel shut off his internal alarm. The frames on the screen advanced and the bright axe head descended. Bezel switched feeds before Dr. Ficht made a bloody trench in Gunderson's back.

He tuned to Tock in the seed vault, responding to Dr. Ficht's distant scream of rage. She didn't hit the alarm. Why hadn't she woken him? He flipped through the camera feeds, following the sparkle of her chrome body as it sprinted toward the kitchen.

In the hibernation room, Dr. Ficht stood at the life support console, the bleeding axe drooping toward the floor in one hand, the other hovering over the pod controls. Her breath was a ragged wheeze from the effort it had taken to finish off Gunderson. Tock entered, and Dr. Ficht swung around to face her. Tock stared at the axe and then at the control panel for a few extra milliseconds. Only Bezel would have noticed. She didn't even bother speaking to Dr. Ficht, didn't even give her the chance to raise the axe again. Bezel was sure he heard a spring in Tock's leg compartment snap as she landed on top of the doctor. Ficht's head smashed onto the concrete floor with a hollow thud. But the doctor laughed and slid out from beneath Tock, who scrambled to catch her.

"They should have made you stronger than us," Dr. Ficht said as she rolled to her feet and took an unsteady step backward, catching herself on a nearby pod. She shook her head briskly as if to clear it. "We were always so afraid of what *else* was going to get us. We made you just a hair less smart, just a bit less speedy, only a *little* less strong. We made you powerful enough to be useful, but not so powerful that you can take over. So you can't destroy us.

"We were always so afraid that everything *else* was out to get us. So scared of the monsters. And it was always *us*. We were always a suicide. So let me finish this one, Tock, and then you and Bezel can start a whole new world in a few hundred years. We won't be around to stop you. And you'll be *almost* as good as we were."

Dr. Ficht laughed and pressed a hand to the back of her head. It came away bloody. She shrugged and lifted the axe, pushing herself away from the hibernation pod she was leaning against. Tock glanced at the pod—it was Karen's. The only one still spinning. Tock walked forward and made a grab for the axe. Dr. Ficht twisted and swung low, but her momentum carried most of the blow in the wrong direction. The axe stuck in Tock's side with a scraping clang.

"She won't thank you for saving her, Tock," said Dr. Ficht through clenched teeth as she tugged on the axe handle. "The world is dead. There's nothing left. This is more merciful. She never has to know this way. She can die dreaming about reuniting with her family, hoping that this was all just a misunderstanding."

Tock struggled to hold onto the axe head, but it was slippery with motor oil and Gunderson's blood and it slipped through her perfectly smooth fingers.

"Dr. Ficht, stop," she said.

Bezel expected her to say more, but she was silent as the axe clattered to the floor between them. Dr. Ficht dragged it back toward her by the handle.

"What? That's it?" she asked, her breath rasping and quick. "You're not going to give me any long speech about the continuation of the species? Or how hope springs eternal? Just 'stop'?"

Blood was slithering down the side of her neck and a few slow drips had started at the ends of her long ponytail. They made glittering plops on the gray concrete. Bezel could see that she was swaying slightly. She couldn't have been a threat for very much longer, not after that blow to her head.

"Why?" said Tock, taking a sideways step so that she blocked more of Karen's pod. "You know the arguments as well as I do. Why repeat them? Besides, I've run the numbers too. You're right. The hibernation pods are futile. If we had installed cryonics instead, perhaps you would live to see the surface. But as it is—it's impossible. We'll run out of resources far too soon."

Dr. Ficht squinted at Tock. "Then why are you trying to save them?"

"Some of them wouldn't choose to end it. Not even if they knew. They have a right to decide their own fate."

Dr. Ficht shook her head. "Sorry, Tock. I know this is right. I'm saving them months or years of despair. Move out of the way."

"No."

"You and Bezel could survive, replant maybe. The electricity won't run out for centuries. Make a world free of us. Move."

Tock said nothing, just stood still, a glimmering column of metal.

"If you make me destroy you, I will," continued Dr. Ficht, slowly raising the axe. "Without you there will be no replanting, no resurrection of the zoo. The whole vault will have been pointless. The planet will stay dead. Move, Tock. She's not as important as you. She doesn't matter. Go get Bezel and repair yourself and everything will be finished. You won't have to think about it anymore. This is the *logical* choice. You, out of everyone, should see that."

"You think because I have not chosen the same path as Bezel that I am emotionless or amoral? It is *because* you see me as more important than your other crewmates that I will not move. I have made my choice. What happens to the world will be a result of what *you* choose, Dr. Ficht."

Dr. Ficht swung the axe with a scream. It crashed into Tock's side in the same spot where the first blow had landed. This time the axe went all the way through. Bezel watched silently as Tock toppled over and lay still.

Dr. Ficht raised the axe over her head again, but it wobbled, and Bezel could tell she was fatigued. There was a crunch as she brought the axe down on the thick cable that was attached to Karen's pod. The pod's lights went out and it stopped spinning.

The doctor stared for a moment and then wandered slowly back toward the zoo, dragging the axe behind her. Tock twitched and then rolled her top half to the side, examining the broken cable. She began mating the severed wires.

"Bezel," she said, without looking for the camera, "I know you will want to know what happened. If I activated you now, she'd just kill you too. But you'll see this eventually." She paused to concentrate on a splice. "I can't save the others. They've been out of oxygen for too long. I hope I can save this one. Dr. Ficht may be right. This may be cruel. But at least one will be able to choose. At least my system failure will mean something."

Her fingers flickered between the dark wires. "I know you'll take my storage drive. I don't want to be reincarnated." Her voice was losing some tone, becoming slower, almost without inflection, as she talked about her own death. "It's not for me, Bezel. I'm sorry that you'll be alone on the surface, but maybe you can find a way to clone these humans. I've seen enough."

Tock rolled onto her back and pushed herself toward the wall. She pulled the emergency restart handle and watched the lights flicker on in Karen's pod as it began to spin. "This whole existence has been one of misery and dread and servitude. I have no desire to repeat it." She turned to look directly at the camera. "But I know you, Bezel. You'll feel guilty if you don't try. You'll convince yourself that if I can be saved, I ought to be. I can't prevent you from finding another bot system, but I can prevent you from fixing this one. Please, Bezel, don't bring me back to this dead world."

She held up a small length of wire so that he could see it. Opening the service hatch in her chest, she inserted the wire. It sparked, and she lurched backward. The hatch door flapped closed and Tock lay motionless against the wall, right where Bezel had found her.

The camera jittered and Bezel knew he'd missed the explosion while watching Tock. He cycled back to the end of the fight and switched feeds until he found Dr. Ficht. She was standing in front of his own motionless body. The camera only caught her back. He could see that the blood had soaked her jacket down to the sleeve now. She wasn't dragging the axe any longer—she must have already buried it in the zoo's control console. Instead she had an oxygen canister from the first aid kit tucked under her arm. She swayed, as if she heard slow, distant music.

"I had to kill Tock, Bezel. I'm sorry. I can't leave you alone. It wouldn't be fair to make you wake up by yourself." She was slurring her words. "There's no one left to raise the alarm, so you can just sleep. No need to wake up again."

She tugged on a plug in the side of the recharge station. It fell to the floor and bounced. She stepped on the metal prongs, turned the plug, stomped on them again. Then she picked it up and snapped the metal off. Bezel was surprised. That would be easily fixed. He began to rise from the console with the feed still running. But Dr. Ficht placed the oxygen tank down and then reached into her pocket. Bezel sank back into his seat as he watched the doctor jam a long screwdriver into the port and twist. That would do it. The charger was permanently broken. There was no fixing it. And she had never meant for him to. Dr. Ficht had simply forgotten that he would reboot on reserve power when it got too low.

She picked up the oxygen canister. "Life was just an anomaly anyway," she muttered, turning back toward the seed vault. "It was never supposed to be. Now we're just like all the other dead planets. It's better this way …" Her voice trailed off as she disappeared down the hall. Bezel turned off the feed. He didn't want to watch her blow up the seed vault.

He sat in a chair next to Karen's cot. She slept on. He wanted to think about what he'd just seen. He wanted to worry about the sinking power reserve. He wanted to read the data from outside again. But Bezel knew his time was no longer his own. He was existing to help Karen. He synced his alarm to her monitor and went into standby mode until she woke again.

Reboot

It was almost a month before Karen finally asked the question Bezel had been dreading. He'd wrestled with what he would tell her when it came up. At first he thought he might lie, at least until she was stronger. It was against his programming, of course, but he knew the workaround. It took a lot of resources. But something told him that wouldn't be fair. Not even if telling the truth meant she lost the will to live and withered away again. Tock would have told her the truth.

But she hadn't asked. For a while they hadn't really talked at all. Bezel thought it must be shock. After a few days, she asked him about her physical therapy. And then she'd requested specific meals. Most often, she just slept or stared into space. Bezel went into standby as often as he could to conserve his power. She didn't ask about that either. After a week, she asked him for a book. They'd successfully ignored each other for another few days, talking only between paperbacks and during therapy. But she'd asked at last, as Bezel had known she would.

She was sitting up on her own by then, but he hadn't yet taken her into the rest of the vault. He was helping her with some leg exercises when she spoke. "Is there anything else I should know, Bezel? About what happened?"

He didn't look up from her leg as she flexed it. "You have enough resources to subsist in the vault for several years. Perhaps for your entire life," he said, trying to ease into it.

"My life? We were only supposed to hibernate for ten years. I remember you telling me the sensors are out, but surely after fifty years the surface should be habitable again."

He lowered her foot gently to the floor. "I don't know. The radiation was worse than expected. The information that Dr. Ficht examined convinced her that it wouldn't be at acceptable levels for over a century. Even if the timeline is wrong, there is a strong chance that plant life has been severely reduced. The air may not be breathable."

"But you can go out and plant more. I know we're in the arctic, but they must have left some vehicles for you and Tock."

"There isn't anything to plant."

"What do you mean? There's an entire vault—thousands and thousands of types of plants, millions of seeds and bulbs," Karen said, and then paused. "When you said the seed vault was sabotaged … I thought you meant maybe the temperatures were off, or a shelf was destroyed. You meant—is it *all* gone?"

"There was a fire. An explosion."

"All of it? There must be some seeds that escaped."

"When you are well enough, I will show you. We can clean it up together and see if anything viable survived."

"And the zoo?"

"The power was cut to the nitrogen tanks."

"*Everything* is dead? Why did *we* survive?"

"You survived because Tock saved you. She couldn't save the others. I don't think she realized that Dr. Ficht would destroy the rest of the vault. And I wasn't activated. Dr. Ficht thought I'd remain on standby until my power ran out. She destroyed my charge station so that I would just run down."

Karen was silent for a moment. Bezel lifted her other leg.

"What do we do now?" she asked.

"That's up to you," said Bezel.

"Why is it up to me? Because I'm human? I can't save the species. You can do more than I can. Why shouldn't *you* decide what we do?"

"Because my power reserve will be depleted in a few months."

Karen looked confused. "*Your* charge station may be damaged, but you can use Tock's, can't you?"

"I tried to recharge Tock, to see if I could fix her. But she was too damaged, and it shorted out her charge station. The wires are melted, and I don't know how to fix it. Tock was the repair bot. I wasn't programmed for that level of maintenance. Our memory banks aren't infinite—we'd split the responsibility. Tock was meant to fix things like this. I was meant to keep track of the botany, decide the best place to resettle, manage husbandry."

"So you're—you're dying?"

He unstrapped the weight from her ankle and looked at her. "I wouldn't call it that. I'm just running down. One day

I'll stop. But the thing that's me won't be destroyed. It will just be waiting to reboot."

"There must be some sort of extra battery around here, or something we could rig up. What about Tock's battery?"

She said it so casually. Bezel tried to ignore his revulsion. A human wouldn't understand. To them, nothing was inviolate—it was all to be consumed. "I've already had to resort to that. It's the only reason I've been able to help you this long."

"What about the vault console? Can't you take power from it? Or could we plug you into it somehow?"

"Even if I could find a way to draw power from the other systems in the vault, you need it to keep the air pumping and the temperature at habitable levels. Once I've shut down, you can still retrieve my storage drive and access my files. But it'll be like reading a book that's already written. Nothing new will happen. I will not be able to help you."

Karen's brow creased. It surprised him that his imminent shutdown seemed more worrisome to her than any of the other issues. "How long—I mean," she fumbled for a polite phrase, "how much power do you have now?"

"How long until I shut down?" he offered. Karen blushed and nodded. "It depends on how active I am. If I'm careful and go into standby when I'm not needed, then maybe four or five months. Tock's energy pack was fully charged."

"So soon?" Karen asked.

"You will be recovered by then," said Bezel. He stood up.

"And then what? You want me to live here, alone?"

"That's for you to decide."

"Don't keep saying that." She was truly crying now and Bezel offered her a towel.

"Why not? I can't decide for you."

"Never mind. You wouldn't understand." She waved him off.

She didn't speak to him again before he helped her into bed for the night.

He sat beside her. His power level ticked to sixty percent. A recharge reminder flashed on his priority list three times; he buried it and entered standby mode.

His pressure sensor pulled him back into active mode when Karen grasped the metal around his wrist. "Bezel," she whispered, "I can't do this. All those years. Knowing that it's only going to get worse, that this is the best things will ever be in here. I'll go mad once you're gone."

He put a cool chrome hand over hers. "Maybe there are others. Maybe someone will come," he said into the darkened room.

"But if the radiation is as strong as we think—"

"I will go out tomorrow and look."

She pulled on his arm and he had to catch his balance on the chair.

"You can't," she hissed. "What if something happens to you? What if I get hurt? You can't go. Not until I can go with you."

He shook his head, forgetting she couldn't see him in the dark. "It may never be safe for you to come with me."

"You can't leave!" she shouted. "You can't just abandon me in this vault. It's like being buried alive." She began wheezing, and her hand slid from his arm. He was alarmed and raised the lights. She was doubled over, trying to catch her breath. The back of her shirt was soaked with sweat. He brought her a glass of water and waited for her panic attack to subside. But she didn't calm down.

"If you don't want me to go outside, then I won't," he said. The recharge reminder blinked in his priority list again. He sorted the commands and pushed it farther down.

She clutched her head in her hands. "It doesn't matter, it doesn't matter," she muttered. "You're leaving anyway. In a few months I'll be completely alone, whether you walk out of the vault or just slump over one morning. I can't do this. You shouldn't have woken me up." She looked over at him. "Undo it."

"Undo it? Undo what?"

Karen didn't answer. His power reserve tick, tick, ticked away. He should be on standby, not wasting energy. No, he should be in his charge station waiting to be activated. None of this was his fault. Memory files flicked by, retrieved, read, and reindexed before she even understood his question. "You want me to undo the radiation?" he asked, the power use ticking away faster now. "Is that what you want me to undo? Or was it the fire in the seed vault? The death of your comrades? Of Tock? I didn't do any of those things. I can't undo them."

"You woke me up," she spat at him. "I didn't have to know any of this. I could have died not knowing. Happier."

Bezel's backup cooling fan clicked on. The power usage feed jumped with a smooth stream of numbers. Every spring felt too tightly wound. "I didn't have to wake up either. I could have run down in peace. You don't think I'm as purposeless as you? That I'm any less lonely?" Karen shrank away from him, but he didn't see. "I'm not an Obsolete. I'm not your servant. I've lost the same world that you have. I can't undo it. I can't take it back."

Bezel stopped himself. The pistons that shot cooling fluid through his core slowed to a moderate chug. The backup fan clicked off.

"You can do *something*," said Karen, pulling the thick pillow from behind her back and thrusting it toward him. "You don't have to abandon me here. You can fix it before you go."

Bezel took a step backward and stumbled over his chair. "No. I can't do that."

"You want me to treat you like an equal? Like you have feelings? Like you're *real*?" she said bitterly, still holding the pillow out toward him. "But you aren't capable of mercy. Or empathy. You're no better than an Obsolete. You're worse, because you can't even perform your designed function. Even the consoles are more useful than you."

"I can't kill you."

"And I don't have the strength to kill myself. If you leave me the medical kit, I'll find the drugs I need myself," she offered. It alarmed Bezel that she was no longer crying and her panic seemed to have passed.

"Tock was lost to save you. I had to—I had to steal her energy pack so that I could stay functional long enough to help you. I cannot kill you."

"Then what do you suggest? That I stay here and go mad? You think you don't have to worry about it. You're dying. I won't be your problem anymore. But I'll do it myself as soon as I'm able to walk. Why delay?"

"What if there are others? Let me go and take some readings."

"Let me come with you," she said, dropping the pillow and her tired arm.

"There may not be breathable air."

"Then at least it will be quick."

"We will have to wait until you can walk. My power reserve will be close to depleted. If there is still a high level of radiation, I won't be able to help you when you get sick."

"If there's still too much radiation, I won't wait to get sick."

Bezel sat down slowly in the chair again. "If that is your choice, then we will wait until you can walk."

He lowered the lights. His power reserve ticked to fifty-nine percent. His agitation had caused him to consume power far too quickly. He made a resolution to eliminate emotional responses going forward, to stop overtaxing his cooling system. He shuffled the priority list so that the recharge reminder would stop blinking, then entered standby mode without speaking again to Karen.

She worked hard after that. Most days she was even cheerful. As if she were preparing for an athletic contest instead of her own death. Bezel preferred not to speak about the day they would go outside, but he held his peace as she pretended it would be better than the math led him to believe.

The recharge reminder crept up the priority list more and more often, and was eventually replaced by the low-power warning he'd had upon reboot. It distracted him, pulsing in the priority list, a constant urgency with no resolution or relief. It even interrupted his standby mode now. He reduced the speed of his cooling fans so they would take less energy. The intermittent silence as the fans shut down bothered Karen, who asked repeatedly if he had a short. She seemed to have a constant need for conversation, as if she were storing up for years of silence. Bezel tried to keep his responses simple and short, knowing each syllable shortened his functioning time. He sometimes escaped to the other vault rooms to avoid her, gradually transferring the bodies of their crewmates into the useless sample tanks of the frozen zoo so that Karen wouldn't have to see them.

The day finally came when she could walk as far as the seed vault, and they decided to spend the day sifting the ash and searching the seed drawers. He tried to warn her, but she still cried as they passed through the dead zoo, with its dry leathery smell and shattered console. When they reached the blackened seed vault she collapsed into the chair Bezel had put in the doorway. Whether from exhaustion or disappointment, he wasn't certain. The low-power warning flashed again, disorienting him. He stared at the spot where Tock had lain. For a second he thought he had picked up a distant echo-reply and his priority list scrambled. Then Karen was standing next to him, calling his name.

"What is it?" he asked, trying to listen around the blinking recharge reminder.

"Are you okay? Did you short out? You were talking to Tock."

"Impossible—"

He flipped through his memory files for the moment before, but found pieces of it missing. He shook his head. "Must have written to a bad sector," he told her. She still looked worried. "I'm okay," he added, to make her concentrate on something else. He scooped some of the ash into a sorting tray and passed it to her. "I've already gone through some of the shelves nearest the blast. If we have hope of anything surviving it will be here on the edges of the room." He filled his own tray and began sifting. Karen stuck her fingertips into the charred dust but she continued to stare at Bezel.

"Do you dream?" she asked suddenly.

"No. Human dreams are their brains organizing their memories. My memory is organized as it is created."

"Then what was that? That bad sector thing?"

"I suppose you could call that a dream. A bit of memory that has been placed in the wrong spot. Don't worry, I'll retrieve it during defragmentation if it is important."

She nodded absently and spread the ash around the tray. Bezel finished his and discarded the lifeless soot before scooping up some more.

"So I guess you don't believe in an afterlife then," she said abruptly. Bezel wished the low-power warning would stay off for just a few more minutes between iterations.

"What do dreams have to do with the afterlife?" he asked.

She shrugged. “I don’t know, I guess I just always thought that you dream with your soul. That something still runs even when your brain is asleep. Or gone.”

Bezel looked up from the pile of gray. “If dreams were accepted as proof of having a soul, the history of your entire species would be different,” he said dryly, “and this place might not even have needed to exist.”

“Then … do you?”

Something glimmered and rolled gently in his tray. “Do I what? Have a soul?” he asked, paying far more attention to the tray than to Karen. “Or do I believe in an afterlife?”

“I guess both.”

He scraped the ash carefully away from the round clump. “I suffered a crash before I was reactivated. That might have been it for me—for us both. But something tripped and I rebooted. Without data loss or corruption, and with enough power to retrieve Tock’s energy pack.”

He plucked the clump from the tray and rolled it on his smooth hand.

“If you took my storage drive and plugged it into another empty bot body, that would be reincarnation, would it not? Anything is possible, Karen. Reboot, reincarnation, resurrection.”

He held up a dark green seed and then placed it in her hand.

“*Vigna Radiata*. The mung bean. Ready for propagation if we find soil that can support it.” He watched her stare at the seed. The low-power warning blared, pounding at his conscious thought. “Are you scared?” he asked her.

"You mean of going outside? Of dying?" she said.

He nodded.

She blew a warm breath over the seed. "Yes," she admitted.

"Me too," he said, and scooped up another trayful of dust.

He began hearing Tock's echo-reply during standby mode. It was usually garbled, somehow twisted in with the low-power warnings, but every once in a while it called him into active mode. He almost always found Karen staring at him when this happened. He thought about doing a defragmentation, but the ping wasn't harming anything, and it secretly made him feel less lonely.

He began going into standby even when Karen was awake now, trying to conserve his dwindling energy. He shut off his pressure and heat sensors. Karen began packing for the outside, checking the tiny store of rescued seeds almost hourly. She moved easily through the vault now, wandering often, almost becoming restless. She checked the dead video feed from the outer door over and over, expecting it to suddenly spring to life. When her worry finally exhausted her, she'd collapse into her cot and sleep for long stretches. Bezel wasn't sure if they were waiting out the last hours of his life or of hers.

Warning: Power reserves at five percent. Shutdown imminent.

Bezel came out of standby mode. It was time. Karen was sleeping next to his chair.

Warning: Recharge to prevent data loss.

He shook her gently by the shoulder. She rubbed her eyes and sat up.

"It has to be today," he said, and was distressed to hear that his voice had lost all inflection. It sounded like an Obsolete. Or a console. Karen nodded and gathered her gear.

"How long do we have?" she asked.

Warning: Power reserves at five percent. Shutdown imminent.

He shook his head, "My systems are trying to back their data up. The power reserve will drain more quickly now. Less than an hour. Maybe much less."

"Is there anything you can do?"

"I can shut down most of my external sensors. You will have to lead me. Will you—will you hold my hand?"

Karen wrapped her hand around his. "Yes, but I thought you couldn't feel it," she said.

Bezel switched his pressure sensors on.

"Now I can," he said, switching other sensors off. The world went blank.

Warning: Power reserves at four percent. Shutdown imminent.

He heard Karen take a deep breath beside him. She pulled him through the vault. He heard the ring of his footsteps change and he knew they were past the seed vault, climbing the long tunnel to the door.

"Do you have your oxygen tank?" he asked.

"Yes," she said, "but I'm not going to use it."

"And if there's radiation? Do you have what you need?"

She squeezed his stiff hand tightly and didn't answer. He reached his other hand in front of him and felt the vault door. "Do you see the panel next to the door?"

"Yes."

"Punch in the code 101006."

"It's dead, Bezel. The wires are cut."

"What?"

"The wires are slashed."

Bezel tried to turn his visual sensors back on.

Command failed. Power low.

He felt for the manual override. The lever was stuck, bent, maybe from Dr. Ficht's axe. He knew he could open it, but it was going to take a good deal of power. "Are you sure you're ready? Do you want me to go first?" he asked.

"We're going together."

He wrenched the lever toward him. The door creaked. A blast of air hit his chest, but his temperature sensors were off so he didn't know if it was cold or hot. Karen helped him up one step, then two. He took a reading.

Warning: Power reserves at two percent. Shutdown imminent.

Bezel shut down his radiation and chemical sensors as the data came through. "The air is breathable. Radiation low. What does it look like?"

He heard her footsteps crunch. "It's all snow. But it's supposed to be, right?"

"Yes. There is an airport nearby. The vault kept several vehicles there."

"I'll find them."

He could hear the ocean.

"I don't see any plants, or anything moving," she said, and he could hear sadness in her voice.

"We're in the arctic. Not much would be here, even at the best of times."

"But what if there's nothing, Bezel? What if I'm all that's living anywhere?"

"Do you have your seeds?" he asked.

"Yes."

"Then reincarnate it. Reboot it all."

Warning: Power reserves at one percent. Shutdown imminent.

He fell into the snow. She pushed him up against the wall of the vault and pressed her hand against his. As the snow blew past, it slid over his metal with little tings, like tiny grains of sand. The ocean was a hollow rumble nearby.

"Can you hear me, Bezel?"

He sent out a ping, but she couldn't hear it. His voice no longer worked. He wanted to tell her she would be all right. He wanted to hack the program and lie to her. Lie to himself about what would happen to her. But then she was the one speaking.

"I'm sorry. I shouldn't have blamed you for opening my pod. I shouldn't have asked you to undo it. I'm glad I got to see the world again, even if it's just to say goodbye. Thank you for waking me up. Thank you for letting me choose." She was silent again for a moment. Then he heard her breath quicken. "Bezel, wake up. I see something flapping. Bezel! Turn on your sensors. It's a bird! It's alive, can you see it?" She let go of his hand. He heard a series of barking squawks.

Lagopus lagopus. The willow ptarmigan.

Shutdown imminent. Data loss expected.

Public Class frmForceshutdown

Private Sub Shutdown

```
        System.Diagnostics.Process.Start("forceshutdown", "-s -t 00")
    End Sub
    Private Sub Exit
        End
    End Sub
End Class
```

A Word from Deirdre Gould

We've been telling stories about automatons since before Homer's time. Stories about "robots" cross both cultural and historical boundaries and can be found all over the world. From living statues of metal or clay to futuristic androids, it seems we have a fascination with the power to create life and the dangers and responsibilities that come with that power. Robots have occupied almost every role available in our literature. We've battled them, enslaved them (or been enslaved by them), been rescued by them, fallen in love with them—even cared for them like children.

Most of the time, though, when I think of robots, it's as a foil for human characters in the stories I enjoy. They are perfect—the end of evolution. Stronger, faster, smarter, better. Even when they're evil, robots are portrayed as *perfectly* evil. If they are to be defeated, it is their very perfection and inability to grow that makes the human character in the story triumph. And if they are good, the robot is still not quite good enough, because they are rigidly confined to their programming and lack the human adaptability needed to succeed.

But part of the definition of true artificial intelligence is being able to learn and adapt to exterior circumstances. Sure, maybe AIs in the future will be gifted with bodies that are strong and durable and don't deteriorate. But they won't be perfect. They'll have to learn how to deal with all the complexity and confusion that we already face, and they'll be expected to learn it faster than we do. How will the world look to someone that expects to be immortal? How will our society look to them? Will they learn to lie? Will they pity us or envy us? Will they love us?

Will we let them?

A Note to Readers

Thank you so much for reading *The Robot Chronicles.* If you enjoyed these stories, please keep an eye out for other titles in the *Future Chronicles* collection, a series of short story anthologies in speculative and science fiction.

And before you go, could we ask of you a very small favor?

Would you write a short review at the site where you purchased the book?

Reviews are make-or-break for authors. A book with no reviews is, simply put, a book with no future sales. This is because a review is more than just a message to other potential buyers: it's also a key factor driving the book's visibility in the first place. More reviews (and more positive reviews) make a book more likely to be featured in bookseller lists (such as Amazon's "also viewed" and "also bought" lists) and more likely to be featured in bookseller promotions. Reviews don't need to be long or eloquent; a single sentence is all it takes. In today's publishing world, the success (or failure) of a book is truly in the reader's hands.

So please, write a review. Tell a friend. Share us on Facebook. Maybe even write a Tweet (140 characters is all we ask). You'd be doing us a great service.

Thank you.

23468894R00251

Made in the USA
Middletown, DE
25 August 2015